BECAUSE OF HATTIE

ROXANNA C REVELL

Roxanna C Revell
x

ISBN: 9781513683188

Original Image by Deposit Photos

Cover Image by Rebecacovers

Proofread by Jessica Runyard

Formatting by Roxanna C Revell

Created with Vellum

DEDICATION

To you, for taking a chance on a first-time author. I hope you enjoy the story that I've created, and if you do then keep in touch, because I'm already working on the next one. It would also be fantastic if you could write a review to help other readers find their way to this story.

Keep in touch for updates on my new projects.

Instagram @roxannacrevell
Facebook @RoxannaCRevellAuthor
Twitter @RevellAuthor

SOMETIMES

Sometimes it's hard to see,
Through the smoke and the mirrors,
The toxicity.

Sometimes it's hard to heal,
When there's been so many lies,
You can't tell what is real.

Sometimes you have to protect your heart,
When once it ripped open,
Was torn clean apart.

Sometimes it's easy to forgive,
When a love is so strong,
That without it,
You can't live.

Roxanna C Revell

CONTENTS

PROLOGUE

I stood still for a moment and looked around my empty flat. Empty, except for the boxes stacked up and waiting to be collected, the remnants of my broken life now packed into fifteen boxes. Then I looked again at the most important box in the room — the box that was yet to be opened.

I'd put my first missed period down to the food poisoning messing up my body. The second? That was obviously down to the stress of the catastrophic destruction of every aspect of my life — job, friends, lover were all gone. The third? The third was now days late and I could no longer ignore all of the signs that had gone unnoticed for months.

There was no sense in deluding myself any longer. I had half an hour before the removal team were due to arrive. So, I picked up the box and took it to the bathroom, already knowing exactly what the test was going to tell me three minutes after peeing on it.

1

Sometimes I sit back and wonder how it all went so wrong — which is actually a massive waste of time because I know exactly where it all went wrong. I'm twenty-five, unemployed, and I have moved back to my parents' house. It isn't even the house I grew up in. I have zero ties to it. No room, that's 'my room.' When my dad retired from the corporate world three years ago, they moved to Clovelly, my mum's childhood home and one of Devon's most beautiful coastal villages. We visited here all the time, so it isn't entirely new to me, but it's a far cry from Muswell Hill. That's where my childhood home is. That's where I grew up. Where I experienced all my firsts, and where it all went so horribly wrong.

Still, Clovelly is their home, not mine, and when they said that I could come and stay with them whenever I wanted to, I'm pretty sure they weren't expecting me to show up on their doorstep with all my moveable possessions, and fourteen weeks pregnant. Nope. They definitely weren't expecting that. Although it wasn't exactly in my plans either.

There were a lot of tears that afternoon, and many, many questions that were mostly evaded. How could I tell them? They knew things had gone wrong before I left London. They didn't really understand it, what with me not giving them any details. Even when I sobbed my shattered heart out over the phone, I knew they had never expected me to leave. I was a fighter; I didn't let people push me around. I never, ever thought something like this would, or could happen to me. Especially because of her. There is always something, some way to cling on and fight back. Only, there really wasn't. She took everything.

I had made my decision to leave before I knew that I was pregnant. Well, I knew, deep down, I just didn't allow myself the certainty of confirming it until the morning that I left. Of course, I felt ill and of course I lost my appetite and felt emotionally all over the place. I had been pushed out of my job and all the people that I called friends — the people that had been by my side since we were children — all hated me. Nobody would listen to me. She had turned them all. I could possibly have handled it, if I had deserved it. If the things that she had told them were true — but it was all lies. They just wouldn't hear it. I know I deserved her wrath, and I'd been expecting it for months. I had hoped the fact that we'd been best friends since the age of five would mean that she would find a way to forgive me, but no. That apparently just made my betrayal that much worse, and my punishment — epic.

So, I ran home, well, not home exactly, but to my parents' home. To the two people that had my back no matter what, and they did, this time the same as any other. They handled it in their usual way. Mum was reactive, just like me, and her emotions were completely clear. Fear, anger, complete and utter confusion, all mixed in with just a hint of disappointment. She had tried to hide that last one, but I saw it. It flickered in her eyes for a moment before the sadness kicked straight back in. My dad wore his mask. The same one that had made his career; he was unreadable. That was his way. He would listen, swallow down any immediate, knee-jerk reaction, and just take it all in. In a really tough situation, he would just nod at you and head out of the door, and that's exactly what he did that day.

As a teenager it used to drive me mad. I was never really that rebellious, but there were a few occasions where I received the screams of my mum and the slight nod from my dad as he mulled it over. I hated it because I didn't get it. I could handle my mum shouting at me and making her feelings very clear, because that was how I was too. I almost needed him to shout at me, and to tell me that I'd let them down, because I knew how to deal with that. Eventually, I grew to appreciate his silence. He was the calm amongst the emotional storms that were my mum and me.

That particular afternoon — the afternoon when I turned their world upside down, I loved him all the more for it. It gave me hope. Hope, that if my dad went away for long enough, he would come back and be able to fix it all. After all, that was what he did. It made him his money — not loads, but enough for him to retire and move my mum back to the place she loved and set up her own tea rooms.

After ten minutes of listening to my mum berating me, fearing for me and just generally despairing; I welcomed the silence that followed as she, completely out of options, emotions and tears, sat silently, waiting for the man that we both depended on to return. To return and fix everything. It had been another twenty minutes before the front door opened, and I felt like I could breathe again. The relief that both my mum and I felt in that moment destroyed the tension that had filled the room.

At first, he said nothing. He put the kettle on, kissed my mum on the top of her head — her usually impeccably neat hair having become a victim of the distress that I'd caused her, and then sat on the coffee table in front of me. I waited for his easy, reassuring smile. For him to put his arms around me and tell me what the solution would be. It was coming. He hugged me close and hard, and then he sat back and took my hands in his. He waited a moment, and then he said five words that shook me to the core. Five simple words that destroyed all hope as soon as they were spoken, when he said, "I can't fix this, Ava."

What he had actually meant was that he couldn't fix it if he didn't know exactly what had happened. Really it amounted to the same thing, because they weren't getting the details any time soon. I wasn't ready. I wasn't ready to see the flicker of disappointment that I'd seen creep out onto my mum's face engulf it completely. I'm still not. Of course, he couldn't fix it, there was no fixing to be done. Still, they pledged to support me every step of the way, and they did. They do.

They took me to the local doctor the next day, and as it was a Saturday we went to her house. That was the sort of place that I'd run to. The sort of place where it was considered perfectly normal to rock up to see your local doctor at their home, uninvited, with your broken, pregnant daughter. She hadn't been what I expected. She was in her early thirties and was very pleasant — lovely, in fact. She'd been born in Clovelly and had moved away to London, thinking that she needed to escape the small village where everyone knew her name, only to find that was everything that she missed when she moved to London. She missed the local chit chat, she missed the smiles and greetings in the streets, and feeling like she knew her neighbours. When she had received word that a very rare and coveted space was opening up at her home surgery, she jumped at the chance to return. She was my exact opposite. Not just the fact that she hadn't completely messed up her life. Unlike her, I wanted nothing more than the anonymity that came with the City that I'd left. The place that had always been my home.

I sat in her cosy kitchen answering her questions with a similar level of vagueness that I'd given my parents. The only question I could answer with true clarity was the date of my last period. It may sound hard to believe given that it took me fourteen weeks to realise that I was pregnant, but I did track them. I was always pretty regular, but my body was definitely sensitive, and it was often my period that was skipped whenever I was recovering from illness. I'd had food poisoning so that explained the first missed period. I was always sensitive to stress too, and I was certainly stressed out. Whenever I've had exams you could guarantee that it would be a no show for a few months. So that was missed period number two and three explained too. That's why I didn't think more of it. To me it made sense.

It had scared both me and my parents a few times in the past, especially when I was with my first love at the age of sixteen. There was some embarrassing explaining, a very fraught mum, an outwardly calm dad, who was secretly ready to kill Nick — the first love — and a negative pregnancy test. The doctor had put my missing period down to the stress of GCSEs, and that was that. That was always that.

Until now.

Julia — I'm not 'allowed' to call her Dr Weaver was brilliant from the start. I'd expected judgement. Well, I'd expected an old man with nasal hair, to be honest. Julia was great, and she could see through it all. She could see that beneath the fear and the evasiveness, that I was hurting. I was later to find out from my mum that a broken heart may have also brought Julia back home, but then that could have just been a rumour created by the village gossips. I dreaded to think what they were going to say about me.

Julia pushed for additional tests and scans as soon as possible. I hadn't been taking care of myself properly, no decent meals or vitamins, and there had definitely been alcohol consumed. Thankfully, my baby was fine. I wasn't sure if that mattered to me back then, which I know sounds utterly despicable, but I hadn't planned it. Not falling in love with their dad, not getting food poisoning — which consequently had stopped my pill from working — and definitely not losing the man I was in love with, along with everything else. It wasn't the baby's fault, none of it was, but it really felt like a big 'Fuck you'! from the universe when I saw that line appear.

That all changed when I heard the heartbeat for the first time. That changed everything. I made a silent promise to my baby that day, that their heart didn't need to hurt like mine. I would always protect them from that.

2

Even though my parents didn't know exactly what happened, they pulled me in, and they took care of me. They tried for a while to get me to talk, the last attempt being on the way back from having my twenty-week scan. I was sitting in the back seat just staring at the photo of my baby boy. I was having a boy. Dad had been watching me in the rear-view mirror, the radio was on but only really in the background because nobody was listening. It was raining really hard — that bit always sticks with me when I think back to that day.

"You know, Ava," Dad said, then he cleared his throat before continuing, "you have us no matter what. Me and your mum. You will always have a home with us. You'll always have food for you and that little fella. It's just that this was so hard for us. A baby is hard," he said.

He looked at me again in the rear-view mirror, almost asking if it was all right to continue. I just gave a slight nod, saying nothing in return. I couldn't, and he continued, "You have me and your mum. You always will," he repeated. He was delaying. He was nervous. He knew I wasn't going to like where it was going. He cleared his throat again, and said, "I guess what I'm trying to ask you, is whether you really have to do this alone? We know this is hard for you. We know you've been hurt."

"Yes, I have!" I snapped. I knew where it was going. He knew from our first conversation six weeks prior that the baby — no, my baby's father didn't know about the pregnancy. It had been one of his first concerns, the one thing that had really made him angry — the thought that a man would abandon his baby. I had assured him that it wasn't the case, but all that did was give him the idea that he had the solution. He thought that perhaps things could be put right if the father was told. It was the "fix" that he so desperately needed to provide, because he had never not been able to come up with a solution before. I had told him repeatedly and emphatically that it wasn't going to happen.

I had told them something, of course. I told them that I'd been in a relationship. That I had been in love, and that it had caused my life-long best friend, Hattie, to not just hate me, but to also turn all of our friends against me. If my parents had their theories, then they were keeping them to themselves. Mum had given me insight into her thinking one night, when she asked me what had felt like such a poignant question.

"Was it wrong to love him?" she had asked.

"It didn't feel wrong. Nothing has ever felt more right," had been my answer. Then I cried in her arms.

It still didn't feel wrong.

It wasn't wrong.

Mum spoke then, bringing me back to the car, and the rain, "Darling, we're just trying to help."

"I'd want to know," Dad jumped in. "If it were me, I'd want to know, and I'd want to be involved."

I couldn't do it then. I knew all the secrecy was killing them. They had thought that we were close, that we were more open with each other than that — and we were, in normal situations, but it wasn't a normal situation. They deserved more from me, but I just couldn't give it to them, so I told them as bluntly and as matter-of-factly as I could manage, whilst holding back the tears that were waiting to flow, "I need you to drop this. The stress isn't good for the baby."

I knew that I'd stooped to new lows using the well-being of their unborn grandson against them. I didn't mean to be a bitch; it was just self-preservation. It worked. They shared a look, no words. They knew each other well enough after over forty years of marriage to just give a look, and the topic was never brought up again.

We pulled up to the house, and the rain seemed to get heavier to coincide with when we needed to get out of the car. We ran quickly through the gate and it nearly fell off its rusty hinges. My dad was retired but his days were full. He seemed to get a lot of jobs done, but for some reason, and much to my mum's annoyance — that rusty gate was always moved down the 'to do list'. My dad opened the white front door — even in the rain it was a truly beautiful little cottage, wisteria growing all around it, it felt safe... protected, and as we stepped inside, we were greeted with the smell of hot chocolate being warmed on the hob. Lucas was there with a wooden spoon in hand, and a big, welcoming smile on his face.

Had I been in the mood I would've laughed at the image before me. Lucas had dark hair, green eyes, and dimples that appeared when he hit you with his smile. He was also a well-built, six foot four, Irish giant. A "gentle giant" he would often say, and watching him stir hot chocolate you could probably believe him. However, my parents had told me that his arrival in Clovelly was shrouded in secrecy. He'd been accepted by the community; he fished, had a hand in carpentry, even pulled the occasional pint at the pub. His good looks — I could admit he was aesthetically pleasing — and Irish charm had helped, but essentially, he'd given the community of Clovelly no choice. He had simply inserted himself into their world. Now, he was in my parents' kitchen — completely forgiven for letting himself into their house, I should add — and making us all hot chocolate, and he was trying, really trying, to insert himself into my world.

It was so much more than my brain could comprehend, and definitely too much for my shattered heart to even entertain. So, when he turned to me with that smile, and asked me, "What are we having then? Boy or girl?" I simply turned on my heel and went straight out into the rain.

3

I had actually met Lucas before I escaped to my parents' house in a state of heartbreak and despair. I had been in a good place back then. It had been in the early days of my relationship, long before it all went so wrong, and I'd come to visit my parents for their anniversary. For some reason they always wanted to include me in their celebrations. Naturally, they did things for just the two of them, but they saw me, their only child, as a big part of their marriage and always invited me to come and stay. Even if I didn't totally get it, I loved it.

It was a Saturday afternoon, we'd had a massive lunch and a couple of bottles of wine between us, and my parents looked utterly content together on the sofa, fingers entwined. As far as I was concerned my parents were the ultimate in relationship goals. For all of their apparent differences in temperament, they worked. They just fit. Dad was from a working-class East End family, and his parents worked tirelessly to get him into university, and to give him the opportunities they never had. He didn't waste it and he repaid them as soon as he was earning. My dad's demeanour in the boardroom was down to his calm, impenetrable mask, but also because of his accent. He'd never shaken it, and it would be easy to hear his voice and think of an East End gangster, as opposed to the COO of an investment company.

Mum was from Clovelly, and she had a fairly sheltered upbringing, but she was confident. She met my dad at university on a night out and was both intrigued and petrified by him at first, but they just hit it off. She'd been unsure about moving to London but had fallen in love with Muswell Hill. However, she had made it clear that one day she wanted to return home.

I hadn't intended to sneak out that afternoon, but they looked so content that I didn't want to ruin the moment. So, I quietly let myself out the front door and headed out for some fresh air, and a much needed chat with the man that I was in love with. Seeing my parents so loved up made me miss him all the more. More than I wanted to allow myself to. I'd just finished speaking with him and was quietly watching the fishing boats just starting to pull up onto the beach. It really is a beautiful place. White buildings, cobbled streets, luscious green trees all around, and hills — lots of hills. It's just like being in a postcard.

I was quite happily in my own world, a world I'd dared to start to believe held the promise of happiness, when a voice broke through my thoughts saying, "Well, hello there, beautiful."

I had turned at the sound of his voice rather than at what he had said. I had always had a thing for the Irish accent, and I wasn't expecting to hear it in Clovelly. As I turned and took him in, I realised that the accent wasn't the only appealing thing about the man that had spoken. The man that was walking ever closer to me. In truth, everything else about him was appealing too, but it didn't matter to me then, because I had just given my heart away.

He smiled a somewhat smug smile, and continued, "Ah, so you know your name I see, Beautiful. My name is Lucas," he said, holding out his hand.

I hated that he thought that I was responding to being called beautiful — I was definitely not that person. I was comfortable in my own skin; with my long wavy brown hair, that had hints of red in the sun, dark brown, doe-eyes, and a heart shaped face. It wasn't the first time I had received such a compliment — but I was not vain, and I didn't want Lucas thinking that I was. I couldn't be sure if it annoyed me more that he might think that, or because I was concerned about that fact that he might be thinking it.

"Actually, my name is Ava, and I turned around because you surprised me," I admonished him. Or at least I tried to.

He smiled, clearly unbothered by my tone, "Well, Ava, I do apologise for any offence caused — that was not my intention," he replied, smiling. "May I be permitted to add that it is a pleasure to meet you?" he asked. Then he paused and looked at me as if I was supposed to respond. I didn't. Yet he waited with an eyebrow slightly raised as if to prompt me.

"Ermm, yes? You may?" I replied. Assuming that must be the answer he was looking for.

"Well, then to be sure it is a pleasure to meet you, Ava."

I couldn't help but think it was a wind up, and I couldn't help but giggle at him. I had never heard anyone talk like him, and his sing-song Irish accent made it seem all the more comical.

"May I ask then, what brings your beautiful self to the lovely village of Clovelly?" he asked, eyebrows raised again.

"You may," was my response. I knew what was expected that time.

"So, what brings your beautiful self to the lovely village of Clovelly?" he asked, smiling again.

He had a smile that could do damage, and I couldn't help starting to smile back, although I quickly caught myself. "You know, Lucas, I'm just not sure that it is any of your business," I replied seriously. I could tell that he was a man that was used to getting what he wanted, but I had no intention of giving it to him.

I had made a mistake though, as Lucas' smile showed me that he clearly liked a challenge. "Well, Ava, as an upstanding member of this community..."

"An upstanding member of the community, you say?" I had practically snorted it out.

"Yes, may I continue?" he replied calmly.

"Can I stop you?" I asked, still laughing at him.

Unfazed, he continued, "As I was saying. As an upstanding member of the community..." he paused, pre-empting an interruption that never came, "I feel compelled. No... I feel that it is my duty to ensure that the village of Clovelly and its residents are kept safe at all times."

There was no holding back my laughter at that. Lucas, however, simply smiled. He seemed to have the gift of coming across as completely sincere when he was clearly taking the piss. That or he was totally mad. That cold thought washed over me for a second, sobering me somewhat, but I couldn't help but engage with him.

"Lucas, do you actually believe that I pose a threat to this village or its inhabitants?" I asked.

His face became serious and he nodded and replied, "Aye. I think you could be very dangerous to a heart or two around these parts," he paused again as if waiting for me to reply, but I said nothing, I had no idea how to deal with him. He smiled again and continued his interrogation. "So, may I ask again, what brings your beautiful self to the lovely village of Clovelly?"

I started to feel as if I was in dangerous territory with Lucas, and yet I found myself unable to stop myself from responding. "You know, this conversation would probably flow a lot more easily if you didn't ask permission to ask a question in full, prior to asking me the question," I told him.

He smiled at that. "That is certainly true," he said, "but then it would also flow more easily if you, well, how should I put this? Oh yes... if you stop being so difficult and answer me bloody questions," he replied. Then he treated me to a full-on smile, and it became very obvious that he was used to having an effect on women.

"Well, Lucas, just so that I can put your mind at rest regarding my intentions — which I assure you are honourable and harmless," I told him. "I am here visiting my parents. And speaking of my parents, they are probably wondering where I am. It was nice to meet you. I do hope you'll sleep easily tonight."

I shouldn't have teased him like that, but I couldn't help myself. I knew it was time to make myself leave, so I smiled at him and walked away. I had only walked a step when he said, "Oh, Ava, I'm not sure if I'll ever sleep well again. Though, when I do, I'm sure the dreams will be sweet."

I couldn't make out if he was for real, but I rallied myself against his charm and reminded myself that he was only trying to get into my pants. That's all he wanted. So, I carried on walking away — and he followed.

"Just as a matter of due diligence — who are your parents?" he asked.

"I'm not sure that's any of your business," I replied firmly. He could not take the hint.

"I just think that I should meet them, is all..." he started to say, but I stopped and turned at that.

He was charming, but I was clearly telling him no — at least I was really trying to — and it started to feel like I was somehow being unfaithful. "Lucas, you seem nice... I think," I told him. "But what possible reason could there be for you to meet my parents?"

He stepped forward, somehow managing to be close without being too close. I was expecting to see his cocky, infectious smile, but instead he looked almost sincere, as he said, "Well, I would like to get to know the parents of the woman that I'm going to marry."

I instantly burst out laughing, but stopped myself when I saw that he still looked sincere. A moment later he grinned again. "You laugh now, my beautiful Ava, but you just wait — the fates have something special lined up for us. You'll see."

I wanted to laugh but for some reason found myself unable to, my feet didn't feel like they wanted to move away either. I got a hold of myself, shook my head, and forced myself to take a few steps back.

"You have a good day, Lucas," I told him. "And perhaps use that charm on somebody that isn't already spoken for. I'm sure it won't be wasted on them."

He sighed, took a few steps back, and finally admitted defeat. "I'll be seeing you again, Ava," he said, before turning around and walking away.

I don't know if he looked back, because I didn't turn back to look myself; I'd just escaped him, there was no way I was getting drawn back in. He had affected me and that had scared me. So, as I walked back to my parents, I made my thoughts go back to London — to where I left my heart. They went back to what had been declared in my little flat just two days ago, and to what I knew would happen when I went back.

So, when I walked through my parents' door that is where my thoughts were, and that was the reason for the smile on my face. I had let my guard down and they hadn't missed it, and they had immediately given me their best mock interrogation faces. I hadn't told them that I had started seeing someone, and I wasn't ready to start lying to them owhich I would have to do. So, when they asked me why I was so happy, I told them that I had just met Lucas.

"Ah..." was their joint reply.

My dad had rolled his eyes and shook his head, and my mum had gone practically giddy. It hadn't been a total lie and it was clearly believable. They wouldn't push me further that day, and Mark... Mark, and the secret we shared, remained just that.

4

I wasn't entirely sure how Lucas and I became an item. Actually, that's not true. I knew how it happened, and why. I just wasn't sure exactly when it happened. Just like I had expected after meeting Dr Julia Weaver the speculation surrounding the arrival of the Swan's daughter from London, had been the talk of the Clovelly gossip circle. Which unfortunately stretched far beyond Church groups and the WI.

In what I can only assume was a total breach of confidentiality; the local chemist had let the information regarding me buying the pregnancy vitamins out. The closest neighbour had talked of the removal van arriving with dozens of boxes. The local shop owner really enjoyed telling the story about me buying a bottle of Sauvignon Blanc, only to then walk down the street, stand for a few minutes, and then tip it down the drain. So, it wasn't long before the pieces had been put together and everyone knew that the Swan's daughter had fled London pregnant, in shame, and had come to Clovelly to call upon the mercy and support of her loving parents. There were, of course, a few variations but that was more or less how the talk went.

The only part of the story I was truly embarrassed about was the wine. I still don't know what drove me to buy it. It was while I was still somewhat at odds with the life growing inside me, and I'd gone in to buy a few essentials, and ended up picking up that bottle of wine.

It was one of my favourites, and one that Mark and I drank together many a night. Maybe it was some sort of defiance. Or maybe I was just missing him, but I bought it, and at that moment I intended to drink it. I still feel ashamed of that memory, even though I didn't even taste it. I opened it, right there in the street and put it to my nose, and I had never smelled anything so repulsive. So, I just tipped it down the drain.

It was just over two weeks after moving in with my parents before I bumped into Lucas, but that was probably because I had tried to hide away for those two weeks — except for the unfortunate wine-related shopping trip. Lucas had been around though. He'd been on the boats, doing jobs in houses, and drinking in the local. He hadn't been hiding, and like everyone else, he had been listening. So, when, at seventeen weeks pregnant, he spotted me walking up one of Clovelly's steep hills with two bags of shopping, he swooped in.

"Ava! You should not be carrying those bags up that hill!" he had scolded me. He was genuinely mad at me.

Well, he had picked the wrong girl. I had grown tired of feeling broken and had decided to focus on being mad instead. Mad at Mark, mad at Hattie, Ted, Will, everyone. I escaped their lies when I left London and then I came here, and the whispering started again. I had hidden away at first, but I needed to claim my life back. I needed to feel some sense of power, and just like before, being angry felt easier than being broken.

I wasn't even showing so I knew the only way that he knew that I was pregnant, was because of the gossip. I knew the gossip would be inevitable, but I was still annoyed about it. So, this man that had only met me once before, telling me what I should and shouldn't do? Well, that was all that was needed to tip me over the edge. I had stood facing him, glaring at him, as I replied through gritted teeth, "What. The. Actual. Fuck. Did you just say to me?"

I had expected him to be taken aback or to at least feel embarrassed, but he wasn't, he walked closer to me, and glared right back as he told me, "I said, Ava. That you should not be carrying those bags up that hill. And I still say that you should not be carrying those bloody bags up that bloody, great big hill! You're bloody preg—"

"PREGNANT?" I shouted. "You're telling me that I cannot carry two bags up a hill because I'm pregnant?"

Lucas had tried to hold up a hand in that moment either by way of apology or appeasement, but he hadn't realised what he had unleashed in me. All the hurt, all the betrayal, and all the lies; everything that I'd been through over the last few months was about to come crashing out.

"Who the fuck do you think you are to tell me what I can and cannot do?" I asked, but I didn't need or wait for a response. "Women run marathons when pregnant. They swim. Go to the gym. They debate in parliament. They do NOT sit at home with their feet up waiting for some man... some, Lucas, to come and rescue them. And they absolutely CAN carry two shopping bags up a bloody hill!" I shouted at him. I paused for breath and then one of my shopping bags split open, because the entire universe was against me.

We both stood there silently looking at the vegetables,

bread and cheese laying on the pavement. I don't think Lucas dared say anything and I didn't know whether to laugh, cry or shout at him some more. I was about to go with the crying option when suddenly Lucas bent down and scooped everything up. He took the other bag from me without saying a word and started to walk up the hill. I was utterly defeated and all I could do was follow him. As much as I hated to admit it, I realised that if ever there was a person that looked like they needed to be rescued, it was me. The truth was that I didn't need to be rescued, I just needed someone else to be on my side. Lucas it seemed, wanted to be on my side.

Once home, I apologised for yelling at him and thanked him, somewhat begrudgingly, for his help, and then we talked. We had an actual, normal conversation between two adults, which was a stark contrast to our first meeting all those months ago, when he had talked in riddles and practically proposed. He told me a little bit about his life in Ireland — Rosses Point to be precise. He didn't give much detail, but I later searched online and found it was a gorgeous coastal village, not dissimilar to Clovelly. He was a brother to three sisters, which he gave as his reason for being so protective of me. He was nice and he was charming, but there was more to him than he let on, I could see that. Still, I decided that I'd let him have his secrets. After all, I had mine.

I couldn't blame Lucas for not giving me many details, especially as I told him even less than I had told my parents. He was nice, but he was new, and I didn't trust him. My fingers had been burned and my wall was well and truly up. I had to tell him something, so, I told him that I edited books and wrote freelance. I loved baking — just like my mum — probably because of my mum, and that something had happened in London that had cost me everything and everyone in my life.

For such a talker he was a surprisingly good listener, and I don't know why, but I felt the need to let him know that I wasn't as penny-less as everyone in the village thought I was. I may have run to my parents pregnant, but not "pregnant and penny-less" as some of the gossip had suggested. I'd had the good sense to rent my flat out before leaving, so I had some money coming in each month. I did something right. I even told him that I only found out that I was pregnant just before I left London, that I hadn't known at the time of the break-up with the father, and I hadn't told him. I found myself going a step further and telling Lucas something that I hadn't even told my parents — that I had no intention of telling the father — not ever. It was going to be the baby and me. Me and my family — the father's family had done enough damage already. With that said, I suddenly felt the need to rebuild my wall — I hadn't even noticed that he'd been pulling it down. However, my need to protect myself from more hurt was strong, so I told him that I needed to rest.

As he got up to leave, I said, "Thank you for this. It's been nice to speak to another human being other than Julia and my parents. Goodbye, Lucas." I put my hand out to invite him to shake it. In my mind, if he did, he would be agreeing to my terms — agreeing to the "goodbye." I had felt a strange mix of relief and disappointment over the fact that he was leaving, and I didn't like it. I needed him to stay away.

He smiled at me, took my hand and looked me right in the eye as he slowly brought it up to his lips and ever so gently kissed it.

I immediately snatched it back. "Lucas..." I started to say, but I didn't get far before he stopped me.

"Ava, I understand," he said. "You're hurting. Heart-broken in fact, and I've got to tell you that part of me wants to find the man that has done this to you and break his face for hurting you like this. Then there's the other part of me that wants to shake his hand." He paused as he saw my questioning expression and that I was about to explode again.

He put his hand up to silence me. "Ava, no. Not because he hurt you. Never that, but because at some point he clearly did something... he was clearly worthy enough — at one point, at least — to earn your heart," he told me earnestly.

I sank back a little. Just like when we first met Lucas surprised me with the words that came out of his mouth. Words were my trade, but in that moment, they had completely escaped me.

So, he continued, "I've made it very clear that I'm attracted to you. It's in the stars, you and me," he said, and he smiled fondly. "That's what my nana would always say. I know that you don't need to hear that, right now. You've got enough on your plate. You and that wee baby are your priority, and you may not like it, but you're my priority too."

With those words spoken I knew exactly how to respond, and said, quite dumbfounded, "Lucas... let's be honest, you are gorgeous. I admit it, you are. When the Gods were handing out looks, charm and prowess they were clearly feeling generous with you," I told him honestly. "But me? I am broken. My life has fallen apart and I cannot even comprehend what will happen next week, let alone what I'm going to do with the rest of my life. What I'm going to do with this baby. Oh, and while we're on that subject... I am pregnant with another man's baby," I told him, pointing to my stomach to emphasise the point. "The entire female population of Clovelly, and no doubt the surrounding villages are salivating over you. Why on earth are you interested in me? It makes no sense," I said, exasperated. What more could I say to him?

He shook his head and calmly replied, "I only see the happy, beautiful woman that I saw smiling at the beach that day. I know how that smile made me feel and I know she's still in there. I know your life is incredibly fuckin' complicated right now. And yes, I know you're pregnant with another man's baby and that that is the sort of thing that might usually send a man running for the hills," he told me honestly. "As far as I'm concerned, that baby is part of you and that makes him just fine with me. By the way, I have a gift and I think it's a boy — sorry to spoil the surprise," he said smiling innocently. "I know you're not looking for that right now," he said smiling gently, "but I also know that you need a friend, and I truly hope that you'll let me be that to you."

I let out a deep sigh and shrugged. "I had friends, Lucas. Good friends, old friends. And they let me down — all of them. Every. Single. One," I told him, and I looked down as the memory of Tasha and Miri walking out of my door came flooding back to me.

It was his turn to hold out his hand for me to shake, I took it as he looked at me with complete sincerity, as he promised, "I won't Ava. Not ever. I'll always be here for you."

He was there for me, pretty much every day. If he didn't come to the house, then I'd see him when I was out walking — I'd started getting out and about more. After having my twenty-week scan I felt a new sense of purpose and I realised that I did love the life, the baby, growing inside me — the boy Lucas had predicted. I knew that I needed to start doing things again, but I couldn't face contacting my freelance clients from before. I had cut myself off from London and from that life. I had changed my number and deleted all of my social media accounts. I doubted that anyone wanted to contact me anyway, but I no longer cared.

Unfortunately, stepping back into writing felt like opening up the door to my old life again and I couldn't do that. Not then. What I could do was bake, and as my mum needed some help in her tea rooms, I was more than happy to bake for her while she tended to the customers.

I was still prime gossip material, even more so because of Lucas' attention to me. People didn't understand it. We were friends, or at least becoming so, but he had let it slip to people more than once that he wanted more. Nobody could really figure out why he'd be so eager to take on a "pregnant home-wrecker" — that was one of the theories going around; that I had been involved with a married man. So, I tried to keep a low profile and hid away and baked cakes. However, I was also eating them, which is why I had to force myself to get out for some exercise.

Considering how upfront Lucas was with me, he somehow managed to quietly sneak his way into my affections. I started to trust him. I'd seek him out instead of waiting to bump into him. I'd cook him meals and we'd chat easily while he washed and dried the pots. His over-protectiveness was still a bugbear of mine at times — just not when it got me out of pot washing duty. I think I realised that he was starting to mean more to me, that I was letting him in, when I was thirty-five weeks pregnant, but I quickly dismissed it as being down to the hormones. He was gorgeous and I was horny as hell. I regularly found my eyes lingering over his torso and wondering if he was so generously built all over.

I had put my wall back up then. I was still hurting. Still angry, and I decided that when you are weeks away from bringing a new life into the world, it's probably not the best time to start a new relationship. Especially when you're quite certain that you're not yet over said new life's father. That's something that I couldn't let myself think about though, it was easier to push all thoughts of Mark far away. I needed to keep that door firmly closed.

It was when Jacob was four months old that I finally let Lucas in. I had been in my own baby bubble up till then — Lucas had been with me, of course. He saw me at my absolute worst. One day, he came in and I was sitting on the sofa in my parents' living room with both breasts out. Jacob was attached to one and a muslin was underneath the other catching leaking milk. In my sleep deprived state, I hadn't even noticed, but he just put the kettle on, brought me a biscuit and then left me to it.

At four months in, when I finally started to feel like I had a handle on things. The opportunity to rent a little two bed terraced house about a ten-minute walk from my parents had arisen, and figuring that they needed a break, I jumped at it. I'd been in for a week and Lucas had been over every day helping me. It was one of those rare moments where the timing just felt right. We'd eaten and he was washing the pots while I fed and settled Jacob, who for once seemed willing to sleep in his moses basket instead of on me. I walked into the kitchen as Lucas was putting the last of the plates away, and I just didn't feel like fighting it anymore.

So, I walked up behind him, wrapped my arms around his waist, feeling for the first time what I'd been thinking about for months and said, "Lucas O'Connor, I think I'm in love with you."

He had turned immediately and pulled me close, his cocky, infectious smile beaming down at me, as he said, "Oh, Ava Swan, I know you are. It's nice that you've finally caught up. If it's OK with you, I'm going to kiss you now."

Even after I confessed my love he was still asking for my permission. Who was this man? I knew the answer. He was exactly what I needed. I smiled at him, trying to mimic his cocky persona and said, "Just get on with it," and he did.

5

I think after my experience with Mark, I had been expecting for the sex to come naturally straight away. Lucas and I had gotten to know each other well and I was comfortable with him, but I realised as we started kissing, and as the clothes were being pulled off. That as into it as I was, and as ready for it as I thought I was. I didn't entirely let myself go. I didn't feel that same uncontrollable need as I had felt with Mark, and I knew that it wasn't just down to my past hurt, because there were other issues too. For one, I was breastfeeding Jacob and when Lucas first cupped my breasts and ran his thumb over my nipples, I'd instantly recoiled. It felt so strange to have them treated sexually when mere minutes earlier they'd been feeding a baby. So, my breasts were a no-go zone.

Lucas' passion, however, was infectious and my need soon caught up with his. He was as large as I had expected him to be and that made me as excited as it did nervous. I felt like he had been waiting so long for me, and I felt ready, so we skipped over the foreplay. He had grabbed a condom from his wallet, and I watched him expertly slide it over his enormous erection. He picked me up and carried me into the living room as if I weighed nothing and laid me down on the sofa.

The fear left me then, and I suddenly felt just as desperate as he was for him to be inside me. To feel wanted again, and to feel loved again. Then as soon as he pushed inside me, I let out a loud yelp which consequently woke Jacob up. It really hurt. I hadn't been expecting that and I felt mortified for both of us. Jacob was screaming so I pushed off the sofa, picked him up, ran upstairs and settled him on the breast again. My phone was in my bedroom, so I decided to contact Julia. Having a doctor as a friend definitely had its perks.

Julia and I had become good friends. She'd guided me through my pregnancy, childbirth and the early days of motherhood, and along the way she helped put the pieces of me back together again, alongside Lucas, and my parents. She had confided in me in the early days, telling me that it wasn't a broken heart that had made her leave London and come back home. It was in fact the other way around. She had left Clovelly with a broken heart and had hoped that a new place would heal it. It had to some extent, but she had missed her home and came back when the chance arose.

The man in question was Peter Harrison — the pharmacist. He had a girlfriend when Julia fell in love with him but had promised that he was leaving her. He had said all the right things, "It was complicated," and he "needed time" and even better he was "scared of what she might do to herself if he left." Julia had given him time; she had been in love and she had believed him. Then he proposed, only, it wasn't to Julia. So, she left.

I wasn't sure if she told me to make me feel less pathetic about my own situation, or if it was because she knew that

I'd understand. Afterwards, I had looked into whether I could actually get him sacked. However, it would seem that telling people about who has been buying pregnancy vitamins wasn't considered enough of a breach of privacy to warrant his dismissal.

I picked up my phone and I sent her a text.

SOS! Was just about to have sex with Lucas & he put it in & it REALLY hurt! I actually screamed! Jacob now awake... he's BIG but it didn't feel like it was that... has childbirth broken me???

Thankfully her reply was quick.

FINALLY!! It's about time! OK - totally normal for the body to be tender. Not broken, just need some time. Take it slowly, don't push it if it hurts — just do other stuff ;-) Use lube. Come see me tomorrow & give me details.

P.S. Are you using protection?? You're very fertile right now. Jacob is gorgeous but I'm not sure you need another one just yet.

P.P.S. Just how BIG are we talking?

I felt reassured, and after settling Jacob again I put on my dressing gown and went to face Lucas. He was still on the sofa but had put his boxers and t-shirt back on. I sat down next to him and told him that I'd spoken to Julia, and I explained that we might need to take that part a bit slower.

He laughed about the fact that I'd been upstairs texting my doctor-friend and pulled me in for a kiss, and told me, "That's OK. We have all the time in the world." We then proceeded to "just do other stuff" — much to both of our satisfaction.

We continued to try to have actual sex whenever Jacob let us, and one day I found it comfortable enough to do it. It felt amazing to finally have him inside me fully, to feel that close to him, and it was good. Lucas was strong, seemed to have endless energy and he was large. I knew I shouldn't compare but I couldn't help it, because as good as it all was in a physical sense, I just didn't feel the same as I did with Mark. It was definitely pleasurable, but he didn't have the effect on me that Mark did, and he didn't make the things happen that Mark seemed to achieve so effortlessly. I just couldn't help but feel like I was getting pulled into Lucas's passion as opposed to genuinely feeling my own.

One day, when Jacob seemed to be attached to me constantly, I made a mental list to try to figure out what was wrong:

- Lucas is gorgeous
- I fancy him
- His penis is massive
- He knows exactly what to do with it
- He's not allowed to play with my nipples
- He's not Mark.

I hadn't been able to stop that last thought creeping in. I shook it off, thought harder and came to a more palatable conclusion, and that was, that I wasn't the same person that I was when I was with Mark. It seemed like a good enough answer, but deep down I knew it wasn't just that. So, I dug a little deeper and decided that Mark and I had been in a bubble. It had just been the two of us. It was real life but not the real life I was living now. Mark and I had the freedom to have sex pretty much whenever and wherever we wanted, as loudly as we wanted. With Lucas, we had to get it when we could in between work, breastfeeding, changing nappies, and during the very small window of opportunity which formed when Jacob was asleep, and when he was asleep, we were scared to be too loud in case we woke him up.

So, ultimately, I decided that it made total sense that it wasn't the same as it had been with Mark, and I decided to stop agonising about things and to just enjoy them.

Things with Lucas were good. He adored me. He adored Jacob. There was no need to create obstacles that weren't there. Only, I couldn't quite shake the fact that they were there.

6

That was four months ago. Lucas and I have been together for four months now, and have been through more than most couples do in four years. We practically live together, and we are raising a baby together. My baby, really — my little Jacob, but Lucas accepted Jacob before he was even born, and if I'm his, then that means that my baby is too. Jacob adores him. With his dark brown hair, he could even pass him off as his own biologically. Except for those eyes. My mum and dad are convinced that Jacob will lose the deep blue and turn brown like me — there's still time. However, I just know that's not going to be the case. They aren't just blue. They're blue like Mark's.

Today starts the same way as usual — I kiss Lucas goodbye, as he reluctantly leaves my bed at the crack of dawn to head out to the fishing boats. I go back to sleep, only to be woken an hour later by Jacob, wanting a feed. I walk. I bake. I chat with people in the streets, because that's something that I do now. The gossiping subsided when Jacob was born, and the entire village fell in love with the beautiful, new, baby boy. Then it stopped completely when Lucas and I went public. Everyone adores and respects Lucas, so even if they have been on the fence about me, the fact that he has chosen me means something to them. So now I'm accepted.

I actually quite like living in Clovelly now. I'm adjusted to the pace of life. I no longer find it strange that people know my name and greet me in the street. I think I'm still a Londoner at heart, like my dad is, and I probably always will be, but Clovelly is my home now, it's my little safe haven. It's the place where I'll — no, we'll raise Jacob, and most importantly, where I'll be able to keep him hidden.

At least, for now.

Things are looking up for me. I've been jotting down some feature ideas while Jacob is on the breast, for a while now. I had to do something after going through several box sets in a matter of weeks. I've made contact with some of my freelance clients, who thankfully remember me — the real me — and just this morning I secured a new project. At least Hattie and her lies didn't infiltrate every aspect of my life.

In fact, it's been more than an ordinary day, it's been a good day, and I can't help smiling as I head home after a late afternoon walk with Jacob. I took him out in the sling because it's by far the easiest way to get him to nap, and I love our afternoon walks, just him and me, our hearts beating next to each other. However, my smile fades as soon as I walk through the back door and I immediately sense that something is wrong.

Mum is in my kitchen cooking dinner and she gives me what seems like a forced smile when she sees me. I smile back, feeling uneasy and walk further in and see that my dad is in my living room reading the paper. He looks up at me to nod his hello, only to hide back behind the local Gazette. Totally normal behaviour really, except it's not.

Mum bounces over, “Darling, hello,” she says. Naturally she's talking to Jacob, not me. “Ava,” she continues, “I’ve spoken to Lucas and he’ll be home in an hour. Dinner is under control, so why don’t you take a shower and we’ll look after this gorgeous boy.”

She puts her arms out, so I take Jacob out of the sling and he gladly goes to his doting grandma. Something isn't right. My parents rarely show up uninvited since Lucas and I became a couple — and dinner? My mum loves to cook but she’s not cooked for me since I was living with her. I’ve had a bad feeling all week. I managed to forget about it during my walk, but that feeling in the pit of my stomach is back now and it’s stronger than ever.

Dad is still hiding in his paper. This is definitely not good and unfortunately, I have a pretty good idea where this is going. Dad spent last weekend in London with his old friends. There was golf, food, alcohol, and possibly Hattie's dad. I haven't dared to ask him who was there, and if Hattie’s dad wasn't there himself, then there would have been people there that know him. I made my dad promise not to mention anything about Jacob. I knew it was going to be hard for him, especially after he’d had a few drinks. He loves Jacob and is always talking about him to anyone he meets.

Not only that, but I'm well aware that he hasn’t quite got over the fact that there is a man out there unaware that he has a baby — and that has never sat right with my dad. I know that, even if he doesn't say it anymore, but I impressed upon him the importance of keeping it a secret, because of Hattie. Hattie destroyed my life. I don't want her to know about my baby. I told him that she would probably find it funny and gloat — but it isn't that. Hattie knows the truth, even though she spread so many lies. So, my dad promised me that no matter what, he would not say a word.

I do as my mum asks and head for the shower. I take my time. This is the time to prepare myself for the thing that I've been putting off since I came here. I knew it would happen at some point. I've not been that delusional about it, but a girl can hope. I let the water wash over me. I love this shower, it's powerful and usually makes me feel rejuvenated. Right now, I just want to lose myself in the water. Here it is warm. Here it is safe.

I check the clock as I get out — another half an hour until Lucas will be home. My parents are clearly planning to wait for him to be here, so I have another thirty minutes. I really hope that time will go slowly. Actually, I really want time to stop.

My stairs lead straight into the living room where my dad is playing with Jacob on the floor. He could play peek-aboo for hours, that boy. Normally, the sight of my dad playing with his grandson fills me with happiness — a sense of pride even. I brought a lot of baggage with me when I came here, and it all got dumped on them. I still feel bad about that, but the fact that I've brought Jacob into their world and given them so much joy and love, makes me feel like I've made amends in some way. However, I feel no joy right now, because my dad still can't meet my gaze, making his attention to Jacob seem more like a distraction than genuine play.

In some random form of role reversal, it's my mum who is wearing a game face. She comes in from the kitchen with a smile, telling me that everything is under control. I smile at her, but the need to escape is rising in me, so I ask, "Did you get any wine to go with the dinner, Mum?"

"Oh, no I didn't actually dear. I'll—" she is about to offer to go to the shop, so I cut in.

"You've done enough," I tell her. Then I grab my bag and head to the kitchen for my shoes. There is no way that she is going to leave me alone with my dad right now. "Red or white?" I ask. Somehow managing to sound casual when in reality my heart is racing, and my gut is churning.

She replies just as easily, "You choose, darling."

This is definitely not going to be good. Mum likes things to be just right and wine is always selected based on what we are eating. The fact that she not only forgot to bring some wine, but is also letting me choose, further fuels the dread that is beginning to take over me. I peek into the living room one last time to make sure Jacob is happy, then head out to the shops.

This is happening. What else can it be? Dad has just been in London and I have noticed that he hasn't been himself all week. There is no other explanation, and I am trying my best to come up with one. I barely look at the wine and I didn't even think to ask what my mum was cooking, so I just pick up two bottles of red and two of white. Jacob wakes during the nights for feeds, and so as much as I may want to, there is no way that I can drink myself into oblivion. However, I am definitely going to need something.

My legs feel like they are made of lead, as I get closer to my house, and for a moment I'm not sure my hand will actually move in order to put the key in the door, but somehow, I manage it. To anyone else the scene before me would seem normal, idyllic even. Mum is now plating up and Dad is fastening Jacob into his high chair. Jacob sees me and gives me the biggest smile. At least by the end of the night he won't think any less of me. Yes, on the outside all seems well, but my instincts are screaming at me that it isn't.

Mum takes the wine from me, she puts one of the bottles of white in the freezer and as she goes to open one of the reds, she says, "Lucas is back early and is in the shower, so we're all set for dinner."

Lucas enters the room completely on cue — I've never known anyone shower as quickly as he does. He walks over to me with his easy smile and gives me a kiss, but immediately senses my panic and a silent question crosses his face. He knows something isn't quite right too, but he doesn't let on. He goes over to my mum and says, "Eleanor, this smells truly lovely. What a treat. Is there anything that I can do to help?"

Mum is dishing up by this point, and replies, "Absolutely not! You just sit yourself down and pour yourself a drink. You too, Ava," she adds, glancing at me.

Dad is now sitting, so I ask him, "Red or white?" The plates are put in front of us and instead of answering me, he turns to Lucas.

"You don't happen to have any of that whiskey of yours knocking around, do you?" he asks him.

"Of course," Lucas replies, "I'll go get it," and he leaves the room.

I start to set aside some of my dinner for Jacob, who is currently chewing a bread roll and will be happy with that until it cools enough. I always feed him from my plate and generally make myself larger portions because of it. Tonight, that isn't going to be an issue though. I know that tonight I'm not going to be able to eat a thing.

Lucas returns with a bottle of his most cherished whiskey and a glass for my dad, who I am now starting to feel annoyed with on top of everything else. I am officially getting the cold shoulder and there is no point in putting this off any longer.

"Whiskey with dinner, Dad?" I ask him. "This must be bad." He says nothing but he swallows hard and I can't leave it there. "You've not looked at me all evening," I tell him. "Are we really going to pretend our way through this meal? Sorry, Mum, it does look really good, but honestly, can you both just say whatever it is that you came to say, because I cannot stand this!" I blurt it out in a mixture of anger and fear. I have tried to avoid this conversation for so long, but right now I just want it over and done with.

Everyone puts their forks down at the same time, except Jacob, who is now demanding my dinner. I give it to him feeling completely envious of his obliviousness. Dad looks at me now, but he is unreadable again. Mum is sitting next to him, on the other side of Jacob, and Lucas is next to me, and the slight nudge of his leg against mine reminds me that he has my back. I hope he still will by the end.

Dad finally speaks, "Yes, you're right," he says. I suck in a breath as he clears his throat and starts. "As you know, I was in London with the old gang last weekend," he says. "Now, just to reassure you. I never said a word to anyone about Jacob, or being a grandad or anything."

I release the breath that I didn't realise that I had still been holding, and I nod in a way of thanks, but to also encourage him to continue — he does.

"As you know, Hattie's dad — who couldn't make it by the way — but as you know, we know a lot of the same people. So that means that they heard stories," he says.

"Stories?" I ask, sarcastically. "Any story in particular?" I don't know why I'm feeling angry about the fact that I'm being talked about back in London, it's not like I don't know what they are saying. That is unless Hattie has added another chapter to her book of lies.

Dad looks at me hard. He clearly isn't liking this either,

and he definitely doesn't like what he has heard. He sighs and continues more firmly, "Ava, all we've had to go on since you arrived is our own imagination, since you have refused to give us any details about what went on?" he tells me. "You tell us you and Hattie fell out and that it was big enough for her to turn everyone against you," he says. "You tell us that she did this through lies, and yet you still refuse to tell us what the truth is. So, then I go to London and I get told what happened by my friends, and what they told me wasn't pretty," he says angrily. Then he pauses to run his hands through his hair. "I'm hoping that what I was told was one of Hattie's lies."

"Why don't you just ask me what you need to ask me," I instruct him.

Mum is now focusing on Jacob, but my dad's gaze never leaves my face, I feel Lucas' leg against mine again... thank God, for this man.

Dad clears his throat and then asks, "Did you have sex with Ted and Will — Hattie's brothers?"

I can't help but let out a sour laugh. I've heard this accusation before, but hearing it come out of my dad's mouth — hearing it here, has made the wounds that I thought had healed rip open again. I look him dead in the eye and answer him as clearly and as calmly as I can.

"No, Dad," I tell him. "No! I did not have sex with Ted or Will. I have never had sex with Ted or Will. Not at the same time, not one after the other, not either of them. Not ever!" I can't tell if he believes me or not but either way he isn't finished.

"So, neither of Hattie's brothers are Jacob's father?" he asks.

"That would be pretty difficult, don't you think? Given

that I. Never. Ever. Had. Sex. With. Either. Of. Them!" It takes all of my strength not to shout at him. The only reason I don't is because of Jacob sitting next to me. Still, I stress every word because I have to make him believe me.

Dad rubs his face now; he looks so tired and I realise that this has been churning around in him all week. It's Mum that asks the obvious question.

"So why on earth would Hattie, your best friend and both her brothers — because they have backed up this version of events by the way," she says. "Why would they lie about you like this? Hattie loves you."

"Hattie loved me," I practically spit back. "I doubt that she does now, and they made up this lie to punish me. Which is funny because Hattie clearly thought that what happened, what really happened, was bad enough to destroy my life, so you'd think she'd just tell the truth," I say bitterly. "But no. She wanted to make sure that I looked as bad as possible. This was how she did it. Her brothers backed her up because they're loyal to her, and I guess they didn't really like the real story either," I tell them seriously.

There is silence for a moment. I know what is coming next, I just don't know which direction it is going to come from. I'm looking from my mum to my dad, so it takes me by surprise when it's Lucas that speaks.

"Ava, everybody around this table loves you," he says. "I personally don't think there's anything that you could do to make me not love you."

Mum is next. "He's right, darling," she says kindly.

We all turn to my dad and he looks me in the eyes and says, "It's time, Ava."

I nod, get up and go to the freezer to get the now chilled wine. I fill my glass and put the bottle on the table. I look at their glasses and motion for them to top them up too, and they do.

"I guess I should start at the beginning," I say, taking a deep breath in.

7

I had a good life in Muswell Hill — I guess I had it quite easy, really. My parents bought their house on Kings Avenue when prices were low and when they saw the direction that property in London was going, they decided to re-mortgage, released some equity, and bought a two-bed flat in need of some TLC in a block on The Broadway. They rented it out for years, but they'd always intended it for me. So, when I finished university in Bristol and returned to London, they signed the deeds over to me and there I was — fresh out of university with a two-bed flat and no mortgage to pay.

I was lucky, I knew that, not just because of the security the flat gave me, but also the freedom it gave me work-wise. I got a rather low paid role as a junior editor with a well-known publisher straight out of uni, whilst also working on my writing in my own time. After a few years the company expressed the need to make cuts, and I offered to go part time. This apparently worked for them as they happily agreed and also took the 'Junior' out of my job title. This gave me the chance to develop writing as a career as well, and so I became self-employed at the same time and started to write freelance for various publications. It was hit and miss at first. Some months I barely got anything, but in time the work came in.

I was also lucky with my friendships. There was a group of four of us that had known each other since school; me, Hattie, Tasha and Miranda. Hattie and I both ended up at Bristol, but Tasha and Miri went in different directions, but we stayed close, and we all came back to London.

Hattie Davidson had been my best friend since the age of five when she moved in a few doors down from me. My mum got introduced to her mum by neighbours and I met Hattie in reception class — so we were essentially thrust together. That worked well for Hattie and me as we instantly adored each other, but not so well for our mums, who couldn't have been more different and not just in age. Hattie's parents were a good ten years younger than mine, but their personalities differed massively too. Hattie's mum, Mary, was quite a piece of work — that's what I'd heard my mum say to my dad one evening and I'd passed that information straight onto Hattie the next day. We both assumed it to be a good thing, and Hattie naturally told her mum when she picked her up after school. Mary didn't seem to share our enthusiasm for the 'compliment' and my own mum — who was standing right next to her at the time — looked like she was about to die on the spot. Neither of them had hoped that our friendship would last, but it did.

Hattie's dad was another matter. All the other dads liked him and so did the other mums. He was kind, smart, charming and very handsome. I was to learn years later, that her parents had got together at university and accidentally got pregnant with Hattie during their third year. They married, thinking it was the right thing to do, and later had two more children — Ted, then Will. They had support from their parents and they both graduated, and Hattie's dad went into a great job.

They were well off, but not happy and there were many times when Hattie would come to me crying after she'd overheard another argument. Tasha, Miri and I were always on her dad's side — or from the age of twelve — her "lovely" dad's side — that's what we had taken to calling him. When our teenage hormones kicked in, we could all finally appreciate why he made our mums blush. None of us liked Hattie's mum, preferring to see her as some cruel wife putting the saint of a man down, and we were all relieved when they divorced a few years later. That was until we realised that we wouldn't see him at our sleepovers anymore.

At twenty-four, confident and gorgeous, Hattie had a great love life — unlike me. She and Nate had been together for almost two years and whether Nate knew it or not she was already planning their wedding. Hattie was a weird mix of both her mum and her dad and not just in looks. Like her brothers she resembled her mum, but she had her dad's blue eyes — they all do. Hattie could be kind, really kind, and that's definitely from her dad.

As far as best friends go, I can't imagine anyone had a better one than me. Hattie just sparkled — that's how I thought of her. Yet, just like her mum, she was a force to be reckoned with. When Hattie was on a mission there was no point in standing in her way. She would trample right over you — no matter who you were. She can't help it; she just becomes completely blinkered and she can't see past her end goal. Some say she's selfish, but it's just Hattie. She didn't mean any harm... most of the time.

However, on the Saturday morning when she showed up

at my flat. The morning when events, beyond anything we could foresee, were about to be set in motion. She was running the risk of annoying all of my neighbours with the incessant manner in which she was buzzing at my intercom. I knew it was her before I even lifted the receiver.

"Hattie, seriously?" I said in mock exasperation.

"Well, hello to you, too," she replied. "Let me in, will you? I really need to speak to you."

Yes, it was definitely Hattie and apparently, she was on a mission. I opened the door for her and welcomed her with a hug, as we always did. I loved that girl, even though I was probably not going like what was coming next. Luckily, Hattie didn't waste time on niceties when she had something on her mind, so I didn't have to wait for too long to find out what had brought her to my door. She took off her coat and gave me her best sweet and innocent look.

"I need to ask you a favour," she said in a tone equally as sweet.

"Really? I'd never have guessed," I replied, smiling.

"It's nothing bad," she quickly added.

I laughed at her and went to put the kettle on. "Just ask me what you need me to do. Wait no — just tell me what you need me to do," I said, and in return she gave me a look of mock offence.

"Ha! Funny. You can say no," she told me with a scowl.

I laughed harder then. "I can? How have you never told me this before?" I replied, and she huffed at me. The banter was clearly cutting into her agenda, so I shook the laughter aside and said, "Spit it out, Hattie."

She was happy to be back on track and she got straight to it. "Well, as you know my dad has returned from his stint in Tokyo," she said, beaming.

I did know. She was thrilled to have him back. Hattie's

dad worked in corporate takeovers and had been based at his company's head office in Japan for five years. I didn't know exactly what he did, but I knew he was high up in the ranks. He came back to London often, but she had missed him. He moved back a few months ago and was working for himself, semi-retired at forty-four — just dipping in and out as a consultant.

"So..." she continued, "he's been on a few dates with this lovely woman called Helen. Honestly, she's perfect for him, but for some reason he's dragging his feet. So..."

"Sorry to interrupt you Hattie," I said, "but you're asking me a favour relating to your dad's love life?" I really didn't like where the conversation was going, and Hattie clearly didn't like me interrupting her train of thought. She gave me a firm look and continued, "If you let me finish, I will tell you."

Yes, Hattie was definitely on a mission.

"So, as I was saying. Helen is just the best, but my dad is dragging his feet a bit," she said, rolling her eyes. "There's been a few kisses here and there but that's it."

I really wanted to know how she knew these details but didn't dare to interrupt her again. She continued, "I've managed to persuade him to cook a meal for her at his house next Saturday night, but my dad isn't really the best cook and I'm planning on this being a seal the deal kinda meal — if you know what I'm saying?" she said, smiling at me conspiratorially. Oh, I knew. I couldn't quite get my head around her enthusiasm to get her dad into bed with a woman mind you. She took a breath and carried on, "So that's where you, my darling, beautiful, amazing Ava. Best friend in the whole-wide-world forever, come in."

"I'm a little lost," I replied, looking at her quizzically.

She looked at me as if I was missing the obvious and

said, "I need you to go to my dad's and cook an amazing meal for him and Helen. I mean, not so amazing that she doesn't believe that he's cooked it, but amazing enough to make her want to jump into bed with him."

That wasn't as bad as I was expecting given the weirdness of the conversation. I could cook. My mum and I would always cook and bake together when I was growing up and I'd developed her love for it, and yes, I was pretty good.

"Right. So, you want me to go to your dad's house next Saturday and cook a meal that is just the right level of amazing to ensure that we don't arouse suspicion, but to also ensure that your dad gets a shag?" I confirmed.

She looked triumphant. "Exactly!" she exclaimed. "So, you'll do it then? Please say yes," she practically begged.

"Hattie, does it not feel a little strange to you that you are meddling in your dad's love life? Is he even that into this Helen?" I asked her. Part of me needed her to see that this situation was not really the norm.

"Helen is great for my dad. I'm not sure why he doesn't see that himself, so I'm just helping him along. It's what loving daughters do," she told me, looking angelic again. "Please, please, please say yes, Ava," she begged again.

There was no point in fighting her. She'd break me eventually and we both knew it. So, I agreed. Hattie was thrilled and continued with her instructions. I was to put together a menu suggestion and then she would make sure that her dad bought all of the ingredients in, along with some wine to match. All I needed to do was show up and cook.

The week flew by. I had a couple of freelance projects on the go, alongside my editing role, so I'd had my head down all week and had almost forgotten about Saturday's plans, until Hattie texted me on Friday afternoon.

Dad has confirmed he's got everything on the list.

Helen is due to arrive at 6:30pm. You need to be LONG gone by then. What time do you need to be there to start?xx

Oh, Hats. I felt a bit sorry for her dad — did he actually want this? From what she had said it sounded like this was all Hattie. Still, I had agreed to help and there would be no backing out now.

Probably from about 2 — it's not too prep heavy but the dessert takes a while. He'll have to do a few things himself like reheat & plate up if the "help" is supposed to be long gone before his future wife arrives. x ;-) I replied.

Wife indeed if I have anything to do with it. OK — will tell him to be ready.xx

I started to feel the pressure a little bit. I may have been joking about him marrying this woman, but Hattie had plans for them and it suddenly occurred to me that it might well be on me — or at least my cooking — if things didn't go her way. I reached for the recipes that I'd printed off and went over them again, making sure that I had all the timings right and hadn't missed any small detail. I was a confident cook and would often wing it a bit instead of following recipes to the letter — the results of which were somewhat varying — but not tomorrow. Tomorrow I was going to do everything by the book. If things didn't turn out the way Hattie had planned then it was absolutely, categorically, not going to be because of me.

Saturday was a nice, mild day for November, so I put on skinny jeans — as most of mine were — and a loose fitting, long sleeved, black V-neck t-shirt. I didn't need lots of layers on if I was going to be cooking all afternoon. My long, layered hair was down but I had a hairband on my wrist, ready to scoop it up when I got started, because it definitely needed to be out of the way. I was a good cook, but I was a messy cook. It drove my neat freak mother insane, but as hard as I tried, I always ended up in a mess and so black tops were always the way to go. I'd been faffing around a bit during the morning and didn't dare be late, so I popped on my trainers and jacket, grabbed my bag. Then, ensuring all timings and instructions were still in there — I'd checked five times already — I headed for the bus stop.

Hattie's dad lived a few streets back from Crouch End's busy high street down a pretty tree-lined road. I knew he'd bought his new home just before he moved back to London and I dreaded to think what it had cost him.

As I walked up the path to the front door it suddenly occurred to me that I could be in for the most awkward afternoon of my life. I hadn't really given it much thought as I was so focused on helping Hattie, but I hadn't actually seen her dad in about ten years. I never went to his house after her parents divorced as Hattie and her brothers lived predominantly with their mum. Because she didn't spend as much time with him, she always wanted to keep him to herself when she was with him. Plus, by that point she'd had a few years of putting up with me, Tasha and Miri always referring to him as her "lovely" dad, so she generally kept us away. I then moved away for university and he went to Japan. He probably remembers me as a giggly little teenager — if he remembers me at all. It dawned on me that my fourteen-year-old self was potentially about to get her fantasies crushed.

Nevertheless, I had a job to do so I pushed it all aside, sucked it up, and rang the doorbell. He opened it after a few moments and there he was. He was wearing jeans with a long-sleeved fitted grey top and his feet were bare. His dark hair was short around the sides and a little unruly on the top. He had the sort of hair that if he ever let it grow would become a full head of curls. There was a little more grey perhaps, but those cheekbones were just as chiselled and those were eyes just as blue. Hattie's dad was as lovely as ever and my fourteen year-old-self did a little dance of joy.

However, I wasn't fourteen anymore, ten years had passed, and my twenty-four year-old-self was experiencing an entirely different set of feelings, and they definitely weren't as innocent. He smiled his kind, boyish smile, and it could have been wishful thinking on my part, but it felt like he was silently appraising me too. The afternoon was definitely going to be awkward, just not in the way that I had been worried about.

He opened the door wider and stepped aside for me. "Ava Swan, look at you. All grown up and beautiful!" he said. "Come in please. Oh, and I know my daughter, so in case she has forgotten to do so, let me just say thank you for agreeing to do this."

He said I was "beautiful". He was probably just being kind, but my heart momentarily skipped a beat and I was tingling in places that really shouldn't have been tingling. I returned his smile and walked past him slipping off my jacket and he took it from me. "Honestly Mr Davidson," I said, and he visibly winced at my words, "it's not a problem. I enjoy cooking and I'm happy to help."

He regained his smile and he laughed as he said, "I think we both know that you didn't have a choice." I laughed back confirming his suspicions. "And please, Ava, no more Mr Davidson, it reminds me of my father. Please, call me Mark."

Mark gave me a tour of the downstairs of the house. He told me that he'd pretty much had it gutted, and I had no idea how he had achieved all of the work in such a short time. These houses were usually all corridors leading into separate rooms, but he'd opened it up. One side was a large living space — formal at one end, but with a cosy, snug area at the other. The stairs acted as a divide, and on the other side, the two rooms that would once have been a separate kitchen and dining room, were opened up to make one large space. There was no door, just an opening, about two doors wide at the bottom of the stairs.

The kitchen was set out with an informal breakfast bar area, there was a sofa near the patio doors leading out to the garden, and nearer to the front of the house was a large dining table. It was an amazing space. The place was full of light and I loved it. Some open plan homes often felt a little cold to me, but it was warm, no doubt helped by the under-floor heating that my toes were very much enjoying. Mark may have only been back for a short time, but the place felt lived in. It felt like a home.

Mark was a bachelor and he didn't really look like a dad to me. Not like mine anyway, but then he was more than ten years younger than my parents. In this day and age many men only just become parents at forty-four, but Mark had three grown up children — well, almost. Hattie was twenty-four like me and had been an accident during the start of her parents third year at university. It wasn't until Hattie was four that she got her first sibling - Ted, and Will came just over a year later.

I had no siblings. My parents had struggled to conceive with me and decided not to push for more. They just thought that if it happened it happened — but it didn't. Hattie's brothers became my brothers — in my eyes anyway. They had both been so young when I met them that I only ever really saw them as little boys — even now. They were men now though — of sorts. Ted was in his last year of university doing an engineering degree and Will had just started studying law. They were both in London living with

Hattie's mum and her husband Tom, but I only saw them occasionally when I went out with Hattie.

I used to spend a lot of time with them, but it had been a bit awkward since last Christmas when we all went out, and at one point they both drunkenly told me that they wanted to kiss me. Ted had actually tried to and hadn't really appreciated my rebuttal. They were handsome boys, it was true, but I would always see them as brothers. Besides, the best part about them would always be their eyes. They had Mark's eyes, but Mary's features — Mark had kept the rest of his attributes for himself. He truly was a gorgeous man and I was finding it hard to remind myself that he wasn't just a dad — he was my best friend's dad.

I saw the perfect reminder when he showed me into the snug and I took in the large photo of the three siblings hanging on the wall. I recognised it immediately as it had been done professionally as part of a family shoot that Mary had arranged.

"I remember when these were taken," I said to him, pointing towards the image.

"Oh, were you there?" he asked. "I was in Japan at the time, so they were just done of the three of them — I believe there were some of Mary and Tom too."

Tom was Hattie's step-dad, he and Mary had been married for six years and they seemed good together. He was in no way as handsome as Mark, but he was probably the kindest man I'd ever met. He made Mary that bit more likeable in my opinion — a bit anyway. She'd found her match whereas Mark had not.

"No, I wasn't technically there, but it felt like I was," I answered. "Hattie brought a USB stick over with every single image that was taken that day so that we could select the ones where they — well, in truth, where she looked her best," I told him and we both laughed. "They were all good if you ask me, but I remember picking this one out. It seemed more natural," I said, smiling at him.

"I think Hattie sent me about twenty photos," he said.

"Twenty!" I laughed in response. "Oh, you got off so lightly."

He laughed and said genuinely, "You really are a good friend to her, aren't you?" It was starting to feel less and less that way. "And you were right, this was my favourite too," he said. Then he smiled at me and my knees weakened another notch. "I may be biased," he continued, "but I'd say that I have three good looking children there."

I laughed and replied, "They have good genes... um..." oh dear, that just slipped out.

"Thank you," he said, smiling back at me.

I was mortified and I could feel the redness creeping up from my neck to my face, shrouding me in embarrassment. I desperately needed to change the subject, so I walked back towards the kitchen.

"You know, I think my mum would divorce my dad and marry this kitchen if she ever saw it," I exclaimed, thrilled to have slipped in a legitimate and seamless subject change.

He laughed at that. "How are your parents? Where was it they moved to again?"

"Clovelly," I replied, "in Devon. It's my mum's home and she always wanted to move back there eventually. Dad sometimes complains about it but he's really happy," I said, and I smiled fondly at the thought of my London-born dad, and how he'd often grumble at the pace of life in Clovelly. "They're happy," I added.

"That's great," he replied smiling, and I could see that he meant it. "Well, it's been a while since I saw your parents, but I don't think I'd like to be held responsible for the breakdown of their marriage," he said, and as he gave a little shudder, I knew straight away what he meant.

"Ah, my dad wouldn't blame you," I told him. "He might have a thing or two to say to your marble finish, mind you." I ran my hand across it, and he laughed again. I liked that I was making him laugh.

"Well, I don't think I would stand in his way," he told me, still laughing. "I've always liked Jonathan, but he has this quietly fearsome streak to him, don't you think?" he asked, smiling. He seemed to be always smiling.

"Dad's a softie," I said fondly. I completely adored my dad. "For a truly fearsome experience you would've had to have met his mum." I shuddered. "Nanny Mae scared me at times and I'm apparently the person that she adored most in the world."

"I can understand why," he said, looking right at me. Then he put his head down and ran his fingers through his hair, embarrassed by what he had let slip. It seemed neither of us had control over our mouths. "I'll get the food out, then shall I?" he said, walking over to the fridge.

I nodded and followed him over. It was definitely time to focus on the food, so I laid the recipe out on the side. Then I scooped my hair up and reached for the band on my wrist, and as I did my t-shirt rose up revealing a bit of my toned stomach. I looked towards him and saw that he was watching me. He was trying to be discreet, still bending down and taking the food out of the fridge, but I saw it — just for a moment. I was starting to think that the appraisal I'd seen on his doorstep hadn't just been in my imagination. It wasn't just him though, my body was practically humming all over.

Mark looked good — really good. I remembered that he was a swimmer. That was how he would wind down after a long day at work, or if he needed to escape another fight with Mary. I was there a few times when he would head out, bag in hand. It had become the norm after a while, but I could see that it still got to Hattie. He had clearly kept it up though, and you could see the muscles in his arms through his t-shirt. He was lean, but muscular, and very nice to look at.

He took the last few items out and said, "OK, so that is everything from Hattie's list. I don't know what order you need things in, but you clearly do," He nodded towards the lists that I'd now propped up in order, and asked, "Are you always this organised?" with an amused smile on his face.

I laughed at that. "Actually, I'm really not and I'm not sure if Hattie warned you but I'm a really messy cook. And I don't mean a bit of food here and there — I mean seriously messy," I told him honestly. "My mum believes me to be physically incapable of stirring anything without splashing half of the contents all over the wall. And those lists? Well, you know your daughter," I said, and I left it there.

He laughed and raised his eyebrows and nodded as he replied, "Indeed I do." He paused for a moment then asked, "So where do you want me?"

I couldn't answer him straight away. Instead, I did my best to swallow down both my smile and my very dirty thoughts.

8

I'd told Mark that it was probably best that he left me to it. From what Hattie had told me about his cooking experience I decided it was better that he kept his distance. I told him it was safer for his clothes too. In truth, I couldn't concentrate when he was too close. Naturally, he had defended himself.

"You know, I have been single for over a decade. Does it look like I've not eaten?" He pointed to his body giving me permission to look him over, and I found myself taking him in from head to toe, and not very subtly. He saw it and smiled, and it was again my turn to be embarrassed.

I quickly cleared my throat and told him, "You look good... healthy, I mean. You know... like you've eaten."

His smile grew and I decided that I'd made enough of a fool of myself, so I turned around and quickly started on the food. Mark walked away to the small sofa near the patio and got busy on his laptop. That's what it sounded like anyway; I didn't dare turn around to look.

After about forty minutes of working in silence, I'd prepped all the vegetables and the meat was marinating. I was in my comfort zone again — cooking, focusing on following the instructions, and on helping my best friend. I had regained control of my body again, or at least I thought I had, but the tingling started again as soon as I felt him approach.

"Jesus, you really are messy!" he said aghast.

"Hey! You were warned," I laughed. "I can't help it. Sorry, this gorgeous kitchen probably deserves to be treated with more respect," I said apologetically.

"If it had feelings then I'm sure it would be happy to be being used for its proper purpose," he said, still amused. "Anyway, it smells amazing. How am I supposed to pass this off as my own, again?" he asked.

"Ah..." I replied "that's the beauty of this menu. It's good but it's simple. Hattie didn't want to arouse suspicion by creating something too elaborate, but..." I hesitated, unsure whether to say what I wanted to say.

"But what?" he asked, smiling. It was a teasing smile, daring me to carry on and I couldn't help but accept the challenge.

"It's supposed to be not so good that she — Helen, doesn't believe that you made it, but..." I took a breath to steady myself, he was still smiling at me, so I forced myself to continue, "but it's supposed to be good enough to get you some sex tonight." I cringed as I said it. "I'm sorry. This is Hattie's plan, or perhaps your plan too, I don't know — but it's definitely Hattie's plan and I'm just a pawn." I put my hands in the air to demonstrate my innocence and burst out laughing, it sounded all the more ridiculous saying it out loud to him.

"Oh, dear Lord." He leant back against the worktop and shook his head. "My daughter is actually engineering my sex life. Is this what it has come to?" He laughed again and looked at me and asked, "Am I really such a lost cause?"

Thankfully, he didn't wait for me to answer and instead he headed over to the fridge and pulled out a bottle of white wine. He walked over to me, as I was positioned right by the cupboard where the glasses were kept, and he looked me in the eye as I edged to the side for him. I probably should've given him more space, but it was hard to make my body move away. He brought down one glass and reached up for another and tilted it towards me. It was a silent question and I nodded my reply.

He smiled and said, "I'm glad I'm not the only one that's going to need alcohol to get through this."

He stayed close, and we drank while I cooked, and I decided to turn the conversation towards safer ground by asking him about his time in Japan. He was happy to share his experiences with me, and it sounded amazing and beautiful, but also a little lonely at times. He may have had the chance to explore but he worked long hours, ate out a lot, often alone, and Skyped with his children.

The wine was starting to make me feel brave, so I asked, "So, there was no girlfriend out there then?" I managed to make it sound like an innocent question but as soon as the words were spoken, I realised that it was something that I really wanted to know.

"You're interested in my love life too?" he replied, giving a mock sigh, but the teasing smile was back.

"I'm here cooking food for your date tonight — technically I'm already involved," I retorted, laughing.

"Hmmm... I guess that is true," he laughed in reply. "Well, I dated a bit but there was nothing serious. I didn't meet anyone that I really sparked with."

"Ah... the elusive spark. You can never quite tell where it

might crop up," I sighed jokingly.

"Exactly," he replied seriously. He was looking right at me again, those deep blue eyes trying to work out what I was thinking. I practically hid behind my wine glass, and he continued, "Sometimes it hits you when it's most unexpected."

"Yes," I answered, "and sometimes when it's most in—"

"Inappropriate?" he interrupted, serious for a moment.

I tried to steady myself with another sip of wine and replied, "I was going to say inconvenient."

He smiled and gave a slight nod and thankfully we were saved by the oven timer — the dessert was ready to come out.

"So, how about you?" he asked. "What's your boyfriend doing while you're here with me?" He kept his tone casual, but his mask was slipping, just like mine.

"I don't have a boyfriend," I replied, keeping my answer purposefully brief.

"How is that possible?" he asked seriously, then he quickly cleared his throat and continued, "I'm sure I remember Hattie saying something about a boyfriend after university?"

"Oh, Harry... We broke up about six months after university," I kept it brief, again.

"Why?"

He clearly wasn't going to let me get away without the whole story, but it was OK, I knew the answer to this. The whole thing had been thoroughly dissected over a few wine filled nights with Hattie — Tasha and Miri too.

"I think when it came down to it, we worked at university but not in real life," I told him, honestly. "He wanted to live in London but part of that journey in his mind meant living in some crappy house share, having no money, but still somehow affording to get wasted every night," I rolled my eyes and paused for some wine and to check if he had really wanted all this detail.

He appeared to be listening intently and so I continued, "He lived with me in Muswell Hill to begin with, but it was like he thought it was cheating or something," I shook my head and shrugged at the memory. "So, when he expressed a desire to live somewhere else, I should've felt sad, but I was actually relieved," I said honestly. "I think I knew then that it was over, but we didn't break up straight away. He moved into a flat in Clapham South. I mean really, he may as well have gone to Jersey or something," I told him and we both laughed; Muswell Hill to Clapham South was a pain of a journey.

"In the end we just fizzled out. No dramatics, we just ended it," I shrugged. I really hadn't been bothered about things ending with Harry. "He actually got in touch about a month ago and suggested going to dinner," I told him, and I swear his face dropped a little, "but I didn't see the point in going there again."

"Why not? Were you not curious to see if there's still something there?"

"No, he's not the one for me," I replied honestly. "I think if you're not sad about a two-year relationship ending then that tells you everything you need to know."

He gave me a knowing nod before shaking his head and telling me, "Well, he's a bloody fool."

"I know. Who would want to give up having a mortgage free flat in Muswell Hill for some dive in Clapham?" We both laughed and we both knew that it wasn't the living situation that Mark had been referring to.

"So, there's been nobody else since then?" he asked, utterly failing to keep his tone casual.

"I've dated a bit but there's not been anybody important," I replied.

We locked eyes again, but he broke away.

"So, what do you think of Nate?" he asked.

Good. A subject change. Talking about Hattie was safe territory. It reminded me why I was there. "I like Nate," I told him honestly. "He's my manager Miles' best friend, which I was worried would be weird at first, especially when Hattie unknowingly set us up on a blind double date." I shuddered at the memory of that awkward evening. "Nate's nice. I like him. What do you think of Nate?" I asked, giving him a pointed look.

"I think my daughter probably runs rings around him," he answered smiling.

"I wouldn't be too sure—"

"You don't think so?" he asked, intrigued.

"I did at first," I told him, "it's usually the way, but Nate has more backbone than he first lets on. I think he's good for her, but—"

"Uh oh, another but," he gave a fake shudder.

"Yes... I don't want this to sound bad, I love Hattie," I said. "I do think Nate is good for her, but she doesn't always choose the things that are good for her."

"Ah, well, she doesn't always make the best choices for me either," he replied.

"Helen?" I asked.

"Yes," he replied a little uncomfortably.

"So, why are you doing this tonight?" I asked him. "Or can you not say no to Hattie either?"

"I can actually," he replied. "Over the phone... when I'm in Japan," he said and we both laughed. "Tonight, is happening because for some reason Hattie seems to think that Helen is the woman for me," he said, looking doubtful.

"I guess when you put us down on paper it looks that way. She is a nice woman. She's smart, attractive. She's nice, but..."

"No spark," I stated.

"No spark," he agreed. Then looking me in the eyes again he continued, "Hattie thinks tonight is about making things happen, but for me it's about finding out for certain whether I want anything more to happen or not," he replied, never taking his eyes off mine.

It felt like our eyes were locked for minutes but in reality, it was probably only seconds. This time it was his phone ringing that snapped us out of it, and he went over to the sofa by the patio to fetch it and then left the room. I used the space to take stock. Food-wise things were going to plan. It was half past five, everything was pretty much done, I just needed to tell Mark what he needed to do and then I needed to leave him to Helen.

The jealousy was creeping in, but so was the guilt. I may have done what I'd promised to do but I had also got a little tipsy and had most definitely flirted with my best friend's dad. Mentally, I'd already had sex with him at least five times over. Lines had been crossed and although I had no right, I definitely didn't want anything to happen between him and Helen. All in all, it was a good thing that it was time for me to go.

Mark walked back into the kitchen and put his phone on the worktop, he gave a short, half laugh.

"That was Helen," he said. "She left it as late as she could to call in the hope that she might feel better, but apparently she's getting over a sickness bug. She called to say that she's not going to make it."

We were staring right at each other and the only response I could think of was, "Oh."

9

I should've left there and then. I should've given him the instructions to reheat the food for another day. Instead, when Mark apologised for wasting my day and suggested that I should at least stay and eat the food that I'd prepared, I'd agreed. I was hungry after all. When he offered me more wine, I should've said no, but cooking is thirsty work.

There were many times when I should've acted differently. I shouldn't have sat so close to him at the table. I shouldn't have allowed his leg to linger against mine. I shouldn't have let him keep topping up my wine glass. When we'd eaten, and he suggested we sit down and look at the photos of the places he visited in Japan — I should've said no. I should've gone home. Instead what I did was excuse myself, head to the bathroom and have a quick splash to freshen up down below. Because that's what you do when you've been on your feet all day, had too much wine, and have fully accepted the fact that you're going to have sex with your best friend's dad.

"More wine?" he asked, as I came back into the room.

I really didn't need more wine, I didn't want to feel sick, or worse, actually be sick so I shook my head and said, "Actually water would be really good. No more wine for me." It was the only smart decision that I'd made all day.

He came back with the water and sat next to me.

"I'm really sorry that your evening didn't go as planned," I said. It was a lie and he knew it.

"You are?" he teased.

"Actually, I don't know why I said that," I told him. The wine was making me brave, so I decided to be honest, "I'm glad things turned out this way. It's been nice."

"I'm glad too," he said smiling at me. "It's been unexpected, but definitely nice."

"Nice, unexpected, and inconvenient..." I had to say it.

"Ava, I don't know how you can possibly feel like this situation is inconvenient," he said, laughing dryly. "My daughter sent her best friend to my house this afternoon — her best friend who is twenty years younger than me. Her best friend, who from the moment that I opened the door to her, all I have thought about is getting her in my bed completely naked." He shook his head a little. "No, absolutely no idea how that could be considered inconvenient."

He was laughing but it was forced. He didn't find this funny. His eyes were locked on mine. We had been flirting all afternoon, we could both feel the tension, and he had put his cards on the table, and it was my turn.

"Better an inconvenience, than inappropriate. Better it be complicated... than wrong," I replied.

"I don't remember ever feeling like this Ava. How can it be wrong?" he asked earnestly.

I didn't want to talk about it anymore. We could paint it whichever way we wanted to because it didn't matter. We both wanted the same thing. Yet he hadn't moved. It was like he was waiting for permission. I was going to have to show him that it was OK — that my need for him was as strong as his for me.

I stood up slowly keeping my right knee against his left leg and turned to face him. I slowly lowered myself onto his lap, gently pushing him backwards. My legs were on either side of his and he put his arms around my waist and pulled me even closer to him, his eyes never leaving mine for a second. My left hand rested on his chest and I could feel that his heart was beating as strongly as mine. I slowly ran my right hand through his short curls, then rested it gently on the side of his face. We both moved our heads towards each other, but he paused before touching me. How could he still be unsure that I wanted this?

So, I decided to make it very clear and told him, "Mark... I need you to kiss me." Then he did.

It started off gently with tentative, exploring kisses but they soon deepened. My hand moved from the side of his face to the back of his head, holding him in place, keeping him on me as our mouths opened and our tongues touched, exploring each other further. He let out a slight groan in the back of his throat and moved to my neck. As his mouth explored my neck and nibbled at my ears, his hands were working their way up my body towards my breasts. There were too many layers between us so I pushed him back for a moment so that I could pull my top off. He took me in greedily, then leaned in to kiss my chest. As he kissed the top of my breasts his hands moved to my back to unhook my bra and it was off in seconds. He sat back and took his own top off.

He was just as toned and defined as I had imagined. He was muscular but athletically so, incredibly firm and rippled, but not imposing. I dragged my eyes from his body back to his eyes. He was taking me in too — now naked from the waist up.

"You are so beautiful," he told me, as he manoeuvred us so that I was now lying beneath him. He kissed me with more force and I met his need with my own. There was no tenderness, no exploring each other slowly. It was about satisfying our need for each other. He moved from my mouth, down to my chest, tasting and teasing both of my nipples before moving down to my stomach. He undid my jeans pulling my pants off with them. His eyes were pure lust, and excitement coursed through my body.

He moved up and lowered himself onto me so that we were kissing again and when he trailed his kisses towards my ear, he spoke softly but urgently, "Do I need to get a condom?"

"I'm on the pill," was my own urgent reply. Even if I wasn't, I'm not sure that I would have been able to let him move away from me, but it was OK, we were covered.

He continued to kiss me as his right hand slid down my body, over the top of my thigh and between my legs. I moaned softly as he touched me and started to explore my centre, pushing slowly inside with his fingers. He smiled — he was happy with what he found. I knew I was soaking wet for him; the entire afternoon had felt like a torturous foreplay session. I didn't need that now. I didn't want that now. I just wanted him inside me.

I smiled back at him and my hands went directly to his trousers. I made quick work of unhooking his belt and his buttons and he took his hands off me momentarily to help pull his trousers off. I saw him fully. He was ready. He was large, thick, incredibly hard, and my body was begging for him. I pulled him back down onto me and we kissed deeply, I tilted my hips up and wrapped my legs around his waist as he pushed into me. Both of our breaths hitched, and we both moaned at the sensation. He filled me completely and I squeezed, tightening myself around him so that we could feel each other even more.

His kisses came hard as he started to push in and out, slowly at first but quickly becoming faster. I tilted some more and lifted my hips to allow him in even deeper and the waves of pleasure started to wash over me. His thrusts became harder and faster and I met each one with my own. We were both breathing hard and moaning and it wasn't long before I felt my climax building. I put my hand on his lower back willing him even deeper and faster and moments later I was completely out of control of my body. I had never climaxed so intensely, and I couldn't hold back my screams of pleasure. Mark was clearly there too but he held back while I rode out the waves of my orgasm before allowing himself his own release.

We both came quickly, intensely and very loudly. I was normally a bit shy about being loud, but I couldn't help it. Considering that in the grand scheme of things what had just happened was a quickie on a sofa with no foreplay, it was the best sex that I'd ever had. He was above me, half propped up with his arm on one side so as not to squash me. We were both breathing hard. He was still inside me and I could feel him pulsing and I couldn't help but squeeze him again, and as my body tingled at the sensation, he too let out another moan.

We both smiled, lying there, we were completely vulnerable to each other. We had completely crossed a line, but there was no awkwardness. I put my hand on the back of his head and pulled him down so that I could kiss him again. They were less urgent this time, we were both satiated, for the time being.

He pulled away slightly and sighed. "Ava Swan, you are completely perfect," he told me. "What am I going to do with you?"

He was close enough to kiss so I gave his bottom lip a slight nip and replied, "I can think of a few things."

He kissed me deeply and then he picked me up from the sofa and carried me to his bed.

10

I stayed until about three in the morning. It was very tempting to stay there, in his bed, in his arms, but we knew Hattie would be in touch in the morning for an update — if she hadn't been already; neither of us had looked at our phones. I couldn't fall asleep there, no matter how much I longed to.

The sex didn't finish on the sofa. Mark took me to his room, I was naked in his bed, just like he'd wanted when he first saw me — like we'd both wanted. After the urgency of our session on the sofa we took our time with each other. There was a lot of kissing... he kissed me everywhere. My second orgasm of the night occurred when Mark was licking my centre and pushing his fingers deep inside me, he was hitting all the right spots and I had completely lost control of my body again.

When the intensity of my orgasm got too much to bear, I had tried to squirm away, but he held me firmly in place and my release was long and very wet. I had experienced female ejaculation before but only with my favourite vibrator. No man had achieved it before, and I was embarrassed that

Mark had literally been covered in it. He wasn't though. He had loved how my body responded to his touch and had thrust quickly inside me.

He wasn't going to be quick to find his release; he took his time. He was taking control of me and I loved every second of it. I had never completely surrendered myself to a man like that, but I didn't give it a second thought. I don't know if it was because he was older or if it was just Mark, but I trusted him entirely. He was still pushing into me, but he stopped kissing me for a moment.

"I love making you cum," he groaned. I loved it too. "I'm going to make you scream again soon. I'm not going to be done with you until these sheets are soaked through."

I tried to laugh, to tease him. I tried to think of a witty retort to challenge him — but he was right. He felt so good inside me — I knew he'd have me out of control again soon. He was driving me crazy and he knew it. The satisfied smile he wore confirmed how pleased he was with himself, and I felt the need to turn the tables and teach him a lesson. I didn't need to orgasm again straight away, we had time and he needed a taste of his own medicine.

I thrust with all of my strength and twisted to the side so that I was on top and I started to ride him slowly and deeply. He tried to sit up, to hold me but I pushed him back down. He smiled, he thought that I was going to ride him hard, I could see it in his eyes. He thought he'd have me screaming again, but that wasn't my plan. I leant forward and kissed him and then I slowly lifted myself off him. He groaned his objection and I gently bit his lip. I looked him in the eye, it was my turn to smirk as I trailed my kisses down his throat.

"Now you're just being mean..." he rasped out.

"Oh, don't be like that," I teased, trailing my kisses lower and lower. "I have every intention of being very, very nice to you."

I may have liked giving him some power, but he didn't hold all the cards. I slowly found my way to his penis. He was struggling, and so I held him firmly, looked him straight in the eye and took him into my mouth. For a moment I let him think that I was going to take it slowly, that I was going to torture him some more, but I didn't. I took him in deep, hard and fast. I used my hand and tongue and worked him from base to tip. He was groaning and grinding against me, his hands grasping my hair, keeping me in place.

"Oh, God... Ava..." he grunted out.

He was close so I upped the pace and increased the pressure with my lips. He came hard, moaning loudly and I swallowed him down. I didn't release him straight away. I gently slid back to the top and kissed the tip. He was watching me in awe the entire time.

"If that was supposed to be a form of punishment... I don't know... just please feel free to do that whenever you want..." he was still breathing hard and struggling to speak, but he leant forward and pulled me further up the bed so that I was face to face with him again and we were kissing, once more.

That was how the night went on. We came hard and then we kissed gently. We did pretty much everything to each other. I'd never felt so confident in bed and it wasn't just down to the wine. That had worn off, it was just Mark. It was Mark and me. Something just clicked with us. He knew how to please me more in one night than Harry had in the two years that we'd been together.

Mark begrudgingly agreed that I should leave and got up to find his phone so that he could book a taxi for me. I started to look for my clothes but realised that they were all downstairs, so I retrieved them and reluctantly got dressed. I saw Mark in the opening to the kitchen, watching me.

"It'll be here in ten minutes," he sighed.

"Thank you. Do you know where I put my bag?" I asked.

"I just saw it in the kitchen... I have a few messages from Hattie," he said apprehensively. "I hadn't realised that she and Helen contacted each other, but she knows she didn't come here tonight."

"Oh... what are we going to tell her?" I asked, already feeling worried.

"You mean you don't think we should tell her that we spent the night having phenomenal sex?" he said, smiling for a moment, but a frown quickly followed. "What we talked about earlier... the inconvenience thing... I know this is complicated. I know that the smart thing to do would be to put this down to a night of madness that we never talk about again," he said, and with those words spoken, my heart sank a little, but then he continued, "But I don't want to. I want to do this again. And I don't just mean sleeping with you — I mean I absolutely want to do that," he said, laughing a little, but then looked at me intensely, and continued, "This... you and me. Talking, eating, you know... just being with you some more. I want that."

I sighed deeply, because it was hard to breathe with my heart pounding so hard. "I want that too," I eventually managed to say.

"Good," he said, relieved. "So, we say that you were here when Helen called, so I suggested you should eat. We talked about life, Japan, work, your parents. All the things that are true — but then you went home."

I gave him a wry smile. "I guess that is mainly true after all," I replied.

I walked past him into the kitchen and picked up my

bag. I looked at my phone and saw that there were three texts from Hattie, but I couldn't bring myself to read them. Mark came up behind me and wrapped his arms around me.

"I'm going to have to tell her that I took some of the wine home and drank the bottle and passed out or something," I told him. "It's the only way I'll be off the hook for not responding to these messages." I turned to him and said, "This isn't what I do you know — lying to the people that I care about. That's not usually who I am," I told him honestly, "but there's no point hurting her when we don't even know what this is between us."

He nodded in agreement. "I know. I don't think I could ever think badly of you, by the way," he said, and he kissed my forehead.

"So, we keep this to ourselves," I said. "We take things as they come. If it fizzles out, then nobody needs to know. Then if—"

"If I fall completely in love with you?" he asked, pulling me closer. "Then I guess we'll deal with that when the time comes."

I wasn't going to say exactly that but as soon as he said it, I knew that falling in love with him was a very real possibility. Yes, we'd had amazing sex, but it felt like there was more to it than that — and he'd said *when* not *if* and my heart was already doing somersaults.

His phone rang alerting us that the taxi had arrived. I gave him my number and we said goodbye, struggling to let each other go, but promising to speak later that day.

As soon as I was in the taxi and away from him the reality of the situation hit me. This was Hattie's dad. It wasn't just complicated; the fall out would be catastrophic. I couldn't help but laugh at how messed up it was. Hattie had sent me to her dad in order to get him into bed with Helen, and I ended up being the one in his bed, shagging his brains out. Yet, it wasn't funny. Hattie would never accept it. She loved us both, but independently. He was her dad and I was her lifelong best friend. We weren't supposed to collide.

When I got in, I felt the need for a shower. I had had a lot of sex and should have definitely washed, but I didn't have the energy. I also didn't want to wash Mark from me. I wasn't sure if I'd be able to sleep, but as I curled up in my duvet, I could smell him all over me. It wasn't the same as falling asleep in his arms, but I fell asleep feeling like he was with me.

11

It was after nine when I woke, and the Broadway was starting to slowly come to life. I checked my phone and saw another message from Hattie and the guilt hit me again. As did the images of what I'd been doing the night before. My body ached; I'd used muscles that I'd not used in a long time and I was a little sore from being well and truly pounded. I could think of no other way to describe the onslaught that had been last night's sex marathon.

I needed a coffee and I needed a shower, but I couldn't delay responding to Hattie any longer, so I read each of her messages. The first had been sent at around five O'clock asking me how it was all going — I'd never even heard my phone. The second was an hour later when she'd found out that Helen had called it off due to being ill and she was clearly *not* happy. The third was sent around nine asking for me to tell her what had gone on and why I wasn't replying. The last, sent an hour ago simply read, **ARE YOU STILL ALIVE?**

I couldn't postpone it any longer; it was time to start the process of deceiving my best friend.

I'm alive! Head is sore as I took a bottle of your dad's wine last night and drank too much & I zonked out in bed. Sorry about Helen. For what it's worth the dinner was yum. I ate with your dad — we didn't see the point in wasting it. Sorry I missed the earlier texts — I put my phone on silent so that I wasn't distracted. Love you.xx

I was officially going to hell, but I was going there caffeinated. I went into the kitchen and boiled the kettle, filled the cafetière, then went for a shower. My body really was tender, but in a good way. My heart was feeling unsteady and my gut was churning with guilt. Calling it complicated was an understatement. However, I knew that I wanted to see Mark again and I knew that when I did, we'd have sex. We liked each other a lot. We probably shouldn't have, but we did. Why shouldn't we explore it? Why shouldn't we be happy?

When I got out of the shower, I dressed in jogging bottoms and a jumper. The coffee was ready, and my phone was flashing with two new messages. The first was Hattie.

You had me worried for a moment. Bloody sucks about Helen but that just means that I need to create Plan B. Love you too.xx

Phew!

Hattie was still in mission mode and so other than discovering that I was still alive, she wasn't really focusing on anything else that I'd said. The downside was that she was still going to try and push things with Helen and I couldn't help but feel annoyed about it. That feeling left me though when I read the next message. It was from a number that I didn't have stored, it was from Mark.

My bed feels very empty without you in it...how did you sleep? Mark xx

A smile engulfed my face. The rules of dating would tell

me that I should wait a while before replying, but Mark and I had already broken all of the rules, and I was missing him. So, I held my coffee close, inhaling the aroma and replied straight away.

I slept well, actually. Probably due to all of the exertion yesterday... I could smell you all night. It was nice.xx

His reply was instant, **Do you have any plans today? I need to see you.xx**

I don't, but Hattie might have — for you that is. She's not ready to give up on you & Helen yet...xx

Again, his response came instantly, **There is no me & Helen. I'll talk to her. Can I call you later?xx**

I liked that.

Helen was not going to be one of the many issues that we would undoubtedly face.

I sat on my sofa, pulled a cushion in, and held it close while I drank my coffee. I didn't have any plans. I liked having the odd Sunday when I could just take the day as it came. It didn't matter that it was a Sunday as there was always lots to do in Muswell Hill — which was good. I was going to have to keep busy as it was the only way to push aside my Hattie guilt, and to stop myself from checking for messages from Mark every five-seconds.

Yet, guilt it would seem, is not that easy to ignore, and as a result my stomach was in knots. Hattie had been my best friend since I was five and I had just spent the night having sex with her dad. Not only that, but I really wanted to do it again, and was more than likely going to in spite of the guilt that I was feeling.

I spent the morning and early afternoon cleaning my flat from top to bottom, constantly checking my phone for messages. After I'd finished with that it was around two O'clock and there was still no word from Mark. I was going crazy inside my flat, so I decided to head over to Carolyn's.

Carolyn Smith was an old neighbour of my parents and she still lived in the same house on Kings Avenue. Her husband died a few years ago and she had got a gorgeous golden Labrador puppy called Cooper to keep her company. It wasn't the most well thought out decision. She may be a fit & healthy sixty-plus-year-old, but her older sister wasn't all that well, and she often had to visit. Thankfully, my flexible working life meant that I could help out, and I regularly took Cooper for walks. I wasn't due to go there that day, but I needed the distraction of my wise friend and Cooper's unconditional doggy-love to make me feel like I wasn't a terrible person. I passed a couple more hours with them, and when I got home at around four O'clock Mark finally got in touch.

I'm sorry. Hattie has been here all afternoon. Are you home? Can I come over?xx

This was yet another one of those moments where I could've or should've acted differently. I could have told him that it had been a mistake and we needed to forget about it. I'd struggled with the guilt all day after all — but no. I followed my heart — or possibly my body and replied, **Yes and yes.xx**

I immediately went to freshen up and change into a fancier set of underwear. Having driven, it only took him ten minutes to get to me, and just hearing his voice over the intercom had me tingling all over, and when I opened my door to him my heart actually skipped a beat. I knew deep down that it couldn't last. I knew that if Hattie found out she'd make it end. I knew I was going to have to give him up one day.

Just not yet.

He walked towards me and kissed me deeply, "How the hell have you got me missing you so much already?" he asked.

I laughed and replied, "That's probably because you're a dirty old man." I was teasing and he knew it, but he gave my bottom a slight slap and pulled me closer.

"I guess I am a bit, aren't I?" he agreed. "Though who could possibly blame me?"

We both laughed and kissed some more. Being in his arms made all of the guilt and uncertainty that had overwhelmed me all day instantly disappear. He pulled away for a moment and looked around the room.

"This is nice," he said, "and very clean. I was expecting a bit of a shit hole to be honest, having seen you cook yesterday." He was smirking.

"Excuse me," I said in mock offence, giving him a slight shove. "I may be a messy cook, but I do know how to clean. Plus, I've been on a bit of a guilt-cleaning mission most of the day," I admitted.

He looked sombre and asked hesitantly, "Do you regret last night?"

"Not at all," I reassured him with another kiss. "Still... I am betraying my best friend and that's a hard thing for me to just forget about," I sighed a little. "You being here seems to make those feelings disappear," I told him honestly, and he smiled at that. "So, how was she this afternoon?" I asked.

He looked a little awkward. "Ah well... I told her that I felt that it was a good thing that Helen couldn't make it," he said. "That I didn't think that she was right for me, that we didn't really spark, and that I was going to end things now."

He was still looking awkward so I knew that there must be more to it than that. "Well, you're still alive so that's a good sign," I said, and he laughed then. "What did she say?" I asked more seriously.

"She ranted a bit about how it was unhealthy to be alone and that I'm going to end up dying a lonely old man," he said rolling his eyes.

I couldn't help but laugh. Hattie certainly knew how to lay on the dramatics.

"After a while, she relented," he continued, "but she had one request... she asked that I at least wait until Helen was feeling better, and do it face to face," he paused again. "I agreed," he said looking at me, clearly worried about my reaction.

"Oh... well, that seems fair," I said, honestly. "None of this is Helen's fault and I can't exactly blame her for liking you," I admitted, and he looked relieved. "Hattie really relented that easily?" I asked a little suspiciously.

"Apparently so... I hope so," he said and then he kissed me again. "So, are you going to give me the grand tour?" he asked, looking around my flat.

"Sure, I have two minutes to spare." I pointed to the space we were standing in and said, "This is the kitchen, dining room and living room. Over here we have a somewhat modest bathroom," I led him down the hallway. "This is the spare room, come-home office, come-wardrobe, and dumping ground. And this... is my bedroom. And that's it," I smiled.

I loved my flat. It was perfect for me, but it was not much compared to his home.

Mark took in a deep breath and exhaled. "It just won't do. There aren't enough rooms," he said seriously.

He had a serious look on his face, and I didn't really know how to take what he had just said, "Well... um..." I stuttered out before he carried on.

"You see, I came here planning to have sex with you in every single room here, and there just aren't enough rooms," he said, smiling, and my body tingled all over.

"Well, I like to consider the kitchen, dining room and living room as their own unique spaces," I replied, smiling.

"Unique spaces?" he asked, eyebrows raised.

"Yes," I continued. "Think of them as individual spaces without walls... without boundaries."

"Without boundaries?" he asked, with the familiar darkness returning to his eyes, and I silently nodded in reply. "I can definitely work with that."

Then he kissed me, and we came at each other with the same level of urgency as we had on his sofa the night before. We were in my bedroom. That's where we started. That's where we eventually finished. He stayed over that night and I slept soundly in his arms.

We saw each other as much as we could the following week, in-between work and social schedules. Thankfully it coincided with a crazy week for Hattie which meant long hours, so I didn't see or hear much from her. She was in marketing and whenever they were close to a new launch, she lost her social life for a few weeks. Sometimes it was annoying, but I was grateful for it then. It meant I didn't need to lie to her face straight away.

I was due to look after Cooper at the weekend as Carolyn had to stay with her sister. Mark came with me on the Saturday and had me bent over her kitchen table trying not to scream out too loudly as we came. On Sunday he had plans with Hattie, so I played with Cooper in the garden for a while and then took him for a walk around Alexandra Palace. I was walking along quite happily when all of a sudden I heard my name being called. It was Hattie, and when I turned in her direction, I saw the entire Davidson family sitting having a picnic. Mark, Hattie, Ted and Will along with Nate and a woman I didn't know. A woman that was sitting next to Mark. It was Helen — it had to be. Of course, Hattie wasn't going to give up that easily, and of course, Hattie would arrange a picnic in the park in November.

I walked over and did my best to quickly find my game face. Hattie jumped up and hugged me and when she was finished Ted and Will followed suit. They liked to hug me at the same time, completely enveloping me and somewhat squashing me. Nate smiled and said hello because he didn't do hugs, and Mark? Well, Mark looked like he wanted the ground to swallow him up. He gave me a quick, apologetic look but he quickly changed it to a polite smile so that nobody saw.

He stood up and extended his hand and said, "Hello Ava," somewhat over politely.

I took his hand, trying to ignore the tingles that were caused by his touch, and said, "Mr Davidson," smiling politely in return. He gave a momentary smirk and released me.

Hattie jumped in and said, "Ava, this is Helen."

Helen stood up and I assessed her as discreetly as I could. She was probably in her late thirties, she had medium length blonde hair, slim, pretty. She seemed nice. Mark had said she was. She put out her hand and I took it and we politely greeted each other as strangers do.

"What are you up to, Ava?" Will asked enthusiastically. "Fancy joining us?" He was giving me his most endearing smile. When would he realise that it was never going to happen?

"Thanks, Will, but no," I told him. "I need to get Coop back and do some work. I was supposed to do it yesterday, but I got side-tracked," I allowed myself to look at Mark for a moment and he was looking right at me. "You guys have fun though, bye." I waved and walked away calling Cooper to come with me.

"I'll text you later. Love you," Hattie said, as I started to walk away. She had a big smile on her face and was clearly pleased with herself.

"You too," I replied, without glancing at anyone else in the group. I walked a little further away and then I heard my phone beeping. It was Mark, I turned around and could still make them out and could see that he was standing a little away from the group.

Please don't be mad with me, I had no idea Helen would be here. This is all Hattie. I am going to use this as my opportunity to talk to her face to face, like I said I would. I DO NOT want her. I only want you.xx

Then a second message came through.

P.S. If you ever call me 'Mr Davidson' again you will be punished accordingly.xx

It was easy to believe him. Hattie had already alluded to there being a "Plan B," and I thought she'd let him off the hook too easily before. Mark's second message may have had me smiling unashamedly, but I didn't reply straight away. In truth, I was feeling a little annoyed. I knew it wasn't his fault that Helen was there, I knew Hattie to be very capable of setting this sort of thing up. Still, it served as yet another reminder that Hattie would never accept Mark and me as a couple.

When I got home, I opened up my laptop. I hadn't been lying about needing to work. I had a deadline and I was cutting it fine, but there was still Mark to reply to, so I picked up my phone.

Dear Mr Davidson, I understand how the situation today could have occurred & I'm not mad with you.xx

I gave a little laugh and started to get to work, but my phone beeped almost instantly with a reply from Mark.

I'll give you some time to work, but I will be round later. You were warned.xx

It felt like electricity was flowing through me, and a feeling of excitement engulfed me. I was already turned on and I had no idea what he had in store for me. I pushed the feelings deep, deep down and started typing. Four hours later I was finished, and Mark turned up at my door. He told me that he'd spoken to Helen and it was sorted. Then without warning he scooped me up, effortlessly carrying me over his shoulder into my bedroom, and I couldn't help but give a little squeal. He threw me onto my bed and started to dish out my punishment. He punished me again and again, and I loved every second of it.

12

As the weeks quickly passed by, there was no denying that Mark and I had moved on from just enjoying each other's company, but at six weeks in I had a wobble. I'd been having dinner with Hattie and Nate at their flat and she just kept looking at me. Eventually, she asked me if I was seeing someone and I almost choked on my wine. She said I seemed different, happier, and naturally she thought that meant that I was "getting some." I'd laughed it off reminding her how boring my romantic life has always been, and in that moment, I hated myself.

I was already lying to her, well, not lying as such, just not telling her something very important. She'd never asked me anything more about what happened at her dad's when I cooked the meal. She was too focused on Helen then. So, this was the first time she'd asked me a question outright, and the first time I lied to her face — and it didn't feel good. I felt awkward for the rest of the night and feigned tiredness in order to leave earlier than I usually would.

I took the bus home, and, on the way, I sent Mark a message.

I'm not sure we should be doing this anymore.

Even as the message was sent, I knew that I didn't really want it to stop. We'd gone beyond being just sex weeks ago. In truth I think it always was more than that anyway. Even that first night I knew it. There was no denying that our desire for each other was always brimming under the surface, but our connection went deeper than that. Whenever he was with me, I felt whole. I'd never really thought that there was something missing from my life, and yet Mark seemed to complete me. He became the person I'd talk to about feature ideas, I'd tell him about books that I was editing at work — the good and the bad — and how I hoped to one day write my own. He was always supportive, always encouraging. He told me that he thought I could do anything I put my mind to, and he made me feel like I could. So even with that message sent I knew that I didn't want it to end.

Thankfully, Mark felt the same and he came over when I got home. I cried when I opened the door to him and he just held me, not saying a word. He understood how I felt, neither of us liked hiding away, but we didn't see another option. We wanted to be together, and not just physically. We talked easily from day one, never really noticing the age gap, and we talked a lot that night.

We talked about his parents because I never really heard much about them from Hattie. I knew they had moved to Scotland, they visited rarely, and they had money. That was about the only thing Hattie ever thought was good about them — the cheques she got for birthdays and Christmas. Mark described them as being cold — cold and controlling, just like the woman he ended up marrying.

I may have never liked Mary, but I could never say she was unattractive — physically anyway. Mark hadn't just been drawn to her looks when they met at university, it was her nature too. It was familiar to him, he knew how to handle it, it had been what he'd known all his life. When she accidentally got pregnant, both families had encouraged the marriage. Both of their families had prioritised keeping up appearances above the happiness of their children — though Mark never really sensed that Mary didn't want it. Mark was never sure that it was the right thing to do, but he'd done as he was told, like he always had. Three children later, he was still playing by their rules, until the day he finally had enough.

He confided in me that he'd always felt guilty about going to Japan, but that he needed to do something for himself. That was the first time in his life that he did what he wanted to do, but he wasn't about to neglect his responsibilities entirely, which is why he travelled back to see his children so often. He told me that he felt like he almost fell into the same trap with Helen — being with a woman that others approved of as opposed to someone that he truly wanted.

"You saved me from that," he told me. "You appeared on my doorstep and you let the light in. You brought life into me. You woke me up," he said, taking my hand in his. "Everything about you is warm. You're the opposite of everything I've ever known, and I know this is hard, but I don't want this to stop."

"Neither do I," I told him honestly, and we'd shared a gentle kiss.

"It isn't just sex, you know," he said reassuringly.

"Yes, you drive me crazy," he admitted. "Honestly, I just look at you and I feel like I want to know all of you. I want to pull you apart piece by piece so that I can figure out everything about you," he laughed a little. "I see your name come up on my phone and I'm excited to talk to you, to hear what you've been doing, what you have to tell me," he said smiling. "You make me happy and I want to make you happy too."

"You do make me happy. More than you could ever realise," I told him. Then I asked, "How have you managed to stay so nice? None of us ever liked Mary, we didn't see why you were with her. We all thought you were lovely," I admitted, a little embarrassed.

He had laughed, but we both felt that it was best not to dwell on how we knew each other before. Instead, he told me about his grandmother, Anna. Mark's mum was cold like her father and she married a man just like him. Her mum had been the opposite and had divorced her husband as soon as her own parents passed away, and she finally felt that she could break free.

It would seem that she'd felt a little out of control when it came to raising Mark's mum, but with her own oppressive parents gone, she felt that she had to intervene with her only grandson. She made sure that Mark had warmth from someone in his life when he grew up. She'd wanted to make him see how families should be and was truly heartbroken for him when he married Mary. She'd refused to go to the wedding, despite his pleas for her to attend. She just couldn't condone it. Still, she stayed in his life, reminding him of what was important, and he in turn made sure that there was balance and warmth in his own children's lives because of her.

"Will's more like you. Hattie and Ted are Mary... but Will is definitely more you," I told him, and he'd smiled at that.

"She would very much approve of you — of us," he said, referring back to his grandmother. "I like to think she's looking down on me and that I've finally done something to make her rest easy," he said, smiling sadly.

The subject was changed on to me after that, about why I'd never truly been hurt by my past relationships ending. I didn't really know how to answer that. I had been in love with both Nick and Harry at some point, and I couldn't really pinpoint when it stopped with either relationship.

Unlike Mark, I had a warm, loving upbringing. My parents were both emotionally present and incredibly supportive of me. The only thing I could ever put it down to, was the fact that I put their relationship on a pedestal. I knew how in love they were, and had always been, and I think deep down I was always holding out for that too. So, when I felt it wouldn't happen with either of them, I started to pull away from them.

I didn't say it to him then, I didn't even fully admit it to myself, but deep down I knew that it felt different with Mark than it did with the others. Like I could actually have found my partner for life in him. What I did say — what we both said — was that we didn't want to see other people, only each other. So that night, instead of ending it, we officially declared ourselves a couple. A couple, that in time could let the people around us in on our happiness — when we felt the time was right.

Like all couples, some days we'd sit on the sofa together in silence reading. We'd go out for meals — but only in areas where we were sure that we wouldn't bump into the people that we knew. We'd have the odd weekend away; Mark telling his family that he was entertaining clients, or visiting friends out of town, and me claiming to be in Clovelly with my parents. Those weekends away were my favourite because we could just be ourselves. We weren't looking over our shoulders, and we could be completely present with each other.

That is, except for our trip to the Peak District at two months in — that's when we had our first fight. Not that it could really be called a fight. As true Londoners we'd headed to the Peaks with a romantic image of the Northern wilderness, but had gone completely unprepared. The heavens had literally opened on us when we were out walking, and we both got completely soaked. We had taken refuge in a little pub which was thankfully quiet, and we bagged the place by the fire and ordered a bottle of wine. Mark had come back to our table with a chess board and when I confessed that I had no idea how to play it, he said he'd teach me. I thought it was going well — I was winning in fact, but then, twenty minutes into the game he burst out laughing, telling me that he had absolutely no clue how to play it either and had made up everything that he'd told me. I pretended to be annoyed at him for winding me up like that. Though really, I hadn't cared because fake rules or not, I was still winning.

After that we moved onto Scrabble but quickly discovered that we were both far too competitive to play that one. So instead we drank more wine, and as the pub got busier with people taking refuge from the storm, we got chatting with those around us and actually had a brilliant day. That night, a little worse for wear, we stumbled into our room at the bed and breakfast and couldn't figure out how to get the heating working. It was freezing so we went to bed in trousers, massive hats and hoodies. We spent the night wrapped together for warmth and probably only slept because we were so drunk.

The next morning, we were both very rough. The drive home was awful, we were both tired and hungover and we hit traffic. That was when we both started getting annoyed with each other. We hadn't really argued, we'd just been snappy and inpatient, and after a while we'd mutually agreed not to speak for the rest of the journey home.

When we pulled up into Muswell Hill he looked at me and said, "Sorry for being a dick."

I laughed at his honesty and said, "Sorry for being an arse."

We kissed and made up, but we knew we needed a good night's sleep, so he headed home and I ran myself a lovely, hot bath.

Mark and I were a couple in every sense of the word, and we did everything a couple would do. We just had to do it in secret, but as our feelings grew it was getting harder and harder to keep it that way. I was starting to resent the fact that I couldn't tell the world that we belonged to each other. I hated hiding away as if what we were doing was wrong. It wasn't wrong. It was complicated, but it never once felt wrong.

We declared our love for each other during the week before I went to Clovelly for my parent's anniversary. He'd stayed over on the Thursday night and we were having breakfast in the kitchen when he just said, "Ava, I'm not sure if you're aware, but I'm completely and utterly in love with you."

I was unwashed and had a mouth full of granola at the time, and I'd almost choked in my haste to swallow it so that I could tell him that I felt the same. A few days later when I returned from visiting my parents, I'd told him how I'd met a potentially crazy, and very tall Irishman that had told me that he would marry me one day. We laughed about it, but the truth was that it only served to remind us of something that we would never have together — a future.

The only people that knew about us were Darren Barton and his wife Lilly. Darren was a seriously in demand criminal lawyer and had been Mark's best friend since they shared a room together in the first year of university. Darren had stuck by Mark through everything — the unexpected pregnancy, his doomed marriage with Mary, and now his relationship with someone twenty years younger than him. He was also godfather to all three of Mark's children. Mark had confided in him about us one night. He knew that he could trust him, and I think he was in need of some perspective.

From what I gathered from the conversation; after the initial back-slapping that was to be expected when your best friend tells you that he's sleeping with someone twenty years younger than him — his daughter's best friend, no less — Darren had told him what he already knew — that Hattie would never accept it. That was always the thing that hung over us. We knew our time was limited, because of Hattie.

We spent one weekend with Darren and Lilly at their cottage in the Cotswolds, and I was so excited to be meeting up with another couple and doing something that a normal couple would do. However, I was also very nervous. Mark and I barely noticed the age difference, but I didn't know what Darren and Lilly would make of me. In the end I needn't have worried. They had been watching us closely that first evening and they saw that we fit. In spite of the age difference and the complexity of the situation, there was no denying that we worked. More still, that we were happy.

On Saturday we all went golfing — another first for me. Mark and Darren could play, Lilly had been "forced to learn against her will'" as she told me — and I had no clue whatsoever. It started off pretty calmly, Mark would help me with my positioning and eventually I'd make a shot. Darren would stand there shaking his head at Lilly as she purposely made a mess of her turn. I thought it was going to be a really slow afternoon, but then Lilly handed me one of the bottles of cola that she'd brought with her. I took a big drink of mine and nearly spat it straight back out. Lilly quickly patted my back, telling the others that it had gone down the wrong hole, but in reality, it was actually the large quantity of vodka that had surprised and almost choked me.

When I finally managed to breathe again, I looked at Lilly and she smiled at me and put her finger over her lips, telling me to keep quiet. She then took a sip from her own bottle, and the little shudder she gave let me know that her drink was just the same as mine. I couldn't help but giggle with her as I drank from my own bottle again, without reacting, and we proceeded to sneakily drink our way to the sixth hole.

When it was my turn, I did my best to walk in a straight line and plant my tee in the ground, but then Lilly tripped over her golf bag and we both burst into a fit of giggles. Mark was standing in front of me and he looked at us both.

"You're both shit-faced, aren't you?" he said, shaking his head, but smiling at us affectionately.

Naturally, we both laughed even harder at that, so he and Darren decided to drive us back to the club house so that they could get on with a "proper game." Once there we actually attempted to sober up and ordered some lunch, and we spent the rest of the afternoon getting to know each other. Lilly was just lovely and so easy to talk to, but that could have been to do with the amount of alcohol she had me drinking. That evening we had more wine with our meal, and were chatting away quite happily in the kitchen when she suddenly went serious on me.

"Ava, you can tell me that it's none of my business...

but I have to ask..." she said. "Have you thought about what will happen when Hattie finds out about this? Whether it's by accident or you come clean — I can't imagine her reaction would be much different. You do know how she'll react, don't you?" she asked, with concern.

I nodded solemnly as I responded, "I probably know Hattie better than anyone so I know exactly what will happen," I told her. "She'll ask him to choose."

Lilly nodded. She'd been thinking it too. "And then what?" she asked.

I could feel the tears threatening to spill over and I could barely bring myself to say the words. "And then I'll leave," I eventually replied.

I hadn't known that Mark had been standing in the doorway listening and it startled me when he spoke.

"Just like that?" he asked sadly. I turned in surprise and there was no stopping the tears from falling when I saw the sadness in his face. "You'd leave me, just like that?" he asked again.

Lilly made her excuses and left, and Mark walked further into the kitchen, stopping just in front of me.

"Not 'just like that' — no," I clarified. "The thought of this ending breaks my heart," I said and there was no stopping the tears. "Hattie will ask you to choose. Ted and Will, too. It will be them or me, and I... I love you too much to put you in that position. I don't want you to have to bear that burden," I told him. "If you were to choose me it would break us apart. I would never be able to forgive myself for destroying your family, and even though I've been lying to her for the past five months, I would never let you choose me over Hattie. I would not take you from her. I couldn't... I can't hurt her like that," I said with my heart breaking.

"We've always known that's what it will come to. Even though we like to ignore it."

He said nothing but his tears fell too.

"That's the reason why we only ever talk about telling them about us," I said. "We've never done it because we know it will be the end, and neither of us wants it to end," I took a deep breath because it needed to be said. "So, yes... No matter how much it will hurt. No matter how much I love you. When the time comes... when that time comes... I will walk away," I told him, and then I let the tears flow fully.

It was the thing that we'd both been too afraid to admit, and it broke both of our hearts just thinking about it. Mark grabbed me and held me close and told me, "I don't ever want to be without you, Ava. I love you so much."

We stayed in that kitchen just holding each other for a long time before heading to bed. That night we just held each other, that night we lay there in fear because we'd fully acknowledged what was to come. That eventually we would lose each other.

The following week I went out with Hattie, Tasha and Miri. We hadn't been out as the four of us in a long time, so we went the whole hog — meal, dancing and shots. Lots of shots. It was such a fun night. I had to be guarded but I was used to that by then, so I still managed to laugh and genuinely be happy. That night will stay with me for a long time. In fact, as nights out go, it was one that will go down in history. That was the night that I got food poisoning.

13

Will's birthday was coming up and Mary and Tom were hosting a garden party at their home in Hampstead. I'd never been warm with Mary and always sensed that the feeling was mutual. I always thought that she'd love it if Hattie and I fell out, but we never did, so she had no choice but to accept that I was around. I'm not sure if I was invited by Hattie or Will in the end, but I was going, and so was Mark. It would be the first time that we would be together with his family. Only, not *together*. We wouldn't be able to let on how well we knew each other, and we definitely wouldn't be allowed to show how in love we were. We were going to have to fake our way through the entire event.

The only plus side was that because I had been roped in to do some baking, since Mary never seemed to mind asking me to do that, and my beloved Golf was in the garage, Mark had been asked to drive me. It made sense as he lived close by and I had a lot of cakes to bring. To everyone else it was intended as a kind gesture; to us it meant that we would have some time alone.

I was really behind with the cakes. The food poisoning two weeks prior had really taken it out of me and my plans to stagger the baking had been scuppered. I still didn't feel perfect, there always seemed to be a queasiness lingering in the background and that too had put me off baking. I had a lot to do in the week leading up to the party, as well as freelance projects to complete, so I had hardly seen Mark and I had missed him. He had been there when I was ill, as much as he could anyway, because Hattie wanted to help too. She felt bad about having been the one to choose the restaurant that "poisoned me", and she came around after work every night for a week to check on me.

Mark would come over during the day and set himself up in my spare room on the days that he was working. When he heard me rush to the bathroom, he'd wait till I was finished, hand me a glass of water, and help me back to either my bed or the sofa. He had tried to come into the bathroom to hold my hair one time, but I never knew whether I'd be sitting on the toilet or puking into it until I got there and I didn't want him seeing *that*. Instead, he waited for me to materialise from the bathroom and helped me the only way that he could.

I felt awful that week and not just because of the illness. It wasn't often that Hattie showed her caring side, but when she did, she went all out. I was always aware of the fact that I was at risk of losing the love of my life. However, along the way I'd lost sight of the fact that I was at risk of losing my best friend too. Hattie could be selfish, headstrong, a bit of a bitch even, if you got on the wrong side of her — but she'd claimed me as hers when we were five and had been by my side ever since. I wasn't sure what life would be like without her in it.

Mark texted me on the morning of the party to tell me

not to wear anything "too sexy," because he was already going to struggle at the party. I'd picked a pretty, floral printed, floaty, knee length dress. It was slightly shaped in a gentle V around the neck, revealing just a tiny hint of cleavage. Pretty, not sexy. It was mid-May and we were having some lovely warm weather, so I went with some dainty wedge sandals and cardigan to match. When I answered the door to Mark, I was instantly hit by how much I had missed him. He grabbed me in a bear hug and groaned.

"That was a long week. Any week where I only see you once is a long week. I love you," he told me, passionately.

"I know and I love you too," I replied, and we kissed. I could feel him hardening against me and my body responded excitedly, but then he looked me up and down with a pained expression.

"I thought I asked you not to look too sexy," he complained.

I laughed, "This is not sexy."

"Everything about you is sexy, Ava, and this afternoon is going to be torture," he groaned out pulling me so close so that I could feel his erection emphasising the point. "I'm not the only one that thinks so either," he said, frowning. "Do you know what it's like hearing my own sons telling me how much they fancy you?" he exclaimed.

Ted and Will — two more people that we were going to hurt. I shrugged off my dark thoughts, gave him a teasing smile and said, "I bet you feel like you've one-upped them, knowing that you can have me anytime you want?"

He laughed at that. "A little perhaps" he admitted, "but I haven't had you all week."

I gently pushed away from him stepping backwards, then sat up on the breakfast bar, slowly opening my legs for him. I looked him in the eye and told him, “Then you'd better have me now.”

He closed the space between us in a second and kissed me hard, first my mouth then my neck, moving down to the top of my breasts. He lowered me backwards and pulled down my knickers, quickly unzipped his trousers, and as he pushed into me, we both groaned at the sensation. This was where he belonged.

He thrust into me hard and fast and it wasn't long before I was crying out my release, with his quickly following. We slumped against each other, propping each other up and panting heavily. It had been fast and urgent, a release we'd needed after missing each other so much. Had we known then that it was to be the last time it would've been different. We would've taken it slowly and savoured every moment.

The drive to Hampstead was a mixture of being nervous over what was to come and giving Mark longing looks. It was nice to be close to him and I was thankful that his car was an automatic, as it meant that we could hold hands as much as possible. We pulled up into a space on the street, it was on street parking only and we couldn't get that close to the house. We sat in the car, but we didn't make a move to get out. Mark gave my hand a squeeze and I wanted to kiss him but didn't dare in case somebody saw.

He smiled at me, trying to reassure me. “It's going to be OK. We can do this,” he said. “Darren and Lilly will be there to keep me distracted. Lilly will probably find it hard not to talk to you though. She likes you a lot, you know?” I smiled at that, I liked Lilly too. “She's known for being an excellent judge of character by the way. Some call it a gift. And you will no doubt have an army of admirers to keep batting away,” he said, and I rolled my eyes at that. “And I'm sure

Hattie and Mary will find some jobs for you too," he said smiling.

"I'm not sure about the 'army of admirers' part, but I'm sure I will have my duties," I replied, starting to relax a little.

"Then I'll take you home, because you can't be expected to carry all the cake tins home after all. And it will just be us again," he said, lovingly.

"I like the sound of that," I told him, smiling adoringly at the man that had my heart entirely. "And you're right. You can't drink a lot because you're driving, and I'm not going to drink a lot because I still don't feel one hundred percent," I told him. "So, as long as you don't keep looking at me like this... then yes. We've got this."

I had no idea how wrong I was.

It was going well, and Mark and I spoke when we were close to each other. I'd arrived with him so there was no point pretending that we were strangers after all, but he mainly stuck to Darren and Lilly as he said he would. They were such good friends. They knew that it was hard for both of us and occasionally I caught Lilly giving me a comforting smile. It was going as planned, we were playing our parts, and I felt myself starting to relax.

Will was tipsy and he asked me for a birthday kiss, so I kissed him on the cheek and patted him on the head, reminding him that he was like a brother to me.

"You break my heart, Ava Swan," he said to me, walking back to his friends.

I laughed at him and replied, "Perhaps, if you had one, Will Davidson."

He mimed a dagger going into his heart and his friends laughed at him and gave him another beer. I shook my head at him and caught Mark's gaze. He smirked and raised his eyebrows, but he wasn't annoyed.

As expected, Mary found jobs for me to do. Apparently, as the baker of cakes it was considered my job to bring the cakes out to the table. I was petrified of dropping them but had successfully brought out the Victoria sponge and chocolate fudge cake without incident. That just left the cinnamon swirls, and as I brought them out I walked past Will's pig of a best friend — Ian Simmons, and as I did he said, "Nice buns!" and slapped me so hard on the bottom that it knocked me off balance, and I gave a little shriek and started to tumble. In my efforts to keep the plate upright and to not spill anything I landed awkwardly on my ankle and gasped at the pain.

I was on the floor holding my ankle, so I didn't see him coming, but Mark was there in seconds and without pausing he grabbed Ian by his shirt and shouted, "Don't you ever touch her again!"

Everyone went silent. Nate came up behind me and helped me up, and I tried to put weight on my ankle, but just winced again at the pain. I saw Mark. He was furious, and he looked ready to kill Ian, who was apologising profusely. It was Darren that stepped in giving Mark a firm look and placing his own hand on one of Mark's arms. It was to try to stop him, but to also warn him about what he had just done. Because to most people at the party, Mark was just protecting a young woman he knew, a woman who had just been publicly groped and was now injured because of it. Yet, to those that knew Mark, really knew him — like Mary, Hattie, Ted and Will, it looked like a man that was protecting what was his. He hadn't thought about it, he had just reacted in the moment. It was primal. He was a man reacting to someone he clearly cared about being violated.

Darren started quietly talking to Mark, but he still hadn't taken his hands off of Ian, who was visibly scared. I scanned the garden and saw that everyone was watching. I'd heard Hattie behind me when she'd shouted at Ian for slapping me, so I didn't have to worry about meeting her gaze, but I locked eyes with Mary. She was standing there looking right at me, arms folded. She gave a slight sneer and shook her head at me. Ted stood next to her looking between us, and I saw the moment when realisation dawned on him. It was the moment a look of disgust washed across his face. They knew, and I knew that I was the only one that could calm Mark down. So, I hobbled forward and put my hand on his arm and spoke as calmly as I could.

"Let him go, Mark. I'm fine... really," I told him softly.

He turned and looked at me and saw the tears that couldn't be contained running down my cheeks. The realisation of what he'd just done dawned on him and he swallowed hard, letting go of Ian without taking his eyes off me. Unexpectedly, it was Tom who came to our rescue.

"Come on, let's take a look at that ankle, shall we?" he said.

Then he and Nate — who had been holding me up the entire time — helped me indoors and took me into the dining room so that he could prop my foot up on a chair. Tom was a doctor and I couldn't tell if he was as oblivious as most of the people outside were, or if he was just being kind. I knew Mark was next to me, silently watching what Tom was doing with my ankle, but I couldn't look up at him. I couldn't look at anyone. I knew what it all meant, and my heart was already breaking. I heard more people enter the room and the door close, but I still couldn't look up.

Naturally, it was Mary that spoke first. "Really, Mark. Your daughter's best friend? What the hell are you thinking?" she asked. She sounded angry, but part of her was enjoying it, I could tell.

Mark didn't acknowledge Mary. He didn't speak at all. He was still looking down at me — angry and hurting.

Tom finished assessing my ankle and looked at me. "It's just a sprain. You'll be fine, Ava," he said, giving me a kind smile.

He knew after all. He was definitely too nice for Mary. I gave him a slight smile, grateful for a friendly face, but the tears still fell. I was starting to feel vulnerable sitting down in a room full of people that were angry with me, so I started to stand, and Mark instinctively reached out to help me.

"No, Dad!" Hattie shouted, and my heart momentarily stopped beating. I thought I might actually be sick on the spot, but I took a deep breath and pushed the urge back down. She sounded furious as she continued, "No! You don't touch her. You don't."

Mark carried on holding me, but I still couldn't look. He spoke firmly, "Hattie...I know this is a shock and I'm truly sorry about that," he told her, "but you don't get to tell me what to do."

"THAT'S MY BEST FRIEND!" she screamed. Then she paused. "At least, she was. Are you going to look at me at any point you fucking bitch?" she scathed at me.

"Hattie, don't do this," Mark warned her.

Will jumped in then and shouted, "What the hell did you expect, Dad? You've been sleeping with Ava? Ava!" He was incredulous, but he was also hurt. "I can't even get my head around this..." he said, and he walked to the furthest corner of the room and leant against the wall.

"I'm in love with her," Mark said calmly.

Mary scoffed, Ted remained silent, Will turned away and Hattie was still staring at me. I still hadn't looked up, but I could feel her eyes burning into me.

"Look at me, Ava," Hattie commanded.

I took a deep breath and wiped away the tears. Fresh ones fell immediately, but I looked my best friend right in the eyes. She was furious, but I could see the hurt there too.

"How long?" she asked. I cleared my throat and answered, "Since... since the night I cooked the meal," it came out as a whisper.

"What? That's what? Six months ago? You've been sleeping with MY dad. You've been lying to me for six. Fucking. Months? How could you?" she shouted, and her tears fell too.

"Hattie, just—" Mark started to say.

"No, Dad! No. I am asking her," she shouted, pointing at me.

It felt like the only chance I had to try to save things, to save my relationship with Mark, and with Hattie. So, I found the strength to speak.

"Hattie... please believe me... I never wanted to hurt you. Never. We have talked about telling you, all of you, so many times," I looked at Ted and Will too. Ted was angry but Will seemed gutted. "But we couldn't. We didn't think you'd accept it... so—"

"So, you just lied to me and crept around? Were you laughing at me?" Hattie asked angrily.

"Hattie, please, you know me. You. Know. Me. When have I ever tried to hurt you?" I asked her desperately. "Name me one time I've not been there for you?" She said nothing. "We didn't plan this. It wasn't a game. We were attracted to each other and we acted on it. We didn't say anything to begin with because we didn't want to upset anyone over something that might have just been a fling... but at the same time we couldn't stay away from each other," I told her honestly. "So, yes, we lied. We crept around, and we kept on doing it because we fell in love and we didn't want it to stop." I looked her right in the eyes because I needed her to see. "I love him Hattie. I really love him... and I love you too."

She was quiet, she was taking in what I said, and it gave me hope. Hope that she really heard me. Hope that she could see how much it was hurting me too.

"You were right," she finally said. "I don't accept this. You betrayed me. Both of you." Then she turned to Nate and he embraced her. She was quiet, but I could see from the way her shoulders were moving that she was crying.

The room was quiet until Mary spoke, "Mark," she said firmly. "I think it's time you and your midlife crisis on legs, left."

She still looked like she was enjoying this. She was finally getting rid of me, but I didn't need telling twice, and I didn't want to be in that room for another minute. Mark wrapped his arm around me, partly to support me but I could feel what else he was doing — he was trying to protect me.

When we opened the door Darren and Lilly were on the other side, looking worried. I was right to have believed that the rest of the party was oblivious. They thought the crowd gathered in the dining room were just making sure that I was OK, and they had carried on drinking and eating. Darren and Lilly, however, knew better. They saw my face streaked with tears, the way Mark was holding me, and the anguished look on his face. Lilly moved to reach for me, her face full of concern but she stopped when she saw Hattie staring her down in the doorway behind me. Darren was looking at Mark, they didn't speak a word, but then they didn't need to. When we got outside Mark picked me up and carried me to the car.

He got in next to me and shouted, "Fuuuuck!" He put his

head on the wheel and turned to me and his tears fell too, "I'm so sorry, Ava. This is all my fault. We were doing fine, but when that little fuck hurt you. When he knocked you down... I just... I didn't even think. I just didn't... I just wanted to rip his head off! He assaulted you."

I looked up at him. God, I loved him. I had never loved anyone like I loved him. It was going to hurt so much. What was coming next was going to break me, but at that moment it was still just us. So, I leaned in and kissed him gently and told him that I loved him. We didn't speak another word during the journey back to his. We didn't speak while we sat together on the sofa, fingers entwined, my head resting against his chest, as he held me as close as he could. I was listening to his heartbeat. I wanted to remember it. How it sounded, how he felt, how he smelled. I was silently taking it all in. I didn't want to forget any of it.

The silence lasted until Mark's phone rang. It was Ted, asking where Mark was, if I was with him, and then telling him that they'd all be there in ten minutes. I excused myself and went to the bathroom with my phone, and I called the local taxi company to come to Mark's house in thirty minutes. I knew why they were coming. I knew what they would say and how long they'd take to say it, and I knew my heart was about to break into a million pieces.

14

Mark opened the door to them without saying a word and they all walked straight to the kitchen, where I was already seated at the breakfast bar. Ted first, he seemed to have taken on the role of leader, then Hattie and Will. I was glad of one thing, that Mary hadn't come with them.

Hattie had regained her composure, but I could see that she had been crying a lot, and I hated that I had been the one to do that to her. Mark cleared his throat and offered them drinks, but they all declined. They were only there to talk. To talk, not listen. I knew there was nothing more that I could say to them to change their minds, so I just sat and waited for the inevitable. Mark came over to me and put one hand on my shoulder and the other on the marble top. I looked down at it — it really was a beautiful kitchen. To the three of them sitting across from us it must've looked like a show of solidarity, but I knew there was more to it. Mark was trying to stop me from leaving.

It was Ted who spoke. "As you can imagine we've done a lot of talking," he said. "You've really hurt us with this, Dad.

You too, Ava. Hattie aside, you know... it doesn't matter," he said, shaking his head. "We could talk about this until we're all blue in the face and get nowhere."

"So, what exactly is it that you are suggesting that we do? How do we move on from this?" Mark asked.

Hattie scoffed, Will remained silent and Ted continued to speak for the three of them. "Well, that's just the point, Dad. We — as in *us*, your children..." He gestured to his siblings, "We can't just move on. Not as a 'we' — not if you're still with her."

I closed my eyes and felt the blow. I had expected it, but it still knocked the breath out of me momentarily.

"Why not?" Mark pleaded. "Why not? This is Ava. You know her, you like her — love her, even. Is it so hard to understand why I would feel that way about her too?" he asked them, but they didn't answer. "We're the same people that we were last week. I'm your father. Hattie, Ava is still the same friend that adores you. So why not?"

"Really? Seriously?" Will asked incredulously. "She is the same age as your daughter. You've known her since she was five, for Christ's sake! It's wrong, Dad. It's just wrong. Not to mention—"

Ted put his hand up to quieten his brother. He could see that Mark was about to speak so he pushed on more firmly with the speech that they had clearly prepared. "Like I said, we could argue about this all night. It doesn't matter, it won't change anything," he said, looking at us hard. "We don't accept this. We don't accept the two of you. We don't accept her" he pointed at me for added effect, but it wasn't necessary. "If she's in your life then we're not. That's what it comes down to."

I breathed hard. They were right on cue and my taxi would be arriving in five minutes.

Then Hattie finally spoke up. "It's her or us, Dad. You have to choose," she told him — as predicted.

It was a good thing that I was sitting because if I hadn't been, I would've fallen. The room felt like it was spinning and my whole body felt like jelly. The only things that I was really aware of was my pounding heart and Mark's hands around my waist. He was holding onto me with both hands. I started to focus back on the room and on the raised voices around me, and I turned to look at Mark. He knew what was going to happen next, because I had already told him. His agony was clear to see as he slowly shook his head at me, pleading with his eyes.

"There is no choice to make," I said, so quietly that only Mark heard me. So, I turned to face the three of them head on. "There is no choice to make," I repeated. "When I told you that I didn't want to hurt you I meant it. This right here is why we kept it a secret. Because we knew it would come to this... and I've already told Mark what I'd do when it did..."

"Ava... please..." Mark begged. His tears fell and his pain was clear for everyone to see. "Don't do this."

I turned to him, held his face and kissed him. Our tears blended together and we both let out a quiet sob. "I have to, you know I do... I love you so much."

I wiped away the tears from my face, his and mine, and turned to Hattie, just Hattie, I only really owed it to her.

"I was never going to take him away from you. I wouldn't do that to you, and I wouldn't do that to him," I told her with complete sincerity. "I love him, I'm completely in love with him, but I love you too and I would never do that to you, no matter what it cost me." She looked away but I could see her tears, and then my phone rang. "My taxi is here," I said, slowly moving off the chair.

"Your taxi?" Mark cried. "When did you...? You're leaving? No! Ava, don't go. Stay. There must be a way we can sort this out. I love you." He looked at his children. "I love her. Surely, we can work this out?" he begged them, but none of them said a word, and so I continued to move away.

Mark grabbed me and turned me to face him. "I love you, Ava. I love you too much for this to be over. It can't just be over," he pleaded.

I cupped his face in my hands, pulled him close and kissed him. It was a kiss of love. It was a kiss of longing. It was a kiss of sadness. It was a kiss goodbye. "I love you," I told him. "I will always cherish this. I will always cherish you. Goodbye Mark."

I stepped back and he let me go, finally succumbing to the reality that he had been trying to fight. I hobbled to the door not caring how I looked. My dignity didn't matter, not when my world was falling apart. I didn't turn around to look at any of them as I left, but the house was silent. Silent, except for Mark who was crying. His heart was broken too.

The taxi driver kept giving me concerned looks in the rear-view mirror and I don't know how I held it together, but I was relieved that it was a short journey home. I opened the door, put my key on the table, closed the door, leant against it and just slid down to the floor. The pain overwhelmed me, and I no longer held it back. There was no way of holding it back. As I laid there, curled up on the floor sobbing uncontrollably, I finally understood the phrase "crying your heart out".

I couldn't say how long it had been, but after a while the tears dried, but I didn't have the desire to move so I stayed there on the floor. That was until another feeling overwhelmed me and I had to get up. I got myself up off that floor and I ran to the bathroom just making it to the toilet in time to be sick.

15

Hattie messaged a few hours after I got home asking me not to involve Tasha or Miri. In fact, she went as far as to ask me to not speak to them at all for a week. She told me that she needed them, and that she needed to "get her head around things." She had stressed that it would be less embarrassing for everyone involved if I didn't tell anyone about what had happened, and for some foolish reason it gave me hope. Hope that there was a chance that we could be friends again. Hope that I hadn't just lost two people that I loved forever. So, I agreed. I promised her that I wouldn't say a word to anyone.

That week was the hardest week of my life. I'd only had two real relationships before Mark, and they had both just fizzled out. The love was gone before they were over, so I had never experienced the heartbreak. I'd never experienced the pain, and I was totally overwhelmed by it. I called in sick, telling work that I was still not quite right from the food poisoning and bought myself the three days off. I couldn't go in. I couldn't look at people. Even Amanda, who was my closest work friend. She was ten years older, single — having been through a nasty divorce — and was probably one of the few people that might actually be able to help me, but I couldn't face seeing her. I couldn't bring myself to find the right words — and what could I say when I'd promised not to tell?

The week went by in a haze. I woke up, had a momentary reprise from the pain, before I remembered, and it hit me full force again. Some mornings I was even sick. I didn't know heartbreak was capable of affecting you so physically. I showered because I liked losing myself in the warmth of the water. I dressed, because there was a part of me that was hoping that Mark would show up, take me back, and make everything right again. He didn't. I ate occasionally when I could no longer stand the noise from my stomach, but it didn't always stay down. I watched television without really watching, but it felt like some company. It took all of my strength not to contact Mark or Hattie. I didn't call my parents because I didn't know where to start, and I didn't call Tasha or Miri because I'd promised not to. I was utterly alone, and I was utterly broken.

I cried a lot. I cried when I woke up, when I went to bed and when I looked in the mirror and saw the face of a girl that just a week ago had been so happy. All that I saw reflected back at me was pain, and I'd lost the person that should have been helping me. Hattie should've been there propping me up, telling me I'd get over it, that the pain was temporary. She should have been plying me with wine and telling me why I was better off without him, but it was the loss of Hattie that I was grieving over too. The loss of my best friend. The pain wasn't just because of Mark. It was because of Hattie too.

Miri sent me a text on Saturday asking if she and Tasha could come by. She said they'd been with Hattie all week "helping her" and we needed to talk. I didn't know what to expect, or what Hattie had told them, but they'd been my friends for so long too, and I really needed them. I made an effort to shower and dress in something other than my leggings. I didn't have the energy to apply makeup and I knew that I looked drained, but I didn't care. I let them in and hugged them both, but when they hugged me back it didn't feel as warm as before. I brushed it off because they looked concerned. There was definitely concern, but there was something else there too.

"You don't look well," Tasha said. "Are you OK?"

"No, not really," I replied. There was no point in lying. "I've really wanted to call you both this week, but I promised Hattie I wouldn't... how is she?" I asked them hesitantly.

"She's gutted, Ava," Miri answered, and her admonishing tone startled me. "She's absolutely in bits."

I gave a dry laugh. "This hasn't exactly been the easiest of weeks for me either," I replied, and the tears started again.

"I can see that... but it's different with Hattie. How could you do this?" Miri asked, incredulously.

I was at a loss. "I... I didn't think she'd tell you. She asked me not to," I told them.

"Actually, she was too upset to speak to begin with," Tasha said, making her disapproval known. "Ted and Will told us what's been going on with them."

"Right, so you know," I said weakly. "You have to know that I never wanted to hurt any of them. It's just—"

"How?" Miri interrupted angrily. "On what planet did you think that they wouldn't get hurt? They're brothers!"

"It's messed up," Tasha added.

"Brothers? I'm sorry, what?" I asked confusedly. "I don't know what you mean by that."

Miri answered, "I mean, how did you think that sleeping with them both... stringing them both along, wouldn't hurt anyone?"

I couldn't quite believe what I was hearing. Was this happening? Was this a joke? I practically choked out the words, "Wait... what? What are you saying I did?" I asked.

"It's not what we're saying, it's what they're saying," Tasha replied with disdain.

I looked at them completely dumbfounded, and asked, "Are you telling me that Ted and Will have told you that I have been sleeping with them?"

"Yes!" they both replied in unison.

I laughed. For the first time in a week, I actually laughed. Miri was angry at that.

"This is not funny. Hattie is gutted. You nearly wrecked their relationship, and she feels like she can't be friends with you anymore. She's heartbroken," she scolded me.

"I am laughing because I don't know what else to do," I answered. "I am laughing because I can't quite get my head around what you've just said to me."

"What do you mean?" Miri asked.

"I mean, that it is a total lie," I said, near hysterics. "That is a lie! I can't even believe this, that is not what happened. Not at all."

"Why would they make that up?" Tasha asked. "All three of them. Why would they make that up?"

"Because I have hurt them and they're mad at me. They're punishing me apparently, although I don't know why because they know exactly how much I'm already hurting," I added bitterly. "Honestly, that's not what happened. I promise you."

"So, what has happened?" Miri asked.

"I can't. I'm sorry, but Hattie made me promise not to say," I answered shrugging, realising that it wouldn't be enough. They looked at each other, and then back to me.

"What are we supposed to do with that?" Miri asked.

"You're supposed to know me. You're supposed to know that I wouldn't do that," I replied calmly. It was no longer funny.

"Then tell us your version," Tasha urged.

I shook my head and the tears fell. "I can't," I replied. "I promised."

"Ava, you know I've always liked Ted—"

"Yes, Miri, I do. Which is just another reason why I wouldn't do that," I implored. Miri just exhaled loudly and shrugged.

"And what about Paul?" Tasha asked.

Oh, no. I could see where she was going. Paul was Tasha's ex. He was a complete player and treated her like crap, but she adored him, and he broke her heart. "What about Paul?" I asked, grudgingly.

"Is it true that you kissed him?" she asked.

"No. It's not," I replied firmly.

"So, after he broke up with me, you didn't bump into him on a night out with Hattie and get off with him?" she asked, but her anger suggested that she'd already made up her mind.

I couldn't believe what was happening.

"That is not what happened," I said, shaking my head. "Yes, Hattie and I saw him when we were out not long after you broke up. He came over to me and he leant in to talk to me. I stupidly thought he was going to ask how you were, like a normal human being would," I told her honestly. "But he kissed me, and I pushed him away. I swear it! Hattie was th—" I stopped myself.

Hattie had been there. She had tipped her drink on him and sent him packing. Hattie knew the truth, but it was clear that Hattie was no longer an ally. She hadn't asked me to stay away for a week to sort herself out. She'd wanted me away so that she could tell her stories.

"I can't believe she's doing this to me," I choked out.

"So, you're the victim?" Miri asked dryly. "You've done nothing wrong and everyone else is lying?"

"I told you I've hurt them, I admit that. I've just not done what they're saying I've done," I replied solemnly.

"Then tell us!" Tasha shouted.

"I promised," I told her again. I didn't know who I was protecting. Whether it was some misplaced loyalty to a friendship that was clearly over, or if it was Mark, but I just couldn't tell them.

"Then what do you expect us to do?" Tasha asked.

"I don't expect you to do anything," I replied. "But I hope that you'll be my friends. I hope that you can remember that you know me and give me the benefit of the doubt. I hope that you can see that I need you too?" I said looking right at them, in the hope that they could see that I was telling the truth.

They looked at each other again. We were a foursome, me, Hattie, Tasha and Miri, but as Hattie and I were best friends, Tasha and Miri were too. They would stick together.

"Ava... Hattie and her brothers have all told us the same thing, and you won't tell us anything at all," Miri said gently. "I'm sorry to see you hurting, I am, but Hattie really needs us right now."

I nodded slowly letting my tears flow unchecked, understanding that they'd made their choice. Understanding that I'd lost them too. After they'd gone, I picked up my phone and pulled up my message thread with Hattie. There were so many things I wanted to say. So many things that I had the right to say — but utterly defeated, I only managed one word... **Why?**

I never heard back from her. Just like I never heard from Tasha or Miri again.

16

On Sunday I decided to call my parents because I desperately needed to hear a friendly voice. It was a very awkward conversation, though. I burst into tears as soon as my mum spoke to me, and I was utterly unable to speak for five minutes. Mum was so freaked out she was about to get my dad to call the police to come and check on me. I eventually managed to get some words out, but not the words that they needed to hear in order to be able to help me. My heart was broken, they got that, but they didn't know by whom and were notably upset that I'd been in a relationship — had been in love in fact, and not told them.

I told them that Hattie had turned on me, was spreading lies about me, and had turned Tasha and Miri against me too. However, I didn't tell them what the lies were, so understandably, they were at a loss. Mum pledged to get straight into the car to come and see me, but I begged her not to. In the end, she said the only things that she could say — the generic break-up phrases such as "it will get easier," "time will heal," "focus on your work" and "get out with your friends." The last one being a little tricky as it seemed that I no longer had any — except for Amanda. At least I knew that I could see Amanda at work the next day. That had made me feel a little stronger, and I knew that I would get up the next day, put on my professional face, and go to work. However, for the rest of Sunday I decided that continuing to cry was perfectly acceptable.

It was hard trying to get into my usual Monday morning routine. Everything just felt empty. Empty and pointless. The traffic was terrible due to a burst water main, and I managed to miss my stop because I'd been staring out of the window blankly. I was late and flustered, and as soon as I saw Amanda, she asked me if I was feeling better, which sent me running into the toilets, where I instantly burst into tears. She came in after me and then followed another awkward conversation where I had to tell a friend that hadn't even known that I'd been in a relationship, that it had ended, and I was heartbroken — but I still didn't give her any details. Looking back things might not have been as bad if I'd just told people what had really happened. In truth, I know that they wouldn't have been. Hattie may have wanted to punish me for breaking my promise, but she was doing that anyway. Still, at the time I had been holding on to some misplaced loyalty to her, to her and the hope that we could get past it. The hope that we'd be friends again, one day.

Like my parents, Amanda still supported me, she became my rock, in fact. I tried not to lean on her too much because I didn't want to scare her away. She was the only person that I had, and I was so scared of losing her too. I still had Carolyn and Cooper and I knew that I could always count on them, but Carolyn had enough on her plate supporting her sister. I didn't want to impose on her too, and I decided from the beginning that I wouldn't tell her about any of it.

Amanda's prescribed "healing process" started small. I'd go to her flat, and as she lived in West London, I didn't have to worry about bumping into anyone that I didn't want to see. Then she eventually got me to a pub for a drink, and then we progressed to going out for a meal. It still hurt to breathe at times when I thought about Mark, and every morning I woke up to the realisation that he was gone. Each time it hit me, it felt no less painful than the first. I started to doubt that it ever would. The stress was also taking its toll on my body causing me to miss another period, and there were times when the constant queasiness turned physical.

Still, having Amanda helped. Focusing on work did too, and I knew that I needed to make it up to them. I'd had a lot of time off due to the real food poisoning, and then the fake one that I told them about, instead of telling them that I was too heartbroken to breathe let alone come to work. I wasn't sure how they'd take that. Then one sunny Monday morning in mid-June, things were set to change again.

It had been a month. A month of no Mark, no Hattie, no Tasha, and no Miri. A month of self-help videos and books that Amanda had forced on me. It had been a month of pain, but also, a month of Amanda. Amanda, who had been through something much worse, and who had started to make me believe that I could get through it too. That in time, that one day, I'd be all right again.

That was until I got into work and saw her on that sunny Monday. I greeted her with a hug, and although she hugged me back, I could feel that she was distant. I put it down to the fact that she'd perhaps had a bit too much of me over the last month, and I decided not to push it. Then at lunch she disappeared a little earlier than normal and that got me worried. I couldn't lose her too, so I sent her a text asking if everything was OK, and she replied saying that we should have a coffee after work.

I didn't see much of Amanda for the rest of the day as she was in meetings, and my gut was churning with worry — I was even sick again. She finally appeared at the end of the day, gave me a smile that felt too forced, and led the way to the nearest coffee shop.

As we sat down with our drinks I immediately asked, "Amanda, is everything OK?" I knew I sounded desperate, but I couldn't help it. "I'm sorry if you feel like I've put on you for the last month, I really am. I do appreciate all you've done for me; I hope you know that?"

"I know, Ava. I know it's been hard..." she sighed, clearly struggling to find the right words. "It's just that I've heard some things over the weekend, and I need to talk to you... what I've heard, Ava. It changes things."

My stomach leapt into my mouth. "OK, talk to me," I urged, whilst trying to hide my panic.

She cleared her throat. "You see, I happened to bump into Miles over the weekend — he lives near me, as you know, and he told me something very upsetting," she said, and she was clearly still upset, I could see that. "You know how Alex and I broke up, don't you?" she asked.

"Well, yes... he had an affair," I replied.

"Yes, he did, and the betrayal took longer to get over than the heartbreak," she said, starting to get angry.

"Amanda, I think I know where this is going, but I told you that Hattie has been lying about her brothers. Anything Miles has heard has come from her."

"I know you said that, but the thing is... that's not what he told me," she said, still looking displeased. I was confused. I didn't think it was possible that Hattie had let the truth out. Amanda continued, "It appears that the reason that you never told me about your relationship, and the reason that you still won't give any details... is because he was married."

I had not been expecting that and I instantly laughed at the ridiculousness of it. That hadn't been the right reaction though as it was a sore subject for Amanda.

"I'm sorry that I laughed, Amanda. I don't think this is funny," I assured her. "I laughed because I was surprised! I was not expecting that. I just... I have no idea..." I exhaled a long breath. "It isn't true. He was not married. He had been married before, but not now, not with me. It was just him and me," I told her honestly.

God, I hoped she could see that I was being honest.

She sighed and put her head in her hands, shaking it slightly. "He said you'd deny it," she told me, looking up at me. Then she continued, "He said that's why Hattie has fallen out with you. It was someone she knew. She knows the wife and that's why she's pushed you away," she said looking sad. "She feels like you used her to get to him, and now their marriage is over. It's over, and that poor woman is going through what I did."

I was utterly speechless. I had not seen it coming, and I was so busy thinking about how Hattie could take things so far, that I'd almost forgotten that Amanda was there.

"Ava!" she said with a harshness that brought me back to the room. "Well, do you still deny it?"

"Sorry, Amanda... I am... I am at a loss here, I really am... yes. I deny it. I was not and have not ever been involved with a married man," I told her. "I have no idea why this lie has started... the one about her brothers has been effective enough." I laughed dryly but I was far from amused.

"Then tell me the truth. Why not tell me what really

happened?" she asked, solemnly. I looked up and shook my head. "I know this seems mad, given the fact that lies are being spread," I said, sighing. "I did hurt Hattie. Not in the ways being said, but she got hurt. It wasn't my intention, but it happened," I said honestly. "So, when she asked me to keep the truth to myself, I promised that I would. I know it makes no sense, but I feel like I need to keep that promise," I sighed as I realised that it really didn't make any sense. Keeping the promise made no sense, and yet, I couldn't seem to find a way to break it.

Amanda groaned. "Ava, what am I meant to do with that?" she asked, raising her arms in exasperation. "I've always liked you, and we've seen each other socially before, but for the last month you've relied on me because you no longer have any other friends — and you've got no other friends because of something you did."

"No," I countered. "I've got no friends because they've taken Hattie's side, they've believed her lies."

"You just admitted hurting her," she snapped back.

"I know and trust me she is paying me back!" I almost yelled.

"Then tell me the truth. Just tell me," she practically begged.

"I can't," I said shrugging helplessly, and as Amanda shook her head at me, a thought suddenly hit me. "Why is it so hard for the people that are supposed to know me to believe me?" I asked.

She sighed as she stood up to put on her coat and said, "Maybe because you won't say anything, Ava, and in my book — in most people's book — that implies guilt." Then she got up and walked away — and I let her.

So, Hattie had won again. I grabbed my own coat and went to the bus stop. Once I was home I sat down and had a moment of clarity. Hattie was out to destroy everything that I had. It wasn't just about getting me out of her life — she wanted to destroy mine entirely. Miri liked Ted, he'd never shown an interest in her, but we'd all been out a few times and she had seen him flirt with me. I never acted on it, and had always reassured her that he was like a brother to me, but it had bothered her, and it had caused a rift before. Ted was her sore spot, so being told that I'd slept with him, and not only that but I'd used him to. That was all that it took to turn her.

I knew that Hattie knew about Amanda's break-up, because it was me that told her. I'm not sure if Miles was in on it, or if she'd lied to him too, but Hattie knew Amanda was looking out for me, that she was helping me, and she knew exactly what wounds to poke at there too. However, Amanda couldn't avoid me in the same way that Tasha and Miri had. She would have to see me at work, and I tried to comfort myself with the belief that I would be able to use that time to get her to believe me.

The next day at work Amanda avoided me, and the next, and the next. I tried to talk to her in the toilets one time, and she told me that it was too close to something that had hurt her, and that she needed time to think. So, I gave it to her, and I went back to being in my flat, and seeing nobody except for Carolyn and Cooper. Carolyn knew that something was wrong, but I never confided in her. I didn't want to burden her, and I was scared that if I let her too close then she'd be taken from me too.

I didn't see much of Miles during those troubled weeks with Amanda, but I wanted to speak to him and had asked his secretary to set up a meeting for me. He often worked from home and spent days in meetings, and as I was only part time it wasn't unusual for me to not cross paths with him in the office for weeks at a time. Then I got in one Monday morning at the end of June, and had an email confirming a meeting in his office at ten O'clock. I didn't know what to expect as I still couldn't figure out if he was complicit or just a pawn, but I knew that I'd more than likely be in a position where I needed to defend my character again. However, I tried to take some strength from the fact that he would need to defend his too.

I entered his office and was taken aback to see Val Turner, our HR Manager standing with him. She greeted me formally and then sat across from Miles, and when I was invited to sit in the chair next to her, the panic started to creep in. I thought I was there to confront him. What could possibly come next?

Miles didn't make me wait long to find out. "Ava, I've asked Val to join this meeting in an official capacity."

"Official capacity. Why?" I asked.

"We've been concerned about your standard of work and commitment recently," he said calmly. "You've had a considerable amount of time off and there have been errors. There have been complaints."

"What?" I asked, trying to remain calm, but my insides were churning, and I started burning up. "I've had time off due to food poisoning and I've not been made aware of any complaints," I replied. "Surely if there have been errors that have led to complaints then I should've been informed so that I could rectify them?"

Val spoke next. "This meeting is about addressing those issues, and to see if we can come up with a plan to move things forward," she said professionally.

"OK, well, can I see details then, so that I know what the issue is?" I asked.

Miles spoke up again. "I'm not sure that's necessary as

those involved wish to remain anonymous," he said matter of factly. "We've been made aware that you are having some personal issues, and it appears that some of your colleagues have been covering for you for a while. As such, there isn't a clear set of documented evidence," he said calmly, never once showing any sign of sympathy.

It didn't add up. "Surely there should be something solid that you can give me so that I can see the errors; I'm honestly at a loss as to what they could be," I told them. "Yes, I've had a lot going on in my personal life... I think you're aware of that Miles?" I asked pointedly. I looked at him hard, but he was still unfazed. "I'm dedicated to this job, and I know that I can turn whatever issues there are around."

"That's great to hear, Ava," Val said kindly, but then she paused. "Unfortunately, it has also been brought to our attention that you may have been dishonest about some of your sick leave."

"How so?" I asked.

"Well, we are aware of the food poisoning at the end of April, but a few weeks later you claimed to still be suffering and took a full week off. I've since been advised that that may not have been the real reason," she said, looking at me closely. "Can you now clarify for us what that was?"

I started to feel defensive — was Hattie really coming for my job too? "Does it matter?" I asked her. "Have I used hours that I'm not entitled to?"

"No, Ava," it was Miles' turn again, "but as mentioned at the beginning of this meeting it does lead us to question your dedication."

"As it happens, I was sick that week, a few times actually. But no, it wasn't down to food poisoning. It was down to a difficult personal matter that I'd rather not talk about," I said bluntly. As angry as I was, there was no stopping the tears that had started to fill my eyes.

Miles and Val exchanged a look, but it was Val that spoke. "I can see that this is very hard for you, Ava, and I would suggest that you take the rest of the day off to think things through," she said, kindly. "However, when you return tomorrow, we will need to discuss putting you on a performance management programme," she added formally. "I'm sure you'll be able to turn things around, but this is standard procedure in these circumstances," she said. She smiled, and her kindness at least seemed genuine.

I silently nodded and left the room and went straight to the toilets to catch my breath. This was Hattie. It had to be — but then I thought more about it and wondered if it was actually on me. I had lied about my absence, I had been distracted, perhaps I had let things slide. Yet, nobody had said anything and neither Val nor Miles could show me. There was one person that might know though, I just didn't know if she'd talk to me.

Amanda was senior to me, so if there had been any issues she would know. I found her at her desk and pulled her aside. "Amanda," I said urgently. "I know... actually I don't know what you think of me right now, but I need to ask you something, and I need you to be totally honest."

She scoffed at my request, no doubt because I hadn't been honest with her, but still, she agreed.

"You are the senior editor in this team. So, you know when there are issues with people's work?" I asked.

She nodded. "Yes, I do."

"And have you been made aware of any mistakes that I've made, or complaints about me?" I asked.

She looked irritated now and asked, "What's this about, Ava?"

"Please, Amanda... have you?" I begged, and she must've seen how important it was to me as she relented a little.

"No, Ava. None," she said honestly. "I had half expected to, given everything... but no. Everything has been fine."

I asked my final question. "And neither you nor anyone else, to your knowledge, has been covering for me?"

"No, Ava. Why would they?" she said, practically laughing at me.

Why would they, indeed.

"Thank you, Amanda," I said, and I walked out.

When I got to the bus stop, there was a fifteen-minute wait for my bus. I was completely on edge and there was no way I could stand there waiting, so I decided to walk up to Archway as there'd be different buses to catch there. As I walked, I played it all through over and over again. Amanda's tone made it clear that she no longer wanted to be my friend. She wouldn't tell me my work was fine if it wasn't, and she clearly didn't think anyone in the office would cover for me. I got on with everyone, but Amanda was the only one that I'd been particularly close with, and when she pulled away, they saw it. Of course, nobody would have covered up my mistakes, and Miles had nothing to show me. It was Hattie, it had to be. She was coming for my job. How far was she going to go with this, and more importantly, how was I going to stop her?

When I got to Archway, I saw a bus approaching, and it suddenly struck me that there was one person that could possibly help — that may be willing to help. I didn't know how I was going to get through it, but it was my only hope, so I ran to the bus stop and joined the queue. Only, this bus wasn't going to take me back to Muswell Hill. This bus stopped at Crouch End.

I had no idea if Mark would even be in, but I had to at

least try. My legs turned to jelly, and my heart was pounding as I rang the doorbell. Moments later I heard footsteps approaching and I held my breath until he opened the door. He stood there in front of me looking utterly shocked. I hadn't looked at his face in the flesh for almost two months and my heart skipped a beat at the sight of him. I still was still in love with him and even now I still wanted him. He looked tired, he looked like he'd been suffering, but it was still him.

"Ava? What... what are you doing here?" he asked awkwardly. "I'm not sure it's a good idea for you to be here," he said, and his words hit me harder than any had ever before. Last time I was here he'd been begging me to stay. I couldn't let myself think about any of that, so I got straight to the reason I was there.

"I'm here to ask for your help with Hattie," I blurted out. "I assume you know the lies she's been telling?"

He looked ashamed. "I do know what she said about the boys, and she knows I'm not happy about it," he replied, with pain evident in his eyes.

I laughed, but I wasn't remotely amused. "You know, I can understand her taking Tasha and Miri. I get that, but Amanda, and now my job? You need to reign her in, Mark."

He looked confused. "What do you mean? What about Amanda and your job?"

"Oh, so you didn't hear that one?" I asked sarcastically. "Well, let me fill you in on what your poisonous bitch of a daughter has done!" I shouted. "She turned Miri using your sons. Miri's always liked Ted so that was her weak spot. Tasha follows where Miri goes so that only left me with Amanda. So, then Amanda hears from Miles..." I paused and asked, "You remember Miles, don't you? My manager, Nate's best friend?" I didn't wait for a response. "Miles told

Amanda that I had been having an affair with a married man, and that I'd wrecked the marriage, leaving the wife devastated. Amanda was cheated on by her husband. She had been left devastated. Hattie knew that." Mark looked utterly shocked, but it didn't end there, so I continued, "So that brings me back to Miles, who today, along with our HR Manager, pulled me into his office to question my dedication to the job. To tell me about complaints about my work, and to put me on a performance management programme — no doubt with the intention of managing me out."

It was clear that Mark knew nothing about any of this. "Ava... Ava that's..." he tried to speak, but I wasn't finished.

"Only, when I asked Amanda — who is the senior editor in my team — she said there hadn't been any problems," I stepped closer to him; I was as desperate as I was furious. "So, Mark, if you ever truly cared about me, get her to stop! Plea—"

"If I ever truly cared about you?" he interrupted angrily. "Ava, you left me. I didn't want you to go. I didn't get the chance to choose, you just left. If I ever cared about you? I love you," he shouted, and then ran his hands through his hair trying to calm himself.

"You know why I left," I choked out. "I left because I didn't want to destroy your family. Because I didn't want to hurt Hattie any more than I already had," I reminded him. "She saw how heartbroken I was. She could see the pain, I know it, and I did it for her. I put her feelings before my own, and it hurt more than anything has ever hurt. Why isn't that enough for her?" I asked desperately, and the tears fell.

"I'm sorry, Ava..." he said, crying too. "I had no idea she was going to do this. She made me promise not to tell, just like she did you, and when I heard what she and the boys had said I went mad at them. I did," he said honestly. "Then they turned on me, telling me that I was choosing you. I had already lost you, and you left so that I wouldn't lose them. So, I decided that I couldn't let it happen," he said sadly.

"So, you think it's OK what she's doing to me? Did you know?" I asked, furious again.

"No! No. I have only heard the lie about Ted and Will. I have never heard anything about Amanda or your job, I swear," he said. I could tell he was being honest, but it wasn't enough.

"So, what are you going to do about it?" I asked.

"What can I do about it?" he replied helplessly.

"So, it's just me dealing with this alone?" I asked in despair. "It's just me that has to lose everything? Do I really deserve this, Mark?" I asked, and then I bent forward a little to try to contain the pain, but the tears were unstoppable.

Mark started to move forward instinctively, but then stopped himself. "You don't deserve this, and I am so sorry that this is happening, but if I speak to her about this then I'll lose them. They're my children."

"So, you won't do anything to help me?" I asked, looking at him hard.

"Ava... please... I am so, so sorry, I—"

"You are pathetic." The words came out of me without emotion. It didn't even sound like me, but I suddenly realised that being sad and trying to do the right thing by others, had done nothing other than make things worse for myself. If I was to face it alone then I needed to be strong, and I couldn't do that when I was feeling broken, so I decided to get angry.

Mark looked shocked and hurt by my words, but I couldn't let that be my problem, so I hammered it home.

"You are pathetic. I regret ever coming here that day," and with that said I walked away.

I walked all the way home stopping only to pick up some wine. As I walked, I got stronger, or at least angrier and I started making plans. I needed to take stock. I got in, opened a glass of wine and checked my bank accounts. I may have been part-time and freelancing on the side, but I had no mortgage. My outgoings were low, and my dad was in finance and the importance of taking care of my money had been impressed upon me at an early age. I could quit my job and be OK for a while... I could. Miles wanted me gone, and I no longer had any desire to stay — but if I was going it would be on my terms. So, after the first glass of wine I opened my work emails and began typing.

Dear Miss Turner,

Further to the meeting today with yourself and Mr Humphreys, I have come to the decision that it is no longer possible for me to continue my employment with Mason and Rogers Publishers. As such I would request that you accept this as my letter of resignation — effective immediately.

There are, however, some matters that I would like to address. These have directly led to this difficult decision, and as such I feel it is my duty to state them.

Firstly, the complete lack of professionalism displayed by yourself and Mr Humphreys in today's meeting was somewhat alarming. I was called into a meeting where it had already been decided that I would be performance

managed due to errors and complaints. Yet Mr Humphreys was unable to provide any evidence of such issues. After the meeting, I spoke with a senior member of staff, who categorically denied that they were aware of any errors with my work. I ask you then, what due diligence was done in order to confirm these claims before they were presented to me? Especially given the total lack of physical evidence.

It is accurate to say that I was dishonest about some recent time off. In truth, I had ended a relationship and was not mentally or emotionally in a fit state to come to work. I apologise for not being honest about this, but it truly was the most difficult time. Thank you for being so understanding.

I would also like to advise you that I am aware that Mr Humphreys knowingly circulated lies about me to a senior colleague. This led to a once pleasant working environment turning hostile.

I have truly enjoyed my time with your company, and I thank you for the opportunity that you have given me. I wish I could say that I am sorry for any inconvenience that my immediate resignation may cause, but at this stage that would be a lie.

I should also add that given the circumstances detailed in this correspondence, I will be looking into whether I have a case for constructive dismissal.

Yours sincerely,

Ava Swan

I sent the email blind copying in Val's boss. Even though I probably had a case, I had no intention to look into constructive dismissal, because I just wanted it to be done. The email would no doubt find its way to Miles, and he'd feed it back to Hattie, and I hoped that she'd see that even though I may have been bowing out, that I was willing to take those that had wronged me down along the way.

With that done, I poured myself another glass of wine and started thinking about my next task — where I was going to go? I knew I needed to get out of London. I could go and stay with my mum and dad for a bit. I could even travel. I could freelance from anywhere as long as there was an internet connection. So, I started to look at my options, and after a bit of searching online I found that flats like mine were being rented out for around £2000 a month.

I could do that. I could rent my flat out and have some money coming in that would fund any trip that I took. Given that I had no mortgage it looked like it would be pretty straightforward. I'd need insurance but that would be easy enough. There were also safety certificates to be done, but it looked like most estate agents handled that part. So, by the end of the second glass I'd decided that I'd go to the local estate agents in the morning and get the ball rolling. I'd call my parents in the morning as well and let them know I was coming, but I wouldn't tell them just how long I planned to stay for until I was there. That was definitely a conversation that needed to be done face to face.

During my third glass I decided to do something that I'd not done since I left Mark — I checked social media. I'd been avoiding it in case it set me off again, or worse, if I saw more lies. I clicked onto Hattie's profile and what I saw was many photos of Hattie with Tasha and Miri — Ted and Will too. They were having such fun. Lots of photos from nights out with lovely captions like, *BFFs for life!* There was also a photo of Ted and Miri getting close with the caption, *Finally!*

I felt a whole new wave of rage coming over me and I was going to make some scathing comments of my own, but then I realised something. Hattie had cut me off from everyone and yet she'd not blocked me here. She wanted me to see this, those photos were for me. So instead of commenting I went to my account settings and hit the 'delete account' button. I then went onto every other social media account I had and did the same. It was actually quite liberating.

With the fourth glass downed, I had to quickly run to the toilet and bring it all back up again. That continued for a few hours until eventually, completely empty of everything, I crawled to my bed and passed out.

17

The next morning, I felt appropriately awful, but I had things to do so pushed on through. I called my mum and told her that I had unused annual leave and would like to come to stay for a while. She was thrilled and it was settled that I'd go there at the end of the following week.

Next, I headed out to see the estate agents. They confirmed that it was as straightforward as I thought. I ended up going with the company that gave me coffee because I'd really needed it, and their terms were all pretty much the same. I went home to start the insurance process and the next day the estate agent came over to photograph the flat. The following day the certificates were sorted, and my flat went on the market — and being a desirable location — it was snapped up in a few days.

While all this was happening, while I was claiming back some control over my life, I started to listen to and focus on my body a bit more. I realised that I'd missed another period — that was three. It wasn't an unusual thing for my body given the situation, but I couldn't shake the feeling that I felt different. I thought that I ought to see a doctor before I went to Clovelly, and knowing from previous experiences what one of the first questions they'd ask would be, I went to the chemist to pick up a pregnancy test. I'd done them before and didn't think much of it, so I put it in the bathroom planning to do it closer to my appointment.

I carried on with my to do list. I needed to pack, I needed to decide what I was taking, what was going into storage and what could be given away or thrown. It took days and making the appointment kept getting moved down the list, and so I never made it to the Doctors. There was so much to do, including getting myself a new phone and number. I must've had the same number for years, but I was starting anew, and I didn't want anyone from the past catching up with me. There was one visit that I needed to make before I went though, and that was to Carolyn and Cooper. I felt bad that I was going to be leaving her in the lurch, she relied on my help with Cooper and I would truly miss them both.

Carolyn was shocked and upset that I was leaving, she had known that things weren't right with me, but I'd chosen not to tell her, so she had no idea that things had gotten quite so bad. I spent an afternoon with her drinking tea in her summer house, with Cooper sitting between the two of us.

"You know, Ava..." she said, tentatively, "I know people that know people, and I heard some things."

I let out a deep breath. "Of course, you have. I wonder if it's something I've already heard or a new story," I replied dryly.

"I know what Hattie and her brothers said that you got up to with them." She shook her head disapprovingly and my heart sank. "That girl. Too much like her mother, that one."

I smiled, relieved. "So, you don't believe it?" I asked her.

"Of course not," she answered forcefully, offended by the suggestion. "You know, one of the things I love about living here. Well, actually, it can be a nuisance at times... Vi at the back is always looking into my house, so if she calls for a chat, I can't avoid her because chances are that she's already spotted me."

I laughed at her, she always digressed when she had a story to tell. I was going to miss this woman.

"Anyway, as I was saying, having Vi there, always peeking in does have its perks," she continued, smiling. "It's nice to know what's happening in one's own home when you're not there." She gave me a pointed look and smirked. "You see, she has a great view into my kitchen," she added, and as she raised an eyebrow and smiled at me, the penny dropped.

"Oh, my God!" I said aghast, almost falling off my chair. "She saw us?"

"If you are referring to you and Mark Davidson going at it on my kitchen table, then yes," she replied, smiling even more.

"Carolyn, I'm so, so sorry. I bleached it about five times by the way," I said, completely mortified.

"Don't be. I had a sex life once, you know," she replied kindly.

"So, you've known this whole time?" I asked more sombrely.

"I have," she replied gently. "I understood that you'd have your reasons for keeping it quiet — I told Vi the same. Not that we can blame you. He's always been quite a man, that one. Awful wife."

"Ex-wife," I corrected.

"Yes, well, I could see that you were hurting and when I

heard what that girl was spreading… I tell you, Ava, I nearly went and had words with her myself" she said, angrily. "Just like her mother. Wants to control everything. Wants to control everything and everyone — especially you."

"Me?" I asked, taken aback. "Hattie didn't control me."

"Oh, she did," she replied vehemently. "She was possessive of you from the day you met. She was just good at making you think that you were helping her. I imagine you being with her dad and doing something for yourself, tipped her right over."

"I hurt her," I replied, honestly. I knew I wasn't entirely blameless. "I walked away for her. For him too. I never wanted to ruin their family... I just—"

"You fell in love, dear," she said understandingly, and she smiled and patted my leg.

"Yes, and now I'm running away," I half laughed. "You know, I keep thinking about my Nanny Mae. What she must think of me for letting Hattie destroy my life. For leaving the City... I wish I had her strength."

Carolyn leant forward. "You mustn't think like that," she said kindly. "This is you taking control. If you stay, then she'll just continue to take from you. She won't let you be happy," she told me vehemently. Then she paused and sighed. "I am going to miss you, and not just for your help with this boy here," she said as she scratched behind Cooper's ear. "This is the right thing to do. Put these bad memories to bed, heal your heart and find your happy."

I burst into tears and gave her a big hug. "I'm really going to miss you too."

We hugged for a few minutes and then said our goodbyes, and as we were walking to the front door she chuckled and said, "I have to say, I wish I could be a fly on the wall when your father comes for them, that's for sure."

"What do you mean?" I asked, a little puzzled.

"Well, Jonathan Swan isn't going to stand for an older man breaking his daughter's heart and doing nothing as his children took her life from her, is he?" she asked, laughing a little.

"I guess not," I replied, thoughtfully. "Goodbye, Carolyn. You take care," I told her, and I walked back to the flat that was still my home — for a little bit longer, anyway.

I hadn't thought about that. Mark had joked once about my dad being scary and I'd laughed it off, but there was some truth to it. He grew up in an East End working-class family and life wasn't always easy. He wasn't a violent man, but he'd had a few "scrapes" as he called them when he was younger, and he'd been boxing since he was fourteen. He was also his mother's son and Carolyn was right, he would not just sit around and do nothing. I had thought that I'd just tell my parents everything when I got there, but with Carolyn's words spoken, I realised that there was no way I could tell them, not right away, at least. I didn't want my dad to get into trouble.

Time flew by, and the morning I was due to leave was upon me in no time at all. I'd spoken to the removal company for about the third time about how they would need to stop off somewhere for an hour. This was to give me some time to break it to my parents that I hoped to stay longer than I let on. I didn't think that arriving with a removal van was the most tactful way of doing it. They probably thought I was mad, but they'd agreed, and charged me more too.

I stood still for a moment and looked around my empty flat. Empty, except for the boxes stacked up and waiting to be collected, the remnants of my broken life now packed into fifteen boxes. Then I looked again at the most important box in the room — the box that was yet to be opened. I'd put my first missed period down to the food poisoning messing up my body. The second? That was obviously down to the stress of the catastrophic destruction of every aspect of my life — job, friends, lover were all gone. The third? The third was now days late and I could no longer ignore all of the signs that had gone unnoticed for months.

There was no sense in deluding myself any longer. I had half an hour before the removal team was due to arrive. So, I picked up the box and took it to the bathroom, already knowing exactly what the test was going to tell me three minutes after peeing on it.

18

Mum has her head in her hands, she's been in tears at times. Hearing the full extent of the pain that I've suffered has broken her heart. Especially as I went through it alone. Dad has remained silent the entire time, his head in hands at some points, his hands curled into fists at others. Lucas is sitting next to me and so I haven't been looking at his reactions. His knee has never broken contact with mine though, so I know which parts of the story have affected him. It wasn't the sex, because I didn't really go into detail with them, understanding that neither my parents nor my boyfriend would want to hear about that. Jacob is here so they know enough. Instead, Lucas reacted when I talked about how in love I had been with Mark. His knee would twitch for a moment, or he would bounce it for a bit whenever feelings were mentioned, but other than that he hasn't responded.

Jacob has now finished throwing his food all over the floor and is reaching for me. He'll be wanting some milk and that gives me the perfect opportunity to get some space. I stand up, scoop him up from his high chair and say, "So that's everything. You know everything now. I'm going to feed Jacob next door. Take however long you need."

Then I walk into the living room leaving the three people that I hope still love me to sit in silence. A few moments later I hear a chair scrape on the floor and footsteps heading towards the back door. That will be Dad going for a walk. I wonder how long he'll be out for this time.

I sit looking down at my baby boy. It's been hard talking about it all. The pain of leaving Mark feels fresher than ever and my anger towards Hattie is still palpable. I didn't realise how much it still affects me — all of it. I just haven't thought about it for so long because I had to push it aside. First to focus on the pregnancy, and to make sure that I was sending the baby "happy hormones", as Julia had instructed. Then Jacob was here, and he made my heart burst with a love so deep that everything else pales in comparison. I realised tonight that my wounds haven't healed, they've just been back benched while I dealt with other priorities. Yet, as much as it still hurts, I wouldn't change any of it. How could I when I have Jacob because of it?

If I'd known the food poisoning had messed up my pill, and I was pregnant while Mark and I were still together, then we probably would've stayed together. However, that would have destroyed his relationship with his children, and worse still, Jacob could've been subjected to their wrath. I didn't know then the cruelty that Hattie was capable of, but I do now and I'm glad that Jacob will never be in her sights. Not knowing until that day and coming here, to my family — that was absolutely the best thing for both of us. So, I can't bring myself to regret it.

I sit and dwell on it all until Jacob finishes feeding, then

I put him on the floor so that he can play. I'm focusing on him, but I'm aware of movement in the kitchen now. Then Lucas walks in, gives me a kiss and says, "Shall I take this one for his bath so that you and your mum can talk?"

Relief floods through me, Lucas is still Lucas, and he's looking at me just the same as before. "That would be good, thanks," I tell him.

Mum comes in next with a tray with two glasses of wine and a cup of tea on it. Gesturing at the tray she says, "I wasn't sure which you'd want."

I smile at her and say, "I think I'll take the tea actually, thanks."

"Good, more wine for me." She's smiling at me too, and she goes to sit on the chair opposite me.

"Are you OK?" I ask.

"Me? I was about to ask you the same thing, darling."

"I'm OK. I'm not going to lie, it still hurts, but this isn't exactly new information for me. You on the other hand..." I say apprehensively.

She sighs and says, "I honestly don't know what to say. I do understand why you didn't tell us — Mark Davidson." She raises her eyebrows. "Your dad would've hauled him over the coals!"

"Are you disappointed in me?" I ask nervously.

"Oh, darling, no," she tells me sincerely. "You met an older, handsome, charming man that you'd not seen in years. I can see how it could happen. I think just about everyone on our street was in love with him when you grew up. You girls all had a crush on him, I remember that," she says, laughing, but then looks at me seriously. "You fell in love and in the end, you put everyone else before yourself. How could I be disappointed in you?" she asks lovingly, but then a frown appears as she continues, "That Hattie, on the other hand... I'd like to get my hands on her."

"Thanks Mum," I say, as my eyes start to fill with tears.

"I'm just so sorry that you went through it alone," she says. "I wish you'd told us. It's our job to protect you and we didn't."

"Please don't put that on yourself. I didn't tell you. I didn't let you help," I tell her firmly.

She has tears in her eyes, as she asks, "But why?"

I take a deep breath. "Honestly, I was going to tell you everything when I got here, but Carolyn got me thinking about how Dad might react, and given how good Hattie was at manipulating everything... I didn't want him to get into a situation where they could have him arrested or something."

"I think it's safe to say that he'd have gone straight there; he's got his mother in him," she says, laughing.

"It wasn't just that though," I say cautiously. "Hattie messed with my head for a bit. She managed to turn everyone against me. People that had been my friends for years just walked away," I say sadly. "And I think that... I know it's crazy, but for a while I was worried that you would too."

"Oh, darling, never," she says earnestly.

"It was when I heard his heartbeat that I realised that I loved him and would always protect him," I tell her. "As far as I'm concerned that means keeping him as far away from that family as possible. After a while, you and Dad stopped asking... I think I'd hoped it would be a secret forever," I say honestly.

Mum sighs again and says, "I understand that, I do, but you need to be aware that things like this don't stay a secret forever."

We both turn as we hear the back door open, and my dad walks into the living room, looking broken. Mum stands and gives him a kiss. "I'll go see how Lucas and Jacob are getting on," she says as she goes upstairs, leaving us alone.

Dad paces the room for a moment then sits where Mum had been sitting. He's looking at his hands to begin with but then he looks directly at me — he's been crying. I don't think I've ever really seen him cry.

He clears his throat and says, "For the past week I've been disappointed in you." I nod, understanding, and he carries on, "I got told things... things that I should've known wouldn't be true, and I started to believe them," he tells me, his regret and remorse written all over his face. "You see, all we've had to go on is what's been in our heads. The amount of times your mum and I have sat down and talked about what could be so bad that your best friend since you were five would turn on you. And, Ava, you just refused to tell us..." he pauses for a moment. He looks so anguished, but he continues, "So, when I got told about Ted and Will, and I couldn't say anything back because I didn't know anything. And I guess it made sense." He shakes his head and a look of remorse sweeps over his face. "I was disappointed in you and you didn't deserve that, and I'm truly sorry."

I go to him and give him a hug and we both cry. We stay like that for a few minutes, then I pull away. "You have nothing to be sorry for," I tell him. "I came here pregnant and didn't tell you a thing, and all you did was support and help me. You have nothing to be sorry for."

He smiles at me and hugs me again, then Lucas and Mum come back down the stairs to let me know that Jacob has had his bath, and is now ready for bed. I take him and go upstairs to feed him to sleep. It doesn't take long, and I'm just settling him into his cot when Lucas comes quietly into the bedroom and sits on the bed. I sit next to him; it's his turn to talk now.

He says quietly, "Your parents have gone home. I think they're exhausted."

I yawn and reply, "I know the feeling."

"Too tired to talk?" he asks.

"Not to you," I smile at him.

He lets out a deep breath. "You really loved him, didn't you?" he asks cautiously.

"I did... but now I love you," I reply, taking his hand in mine.

"I know," he tells me, "and I love you, so, so much." He pauses for a moment before continuing, "It just sounded so intense. I'm honestly struggling to see how I compare."

"It was intense," I admit. "Though I think that was because we knew it always had a time limit. We were in our own bubble," I say. "You, me, and Jacob — this is real life, and real life, especially with a baby, has distractions."

"I know, and believe me I wouldn't be without that little man. He's my boy," he says, but it almost sounds like a question.

"He is yours," I reassure him. "You are his dad."

"And you?" he asks, looking deeply into my eyes.

"I'm yours too," I tell him before we kiss.

We quietly and gently make love and I fall asleep feeling relieved. They all know now, and I haven't lost them. I hadn't realised how much of a burden it has been, this secret, and I'm hopeful now that things are going to be just fine. Yet, even in my hope, a shadow looms over me. Because now that I've let the past back in. Now that I've allowed myself to feel it all again — the love and the pain — I know that no matter what I tell Lucas, or what I tell myself. The truth is that there is no comparison between my feelings for

Mark and my feelings for Lucas. I wish that there was. I wish Lucas could make me feel alive in the ways that Mark did. I wish I could replicate the feeling of completeness that I had with Mark — but no matter how hard I try, it just isn't happening.

19

JONATHAN

Jonathan Swan had thought about it over and over all week. Should he go?

Yes. No, absolutely not.

Ava didn't want him to interfere. Still, he couldn't shake it, it was his upbringing, he kept hearing his mum's voice telling him, "Family looks out for family." She had lots of sayings like that. So, he decided he was going.

He didn't tell Eleanor what he was planning to do because she'd have stopped him. So instead, he told her that he was going to spend the day fishing. It would be an all-dayer — early start and late finish. So, when he headed out that morning, he put his fishing gear into his car, and then started the long drive to London. He'd got Mark's address from a mutual friend, and although it was a long trip to make in one day, he didn't intend on being there for long, and as far as he was concerned, it needed to be done. He'd simply say his piece and then leave.

He knew it could be a wasted journey. He was showing up unannounced on a Saturday afternoon, so there was a good chance that he wouldn't be in. As it turned out,

Jonathan was in luck, and he could see movement in the house as he walked up to the door and rang the bell. It was one of the boys that answered the door. Jonathan hadn't seen them for a while but from his age he took him to be the youngest. "It's Will, isn't it?" he asked, smiling kindly at him.

Will smiled back but was clearly confused, he didn't recognise the older man standing in front of him. "Yes, it is," he replied. "Sorry, have we met?"

"Yes, we have, son, but not for a long time. I'm Jonathan Swan," he said, reaching out his hand politely.

Will looked suitably worried but took the offered hand giving it a weak shake in return. "Lovely," Jonathan said, smiling firmly. "Now, be a good boy and step aside."

Jonathan didn't wait for a response or invitation, he just stepped forward and walked past Will. He was in a lovely open plan living room, but he could hear voices in the kitchen and so he headed in that direction.

Will came up behind him. "Dad, this is—" he started to say.

Mark looked up and swallowed hard. "I know who it is, Will," he said calmly. "Hello Jonathan."

Mark was still a handsome man, and Jonathan could see why his daughter would have been attracted to him. He could see why Mark would be attracted to Ava too, she was beautiful. Beautiful, funny, kind and smart. He looked at the rest of the people in the room — Will had gone over to the table and he saw that they were all there — Hattie, Ted and Will. He recognised Miri as well, but he'd never met the man sitting next to Hattie. It really was turning out to be a lucky trip, after all.

"Isn't this cosy," Jonathan said, overly politely. "Hattie, Ted, Will," he nodded at them. "Good to see you too, Miranda," he said, and then he looked towards the unknown man and put out his hand. "Nate is it?" he asked, walking over to greet him.

The man looked worried and had no clue what was going on. "No, I'm Miles," he replied cautiously.

"Oh, Miles," Jonathan said, feigning friendliness. "Work in publishing, do you?" he asked eagerly.

"Uh, yes... I do," Miles replied nervously.

"Of course, you do," Jonathan said, still the epitome of politeness. Then he added, "Cunt," more bitterly.

Miles almost jumped out of his skin and looked to Hattie for an explanation, but Hattie had been unable to look at Jonathan even once since he walked into the room.

It was Mark who provided it. "This is Jonathan Swan, Ava's father," he said.

Jonathan noticed Mark's voice hitch a little as he said Ava's name, but other than that he seemed resolute. He'd obviously been expecting a visit sooner or later.

Mark sighed, and asked, "Can I get you a drink, Jonathan?"

"No thanks, Mark," he replied, looking at him hard. "I don't think I can stand to be in this house for too long. I'll say what I need to say and be on my way," he told him, and Mark just nodded in reply.

Jonathan wasted no time getting started. "You see, two weeks ago I came to London and was given some rather disturbing information. I was told that my daughter had been sleeping with both of your sons," he said tensely. "And you see, Ava has not said a peep about what happened here for the entire time that she's been in Clovelly. Other than something happened to make Hattie here turn on her..."

"For good reason," Miranda interrupted.

Jonathan turned to her. "Quiet please, Miranda, the grown-ups are speaking," he told her calmly.

Miri harrumphed and turned to Ted for support, but he had the good sense not to say a word.

"So, as I was saying..." Jonathan looked across the table to see if anyone else would interrupt him — they didn't. "When I heard this story, I had no choice but to believe it — what with Ava being so secretive," Jonathan swallowed hard, his remorse was clear for them to see. "And for the first time in her life, I was ashamed of my little girl. And when I confronted her, she saw that. She saw it, and I can never take that back," he said, starting to get angry.

"I understand—" Mark started to say.

"Good," Jonathan interrupted. "Good. You see Mark, now that she's finally opened up to us, I feel like I finally understand things too," he said, looking him dead in the eye. "I understand why you'd fancy my daughter. I even understand why she'd fancy you. I understand why you'd have sex with her," he heard Miri gasp, but he ignored her. "I understand how you'd fall in love and decide to keep your relationship a secret. I understand all of that — really, I do," he told him firmly.

Mark looked visibly ashamed and Jonathan looked over to the others at the table. Hattie had her head down and was crying, and Miri was glaring at Ted.

Jonathan continued, "Really, what the whole situation comes down to is this. You fucked Ava," he said, pointing at Mark, "and then your children fucked her over."

Mark nodded, "I know and I'm sorry."

Jonathan knew Mark wanted to say more but he didn't let him continue. He quickly turned to Hattie and said, "What about you Hattie? Are you sorry?" She still couldn't look at him. "Are you sorry for turning all of her friends against her? For ruining her life?" Jonathan still got no reply.

"Ted, Will? How about you? Looks like you've done all right out of this, Ted," he said, gesturing to Miri.

Miri was furious and shouted, "Not anymore! I just don't believe this Hattie, how could you?" She stood up and grabbed her things, then she looked at Hattie again and said, "She was nothing but a friend to you. How could you?" She got no answer either, and she left.

"It would appear that for someone that likes to tell stories, that our Hattie, here is lost for words today," Jonathan said sarcastically. Then he turned back to Mark and added, "You must be so proud of them," Mark said nothing, but he didn't look proud. "So, as I said before, there are many parts of this that I understand. But what I just can't get my head around is this; she came to you," he said, pointing at Mark again. "When her life was being pulled apart at the hands of your children, she came to you for help."

"I know and believe me—" Mark started to reply, but Jonathan put a hand up to stop him.

Jonathan saw that he looked ashamed, ashamed and sad and that pleased him, but he wasn't finished. "You claimed to love her?" Mark nodded and Jonathan continued, "You should've intervened. You should've had her back. She put you and your family first, breaking her own heart in the process, I might add. You should have had her back!"

"I know... I did—"

"No." Jonathan put his hand up to him again. "No more. I've said what I needed to and now I think I'll be on my way," he said, turning to leave.

"How is she?" Mark practically blurted out.

"How is she?" Jonathan repeated aghast. "Well, at first she was a heartbroken mess. But she's a fighter at heart, and she turned her life around. Got herself a nice boyfriend,

Irish — big bastard he is. I wouldn't recommend any of you showing your faces, that's for sure. Worships her he does. Protects her."

Jonathan could see that his words stung but he didn't care. He was done. He turned and walked out the door and walked towards his car, only to find Miranda standing outside on her phone crying. She hung up when she saw him.

"Mr Swan... I've just been speaking to Tasha," she said, still crying. "We can't believe it. Can you please tell her how sorry we are?"

Jonathan looked at the young woman standing in front of him, he'd known Miri a long time and she was clearly hurting. He didn't know if it was over Ava or Ted, but she was hurting. He cleared his throat and said sympathetically, "I'm afraid I can't do that. If I did then she'd know that I came here today... and she doesn't need to know that." He smiled and started to walk away.

"What if we came to see her?" she asked, and Jonathan's blood ran cold. "She doesn't have to know about today."

Jonathan couldn't let them come to Clovelly. If they did, they'd find out about Jacob and he didn't think that was something that they'd keep quiet. So, he told her, "I don't think that's a good idea. What's done is done."

"But we've known her for so long..." Miri tried to argue, but Jonathan stopped her.

"Didn't stop you turning on her though did it?" Miri looked ashamed, but Jonathan felt he needed to do more. "I may be a bloke, but I know a bit about women," he told her, "about how they work, and their friendships. And I know that affection and jealousy often go hand in hand." Miri clearly wanted to protest but Jonathan pushed on. "I think it was convenient for you to have a reason to be rid of my daughter. She was a friend, but she was competition — in your eyes, anyway," he said.

"She never wanted Ted, but he wanted her. Then she was gone and suddenly he's yours."

"I... I..." Miri didn't know what to say so Jonathan hoped to put the final nail in.

"She's moved on," he told her. "Let her go now. Just like you let her go then."

Jonathan walked away feeling awful about hurting Miranda, but he had to keep her away. They couldn't come to Clovelly. He sat down in his car and breathed hard. It had taken all his strength not to slap the lot of that family — but he felt better. He'd done what he'd been unable to do for all this time — he'd defended his daughter and he'd done it all without mentioning Jacob. His mum would be proud. He shook his head trying to get rid of the last of the anger, took a drink of water and started his long journey home.

20

It's been four months since telling my family what happened. Jacob is one now, and I can't believe how time flies. Life is good, I'm writing freelance again and when I'm not doing that, I'm baking in the tea rooms. Mum both loves and hates having me in her kitchen because I'm still a messy cook, and no matter how hard I try, I don't think that will ever change. The Swan is doing well, we've gained a reputation as a place to visit for tourists and locals alike, so business is good.

It's a standard Thursday afternoon. Mum is looking after the customers and I've been baking scones for what seems like hours, mainly because the clean-up takes just as long as the actual baking. It's three o'clock and I'm finally done so I head out into the front to say goodbye and go, but then I hear a voice.

"Ava! Is that you?" a woman asks. I turn, startled, and for a moment I almost don't recognise her. Seeing her here seems so out of place.

"Lilly? What are you doing here?" I ask in shock, and she gets up, arms stretched wide.

Lilly Barton, wife to Mark's best friend is here, in my tea rooms, embracing me like we're old friends. Which I guess we are, but that doesn't stop my heart from dropping into my stomach.

"Oh, my goodness! It's so lovely to see you," I tell her. It's only a half lie, she's only ever been a friend to me, but this is dangerous. If she sees Jacob, then she'll know. He looks more and more like Mark each day.

"You too," she says genuinely. "You look so well."

"Actually, I look a mess, I've been baking all afternoon," I say. Pointing up and down my clothes which are covered in flour.

"My friends and I have been doing a bit of a coastal tour. We're heading back to London tomorrow," she tells me, smiling.

I breathe a sigh of relief. One day. Surely that's manageable? "Where are you staying?" I ask, expecting her to tell me that she's staying at The White House. It's a popular hotel that is far enough away from my home to not be a problem.

"Oh, we're in a delightful bed and breakfast called The Lilacs," she says warmly. That isn't so good, it's only five minutes away. "We've just checked in and they said that this was the place to come for a late lunch. They were right, it's lovely," she adds genuinely.

"Thank you" I say, and I see my mum walking over to us. "This is my mum, it's her place, I'm just the help."

Mum smiles warmly, she's so natural with customers. "Hello," she says offering her hand. "I'm Eleanor Swan."

Lilly takes her hand. "I'm Lilly Barton, it's lovely to meet you. Such a great place you have here," she beams. Lilly was always lovely.

"Lilly Barton?" Mum asks quizzically. "I feel like I know that name."

"Lilly is a friend from London, Mum, I've mentioned her once or twice," I say. I try to glare at her, to tell her to drop it, but she's too distracted trying to place Lilly's name to notice.

"Yes... my husband, Darren, is Mark Davidson's best friend," Lilly says, looking a little uncomfortable.

"Oh... right. Of course," Mum says, trying to sound calm, but she looks at me now and she's clearly just as nervous as I am.

Just then, the bell rings to let us know that the door has opened. It's a light, little jingle that's usually so inoffensive, but is currently sending shivers down my spine, and then I hear my dad speak.

"This little fella is missing his mummy," he says, as I turn around to see Jacob trying to run towards me with his arms out.

"Mumma!" he shouts excitedly, jumping into my arms. I give him a big hug, trying to mask the fear now coursing through me, and I slowly turn and see Lilly looking right at me, mouth open wide.

"Oh... you have a baby?" she asks, surprised.

Dad jumps in before I can speak. "Baby? This big boy just turned one," he says, ever the proud grandad. He has no clue of the significance of what is unfolding in front of him.

"One?" Lilly asks, as she silently does the maths. She and Darren never had children, but she knows enough to work it out. She knows when I left London, and she knows that I couldn't have a one-year old child had I not already been pregnant when I left.

"One," she says again. It's a statement this time. She's worked it out. She smiles again and turns her attention to Jacob, who until now has been resting in the crook of my neck. “Well, look at you, beautiful boy. What's your name?” she asks.

He smiles and giggles at her, giving her the best view of those blue eyes.

“His name is Jacob,” I answer, grateful that she's looking at him and not me. Standing before Lilly now I feel something that I haven't felt before. Guilt. I've kept this a secret for the right reasons as far as I'm concerned, but standing in front of someone that cares for Mark, I feel guilty.

“Look at those blue eyes,” she says, looking into my dark brown ones. “He must take after his father.”

I try, but I can't read her, if she's angry she isn't letting it show.

Then she continues, “Sorry to steal her from you,” she says, looking at my parents, “but, Ava, can we have a word outside, please?”

I just nod my response and my mum leans in to take Jacob from me. Even if my dad is totally unaware, Mum knows what is about to come and she gives me a supportive smile. Unfortunately, it isn't quite enough to mask her own fear.

I follow Lilly out onto the street, and she leads the way, walking a little further away from the tea rooms so that we can't be seen.

She stops, turns to me taking a deep breath and blurts out, “He's Mark's, isn't he? Your son? Mark's the father?” She is annoyed after all. I nod silently, unable to find my voice. “I don't really know why I'm asking, he's the spitting image of him,” she shouts. She paces around running her fingers through her hair. “How could you do this to him?” she asks angrily. “I know you were hurt, but keeping a baby a secret is a pretty hefty punishment, don't you think?”

With that I find my voice. "It was not about punishing him, that's never been the reason," I counter.

"Then why?" she asks, still angry. "How could you keep this from him? You were pregnant in London, when you were still together, even? Why wouldn't you tell him?"

"I didn't know until the morning I left," I shout in defence.

She has her hands on her hips and she scoffs at me, "I may not be an expert, but I don't see how you couldn't have known."

"Lilly... throughout my life, whenever I've been ill or stressed out, I've missed my period. GCSEs, A Levels, my degree — I didn't have a period for months." She doesn't look any less angry, but she is at least letting me speak, so I continue, "I got food poisoning on a night out. That stopped the pill working and that's when I got pregnant, and yes, Mark and I were together then — but I swear, I didn't think anything more of it. Then not long after that everything fell apart. I lost Mark—"

"You left him," she counters.

"I gave him up to spare anyone any more hurt and to stop him losing his children, like I always said I would. I didn't want it to end." She says nothing but gestures for me to continue, so I do, "So, yes, I left him, and as if that wasn't hard enough Hattie decided to destroy my life. I assume you're aware of what she did?" I ask her.

"I am," she replies somewhat more solemnly.

"I was so stressed all the time," I continue, "I didn't even notice the second missed period at the time, and when I did, I didn't question it because of everything that was going on. Then the third..." My tears fall now, and I see Lilly soften a little, but I need to make her see. "It was only after Hattie came for my job, and I went to see Mark to ask him to help to make her stop... it was only then that I realised that I needed to turn all of the pain into anger, so that I could take back control of my life," I say firmly. "That's the only time I actually took a step back to think about it. I bought the test, but I didn't do it until the morning that I left," I tell her honestly, then I laugh dryly. "Looking back, my body was practically shouting it at me. I was physically sick some days and queasy most. I was worried, my gut was always churning. I never... I never knew what Hattie was going to do next," I tell her, and the tears fall full force.

She sighs heavily and moves towards a bench and sits down. She puts her elbows onto her knees and rests her head in her hands. I sit next to her and we remain silent for a few moments, until she speaks.

"Ava, I am truly sorry for what you went through. You didn't deserve any of it. All you ever did was make him happy. Darren and I were dubious at first, but seeing you together... you just worked, you just made sense, and you clearly thought as much of him as he did of you," she says, as she looks at me and smiles sadly. "I do know what Hattie did," she says. Then turning stern, she continues, "I told her myself that it was completely out of order. Unfortunately, she didn't seem to care, or at least she didn't want to hear it."

"I'm well aware of what Hattie is like when she's on a mission," I reply. "I just never thought her mission would be to destroy me."

"For what it's worth, Mark did intervene. After you saw him, he got them to promise to stop," she tells me.

"I didn't know that," I say, not knowing how to feel about it.

"He never got a chance to tell you," she replies. Then she sighs again as if she's hesitant to say what's coming next. "He was a mess. You may not want to hear it, but he was a mess for a long time..."

"You're right," I interrupt her. "I just... I can't."

"I get that..." she answers, then she pauses again. "I understand why you didn't say anything when you found out," she tells me, "but why not later in the pregnancy? Why not when he was born?"

"I was angry with him when I left London," I admit. "Anger was easier to bear than the pain. So, when I found out that I was pregnant..." I look right at her and ask, "Do you think I was happy about it? Do you think I saw it as an opportunity to get Mark back?" I pause, but I'm not really waiting for an answer. "I thought the world was out to get me. It pains me to say it now, but I was completely indifferent to the baby I was carrying. I certainly wasn't in the mindset to be able to tell Mark about it. I didn't want to be having his baby," I tell her. "But when I heard the heartbeat, that just changed everything. I had an innocent baby growing inside me, and it was my job to keep him safe, and that meant not telling Mark. I couldn't tell him because of Hattie."

She closes her eyes and nods. She understands, but I'm not finished. "If Mark knew, Hattie would know, and I wasn't prepared to let her anywhere near him. I'm still not. She will never be part of his life. She's poison!" I say with venom of my own. "That's why I've never told him."

Lilly lets out a long breath and moves closer, then she puts an arm around me and pulls me into her shoulder. "I love Mark — his kids too, they're all my Godchildren," she tells me. "We may not have spent that much time together, but it was enough for me to really like you. Enough for me to know you're a good soul, Ava. You've been through so much and I'm so sorry for that," she says, sighing again. "I wanted to reach out to you so much that day at Will's party. We knew what was happening in that room and when you came out, I could see how much pain you were in," she says sadly. "Then I saw Hattie looking, and I thought that if she knew that we were friends it would make things worse."

I let out a deep breath. "I'm not sure that anything could have made it worse," I tell her.

We sit quietly for a few more minutes and then I pluck up the courage to ask, "When did you say you're going back to London?"

"Tomorrow afternoon," she replies.

"You're going to tell him, aren't you?" I ask, already knowing the answer.

She lets out a deep sigh, and says, "I think you know that I have to."

It's hard to swallow as I sit, leaning against her shoulder. Lilly seems in no rush to leave either and eventually it's Lucas' voice that snaps us both back to attention.

"Ava!" he shouts sounding panicked. "I've just seen your mum, are you OK?" he asks looking hard at Lilly. I don't like that. She doesn't deserve that.

I stand up to meet him and tell him, "I'm fine, Lucas. Don't worry."

Lilly stands too and starts to extend her hand. "Hello, I'm Lilly—"

"I know who you are," Lucas spits back.

"Lucas," I admonish him. "Lilly hasn't done anything wrong. Please don't speak to her like that."

"She's going to though, isn't she?" he asks angrily, and he looks at her again. "Aren't you?"

I've never seen Lucas so angry. I put my hands on his stomach to try to calm him but it's also starting to feel like I might need to hold him back. I turn to Lilly, giving her a look of apology.

"Lucas, you must be Ava's boyfriend?" she asks in a more friendly way than he deserves.

"Yes, and I'm Jacob's dad too. The only one he needs," he fumes.

"Lucas," I say, trying my best to calm him.

Lilly speaks again, "I'm sorry, I understand that this is a difficult situation, I really do. Mark is my husband's best friend, I see him all the time. I can't possibly not tell him."

"You could try," he scathes at her.

"Lucas!" I shout, as I push him back. "Enough! This isn't Lilly's fault, and she does not deserve to be spoken to like this. I cannot ask her to lie to her husband, which is what you're suggesting amounts to. I can't do that."

"Oh, you could, if you really wanted to," he practically spits at me.

"If I...? I can't even believe what I'm hearing, right now. Do you think I haven't always known that somehow, one day, the truth would come out?" I ask him. "I didn't move to another country, we're five hours away from London," I say, exasperated. "Look, whatever comes next we'll face together, like always. But right now, I think you need to go off and cool down somewhere," I tell him, and he looks at me again but doesn't move. "Lucas, please... I'll see you in a bit."

He eventually walks away shaking his head, then he turns back to scowl at Lilly one last time, and I glare at him in return. Once he's gone, I turn to her, expecting her to be upset, but instead she's looking at me as if she's concerned.

"I'm so sorry, Lilly, you didn't deserve that. I've never even seen him like that," I tell her apologetically.

"It's not your fault," she replies calmly.

"I should probably make sure he's OK and let you get

back to your friends. They must be wondering where you are," I tell her.

Lilly walks over to me and gives me a big hug. She lets out a deep breath and tells me, "I'll explain it to him the way you did to me. He knows what his own daughter put you through."

"Thank you," I practically choke out.

She lets go of me and gives me a concerned look again. "You take care of yourself, Ava," she instructs me, and I nod at her and let her go back to the tea rooms.

Instead of going after Lucas like I said I would, I return to the bench and sit down again. I did know that one day this would happen. Mum was right, this isn't the sort of thing that stays secret forever. I'm not sure exactly what is going to happen next, but I know one thing for certain, I need to prepare myself for the fact that Mark will be coming here, and no doubt very soon. I don't know exactly what that will mean, but I know one thing for certain — nothing will ever be the same again.

21

LILLY

Lilly spent the rest of the afternoon in a bit of a daze. She had glossed over the details of her conversation with Ava when she returned to her friends. Her mind had been in a million places at the pub later in the evening, and she could barely follow the conversations happening around her. On the one hand she regretted coming here, she didn't want to be the one to bear this burden. On the other, she was glad it had been her. There weren't many people from Ava's past that knew the truth, or would have treated her fairly. Lilly may have been mad with her initially, but in the end, she understood why she had made the choice that she had.

Lilly could see that her friends were wondering what was going on, so she decided that she needed to snap herself out of it. She made an effort on the journey home and became part of the group once more — it had been a fun trip away and a long time in the planning. She'd actually managed to put it all to the back of her mind for a little while, and then she received a text from Darren.

What time are you going to be back? I've missed you. I

know it's your first night back, but Mark will be here. We've been sparring this afternoon & he seemed out of sorts. Sorry, bad timing, I know. We'll have a large glass of something waiting for you, along with takeaway.xx

Everything came hurtling back. Mark would be there when she got home, that would mean no time to talk to Darren about things first like she had hoped to. That was her plan, to tell Darren so that he could figure out the best way to tell Mark, because he knew him better than anyone. She was counting on the fact that he'd help her through it, but that wasn't going to happen. Lilly knew she couldn't see Mark and not tell him. No — she'd have to tell them both tonight.

She typed her reply, keeping it light, **That's fine, you know I love him more than you ;-) Should be back by 6ish. Make mine a G&T. LARGE.xx**

Darren replied, **You don't love anyone more than me and you know it. Large G&T? Everything OK?xx**

Everything's fine. Love you.xx

You too.xx

She put her phone away and carried on listening to the chatter around her, completely unable to pretend like she was trying to be involved.

Lilly walked through her front door and put her suitcase down. She could hear the two friends laughing in the kitchen. It was a familiar sound, well, perhaps not the laughing part. Mark had relied on them a lot after the break-up with Ava, especially after he discovered that she'd left London. It's not that he blamed her, it was just the first time he admitted to himself that there was no hope of getting her back. Ava may not have wanted to hear about Mark's pain, but it had been hard for him — really hard. He truly loved her, and it took him a long time to come to terms with it being over — but Lilly still didn't think that he was over her. He might be able to laugh again but it had taken time, and Lilly was about to reopen those wounds and drop a bombshell on him too.

She walked into the kitchen, Mark was closest to her and greeted her first with a hug, and then Darren went over and kissed her. She grabbed hold of her husband tightly, and he looked at her with concern and asked, "Is everything OK?"

Lilly let out a deep breath, she had butterflies, and she had no idea how to do what needed to be done.

"No, not really," she replied.

Mark handed her a drink. "One scandalously large G&T, as requested," he smiled.

She took the drink and walked over to the table. They'd ordered Chinese — all of her favourite items. She opened a bag then set it aside because there was no way that she could eat it at that moment. Instead, she took a big gulp of her gin.

"What's going on, sweetheart?" Darren asked, looking concerned.

"Was Cheryl's endless chat a bit too much to bear for eight days?" Mark asked laughing, trying to make light of it.

Lilly downed the rest of her drink then raised her glass to Darren. "Can I have another please?" she asked him.

"Yes..." he replied cautiously.

Both men glanced at each other, they knew Lilly well enough to know that something was really wrong. She sat at the table and Darren returned with another drink moments later.

"Thank you, she said. Then she asked, "What are you drinking, Mark?"

"Ermm... nothing yet..." he replied awkwardly, then he

gestured to the door. "I can head home if you two need some space?"

"No. You need to be here actually, and I think you're going to need a drink. Darren, get the Scotch."

"What's going on Lilly?" Mark asked, looking worried.

Darren returned with a bottle of Scotch and two glasses, then sat on the other side of Lilly and put her hand in his. "Talk to us," he gently urged.

Lilly took a deep breath, and started, "I have absolutely no idea how to do this. I was going to speak to Darren first but you're here now so I can't not say it," she looked at Darren and then to Mark.

"Then say it, Lilly," Mark said, trying to encourage her.

She cleared her throat and took another gulp of gin. "Well, as you know we did a mini Devonshire coastal tour. What I'm not sure that you know is that our last stop was Clovelly," she said, looking directly at Mark. "I saw Ava."

Mark swallowed hard and looked down before asking, "Is... is she OK?"

Lilly put her hand on his to reassure him. "Yes, she is, it's not like that," she told him.

"Then what? What's going on?" he asked more urgently.

Lilly let out another deep breath and said, "She... she has a baby."

"Oh?... Oh..." Mark said, looking pained. "Well, Jonathan said that she had a boyfriend, so I guess..."

"No, Mark," Lilly jumped in. "The baby is one. He's one. Think about it. The boyfriend isn't the father... you are."

"What?" Darren and Mark both said together in shock.

"He's just turned one. She was pregnant when she left London. He's yours," Lilly said as calmly as she could, then she took another large gulp of her drink.

Mark took a large drink of his Scotch and started pacing

the room, running his hands through his hair. He quickly turned and went back to the table. "She just told you all this?" he asked incredulously.

"She didn't have a choice, I saw him," Lilly replied.

"You saw him?"

"Yes, in tea rooms that her mum owns," she answered. "Mark, even if the dates didn't add up, he looks just like you. There'd be no denying it to anyone. So, I made her talk to me about it."

"What a little Bitch!" Darren shouted furiously.

"Darren, don't," Lilly implored.

"Don't? Don't? She's kept the fact that Mark has a child from him for a year! What do you expect me to call her?" Darren shouted.

"She had her reasons—" Lilly tried to argue back, but Mark interrupted.

"What reasons? Why? Was this to punish me? Why?" He was angry but there was pain there too.

"Look, I know this has come as a massive shock, but could you please let me explain things?" Lilly pleaded.

"You're defending her?" Darren asked in disbelief.

Lilly raised her hand to quiet her husband and looked at Mark. "Mark, will you please hear me out?" she asked.

He sat down again and took another gulp of his drink and nodded.

"OK. I'm not sure if you remember but she got food poisoning on a night out?" Lilly asked.

Mark nodded. "Of course, I remember I was worried sick about her."

"Well..." Lilly continued. "That's how it happened. She didn't know. Apparently missing periods is normal for her when she's ill or under a lot of stress. Did you know that?" she asked him.

"Yes, she told me that once," he replied, still looking into his glass.

"She didn't take a test until the morning that she was leaving. Obviously, it was positive, and she wasn't exactly happy about it. She didn't want to be pregnant..." Lilly said, then she paused for a moment but Mark said nothing so she carried on, "She didn't say anything because she couldn't face it at first. She couldn't face you. Then one day things changed, and she realised that she loved the baby... and she wanted to keep it safe."

"Am I not safe?" Mark asked bitterly.

"You might be... but can you say the same about Hattie?" Lilly asked.

"Hattie?" Mark laughed bitterly. "She didn't tell me that she was carrying my baby because of Hattie," he nodded, taking another sip. It wasn't a question, he said it as if he was stating a fact. His glass was empty, so he tilted it towards Darren, and he topped it up.

"Honestly, Mark, I believe her when she says this wasn't about hurting or punishing you. She just didn't want Hattie to know anything about him, and in order to keep her away, she kept you away too," she told him. Then she put her hand on his and continued, "I'm not saying it was right. I'm just saying it wasn't malicious."

Lilly felt like she had said all that she could and that she'd kept her word to Ava. Mark sat silently for a while, occasionally taking a sip from his glass. Darren had gone to him and had put a supportive hand on his shoulder. It always warmed her to see how close they were.

Eventually, Mark spoke. "On the days when I allowed myself to believe that we could actually have a future together, I'd often think about having a baby with Ava... I bet she's a brilliant mother," he said, smiling warmly. "What's his name?" he asked, turning to Lilly.

"Jacob... he's called Jacob," Lilly smiled.

"Jacob. That's nice," Mark smiled. "Did she by any chance say anything about what happens next?"

"No," Lilly replied. "She knew that I wouldn't be able to keep this a secret. She didn't even ask me to. She doesn't expect me to lie to my husband for her."

"No, but then it's not like her to expect people to choose her is it?" Mark replied. He smiled but it didn't reach his eyes.

"No... I guess not," Lilly agreed. "So, I can only assume that she's doing what she needs to do to prepare herself for seeing you again. Mark..." Lilly added hesitantly. "The Hattie thing is a big issue for her. I know it's a big ask, but you can't tell Hattie or the boys. Not yet, at least."

"Of course, no... I... I understand. They won't be happy about this," he said, laughing bitterly. "Serves them right, I guess."

Lilly shifted in her seat a little and took another gulp of her drink.

"There's more?" Mark asked with concern.

"Um... well... there's something else that's been bothering me... it's probably nothing. But..." she paused.

"Lilly, please," Mark quietly urged.

"Her boyfriend — Lucas. I saw him too, she told him. "Aside from the fact that he was somewhat rude and aggressive towards me..." Darren raised his eyebrows. "It's OK," Lilly quickly added. "Ava defended me. She told him to back off and he did. It's just that... I got a really bad feeling about him. I just... I just can't shake it," she said, and neither Mark nor Darren missed the flicker of fear in her eyes.

Mark and Darren shared a look, they didn't just joke about Lilly being good at reading people, it was a genuine gift. If she had a bad feeling about a person then there always turned out to be a reason for it, and if she thought that there was something off about Lucas, then eventually they'd find out that there was.

22

MARK

Mark woke up on Saturday morning with a heavy head, and as soon as clarity descended upon him, his heart felt heavy too. He had a child, another child, one he'd never met, and the woman that he was still in love with was the mother. Mark had gone through every emotion possible the previous night. After Lilly's bombshell they all drank a lot, and Mark got angry, first, at Ava for keeping it from him, and then at his other children for causing it. Then he felt loss, a deep loss for the time that he'd missed out on. That was something that he'd never get back.

Eventually, he had worked, or drank his way to feeling determined. He would go to Clovelly, he would make things right, and he would see his child. Then, all slightly worse for wear they reheated the takeaway and ate every last bit. Lilly bowed out shortly after, claiming she wanted to leave "the men" to it, but they both knew that she never liked to admit defeat. Lilly was small and mighty, but she couldn't always handle her drink.

Darren and Mark had carried on a little longer, but both

had stopped drinking. They had talked realistically, Darren getting to the point as always by asking him what his game plan would be, and advising that he took his time. He even suggested that Mark sought legal advice before going to Clovelly. The truth is that Mark didn't know what to do for the best and he had no idea what to say to Ava. He knew her well enough to know that she wouldn't keep his baby from him out of spite — but this was big. So big, and yet he couldn't blame her. After everything she was put through, everything she survived, everything she escaped... why the hell would she want to invite that back in at the most emotional, and scary time of her life? As hurt as he was, he realised that he couldn't be angry with her.

Darren had also asked him about the boyfriend. Mark couldn't quite mention his name, so he remained 'the boyfriend,' but they had taken Lilly's concerns seriously. Mark decided that he would see what the situation was for himself before making any plans, but Darren had advised caution, telling Mark he needed to "watch his back" while he was there. Mark had laughed that off, reminding his friend that he spent too much time with criminals — but he'd be cautious, nonetheless.

Mark wasn't exactly the same man that Ava left. It had broken him, and for a long time he was a shadow of himself. He would look in the mirror and not even recognise the face looking back at him. Then one day, the day after Ava had told him that he was "pathetic," he decided things needed to change. Prior to that afternoon, he had held onto the fact that the last words that Ava had spoken to him had been words of love — she would "always cherish" him, she had said. Even at his lowest moments he was still able to find comfort from those words, but that had been taken away from him because of his children, but also because of him

— he let her down. He let her walk away thinking that she was all alone.

Mark had called Hattie, Ted and Will to come over the very next day. He sat them down and told them they were done. Nothing more was to be done to Ava. Having told them how he'd come to find out about the latest lies, they accused him of choosing her over them, and they once again dangled the threat of losing them. However, he wasn't the same man they'd been dealing with previously, so he'd hit them where it hurt, telling them that if any one of them did one more thing to Ava — anything — no matter how small. Then all three of them would be cut out of his will. He still laughed at the look of utter shock and fear on their faces. It was two weeks before they spoke to him again, but he hadn't cared. He used those two weeks to take up boxing with Darren.

He was swimming again, eating right, and trying to get his head in order. He was back in shape and feeling good — physically anyway. He'd also hoped that he'd given Ava the break she needed. Whether she knew it or not, he knew that nothing more would be done to her. He had planned to tell her what he'd done for her when he had got himself right again. He had just needed a little more time.

When his children did eventually speak to him again they agreed to leave Ava alone. Hattie had called him and suggested that she and the boys meet him at the weekend, but he had felt the need to make them squirm more and had suggested the following weekend instead. It was agreed. They'd have a picnic at Alexander Palace, and Mary and Tom would join them too, along with Miri. Miri was inexplicably joined at the hip with Ted at that point, because as far as Mark could remember, he had never mentioned being interested in her before.

So, four weeks had passed since Ava arrived on Mark's doorstep, and he was finally feeling ready to go and see her to apologise. He was ready to make her see that he was still the man she had loved, and not the man she regretted. Then that all changed on the day of the picnic when they crossed paths with Carolyn walking Cooper. They all knew her connection to Ava, her fondness for her too, which Mark was personally reminded of when she scowled at both he and Hattie on seeing them.

It was Mary that spoke first, being an old neighbour. “Carolyn, look at you,” she said with false affection — Mark could always tell. “You haven't changed a bit.”

“I dare say neither have you, Mary,” Carolyn had quipped back. “You're all here, I see,” she added with a rather unimpressed expression.

Mary was never good at dealing with people that made it clear that they didn't like her, and it always put her in attack mode. “I'm surprised to see you out, I thought Ava Swan helped you with this?” she asked, and then she added, “Has she let you down?” just to make things worse.

“That young woman has never let me down a day in her life,” Carolyn replied, fuming. “I certainly miss her help, but I can't exactly expect her to travel to me now, can I?”

“What do you mean?” Miri asked. “She's just up the road.”

“I'd hardly call Clovelly ‘just up the road’ young lady,” Carolyn had replied bitterly.

“Oh, well... I'm sure she'll be back to help after her visit with her parents,” Miri had replied, clearly unnerved by the older woman she was barely acquainted with.

“Back from her...? Oh...” Carolyn paused, and a smug smile spread across her face as she said, “You don't know, do you?”

"What don't we know?" Mark asked, concern was starting to creep in.

"Well, she never said it was to be a secret, so I suppose it's OK to tell you now. Although I must add that I can fully understand why she wouldn't tell you," she said, pausing again to give Hattie and Mark a pointed look. Then she continued, "She isn't 'visiting', she has moved there. For now, anyway, she's not sure where she'll go next."

At that moment, Mark's heart jumped into his throat and the blood pulsing in his ears was almost deafening him, but he forced himself to listen to the rest. "She left two weeks ago," Carolyn told them, as if it was nothing.

"But... she's coming back?" Hattie asked shakily.

Carolyn pinned her with a cold, disapproving look. "For her sake I hope not. I doubt it too considering she's rented out her flat. The tenants are already in under a twelve-month contract," she told them triumphantly. "I told her to go and find herself some happiness and to not look back on the nastiness that has taken place here," she said fiercely, and then she looked at the shocked faces around her.

Mark was glad to be wearing sunglasses so that she couldn't see the full effect that her news had on him.

"Well, I think it's best I be on my way," she said, and then she and Cooper slowly walked away.

After Carolyn had gone from sight, Mark's family seemed to find their voices... there were lots of questions, "Did anyone know? Do you think she'll come back? Why was she so mad with you, Hattie?" — that had been Miri — the only one in the group still unaware of the truth. Mark couldn't read his daughter that day, not that he ever truly believed he could, but he thought he saw a glimmer of guilt, shame and sadness before her wall went up again. Then they had all turned to look at Mark who was just standing there, his sunglasses completely failing to mask the tears that were falling.

It had been Will that tried to reach out to him, but Mark had put up a hand to stop him, telling him, “No. We’re done here.” Then he walked away from them and called Darren on the way home, and he and Lilly had driven straight over to Mark’s house.

Mark had been in despair that afternoon. He'd been working on himself, taking his time to become the man Ava needed again, only to discover that it had all been in vain. She'd simply had enough and left. On discovering that she was no longer on social media and her phone number was dead. Darren had encouraged him to try to respect her choice, to let her go, and to give her the space she so clearly needed. It took time, but eventually he had accepted it, but that's all it was.

He accepted it, but he was never at peace with it. Not a day had gone by where Mark had been at peace with losing Ava. Now, he was going to find her, only it wasn't because of her, it was because she had had his baby, and he was going to claim his right to see him. He felt guilty admitting it, but he truly hoped this would be his chance to claim her back too.

After returning home to shower and pack an overnight bag, he got in the car and started his journey. He'd had some food, tried to shake off the whiskey and make himself look presentable. He'd picked up his razor but suddenly realised that he was sporting the short stubble that Ava had thought was sexy, so he decided against shaving. Having left Darren and Lilly at the crack of dawn and getting ready as quickly as he could at home, it was around half past nine when he left London. He checked the route on the Sat Nav and all being well, he could be in Clovelly by half past two.

It was a long journey, but it had been smooth. He'd stopped for coffee and a bit of lunch, but nerves had prevented him from eating much. He arrived in Clovelly with no information other than the fact that Ava's mother owned the tea rooms there. So that's where he intended to start. He found a place to park and checked how to find the tea rooms on his phone, then realised that he'd completely forgotten to book somewhere to stay. It was January, not exactly peak tourist season, so he decided that he had time to sort it later — the priority was making contact with Ava.

He sat in the car park for a while, plucking up the courage to open the door, and while he sat, mentally preparing himself, he also took in his surroundings. It really was a beautiful place; he could understand why Ava would feel safe here. It wouldn't be his bolt hole of choice — he'd secretly bought his about two months ago — but Clovelly was beautiful. Such a great place for a child to grow up, he thought. It was close to three O'clock when Mark finally walked up to the front door of the beautifully lit tea rooms, and the sign told him that they were open until six O'clock. It suddenly dawned on him that he had no idea what he was walking into, she could be there, or it could be her mother, he could even be about to face Jonathan again. As he stepped inside, he saw that the place was currently being run by two young women, along with one older lady.

It was the older woman, Linda —according to her name badge — that caught his gaze and smiled at him. She walked over to greet him and offered him a table near the front. He took note of where the kitchen was and opted for a seat towards the back, which seemed to offer the perfect view of the front door, counter, and kitchen door, whilst managing to offer Mark some privacy. He'd bought several newspapers on the way, not knowing how long he might be waiting there, and ordered the 'Tea for One' option from the menu. Linda made a suggestive comment about his solo status in a lightly flirty, yet jovial manner, and although he had no interest in her, he smiled and played the part. After all, if neither Ava nor her parents showed up, then he may need to try to get some information later. So, it was best to keep her on side.

Mark opened his paper straight away, as much as to use it to hide behind, as to give him something to do. His platter arrived after ten minutes and it looked amazing. He'd learned from Linda that they did all the baking themselves, and he looked at the selection of cakes and felt closer to Ava already, wondering which she had touched. After a few minutes one of the younger girls named Melanie, came over to ask how he was getting on.

"Everything is delicious, thank you, Melanie," he replied, and when the young girl smiled at his charm, Mark saw his opportunity. "I understand that the mother and daughter that run the establishment do all the baking themselves. It's absolutely excellent, will either of them be here today?" he asked politely.

"Oh, I'm not sure," Melanie replied. "Ava sometimes comes in on a Saturday, but she's not been in yet — it all depends on what needs baking and when. Let me check with Linda and I'll let you know."

Melanie walked away not knowing how much hearing Ava's name had affected Mark. He saw her talk to her older colleague then she dutifully walked back to him. She tucked her hair behind her ear, and he greeted her with a warm smile.

"Actually, as it happens, Ava... sorry she's the daughter, Eleanor Swan owns the tea rooms," she told him, as she tucked her hair behind her ear again. Mark held his breath waiting to hear what she'd say next. "Anyway, she didn't finish decorating all of the cakes that she was due to do yesterday, and is most likely popping in soon to finish them. Shall I send her over when she arrives?" she asked, beaming at him.

Mark beamed right back making the young woman blush. "No, no..." he replied, still smiling. "It sounds like she'll have a lot to do so I won't bother her. I'll just leave a feedback card or something," he told her, looking back down at his paper.

"OK, thank you," Melanie said, tucking her hair behind her ear once more. "Please let me know if there's anything more I can help you with."

Mark nodded kindly and she walked away blushing. This was good. It would be Ava that he would see first, and judging by the cross-generational effect that he was having on the staff here — he'd made the right choice not to shave.

From that moment on, every time the bell jingled, letting him know that somebody had arrived, Mark's paper shot up to cover his face. It jingled three times before it was to signal Ava's arrival and he could've sworn the bell sounded different when she walked in. He had been making a point of keeping the newspaper up high enough to cover his face until he could hear the conversation, as opposed to peeking over the top of the paper. He had previously decided that was too risky and would look a little strange. He would then slowly, nonchalantly, move it down when he heard only customers being greeted — but this time it was different.

"Hi Ava," one of the younger girls said, and Mark could barely breathe, knowing that he was about to hear her voice for the first time in well over a year.

"Hi Bea," she replied cheerily, and those two simple words made Mark's heart skip a beat. He listened as she greeted the others with the same level of friendliness and enthusiasm.

"I'm only going to be about an hour, Linda, so I shouldn't cause too much chaos in there," Ava told them.

He could hear her walking toward the kitchen door, but then she paused as Linda replied, "Is that an hour to bake and then an hour to clean?" Linda and both girls laughed, and Mark smiled at the memory of Ava completely destroying his kitchen that first night, and her own many a night after.

"Ah, good point," Ava replied, clearly unfazed by the banter. "Well, Dad can only have Jacob for an hour and a half so I'm planning on it being for both... wish me luck?"

"Good luck!" all three replied at once and then burst into a fit of giggles.

Mark couldn't wait any longer and allowed himself to peek a tiny bit. There she was, standing in the doorway to the kitchen, facing the others and laughing with them. Mark could see the side of her face and his breath hitched. She was still the most beautiful woman he'd ever seen. As she scooped her hair up into the same messy bun that he'd seen her do so many times before, he saw the neck that he'd once been allowed to kiss freely, and as she turned to go into the kitchen, he caught a glimpse of her eyes, and he realised that he was probably the only person in that room that could see it. The only person that could see that although she was smiling at them, the smile hadn't reached those beautiful eyes.

He didn't expect anyone else to notice, because when Ava gave you her megawatt smile you instantly smiled with her; it was infectious. Mark also knew that Ava had no idea of the effect that she had on people, because she'd lived in Hattie's shadow all of her life. Not because she was less pretty or popular, or even less confident. She just always seemed happy to let Hattie shine. Naturally, because she seemed to know that's what Hattie needed. Once the door to the kitchen was closed Mark pulled the paper back down and watched the after effect. They were still smiling. She'd lifted them. That's what Ava did, she lifted people.

Mark knew what he needed to know. She'd be there for an hour but there would only be another half an hour window in which she wouldn't have Jacob. Hearing her say his name had moved Mark and brought on a new wave of excited nervousness. He was eager to see his son, but he knew he had to see Ava alone first. She would want to talk it through before letting them meet. Somehow, he was going to have to get into that kitchen — but it would have to be when all three of the women were looking in an entirely different direction.

Twenty minutes passed with no opportunity, and then Linda came over asking if he needed any more tea; he did. That was one person who would be behind the counter facing the front door, but there were two more. His prayers were answered when moments later an elderly man walking with a frame appeared at the door, clearly a local as all three jumped into action to help him. Mark seized his opportunity and swiftly went towards the kitchen door, opening it as quietly as he could.

It was a quiet door, he was grateful for that, no little bell to signal his arrival. There was a small area for staff to put their belongings on the right by the door, and then the kitchen curved round to the left. He held the door so that it didn't bang closed, then taking a deep breath, slowly walked around the corner.

She didn't hear him come in. She had her back to him, and she was concentrating hard, decorating some small sponges. He always knew she could bake, but watching her working with those beautiful, delicate creations was quite something. He hadn't known she was that good and he watched in quiet awe. He knew he shouldn't, but he decided to steal those few moments, while she was still unaware of him, to study her some more. You wouldn't think she'd had a baby, her body looked just the same, and it was having the same effect on him that it always did. He had wanted her from the moment he saw her on his doorstep, and the time apart had done nothing to lessen his desire for her.

Mark started to feel that watching her that way, when she wasn't aware, was somehow a violation, and he changed his focus to something else. He forced his eyes to move from Ava and onto the workspace around her. It was a mess. Food colouring and icing sugar all over the place. He knew he couldn't stay silent any longer, so he chuckled and said, “Jesus, you really are messy.”

Ava jumped at the sound of his voice, almost sending a tray of just-decorated cakes flying, but she managed to grab them just in time. Then she seemed to freeze to the spot, but Mark could see from her shoulders that she was breathing quickly. He waited for what seemed like a lifetime for her to turn and face him, but eventually, she did. She looked tired, sad, and perhaps a little guilty. She looked at him with those beautiful brown eyes. They were the opposite of his blue ones and he always saw them as the epitome of her character. There was always something new to discover, a part of her soul yet to be revealed.

Those dark eyes run deep, keeping it all hidden, and you never quite get to the bottom, and unless he was mistaken, those eyes were currently taking in his new physique. He'd been boxing with Darren for well over a year now and he knew he'd gained more muscle on his shoulders and arms.

He also knew that the women at the gym appreciated it. Mark had never been vain, but he was aware enough to know when he was being checked out.

He saw her suddenly right herself and as her eyes met his, he said, “Hello Ava.”

It seemed to take her a few minutes to find her voice, but she eventually replied, “Hello Mark.”

23

It's been a hard couple of days and seeing Lilly has changed everything. As I sat on the bench after Lilly left, I couldn't really get my head around it. The secret that I've kept for so long was about to come out, and amongst all the things that I was feeling, I hadn't expected to feel relief... and it shook me. After telling Lucas and my parents about Mark and everything that happened months ago, I felt relieved about the fact that they hadn't disowned me — but this was different.

Mainly, I'm completely petrified. I hope Lilly will pass on what I said — she seemed to get it, and yet now, the idea of saying those things to Mark, to the man that I've denied being involved in the first year of his son's life. They just don't feel adequate anymore. My reasons were real enough, but now I'm not sure if there was ever truly a justification for what I've done. I'd never felt guilty about it until that afternoon with Lilly, but now I can't shift it and I keep getting hit with the overwhelming feeling that I should've told him. I know why I didn't, why I couldn't, but I'm now questioning if I was right, and that's something I never doubted before.

To top it off I'm angry with Lucas, but because my emotions are all over the place, I can't help feeling guilty about what this must be doing to him too. Especially for him to have acted that way towards Lilly.

I did eventually get off that bench, and after asking my parents to have Jacob for a bit longer, I headed home. I was ready to let Lucas know exactly what I thought about the way he had spoken to her. I really wouldn't have believed it if I'd not seen it. Lucas is the peacekeeper; the light-hearted one. I wasn't sure what to make of angry Lucas, but I was going to start by giving him a piece of my mind. Then I saw him sitting at my kitchen table, head in hands, crying.

He cried in my arms for an hour sharing all of his fears. He knew that Mark would come back into my life now and he believes I still have feelings for him. He thinks he's going to lose us both. I reassured him over and over about the fact that if Mark wanted to be a part of Jacob's life then I couldn't stop him, but that's all it would be. He would become part of Jacob's life, but Lucas would remain there also — with me. Eventually, he calmed down and tried to take me to bed, but I said no to that. I felt bad about how he was feeling but couldn't shake my annoyance about how he'd treated Lilly. I was certainly not ready to have sex with him.

I thought he'd understood, and he stayed over, like most nights, but when I rejected his advances on Friday morning, he got angry again. I tried to explain that Mark's impending arrival was playing on my mind and I'd hardly slept, but he didn't seem to hear it. He stormed out of the room, leaving me somewhat bewildered. By the time I came down for breakfast with Jacob he was getting ready to head out. Apparently, he was needed to cover a shift on the boats. By that point I didn't argue for him to stay, but it well and truly messed up my plans, because he was supposed to have

Jacob while I baked at the tea rooms. Mum is away for a long weekend with some friends and Dad was busy most of the day. He helped as much as he could, but I didn't finish the cakes, and that's why I'm heading back there at this time on a Saturday afternoon.

I've not seen Lucas since yesterday morning, and as he's always busy at the weekends, I can only rely on my dad again. I have precisely an hour and a half to get it all finished, including the clean-up. I always make a massive mess decorating French Fancies. Icing them is quick enough but they always drip. It's drawing on the tea room's swan logo that takes time. It's not too intricate, but it's not easy to start again if you mess it up, so it takes time and concentration, and I'm severely lacking in both today.

Clovelly is cold and windy in January, and it is bitter outside, but today I'm enjoying the blast of the fresh sea air. My stomach has been churning ever since I spoke with Lilly. I've got no idea when she'll tell Mark, or how long it'll be before he comes here, and the uncertainty is killing me — but I should have at least a few days to try and get my head in order.

I walk through the door and I'm pleasantly surprised by how busy it is. The Swan has got a reputation as a tourist destination, but there aren't too many of those in January. Linda, the Assistant Manager, is in today, along with Bea and Mel. Linda is my mum's best friend and helped her with the place more or less from day one. I felt like she had her nose put out a little bit when I came here, but after she realised that I was happy to just hide away and bake, she seemed to warm to me.

"Hi Ava," Bea says as I walk in.

I greet the others and head to the kitchen, but I know I'll not be able to escape the near constant teasing about how much of a mess I'll be making in it. It comes from Linda and I laugh along with them. I don't mind really, but I don't find much joy in them today; there's just too much on my mind.

I've done a lot of prep already but there's still some icing to be mixed, so I get to that quickly as I'll need to let them have as much time to dry as possible before I add the logo. Other than tipping the icing sugar over I don't have any major disasters, and I'm pleased when I finish that part in about twenty minutes. Now it's time to decorate the ones I iced yesterday. It's a delicate job so I always have to focus on this bit.

The monotony of the task is good for me right now and I'm happy to lose myself in it, but then someone suddenly speaks behind me, and I jump so hard that I almost send the entire tray flying. I grab it and straighten it up before it tips onto the floor, and then I lean into the counter with my back facing the spot where the voice came from. I'm completely frozen, except for my heart, that is pounding out of my chest.

My mind is racing. "Jesus, you are messy," he just said. Mark just said. Exactly as he said it in his kitchen when it all began. Why is he here already? Lilly would've got home yesterday evening. Had she really told him so quickly? Oh, God, he's here already. I'm not ready. Nowhere near ready. I didn't want it to be like this, it was supposed to be controlled, planned, and I wasn't supposed to be covered in pink icing. I wonder how mad he is. Only he didn't sound mad. That's not what I'd say to someone if I was mad. If I'd just found out my baby had been hidden from me. My mind hurtles on like this for what feels like an age. I need to turn and face him — it's the only thing to be done. So, I stand upright, and slowly turn towards the man that I've spent all this time hiding from.

There he is. Only, I'm not sure which Mark I'm looking at. He's not the Mark I last saw — he looks strong. I only saw weakness in him that day. Still, he's not the Mark I first met either, he's more like that, but he seems different. He looks good, very good, and I feel my body completely betraying me by reacting to him in the same way as I did on his doorstep. I allow my eyes to take him in, he's bigger than before, especially his shoulders and arms. He's more defined, more muscular. His shirt seems to perfectly mould to him, and my eyes follow the path that his abs lead all the way back to his face. He is still gorgeous, and I am clearly still attracted to him. This is not a good start, but it's easier to focus on the warmth spreading to my core, than it is to think about what is currently happening to my heart.

I mentally check myself because this isn't why he's here. He's here because of Jacob, so I take a deep breath and try my best to get control of myself. He seems to notice, and he breaks the silence between us with two simple words.

"Hello Ava," he says.

I just look at him for a few more moments, still quite unable to comprehend the fact that he is here already, but eventually, I reply, "Hello Mark."

With the first words spoken I feel unable to stop there. "I wasn't... I wasn't exp—"

"You weren't expecting me?" he interrupts, eyebrows raised.

"No. I mean yes... I was expecting you... just not today," I reply. "Lilly didn't say when she'd be seeing you. So... so, I guess I thought that I had a few days."

"To prepare?" he asks.

"If that's even possible... but yes," I tell him honestly.

"I was at Lilly and Darren's when she got home last night. I think she wanted to speak to Darren first so that they could... break the news," he says, and as he pauses, he looks me in the eyes, and I feel the guilt kick back in. "But I was there so she couldn't keep it in."

"Yes. Right... I..." I know the words that I need to say but it's hard to form them. "I'm sorry," I eventually force out.

Mark lets out a deep sigh. "For which part exactly?" he asks.

"What did Lilly tell you?" I ask him.

"How it happened, when you found out, and why you didn't tell me," he replies. He's calm, why is he being so calm?

"Why are you so calm?" I squeak out. "Why aren't you shouting at me? Or calling me names? Surely I deserve it?"

"Oh, Ava..." he says, and he runs his hands through his hair. His curls are short again. "I was mad at you. When I found out, I was mad at you. I just couldn't believe that you'd do that to me. Then the more I thought about it, the more I remembered just how hurt you were that day when you came to me for help. When I thought about all you'd endured at the hands of my children," he looks down and shakes his head. "I realised that I couldn't blame you."

"I need to say something, before this goes further," I tell him, and he nods for me to continue. "My reasons for not telling you were about self-preservation, OK? I wasn't trying to punish you." I pause and give him my most sincere look, and he nods again. "I'd taken all I could take and then all of a sudden there was a baby, and it was my job to protect it. I couldn't let the world I'd just fled back in. I just couldn't, and I never felt guilty about it, Mark. Never," I admit. "I was only thinking about keeping him away from the bad." I pause for a moment to hold back the tears, then continue, "I only realised when I saw how upset Lilly was, that I'd completely lost sight of the good." I look him in the eyes and say, "I never let myself think about what this meant for you."

"Ava, listen..." he tries to say.

"No, Mark, sorry, I know I'm rambling, but I need to finish," I tell him.

"OK," he replies, and I continue.

"I never once thought about what this meant for you. I ran away from London and then I hid from the truth. The truth, that I have kept you from knowing your son." I embrace the guilt that I deserve to feel. "You've missed out on a year of his life and I can never make that up to you," I tell him guiltily. "And now, the reasons that I had for doing it... they just seem like utter bullshit now that I'm standing here in front of you, and I'm sorry," I tell him sincerely, and I turn to the counter to wipe away the tears that have spilled over.

"Ava, I... yes, it's true. That's time that I can't get back, and it hurts, it really does," he says sadly. "But I'm here today... I'm hoping that we can talk about me being in his life now. I want to look to the future."

"How are you not angry with me?" I ask, as dumbfounded as I am in awe.

"I don't know. I probably should be... I'm just not," he says, giving a slight smile.

"We should go to mine," I tell him. "Dad is looking after Jacob for a while longer and..." I pause, feeling strange about mentioning Lucas to Mark.

"And Lucas...?" Mark says it for me.

"Uh, yes. I'm not actually sure when he'll be back, but he's probably been working all day, and might well be back around dinner time," I tell him, trying not to give away the fact that I actually have no clue what Lucas is currently up to.

"OK. So, it'll be just us for a bit... trying to figure things out," he confirms.

"That'll be enough time, won't it?" I ask with a smile, trying to break the tension. It works, and he laughs. A small laugh, but still a laugh.

"Can you give me a few minutes to clean up this mess though?" I ask, pointing to the counter covered in icing. "I can't leave it like this."

"I'll help," he says, rolling up his sleeves as he walks over, and my eyes are drawn to his newly muscular arms again. "I'm not sure I dare go out there on my own, anyway. I sneaked in here when nobody was looking and will probably be in trouble..."

"Oh God!" I sigh dramatically.

"What?" he asks, amused.

"I'm going to be walking out there and leaving with you, and I'm pretty certain I saw Jessica Miller out there. She's the worst gossip here."

"What are you going to say?" he asks, even more amused now.

"As little as possible."

It didn't take long to clean up. I looked at Mark a few times just to make sure this was actually happening. I hadn't expected it to happen yet, but I hadn't expected it to happen so calmly either. I had been bracing myself for a fight. I went to great lengths to avoid touching him during the clean-up, but he reaches for the door as I reach for my coat, and as our arms touch, just for the slightest moment, it feels like a jolt of electricity is flowing through me.

"Ready to face the music?" he asks, smiling ruefully.

I nod, taking a deep breath, not just to ready myself for walking out the door, but also to recover from his touch.

As I walk out, I nearly plough straight into Linda.

"Oh, have you done alre—" she starts to say, but then she takes in Mark standing behind me and changes her direction of thought. "Oh, I say, we were wondering where you went to," she beams at him. "We don't tend to let customers into the kitchen, mind you."

"Linda, I'm afraid something has come up and I need to go," I say as calmly as I can.

"I've got some more Fancies done but obviously not as much as I needed to, so I'll arrange to come in again."

"Oh..." she says, looking confused. "Is everything all right, Ava? Do you know this gentleman?" she asks, gesturing towards Mark.

"Yes, I do," I reply, trying to remain nonchalant. "This is Mark. He's a friend of the family from London and we've got some stuff we need to talk about."

"I'll just settle my bill," Mark says, moving around me to get to his coat.

"There's no need," I say. "Linda, could you please just charge it to me?"

"Of course," she replies — but then looking concerned, she adds, "Do you need me to speak to your dad?"

"About putting some cakes on my tab?" I ask, smiling at her. I know her meaning, she wants to make sure I'm OK. "No, Linda, it's fine. Everything is fine. Oh, and don't worry, I tidied up," I smile at her, trying to reassure her. The last thing I need is her raising the alarm.

I look towards Mark, his coat is on and he is in the process of leaving a very generous tip on the table, then he nods that he's ready to leave. I try to cover the short distance from where we are standing, to the front door as quickly as I can, but it seems like everyone wants to get in my way. People are getting up to leave and putting their coats on too slowly. I almost knock Mel flying as she turns to walk to the counter, having just taken an order, and right by the door, as I thought, is Jessica Miller.

I almost think I've escaped her, but just as I reach for the door handle, she jumps up and asks, “Leaving so soon, Ava?”

I let out a discreet expletive under my breath and turn to greet her with my best ‘be nice to all customers’ smile that my mum has made me practice. “Yes, Jessica, sorry, can't stop to chat,” I reply, still trying to escape.

She's next to us in a heartbeat and she's also giving me her best false smile as she says, “The thing is Ava...” She does this thing where she'll lean into you like you're having a discrete conversation, only she never speaks quietly enough for it to actually be discreet.

“The thing is,” she continues, “that I can't help noticing that your very handsome gentleman friend here...” she pauses and smiles at Mark in a way that I think is supposed to be seductive, and I have to fight back the instinctive reaction to claw at her. Then she continues, “It's just that he really does have a look of your Jacob about him. Don't you think?” She looks directly at me, all pretences and niceties now gone as she fixes me with a more challenging gaze.

I want to slap her in her smug face but instead I shrug my shoulders and smile my sweetest smile and say, “Hmmm...” as we walk out.

After Mark and I have walked a little further up the road I turn to him and say, “And so it begins. Welcome to Clovelly, Mark.”

24

It's only a ten-minute walk to my house and we walk it in silence. I open the front door and switch on the light to reveal my front room. Most people use this space as a dining room, but I use it as an office and to store toys — and today it's actually not too untidy. I lead him through to the kitchen, it's a pretty good size with a window at the side and a door leading to the utility and back door — that's the way we usually come in. The living room is behind the kitchen at the back, but I don't bother showing him around. I put my coat on a chair and put the kettle on to boil. "Would you like a coffee, or did you fill up on tea?" I ask him.

"Actually, a coffee would be good, thanks," he replies, not looking at me, but at a large photo of Jacob on the Welsh dresser. I pick it up and hand it to him.

"He's about nine months old there," I tell him.

"Look at him," he says, clearly in awe of his child — seeing his child for the first time. I feel choked up just watching him. "He's gorgeous!" he exclaims, as he turns to smile at me.

I move back to the worktop to put the coffee into the cafetière. "Well, that's very modest of you to say, since he's the spitting image of you," I tease.

"Oh, I don't know, I can see you in there too," he says to me, whilst not taking his eyes off Jacob's face.

"Everyone told me his eyes would probably turn brown like mine, but I knew they'd stay blue."

He gives a small laugh and says, "It is a family trait."

The kettle boils and I pour the water into the cafetière then turn to him. "If you don't mind, I'm just going to change out of all this icing sugar while the coffee is brewing. There's more photographs on there," I say pointing to the Welsh dresser, "just help yourself."

"Thanks," he says, and I quickly head upstairs.

I get to my room and switch out of my black trousers and top into blue jeans and a dark blue, ribbed V-neck jumper. Everything is fitted, but then most of my clothes are. Mum tells me that I 'snapped back' into my pre-baby body because of my age, DNA and breastfeeding. I personally think navigating Clovelly's steep hills with Jacob either attached to me or in a pushchair helped a bit too. I definitely didn't feel like I 'snapped back.' It was a long time before I felt like me again — or a version of me that I vaguely recognised anyway. I look in the mirror, take my hair out of its bun and brush it through. I pause for a moment to look at myself with fresh eyes and then chastise myself; it doesn't matter how I look.

I get back to the kitchen and Mark is now holding another photo, it's of Me, Jacob and Lucas and the fact that he's holding it makes me feel guilty again. He watches me as I start pouring the coffee.

"Lucas, I gather?" he asks, giving the photo a slight tilt so that I can see.

"Yes," I say, handing him his coffee.

"You remember how I take it," he says smiling at me. It appears I do. I didn't even think about it. "He's very handsome," he continues. "When you told me about the crazy Irishman that practically proposed to you that time you visited, I don't remember you telling me how handsome he was."

"I'm surprised you remember that," I say, taking a sip of my coffee and sitting at the table opposite him.

"I remember everything," he says, looking serious for a moment, but then he switches to humour again and continues, "And you definitely didn't say how good looking he was."

"Well, I guess it didn't really matter to me at the time," I reply.

"How did you two get—"

"Mark... I'm not sure we should be talking about my boyfriend."

"Just trying to find out about the man that's been raising my son," he replies.

Touché. "Oh... that's fair enough, I guess," I reply nervously.

"Sorry Ava," he says, shaking his head. "You're right, and we don't have much time, so let's talk about our son."

Those words play around my head for a moment... "our son."

"I want to be in his life," he continues. "I'm hoping we can work this out without having to go through the courts."

"I don't want to fight you on this," I quickly say. "It's only fair... it's only right that you see him."

"So, we can start today?" he asks eagerly.

"I'm not sure it can be avoided. Dad will be bringing him back any moment," I tell him. "I don't have all the answers, I guess we'll figure them out as we go along. But there are a few things that I do know," I pause, take a deep breath and say, "Jacob thinks of Lucas as his dad."

"That's to be expected," he replies calmly.

"Yes... so, I don't think we can just say to him 'hello, this is your daddy' straight away," I say nervously. "I think at first you need to be Mark, and then when he knows you better then we can start to talk about you being Daddy." I look at him closely and ask, "What do you think?"

"Yes, that makes sense," he says, taking a breath of his own, then he continues. "I'm not looking to push anyone out. He's had this life for a year, and yes I'd like him to eventually know who I am, you know, build up to him staying with me," he says and then he sees the look of panic on my face, and quickly adds. "In time... When he's ready. When you're ready. I want to be Daddy one day yes... but right now I'll settle for being in his life."

I smile at him. He seems more and more like the Mark I remember. The Mark I fell in love with. The Mark I am... no... I shake that thought away.

"I'm not sure I'm ready to go back to London yet," I tell him. "I know it's a lot to ask you to travel all the time, but I'm not sure I can go there yet... sorry."

"It's no problem at all," he answers, smiling reassuringly.

"So, how do we do this?" I ask. "What's next?"

"Well, I'm here now so if it's possible, can we do something tomorrow?" he asks.

"Tomorrow's fine," I agree.

"And next weekend?" he asks eagerly. "Is every weekend too much?"

"Mark... I owe you a year," I say, and I shake my head as I try to push back the guilt, I feel at saying those words. "Of course, there will be times when I'll need to work, but I'm sure that between me and my parents someone can always be with you... oh..." I stop myself. "I didn't mean to imply that you must be supervised at all times."

"No, that's OK," he says genuinely. "He doesn't know me yet."

I feel awkward about what I want to say next and my fingers tap against the coffee cup that I've been holding onto for support.

"What do you need to say?" he asks me.

I look up at him. "I have a condition," I tell him.

"Oh... yes... maintenance, of course... I'm not sure what the rate is but of course, I'll pay it," he says.

I laugh at him. "No, Mark, that's not my condition. And thanks, but I don't need your money."

"I'm not suggesting you need it. I just feel obligated to help support him," he clarifies.

"I'm fine there, honestly. If you want to do something, then just set him up a savings account or something. Just speak to my dad first because he's doing things with ISAs that I find a bit confusing..." I say brushing it off.

"If that's what you want, then yes, that's a good idea...so what's your condition?" he asks, looking more serious.

"Well..." I say. "Technically, there are three of them. They go by the names Hattie, Ted and Will Davidson."

"Ah..." he says, understanding my meaning. "You know, he is their half-brother."

"No," I say firmly.

"They'll find out one day."

"No," I say again. "They're not to be involved."

He puts down his coffee and reaches for my hand, and after the initial shock of his touch wears off, it feels comforting, it feels natural, and I welcome it.

"Things didn't work out so well the last time we kept a

big secret," he says looking at me with what seems like regret. "I'm not saying they need to know now, and quite frankly; I don't want to tell them now. I would like to get to know my son without worrying about their drama," he says honestly. "But one day... further down the line, they will need to be told."

"And if they try to hurt him?" I ask

"They wouldn't do that," he reassures me.

"And what about me?"

"I know for certain that they won't hurt you," he says, giving a slight laugh.

"History suggests otherwise. How can you be so sure?"

"Because the day after you came to see me. The day I acted like an utter coward and let you down." He looks at me remorsefully. "Well, the next day I invited them over and I told them that if any one of them did anything else to you, then I would disinherit the lot of them, and that still stands."

I instantly burst out laughing. "Oh, my God, I wish I had seen that."

"I only wish I'd done it sooner," he replies more solemnly.

At that moment I hear the door open and I turn, still smiling, expecting to see Dad and Jacob, but it's not. "Lucas!" I say, somewhat surprised. He looks at me and I watch as his eyes trail down to the table where my hand is still entwined with Mark's. He slams the door shut as he steps further in and he looks so angry. Again.

"Doesn't this look cosy," he tells us, through gritted teeth.

25

"Lucas... this... I take my hand back and stand up. "This is Mark."

Mark stands and stretches out his hand. "Hello Lucas. It's good to meet you," he says kindly.

I turn to see that Lucas has his arms folded across his chest and is glaring at Mark. "Lucas?" I say almost pleading, and he looks at me. "Can we try and be civil about this, please?"

"Civil about what exactly?" he spits back at me. "Civil about the fact that this man is here to take my son from me? Or, civil about the fact that you've been sitting here, all cosy and holding hands all afternoon?"

"I know how that must have looked but we were talking about something difficult... he was just offering comfort," I tell him, trying to keep the situation calm.

"Comfort? Really? That big smile you were wearing when I walked in suggests differently, Ava. Don't you think?" he asks snidely.

He moves towards the end of the table and takes his coat

off, putting it on the chair as if to claim his spot as the 'head.'

"I can't say that I've seen you smile like that for me, these last couple of days," he says.

"That's probably because you've been acting like this for the last couple of days," I admonish him.

He's unfazed. "So, what have you two been talking about whilst sat all cosy-like, around the table?" he asks, sneering.

"Jacob. We've been talking about Jacob." I'm really starting to feel exhausted by him. "Actually, Lucas, why don't you just go upstairs, take a shower and come back down as my boyfriend, and not the stranger that I'm looking at right now?"

"Stranger?" he asks, smiling unnervingly. "I'm the same man you woke up next to on Thursday morning, Ava. I'm the same man that took care of you the moment you arrived here. The same man that helped put the pieces of your sad little heart back together after this one here, broke it," he says pointing at Mark. "I'm the same man that put you and that baby that was growing in your belly first, and I'm the same man that has helped you raise him since the day he was born. Is that the man you're talking about, Ava darlin'?" he asks in an eerily calm manner.

"Honestly, Lucas," I say, shaking from anger now. "I know this is so hard for you. I know you're worried that you're going to get pushed out, but that's not what's happening here."

"I'm not looking to take your place, Lucas," Mark says. "Jacob thinks of you as his dad, I understand that. You're important, but he is my son and I am going to be part of his life."

"We'll see what the courts say then, won't we," Lucas snaps back at him.

"Lucas, no," I tell him. "We're not going down that route. Nobody wins and Mark has rights. Legally, we wouldn't have a leg to stand on. Anyway, I don't want that. We've agreed how to take this forward."

"Oh... you've agreed, have you?" he asks angrily. "The two of you? You didn't think to wait for me?"

I hadn't even thought to include him, perhaps I should have. I know I talk about him being Jacob's dad, but in truth, Jacob's just mine, he's always been just mine.

"Lucas, I'm sorry but the fact is that ultimately, this is my decision... not yours," I tell him.

"Well, that's fucking convenient isn't it!" he shouts at me. "So, I'm just supposed to sit back while he takes what's mine? While he wins?"

"Lucas... what? Wins? This isn't about winning or losing, and if it were then surely you can see that you already have the upper hand?" I ask, trying to make him see sense. My sympathy for him is waning and I'm close to losing it with him now. "Jacob already thinks of you as his dad. You've known him from the start. Mark hasn't even met him yet."

"And what about you, Ava?" he asks, too nastily for my liking.

"What about me?" I ask, through gritted teeth.

"How do we determine which of us wins there? Or do we just see who gets to take you to bed tonight?" he asks, looking at me as if there is actually a chance of that happening.

"Lucas, I won't be going to bed with anyone tonight. You know what? I take back my previous offer." Fuming now, I shout. "Go shower at your own place and get out of my house!"

He laughs at me, and says, "Why? So, you can go and fuck him on the sofa again? You're a slut."

My mouth hangs open in shock and I'm literally lost for words.

Mark isn't though, and he steps forward and shouts, "Now you've gone too far!"

Lucas moves forward too, and I rush to put myself between them.

"You've absolutely gone too far there, my son." Dad's voice stops everyone in their tracks, and we all turn to see him standing in the doorway between the kitchen and the utility. A quick glance reassures me that Jacob is in the pushchair behind him, unable to see what's happening. I have never been so relieved to see my dad in my entire life.

"I don't take too kindly to people using words like that to describe my little girl, Lucas," he says calmly. "I think you know that." Dad looks him dead in the eye, Lucas only gives a dry laugh and steps back a little. "Now, I think she just asked you to leave and that's what I suggest you do."

"I'm just supposed to walk away am I, Jonathan?" he asks him, laughing still.

Laughing but clearly angry.

"No. You're supposed to be here," he says to him seriously. Lucas looks confused, I am too, and I shoot my dad a look. "You're supposed to be here as the man that she can rely on. The man that I took you to be. The man that I can trust to take care of her," he tells him firmly. "But you're not that man right now, are you? So, I suggest you get yourself gone and go and find him, because right now, you're not welcome."

"Jonathan—"

"If I have to say it again Lucas, we are going to have a problem," he tells him firmly. "It's only because I know you're going through a tough time with this that I'm not already teaching you some manners about what you just called her."

Lucas laughs again, looks at each of us, picks up his coat and walks out the front door. I let out a deep breath and go over to hug my dad. There have been times in the past when having a tough, East End dad has come in handy, but I've never been as grateful for it as I am right now.

"Thank you," I whisper into his ear.

"Just doing my job, sweetheart. You OK?" he asks, kissing my forehead.

"Yes. Bit shaky and confused, but yes. Glad you got here when you did, mind you," I tell him honestly.

I let him go and walk into the utility. I paint a smile on my worried face and try to push away everything that I feel about what just happened with Lucas — which I cannot really begin to comprehend right now, anyway. I don't want my little boy to know about all of the hurt and anger. I always feel bad about the stress he must've gone through in those early months of pregnancy, when I didn't know and didn't take care of either or us. Now, I try my best to keep everything calm and happy around him.

"Jakie Baby," I say, as I bend down to unclip him from the pushchair.

"Mumma," he giggles in return, kicking his legs excitedly. He's wearing his winter suit, so I keep him in the utility while I take him out of it — it's warm in the kitchen. As I'm doing it, I half listen to the conversation happening behind me.

"Mark," Dad says politely, but not really welcomingly.

"It's good to see you again, Jonathan," Mark replies a little more warmly.

"Right. You're here now then. I told you that you wouldn't get a warm welcome," Dad chuckles.

"You missed out something rather crucial that day, mind you."

"Yes... Well, it wasn't my place, was it?" Dad replies.

"I guess not," Mark tells him.

"You look like you've been doing more than swimming. Have you been in the ring?" Dad asks.

"Sparring mainly. I've been boxing with Darren for about a year. I still swim though," Mark replies.

So that explains the muscles. An image of Mark in the ring getting all sweaty whilst battering his opponent enters my mind and sends tingles through me again, but I quickly force those thoughts away.

Jacob is now free from his suit, so I scoop him up and walk into the kitchen. Mark is standing there expectantly with a big smile on his face, and I walk towards him slowly, feeling the weight of each step. I don't stop until I'm right next to him and the two of them are close enough to touch.

"Jacob, this is Mark," I say, and Jacob just giggles and buries his head in the crook of my neck. "Mark, meet Jacob... your son," I practically choke that last bit out.

Mark can't hold back his own tears as he reaches out his hand to give Jacob a little handshake. "Hello there, Jacob... it's so lovely to finally meet you."

26

I eventually put Jacob into his high chair and pass him a breadstick while I go to the fridge and get out last night's dinner to reheat for him.

"Home-made moussaka," I say to Mark. "There's enough to go around if you'd like some?"

"Thanks, but no, it's a bit early for me and I'm still full of sandwiches and cake," he says.

"You've been to the tea rooms, then?" Dad asks him.

"Yes, it was the only place I could start. It's absolutely fabulous, you must be so proud of Eleanor," he replies, then quickly catches flying breadstick.

"I hope you're not too fond of that shirt?" I ask him, laughing.

"He can mess up as many shirts as he likes," he says smiling at Jacob, then at me.

Dad clears his throat. "Yes, I'm very proud of her, and she loves it. Even more so now she's got an extra pair of hands that she trusts in the kitchen," he says. Then he comes over and gives me a slight squeeze on the shoulder. "What are we going to do with that boy?" he asks me. "At this point, Dad, I'm going to need you to clarify which "boy" you're referring to."

"Lucas. This isn't like him and I honestly don't like it. I can cancel my plans tonight and come and stay with you?" he asks with concern.

"No, Dad, no. You've had this planned for ages," I tell him. "And I don't know, is the answer to your question," I shrug. "This is so unlike him, and I honestly don't know what to make of it."

"Right, well, any sign of trouble and you call me," he instructs me. "And what about this one?" he asks, pointing to Mark. "Is he going to be trouble?"

"Dad..." I say, shaking my head at him. "He's right there."

Mark laughs. "It's fine, and no. I'm not planning on being any trouble," he replies. He's still playing with Jacob and I take his dinner out of the microwave to let it cool.

"So, are you sticking around for long?" Dad asks Mark.

"Christ!" Mark suddenly says. "I haven't actually booked anywhere yet. I just thought I'd sort it when I was here and then forgot all about it."

"I'm sure Ava can point you in the right direction," Dad says, moving to hug me — but I stop him, suddenly remembering what I'd heard him and Mark talk about when I was with Jacob in the utility.

"Hang on, Dad..." I say. "When you two were talking before, what did you mean about telling Mark that he wouldn't be welcome? When did you tell him that, exactly?" I ask him.

"You don't know?" Mark asks, clearly surprised.

"Know what?" I ask, looking between them both. "Dad?"

Dad looks a little nervous, then answers. "I may have paid Mark a little visit in London after you told us everything that happened," he says, looking at me and shrugging as if it were nothing.

"Dad? Are you serious?" I throw my hands in the air. "What were you thinking? One of the reasons I didn't tell you was to stop you from going there and getting into trouble," I sigh, completely exasperated with him. "Does Mum know?"

"No, she doesn't, and I'm sure Mark here, will confirm to you that I was an absolute gentleman, won't you Mark?" he asks, and we both look at him.

"He was perfectly polite and calm," Mark nods in confirmation, "and somewhat terrifying," he adds smiling.

"Dad!" I groan out.

"Ava... I wasn't there for you when you needed me, and your Nanny Mae would be turning in her grave if I hadn't gone to defend you, and you know it," he says looking at me seriously. "I said my piece to those that had done you wrong, and then I left."

I let out a deep breath and start to relax. I can never stay mad at my dad for long. "Right, well thank you, I guess," I say, and I give him a big hug and kiss him on the cheek. "You better go, or you'll be late."

"I mean it, any sign of trouble and you call. Oh, and maybe we could keep the details of my little visit between us? No need to upset your mum?" he asks innocently.

I laugh and nod at him, and he leaves, raising a hand to Mark. I take Jacob's plate over and sit down on the other side of him, opposite Mark.

"What really happened?" I ask him.

"More or less what your dad said," Mark answers, smiling. "It was a rare afternoon when everyone was at mine and Will answered the door. It took him a while to get over the shock," he adds laughing. "Miranda was there and Miles too—"

"Miles?" I ask in surprise. "What was Miles doing there?" I say it with distaste, his name feels disgusting in my mouth.

"Oh yes, well, Nate broke up with Hattie not long after you left. He wasn't happy about all of the lies. She quite quickly got with Miles. Very quickly actually," he says, then he looks at me. "I see you smirking, you know, there's no need to hide it. Would it make you even happier to know that Miranda dumped Ted after hearing the truth?" he asks, grinning at me.

I put my head down to try to hide my pleasure and he laughs at that. "I guess if anyone is allowed a moment to rejoice in their misery, it's you. Not that Ted ever seemed that bothered by it, to be honest," he adds.

"No, Mark. Don't take away what little pleasure I can get from this. Ted was heartbroken, wasn't he?" I ask him, giving him a look.

He plays along. "Of course, what was I thinking? He was crying on the floor like a baby for days," he says, and we both laugh.

"Now that's more like it," I tell him as I get up to get some water for Jacob. "Oh, and I told you Nate had backbone."

"Yes, you did," he says, and he smiles at me fondly as I sit back down.

We sit in silence for a while, both of us just watching Jacob, who is getting in a mess, but very much enjoying mushing his moussaka into his face.

"I usually eat something with him," I say, breaking the silence. "It's supposed to help encourage him, but I'm not feeling all that hungry, right now," Mark looks like he's about to say something, but I beat him to it. "Oh! I should get a photograph of you both, pass me your phone." I reach out my hand and Mark smiles and takes his phone out of his pocket and passes it to me.

"Be sure to get my good side," he says jokingly.

"You'll have to remind me which side that it is," I retort, and we both smile.

I take a few photos of them both. Jake's a real poser and they look so natural together. In fact, I'm suddenly struck by how natural this whole situation feels. The conversation flows easily between me and Mark, as it always did. Having him here again feels warming. It's hard to describe it, but with all the talk about putting my heart back together, I've never thought about whether it had healed. It's starting to feel like it was simply stitched back together, functioning but ultimately still broken. Now he's here, and we're talking and bonding over our child, and it feels like it is starting to truly heal. It's strange. This whole day has been strange and in no way how I expected our first meeting to go.

Mark snaps me out of my thoughts. "Ava, I need to ask you about Lucas," he says, looking at me seriously.

Lucas... How is it that I've not been thinking about him? Mark continues, "What was that? Is that how he always is? Because Lilly said—"

"God, Mark, I know, he was completely out of order with Lilly. In fact, he's been completely out of order since then."

He continues to look at me seriously, concern clear on his face.

"Honestly, I'm not some abused woman defending her man. He is never like this. I have never seen him like this with anyone. Everyone here worships him. He's the joker, he's reliable, he's usually all about protecting people," I say honestly. "Although, we've never had to deal with anything like this. This isn't exactly the norm, is it?"

"I suppose not," he replies.

"I guess I've never really seen him in a stressful situation... and apparently he doesn't cope with it well," I say as I roll my eyes at the massive understatement.

"I can understand how the fear of losing you might make him feel, Ava. Trust me, I can," he says, looking pained. "But what I just saw; that wasn't right. He cannot behave that way towards you."

I sigh and put my head on the table for a moment, and when I eventually look up our eyes meet. "I know, and I will tell him that... when I eventually speak to him again," I say, giving him a half smile.

We're still looking at each other so I completely miss the cue that means Jacob has finished the eating stage of dinner time, and is about to launch some food, and as he does it splatters right across Mark's chest. I burst out laughing and quickly scoop up the remains of the food so that he can't do any more damage. I look at Mark who is also laughing and he gets up to go to the sink, I follow him and grab a cloth.

"Here, let me," I say, still laughing and trying in vain to scrub the red sauce off the pale blue shirt. "We can probably save it if we get it in the sink to soak now."

Mark's laughing too and he starts to unbutton his shirt. I'm busy filling the sink with hot water and I don't see him do it, so when I turn around and he's standing in front of me shirtless, my mouth practically falls open. He looked good before, but now, even more sculpted and more muscular, he resembles something from Greek mythology. Every part of my body wants to touch him and the throbbing in my core is too much to bear. I drag my eyes up to his face and I can see from the look in his eyes that he knows exactly the effect that he's having on me, and he's enjoying it.

Thankfully, Jacob chooses that moment to squeal and I break myself free from Mark. "He'll be wanting some yoghurt," I say, and I go to the fridge and stand there for a moment, welcoming the cold against my burning face. I give Jacob a yoghurt and spoon. Which is pointless really as he will only use his hands to scoop it out and then paint his face.

"On second thoughts," I say to Mark, "I'm not sure that there's anything here that will fit you — if you get your shirt wet, I mean."

He smiles and puts his shirt back on. "That's fine, it's just a shirt. It can be a souvenir from our first food fight," he says, giving a little laugh, and I let out a breath in relief.

I can cope better with these crazy feelings when he's fully clothed. I smile at him then remember something else. "Oh! We've not looked into where you're staying."

"Oh, bloody hell. I keep forgetting about that. Where do you recommend?"

"Well, the White House is the main hotel here, there are more that are further afield, but it depends how far you want to travel," I tell him. "That's probably the best place to start though," I get my phone and give him the number and he calls them.

"Fully booked," he says.

"OK, well, there are quite a few bed and breakfasts, but they don't tend to do last minute bookings. The Lilacs is just up the road, that's where Lilly stayed. Shelly might be willing to do me a favour if she's got the space — I'll give her a call," I tell him.

I step into the living room and call Shelly; she runs The Lilacs and is really nice and is always itching to babysit for me. I've taken her up on the offer once or twice and the payment is always the same — Devils Chocolate Cake. After a quick call and a bit of grovelling she agrees. She has one room available and Mark can have it if he can be there in thirty minutes and out again early on Sunday. I'm not sure what it is going to cost him, but I'm going to be up to my elbows in chocolate cake for a while.

I walk back into the kitchen and see that Mark is now expertly cleaning the yoghurt off Jacob and I feel my heart swelling again. "Anyone would think that you've done this before," I say to him, smiling. "You can stay at The Lilacs, but you have to be there in half an hour and out by nine thirty tomorrow morning. Where are you parked?"

"In a car park, about a twenty-minute walk away," he replies.

"I'll drive you," I say, and I scoop Jacob up and we all get into my car.

"You upgraded the Golf?" he asks as we get in.

"Don't!" I reply dramatically. "It still pains me, but it was starting to need too much work, so Dad eventually persuaded me to let it go."

"Shame. I have some rather fond memories of that car," he says, giving me a cheeky smile.

I roll my eyes and smile back at him, but I'm glad it's dark so that he can't see me blushing. I know exactly which memories he is referring to, and they're memories that I really shouldn't be thinking about.

I get him to his car in about five minutes and we agree that after he's checked in that he'll come back to help bath Jacob. I get about twenty minutes just Jacob and me and I use them to try to figure out what's going on because I have no clue. It all seems too surreal. Mark is here and he's being nice, really nice, when I thought he'd be furious. Lucas, on the other hand. Lucas, who I've relied on since I came here. Who I had expected to be strong and have my back, is coming apart at the seams. Shouting at Lilly was bad enough but what he just did to me — calling me a slut. I'm as confused as I am angry and I've no idea how we turn this around.

Then there's Mark. All this time I've been holding onto the image of Mark as I last saw him. Mark when he was hurting, when he was weak, and when he let me down. Only, now I've found out that he did help me, albeit too late — but now he's back and he's the Mark I fell in love with. Only from what I've seen from his body, he's that Mark but with a sexier upgrade. Not that I didn't find him sexy enough as it was.

I'm still dwelling on it all when I hear Mark knock at the door. When I see him my body warms, my heart swells and my gut churns. This is all too much.

"It's just occurred to me how hungry I am," I say to him lightly, trying to mask the inner turmoil. "I'm going to warm up leftovers, would you like some?"

"Actually, that would be great," he replies. Then he heads through to the living room to play with Jacob while I warm up some food for us.

"You might want to season it, I make everything Jacob-friendly these days," I say, handing him the salt and pepper.

"Soo... ummm... Shelly is somewhat intrigued about me," he says, smiling a little.

"I bet she is," I reply, raising an eyebrow. "I know how quickly rumours spread here. Trust me. I gave them a lot to talk about when I showed up here pregnant."

He turns solemn. "I'm sorry you went through that alone. If I'd have known—"

"Mark, don't. You didn't know because I didn't tell you.

Just like I didn't tell my parents about everything. Anyway, I wasn't alone. My parents were great, and Julia — she was my doctor and we're actually really good friends now... and..." I pause.

"And Lucas?" he asks tentatively.

"Yes. Lucas was there for me too. He was a friend. He let me know that he wanted more, but he knew I couldn't. So, he was a friend," I tell him honestly.

"He bided his time."

"No. Come on, that makes it sound so creepy," I say, shaking my head. "I get that you might think badly of him, he's not exactly shown himself in his best light—"

"His best light? What I saw today was downright abusive."

"I know. OK, I do, and if that is how he always is we would've ended a long time ago — believe me," I tell him, then I pause, unsure how to continue. It seems weird saying this to Mark, like I'm betraying him somehow. "I just feel like I need to give him the benefit of the doubt. This is hard for him. He... he loves us. He's done so much for me, I can't just turn my back on him."

Mark looks down and swallows hard before asking me, "Do you love him?"

"Mark..." I sigh. "Please, don't."

"It's a simple question," he replies.

"Not when it's you that's asking," I tell him, and then I look down at the remains of my dinner, no longer able to eat a thing. "I'm going to run his bath."

We bath Jacob together without saying another word about it, and he leaves before I settle down to feed Jacob to sleep. We switch numbers — although his never changed — and agree to make plans in the morning. Jacob falls asleep easily, and now it's eight O'clock and I have nothing to do but think and feel.

Mark

Mark leaves after Jacob is in his pyjamas and heads over to The Lilacs. He sits in his room, it's small but nicely decorated and has everything he needs for the night. Except a beer. He could really use a beer right now. He picks up his phone, he's missed a few calls and messages from Darren, but now it's time to talk. He makes the call and Darren answers quickly.

"Hey, you left early this morning. How are you?"

"Yes, sorry I left without saying goodbye. I'm good," Mark says, then he adds, "I'm in Clovelly."

"Of course, you are," Darren half sighs, half laughs. "It's always nice to hear when my professional advice has fallen on deaf ears."

"Professional advice?" Mark laughs. "Here I was thinking I was speaking with my best friend. Should I expect an invoice?" he asks, jokingly.

"It's in the post," Darren replies, feigning seriousness.

"How about I just restock your supply of whiskey?" Mark asks.

"Works for me," Darren replies, laughing. Then he asks, "Have you seen them?"

"Yes. Yes, I've seen them. I've just left them, actually," Mark says to his friend, unable to stop himself from smiling.

"It's gone well, then?" Darren asks.

"Yes, it has. She's not going to stop me seeing him — quite the opposite in fact."

"That's good, mate. Really good," Darren replies genuinely.

"He's so gorgeous, Darren. So happy. She's so good with him," he tells him. "You should see him."

"I can't wait to," Darren replies genuinely.

"And Ava—" Mark adds hesitantly.

"Mark," Darren sighs. "You're supposed to be there for your son, not your ex."

"I know. I am. It's just... she's just the same. We're just the same!" Mark tries to argue.

"Mark. I'm not going to lie to you, I'm worried. You know I'm just looking out for you, but the truth is that you've never stopped loving her," Darren says seriously. "She still has your heart."

"Yes, she does, and unless I'm mistaken, I still have hers too," he replies.

Darren groans. "And the boyfriend?" he asks.

"That's why I'm calling. Lilly was right. Something is not right there," Mark says seriously.

"And it's not possible that you're seeing what you want to see?" Darren asks.

"I didn't want to see what I saw today, Darren. I don't ever want to see anyone treat her the way he did. It was much worse than what Lilly described," Mark says vehemently.

"OK. I trust you both. What do you want to do?" Darren asks.

"I'm going to need some of your contacts. He needs looking into," Mark says firmly.

"Leave it with me. There's someone that owes me a favour."

"Thanks, I really appreciate it. Talk soon," Mark replies, then he hangs up.

He takes a shower and watches some TV, and two hours after speaking with Darren he receives a text from him.

He's on board. Be at my office at 11 on Monday & we'll go from there. D.

He's about to reply but then another message comes through, a message that has him smiling from ear to ear.

It simply says, **Good night Mark.x**

He replies instantly, **Good night Ava.x**

27

It's been five weeks since Mark came back into my life, and for four of those weeks I've seen him every weekend. After the first, unannounced visit, he now travels down on a Friday evening so that he can have as much of the weekend with Jacob as possible.

I finally saw Lucas on Wednesday — three days after the stand-off in my kitchen. We went three days without any contact, and the longer he stayed away the angrier I got because I was owed an apology. Then, on Wednesday, he caught up with me after lunch when I was walking with Jacob, and he apologised straight away.

He said all of the right things. That he was out of order, jealous, lost his mind for a moment, and would never hurt me like that again. He told me that he has never loved anyone the way he loves me, and because I felt like I needed to give him a chance, because I felt like it was right to try to make the relationship work, and because I couldn't say those same words back to him — I took him to bed.

I spent the rest of that week convincing myself that I'd made the right decision. That trying to make it work with

Lucas was the right thing to do. Then I spent the entire weekend with Mark, feeling like I didn't need to make any effort at all, because we still just fit. We still worked. The only things that I found hard to do were to not stare at him for too long, avoiding touching him, and not thinking about the things we used to do together. That did take serious effort. I did make one exception for the self-imposed 'no touching rule,' and that's late on Sunday afternoons when he leaves, and we hug goodbye. That's the moment I long for and loathe in equal measures.

It started off quick and light, but as each week passes, we're holding on that little bit longer, closer and harder. I feel his heart pounding as hard as mine is. I feel his short, shallow breaths, as like me, he fights against what his body wants, and I know that if either one of us were to tilt our heads just slightly, then we'd be kissing. I also know that I'm still completely in love with him, and that he's the man I want to be with. I knew it when I stood on his doorstep, what feels like a lifetime ago, and it would seem that nothing has changed.

So, this is how I've spent the last five weeks; fooling myself into thinking I want to be with Lucas Monday to Friday, and then knowing exactly what I want on Saturday and Sunday, when I'm with Mark, but being too scared to admit it.

Until now.

Lucas hasn't lost it with me again like he did that day, but the cracks are starting to show. It's almost as if the Lucas I'm seeing now is the real him and the Lucas I thought I knew was a lie. He snaps at me, he's less patient, not just with me but Jacob too, even with the people he's working or drinking with. I don't think it's just that I'm seeing him differently now, I have tried, really tried, to gloss over the cracks, but they just keep getting deeper.

I know what the right thing to do is, I just need to find the right time to do it. Which isn't going to be today. It's Saturday, but there will be no Mark as it's Hattie's birthday and he has to be at Mary and Tom's for her party. So, this evening I'm going for a long overdue drink with Julia at our local. I was going to ask my parents to babysit but Lucas has been on his best behaviour for the last few days, and has insisted that he'll stay over and look after Jacob. I was torn, but I agreed, because I know that I'm about to take Jacob away from him. I'm taking both of us away from him. I settle Jacob down for bed and head downstairs. Lucas is eating dinner in front of the TV, but he gets up to kiss me.

"You have a good night, darlin'. Don't drink too much mind you, I know what Julia's like. But you deserve a break," he says kindly, and I feel like the most callous person on the planet.

"Thanks. Make sure you call me if there are any problems, or if you can't settle him if he wakes," I say, then I head out.

When I get to the pub Julia is already there with a bottle of Prosecco on the go. I get a few looks as I sit down, because most people have figured out that Mark is Jacob's biological father. The lovely Jessica and her not so quiet comments that first day got the ball rolling, and naturally, as people have seen us together and seen him with Jacob... well, it's been pretty easy to connect the dots. I just ignore them, because I know this is nothing compared to what they'll be saying when I eventually break up with Lucas.

"How are you?" Julia asks, as I sit down and pick up the glass that she's poured for me.

"I'm OK, how are you?" I reply.

"Um... well, I'm OK too, but as you just drained that glass in two-seconds flat, I think you need to give me more than 'I'm OK,'" she says looking at me pointedly.

"I'm thirsty?" I offer as a response.

"Talk to me," she instructs me.

"Aren't you sick of my drama, Julia? In fact, aren't you sick of everyone's drama?" I've genuinely no idea how she copes being a doctor here, a lot of the time people go to see her for some sort of confessional, as opposed to actually having a medical issue.

"Well, if you look behind you..." she says, and I turn to look, but she stops me. "No, don't actually look. Peter and his wife are in here," she whispers.

"Oh... do you want to leave?" I ask, knowing that even though she doesn't love him anymore, she still gets annoyed at the way he treated her.

"No way!" she almost shouts and people look over once more. She crouches down a bit and goes back to whispering, "I just mean that I'd rather focus on your drama than on that utter prick."

I can't help but laugh at her. I feel so lucky to have her as a friend, especially after my previous experiences. I speak in a low voice too because this pub has many ears. "You may regret asking me that... where shall I start?" I ask her.

"Lucas. Start there."

"I'm going to break up with him."

"Wowsers!" she exclaims. "Is this because of him and how he's been behaving, or because you're in love with Mark?" Julia is never one to beat around the bush.

"I guess, it's both," I tell her, and she nods at me. "I care about Lucas and I have tried these past few weeks to make it work. To make it feel right again, but I've realised that I shouldn't have to try like this. If I don't feel it, I don't feel it. I can't force it," I tell her honestly. "And yes, he's behaving differently, and I just don't see him the same way as I used to. It's like he's not the same person."

"And you're in love with your ex, again," she states.

I let out a deep breath and tell her, "I honestly don't think I ever stopped being in love with him in the first place."

Somehow, we manage to make that one bottle last, probably because we are talking more than drinking. I still don't drink much because I have Jacob to take care of, but we sneak in a cheeky Baileys when they call last orders. Julia gives me a big hug as we leave and reassures me that I'm doing the right thing, and we head home in different directions. It's only a short walk, but I feel apprehensive the whole way. I shouldn't have let Lucas look after Jacob tonight. It's late now and he'll suggest staying over, which means I'm going to have to make up an excuse for why I don't want to have sex with him.

As I get to the front gate, I think that I can hear Jacob crying and the hairs on the back of my neck stand on end. I rush to the back door; I can hear him clearly now and he is hysterical. Why didn't Lucas call me if he couldn't settle him? I told him to call me. As soon as I open the door to the kitchen, I see exactly why Lucas didn't call me. He is slumped over my kitchen table with an almost empty bottle of whiskey in front of him and an empty glass still in his hand. I go over to him and shake him and he lets out a slight grunt.

That's enough.

He's alive and that's all I need to know, so I run upstairs to Jacob's bedroom.

"Jakie! Oh, my baby, I'm so sorry. I'm here now. I'm here," I say as I reach for him. He is bright red, his eyes and nose are streaming, and the top of his sleep bag is soaked from all of the tears. I pick him up and hold him close. Oh, God, how long has he been crying like this? I rock him and kiss him and soothe him, and his sobbing slowly starts to subside.

Then I smell his nappy, so I take him to his changing table and strip him off. I see that the poo in his nappy has started to harden and he is so sore, and then I let out a cry of my own at the realisation that he has been like this for hours. My baby boy woke up, and probably cried because he was dirty, and then he cried and cried and cried, because Lucas was too busy drinking himself unconscious to come and help him.

I burst into tears and hold Jacob close. "I am so sorry baby, I am so, so sorry," I look at him and kiss him all over. "It's OK now. Mummy's here. Mummy's here."

I put him in fresh pyjamas and take him to my room, I lay on the bed with him and he latches on. He's making these horrible hiccupping sounds. I've only ever heard them once before when he was younger, when I got stuck in traffic and he started crying in the back of the car and I couldn't get him out to comfort him. It broke my heart then and it's breaking my heart now, and I instantly blame myself. Why did I trust him? Why?

The self-blame stays with me and I lay there questioning everything, until Jacob falls asleep. Did I turn his monitor on? Yes, I did. I remember. It had no charge, so I plugged it into the charger in the living room. It was on, it was definitely on because I looked at Jacob sleeping before I left. I'm sure that as I came in, I only heard crying coming from upstairs. Did I hear it over the monitor too? I don't remember.

Jacob is asleep now and as I watch him, I'm suddenly hit with a new train of thought, and panic courses through me.

What if something had happened? What if he was crying because he was ill, or hurt? What if there had been a fire? Lucas is unconscious in the kitchen after choosing to drink himself senseless, knowing that he was in charge of a baby. *My* baby.

All I feel now is pure rage. I put cushions at the edge of the bed and go downstairs. The monitor is where I left it, still charging, but switched off. Did he switch it off? It was definitely on when I left. I go into the kitchen and he is still unconscious, only now he's snoring too. I shake him — nothing. I shake him again, harder — still nothing. I growl in frustration and shout at him, "We are done. Do you hear me? We are done!"

He's still dead to the world and the anger now comes out of me in tears. I grab a bag from the utility and go upstairs. He keeps some clothes here, so I find them and shove them into the bag. Then I head to the bathroom, his toiletries are next, I even check the laundry bin. I want it all gone. Once I'm satisfied that I've gathered up everything that is his, I take the bag downstairs and dump it on the floor next to him. I go back to my room, lock the door and curl myself around Jacob, keeping him safe. I will myself to go to sleep and eventually I drift off listening to Jacob's quiet breaths next to my head, and feeling the gentle rise and dip of his stomach under my hand.

Jacob wakes at seven in a lovely mood and I feel both relief and envy over the fact that he seems unfazed by the events of last night. I take him to the bathroom with me so that I can shower — I want to be dressed before I face Lucas. When we get downstairs, I leave Jacob in the living room and take his high chair through to him. I don't want him in the kitchen. I'm too wound up to eat but I make myself a coffee and take another look at the piece of shit still passed out on my table. Jacob seems very happy having breakfast with the TV on for a change, but by half past eight I've had two coffees and Lucas still hasn't moved. I can still hear him snoring and I can't stand his presence here, any longer.

I go into the kitchen and I shove him hard, and he grumbles, so I do it again harder and he wakes with a start. I'm glad I had the good sense to move the glass and bottle or they would've been knocked to the floor and that's another mess that I'd have to clean up.

"What the...? Ow..." he tries to say as he puts his hand to his head, then his neck, and then his back, as he takes in his surroundings. "Did I sleep here? Why didn't you try to move me?" he asks groggily.

"What happened last night, Lucas?" I ask bluntly.

"I guess I drank too much...?" he says, and he gives a slight laugh, but then he looks at my face and if he's sober enough to read it then he'll see nothing but contempt. "What?" he asks, clearly confused.

"Where was I last night, Lucas?" I ask him firmly.

"All right, give me a minute... you were at the pub," he replies, still rubbing his neck.

"And what were you doing last night Lucas? Where were you?" I ask, as the anger builds again.

"I was here... with Jacob. I was looking after Jacob," he replies defensively. Either he's still drunk or he genuinely doesn't think he's done anything wrong.

"No, Lucas!" I scream at him. "You can't actually look after a child when you're passed out drunk. I got home and I could hear him crying from the street. From the street!" I tell him, hysterically now. "And I walk in, and you are passed out drunk, hugging a bottle of whiskey. Why? Why would you do that?"

"Look... yeah... OK... I see that," he tries to say, but I'm nowhere near done with him.

"He must have been crying for hours. He had dry shit stuck to him, his bottom is red raw," I tell him and then I burst into tears at the memory. "Oh my God... anything could've happened. If there had been a fire you wouldn't have had a clue. No clue and I'd have lost him. Do you know how much I hate you, right now?" I can't stop the tears now, just thinking of what could've happened.

Lucas tries to stand, but then winces, thinks better of it and sits back down. He holds up his hands, and says, "But that didn't happen, he's fine, isn't he? He's fine."

I force back the tears, not wanting him to mistake them for weakness and firmly tell him, "Get out."

"Ava—"

"Lucas. Get out now. Take your things and go. This is it. We're over," I tell him, as calmly and firmly as I can.

"Oh, come on. I drank too much."

"You put my son in danger," I counter.

"He's fine," he argues back.

"Get out. We're over," I tell him again, speaking louder this time.

"OK, OK, I'll go, we can talk about this later," he says, getting up again, but then he catches sight of the bag on the floor. "What's this?"

"Your things. Take them and go," I tell him.

"Seriously, Ava, let's just calm down."

"What aren't you hearing? We. Are. Over. I don't want to be with you. I was going to try to find the right moment to end it, and I was going to do it nicely, but not now. Not after this," I tell him. "Get out of my house, out of my life, and away from MY son!" I shout at him, but he still doesn't move. "NOW!" I scream. "Get out now!"

Jacob cries out and I run to grab him, and at the same time the doorbell rings. I carry him past Lucas — who is still standing there motionless — to open the door to see Jeff from next door and he looks worried.

"Is everything OK here?" he asks.

Normally I would lie so that I didn't make a scene or fuel the gossip, but Lucas still hasn't moved, and I want him gone.

"No, Jeff, can you please help me make Lucas leave. I don't want him here," I tell him as I step aside to invite him into the front room.

That clearly wasn't what he was expecting to hear, Jeff is about half the size of Lucas.

"Oh, of course..." he replies nervously, and he clears his throat as he walks towards the door leading to the kitchen. "Lucas, mate... Ava wants you to go... this is her home, so you need to do as she asks," he says, and then he looks at me hopefully, but it was a weak attempt and Lucas still hasn't moved.

A thought comes to me and I ask, "Jeff, did you hear Jacob crying last night?"

"Oh, yes, we did actually," he replies.

"And how long was he crying for?" I ask, bracing myself for his answer.

"Well... I'd say at least three hours..."

I feel the bile rise and for a moment I think I'm going to be sick. Three hours. I was only gone for about half an hour more than that. I am shaking all over and the tears fall fast and hot.

"Jeff, please hold Jacob for me for a moment," I say as I pass him over and I walk into the kitchen.

I stand in front of Lucas again and take a deep breath. "If he woke up and started crying half an hour after I left... you would've still been sober," I say, and he looks at me now, but still says nothing. "Did you hear him? Did you hear my son crying out for help and ignore him? Did you turn his monitor off so you could carry on drinking undisturbed?"

I ask him furiously. The look of guilt on his face is all the confirmation I need, and I scream at the top of my lungs, "GET OUT, GET OUT, GET OUT!"

He is already standing, and, in my rage, I find the strength to shove him backwards. He doesn't put up a fight and so I keep shoving him until he is all the way out of the door. He just stands there staring at me blankly as I run back to get the bag with his things in, and then I launch it at him, slam the door shut, and burst into tears. Jacob is crying too so I take him from Jeff and go to the living room to comfort him. I just sit there, tears falling, stroking his head, reassuring us both as he feeds.

I'd almost forgotten that Jeff is still here until he suddenly appears in the doorway to tell me that my parents are on their way.

28

JONATHAN

Jonathan sat on the train early Tuesday morning with a coffee in hand. His journey to London wasn't the same as last time. He was going to see an ex-colleague and long-time friend, Antony Riley to look at some investment opportunities. It wasn't rushed or unplanned, he would be staying the night with Tony and they'd no doubt be going out for a slap-up meal. He was looking forward to it, and it was a welcome distraction after the last few days. Good timing too as he wanted to look into whether it might be the right time to sell Ava's flat and reinvest elsewhere. He trusted Tony's judgement as much as his own, especially with Ava's money, Tony was her Godfather, after all.

Still, he couldn't quite shake the unease he was feeling about leaving Clovelly. Ava was distraught about what happened with Lucas — not the break-up — but what happened with Jacob. She blamed herself for what could've happened, beating herself up over and over. He was glad she was staying at their house for a while; she needed her mum, whether she'd admit it or not.

He got into St Pancras and took the tube into the City. Tony had done very well for himself. He'd never married, loved the bachelor life, and lived in a very swanky flat. It felt good being back in London. Jonathan had grown to love Clovelly, but London would always be home. He got to Tony's building and was buzzed in and Tony greeted him at the door. Tony was about five years younger than Jonathan and he took care of himself. He was a good-looking chap and looked much younger than his years, but Jonathan had always put that down to his single status. He was recently starting to understand that children definitely aged you.

"Jon," Tony said, reaching out to shake his hand and then pull him into a hug. "It's good to see you. Come in."

"It's good to be here, Tony. I'm looking forward to hearing what you've got to tell me, I feel like I've been out of the game a bit recently," Jonathan replied cheerfully.

Tony led him into his home then he turned and paused. He looked at him sighing and said, "Jonathan, I'm afraid I've got you here under false pretences."

"What are you talking about? There's no investment?" Jonathan asked, confused.

"No, there is, but that's not the only reason you're here," Tony clarified.

"Go on," Jonathan encouraged, laughing a little, if it was anyone else, he'd be feeling nervous.

"He said it was important... about Ava... so, I agreed," Tony told him seriously.

"I think you need to tell me straight here, Tony," Jonathan said, starting to get annoyed. The mention of Ava had him spooked.

"Just come with me. They can explain," Tony said, and he led Jonathan into the kitchen.

There was a big island in the middle and three men

were sitting around it. Two of them he didn't think he'd ever met before and one he knew very well. He walked over to him and he stood up to shake his hand.

"I'm sorry for the secrecy, Jonathan, but I wasn't sure you'd come if I'd asked," he said honestly.

"Right. Well, I think you'd better tell me what all this is about don't you, Mark?" Jonathan replied firmly.

Mark nodded and introduced him to one of the men. "This is my good friend, Darren Barton, he's a..."

"Yes, I've heard your name before," Jonathan said, shaking his hand. "Your reputation precedes you," he said smiling. Then he added, "Am I in need of a lawyer?"

"I should hope not," Darren replied, and he smiled as he shook his hand. "And it's a pleasure to meet you too. I've heard a lot about you. All good, I should add."

Darren took over to introduce the third man. "This is Mike Rogers, he's an associate of mine."

"Nice to meet you, Mike," Jonathan said, shaking his hand. "I'm sorry, but I can't say that I've heard of you," he said, smiling politely still.

Mike smiled back. "In my line of work, that's actually a good thing," he replied.

"And what exactly is your line of work, Mike?" Jonathan asked.

"I'm an investigator."

"Right." Jonathan took stock. "So, I'm standing in a room with an investigator, a criminal lawyer, and the father of my grandchild, and I'm being told that you have something important to tell me about my daughter?" he said, then he looked at Mark. "I suggest someone starts talking."

Mark sat back in his seat next to Darren, Tony and Mike sat too, so Jonathan followed suit. Then Mark cleared his throat and began.

"Mike has been looking into Lucas, at my request," he said calmly.

Jonathan laughed and rubbed his face. "Jesus, Mark, if you wanted to get rid of the competition then you could've saved yourself some money by just waiting for a bit. Ava broke up with Lucas on Sunday," he said, raising his eyebrows. He'd expected Mark to look happy but if anything, he looked concerned.

"That's good," Mark finally said. "Unfortunately, it doesn't necessarily make the situation any better."

"What situation is this, then?" Jonathan asked. Then he added, "Tony, have you got anything open? I've got a feeling I'm going to need a drink."

Tony went to the cupboard and brought out a bottle of Bourbon and a glass for everyone at the table. Mike declined and reached into his bag and brought out a file.

"Both Mark and Lilly — Darren's wife — expressed some concerns about Lucas," Mike told him. "Specifically, regarding his aggressive behaviour, and I was asked to look into him." He pressed a hand onto the file, and continued, "I'm afraid Jonathan, that what I've found is serious and quite disturbing."

"Jesus..." Jonathan sighed out, and he took a big sip of his drink.

Mike opened the file. "I always start my investigation by following the Target's movements. It allows me to learn their patterns so that I know when I can safely enter their place of work or residence, in order to gather information."

"Right," Jonathan said, "so why am I looking at a load of photos of my daughter and grandson?"

"Because her movements are his movements," Mike replied. Jonathan looked confused, and Mike clarified, "Lucas has been following Ava."

"You what?" Jonathan replied with concern.

"See here?" Mike showed him a zoomed in image. "That's him in his van watching her when she went to the shops on Thursday the fourteenth, and here are some others." He showed Jonathan more photographs of Ava either alone or with Jacob, just going about her life, and in all of them Lucas was there in the background watching her. Jonathan felt sick.

Mike continued, "These photographs have been taken over the last four weeks while I've been doing my surveillance. I obviously cannot say when this started, whether it's as a result of Mark coming back into Ava's life, or whether it's been happening for some time — but he appears to know what he's doing. She's never seen him," he confirmed.

"Didn't see you either, did she?" Jonathan replied bitterly.

"That's the job," Mike replied, unfazed.

Jonathan took another sip of his drink and thought for a moment. "Right. Well, we've learned recently that he's a bit of a loose cannon, but it's over now. I'll talk to Ava and we'll see about getting a restraining order."

"That's not the worst of it," Mark said, and Jonathan could see that he was concerned.

Mike continued, "I gained entry to Lucas' residence and workshop. He does everything cash in hand, no taxes. I also found links to other coastal villages and I tracked his movements. Since leaving Ireland eight years ago he's moved from place to place, only really staying for a year at the most," he told him. "It's always the same; bar work, boats, carpentry — always cash in hand. Always moving on before questions are asked. He appears to have stayed in Clovelly much longer than anywhere else, but I put that down to..."

"Ava," Jonathan interrupted. "He's stayed because of Ava."

"Yes. I believe so," Mike confirmed, then he paused. "Jonathan, this next part is the most concerning. I need you to be prepared," Mike said firmly.

Jonathan sighed, put his head in his hands and whispered, "Fuck me," to nobody in particular. Then he looked at Mike and nodded for him to continue.

Mike pulled out a photo of two driving licenses, both had Lucas' face on them.

"What am I looking at here?" Jonathan asked.

"I found both of these driving licenses concealed in his place of residence. Look at the names." Mike instructed.

Jonathan did as he was asked and he read them aloud, "Lucas O'Connor and Jamie O'Connor?"

Mike then handed him images of two birth certificates. "He had these too. Look at the names — the date of birth as well," he instructed again.

Jonathan looked and saw the same two names — Jamie and Lucas O'Connor with the same date of birth. "What am I looking at here?" Jonathan asked, confused. "Are they fakes?"

"No, they're real," Mike answered. "Lucas and Jamie are two separate people."

"So, what is this?" Jonathan asked more urgently.

"The birth certificates are registered in Dublin," Mike told him, "so that's where I went. That's where I found these." He pulled out a copy of a death certificate and a newspaper cutting.

Jonathan looked closely at both. The certificate had the name Lucas O'Connor on it, and from the dates he could see that he was seventeen years old when he died. He shook his head and picked up the newspaper article. There was a photograph of two boys — two Lucas' — much younger, but it was still him. Only not just him, the photo was of Jamie and Lucas O'Connor — twin brothers. According to the article they had gone swimming in a lake on a hot day, and they got into difficulty. Jamie was rescued, but Lucas drowned.

Jonathan put the paper down and looked at Mike. "For the purpose of absolute clarity... because I've got to tell you I am having difficulty taking in what I'm seeing here. You need to tell me in black and white what all this means."

Mike cleared his throat. "Jamie and Lucas were identical twins, but from the information I gathered they were very different people. Lucas was the friendly, happy-go-lucky type, whereas Jamie had more of an edge. He was quick to anger, and he got into trouble, but Lucas kept him from going too far — but then he died, and Jamie took it very badly," Mike said calmly. "He spent time in a young offenders' facility, where it seems he went from bad to worse. He didn't go to prison as an adult, but he was into some bad stuff with some bad people. When it looked like the trouble was coming to his doorstep he fled to England. Once here he took on Lucas' identity — right down to his character, but from what I'm hearing now, he's struggling to maintain it, and Jamie — who he really is — is starting to come out," Mike said, still calm.

Jonathan took it all in, nodding slowly then he asked, "Is he dangerous?"

"I'm not a psychiatrist," Mike replied, "but I do profile people — I know people. Violence against women isn't evident in his past. If anything, he is more likely to be a danger to himself, and possibly to someone he thought was standing in his way." The whole table turned to look at

Mark, but he didn't look surprised — he's already heard this.

Mike continued, "However, I wouldn't want to completely rule out the possibility that he could harm your daughter, at this stage."

Jonathan let out a deep breath. He got up, downed the rest of his drink, turned to Mike and shook his hand. "Thank you for doing this, Mike. Excuse me please, gents, I need some air."

They let Jonathan sit out on the balcony undisturbed for half an hour, but then Mark joined him.

"Darren and Mike had to go, they said to say goodbye," Mark said to him.

"Right," Jonathan replied. "Not working yourself, today?"

"Not today. The rest of the week, yes. I've actually got a lot on this week," Mark replied.

"That's good," Jonathan told him sincerely.

"Jonathan, I'm sorry that we ambushed you like this... that we've put this burden on you," Mark told him genuinely.

"Don't be," Jonathan replied. "I needed to know this. She does too — not just yet mind you. I'm glad she's staying with us right now, that's for sure."

"Why is she with you?" Mark asked, concerned.

"Oh... she's waiting for the landlord to change the locks at hers. She'll go back then," Jonathan told him.

"What happened? Was the break-up that bad?" Mark asked him.

"Look, Mark. I'm not comfortable discussing my daughter's life behind her back. There's been enough of that," he said firmly. "What just went on in there, that's different, but

I'm sure she'll tell you herself anyway, so let's just leave it at that."

"I understand," Mark replied, and he handed one of the glasses of bourbon, that he'd brought out with him to Jonathan and sat down next to him.

"El and I have been watching you two, you know. The way you are with each other. It just seems so natural," Jonathan told him. "When Ava told us everything we were surprised, but we understood. Half the women on the street were in love with you back in the day. I could see how it happened. You're still a handsome man — I don't mind saying — and she's..."

"She's perfect," Mark answered for him.

"I think so," Jonathan replied, smiling. "Still, I have always wondered about something."

"Go on," Mark urged cautiously.

"Did it not ever feel strange being with someone exactly the same age as your own daughter?" Jonathan asked.

Mark let out a slight chuckle. "Hmmm... well, honestly, I never really thought about her age," he admits. "It had been almost ten years since I'd last seen her, so when she appeared on my doorstep, it was like meeting her for the first time, and she just blew me away," Mark said in awe. "She was so easy to talk to, and before I knew it, we were flirting and then — well, you know what then."

"I know as much as I need to know, thanks," Jonathan replied.

"She's just so different to Hattie that at times it was hard to imagine that they were even friends, let alone the same age," Mark told him honestly.

"She's always been an old soul," Jonathan said lovingly.

They both sat quietly for a moment, taking a sip from their glasses, then Mark said, "I'm planning to ask her if she wants to bring Jacob to me this weekend. Tom and Mary are taking Hattie and the boys on holiday, so, if there was ever a time when she could come here and not worry about seeing them — this is it," he said, then he paused and cleared his throat and continued, "And under the circumstances it might be good for her to get away for a bit."

"Yes. Yes, it would," Jonathan replied. "No doubt she'll say no to begin with, but I'll help to persuade her. It isn't this place that she has a problem with, just a few of the people in it," he said, and then he took another sip of his drink. "Then I'll talk to El about how we go about tackling this. I'd appreciate it if you didn't say anything to her yet," he added.

"I don't plan to. This is why I came to you first," Mark agreed.

They sat silently for a while and then Jonathan asked, "Did Ava ever tell you how my parents met?"

"No, I don't think she did," Mark replied.

So, Jonathan started his story. "It was a Saturday morning and my dad was walking down the High Street, and as he approached the fishmongers, he heard this young woman bellowing about being ripped off," he chuckled. "Giving the shop assistant hell, she was. Dad braced himself as he heard the voice coming closer — he was ready to meet some battle axe-type. Instead, out walked this beautiful young woman," Jonathan said smiling. "And as she came out, she saw an elderly lady waiting to cross the road, and she instantly switched from angry to caring and practically stopped the traffic to help this old dear across, she did." Jonathan laughed at the story he'd heard so many times that it felt like he'd been there. "Then she walked right back over, shouted at the fishmonger again, and then walked towards my dad, and as she passed him, she smiled at him," Jonathan said fondly, "and my dad was smitten from that moment on. He followed her home and asked her out, and two weeks later he proposed."

"That's lovely," Mark replied genuinely.

"I think so," Jonathan said smiling. "She was eighteen, he was twenty-two and not really looking to settle down, but he knew he had to be with her." Jonathan took another sip of his drink and asked, "I assume you know who inherited Mae Taylor's smile?"

Mark smiled knowingly and replied, "I think I have a good idea."

Both men were smiling and quietly sipping their drinks. Then Jonathan turned to Mark and said, "You're going to look after her this time, aren't you?" It wasn't a question.

"I didn't want to lose her in the first place," Mark replied. Then he drank the rest of his drink and said his goodbyes, leaving Jonathan to sit alone once more. To sit alone, trying to figure out how the hell things could be fixed this time.

29

I'm driving to London. I can't quite believe I'm doing it, but I am. Mark called on Tuesday to ask if I'd bring Jacob to him this weekend. He told me Hattie and the boys are away with Mary and Tom, so there's no chance of bumping into them. He also suggested that Darren and Lilly would love to see me and meet Jacob, and perhaps we could all have dinner on Saturday night — tomorrow night. My initial reaction was "no," but he asked me to think about it. Then Dad came back on Wednesday night after seeing Uncle Tony, and he just kept telling me that it was a good idea.

On Thursday, I told Mark about breaking up with Lucas and about what had happened. I felt that as Jacob's dad he should know. I was still feeling guilty and had expected him to be annoyed, but he was understanding. There was no anger in him, but I did sense concern. He suggested again that London could be a good option — it was "good timing," he said. He sounded just like my dad, and if I didn't know any better, I'd say they were conspiring. So, I agreed. I couldn't avoid my home town forever, nor could I expect

Mark to always travel to Clovelly, and if the people I don't want to see are miles away — then why not.

I decided to call Carolyn to see if I could visit her and Cooper, and as soon as I heard her voice, I realised just how much I've missed both her and that crazy mutt. I told her about Jacob, and she insisted that we spend a night with her. So that's why I'm travelling there today — Friday, instead of tomorrow morning. It's a win, win really. I get to spend time with the one person in London that didn't turn on me, and I'll be there early in the morning on Saturday to see more of Mark, without having to get up ridiculously early.

I finally pull up outside Carolyn's house mid-afternoon and I sit outside for a bit while Jacob sleeps. It's been a five-hour drive and he's chosen the last thirty minutes of the journey to sleep. At least he's been content. Driving with a miserable one year old is not fun. My stomach has been churning the entire time. I'm nervous and excited. I'm nervous about seeing Darren and Lilly. Lilly will probably be OK if our last meeting was anything to go by, but Darren. Darren is Mark's best friend, they're like brothers, and I'm not sure he'll be as forgiving of me.

Then there's Mark. Lucas is gone now. It may be barely a week since I ended things, but given how it ended I don't feel like I owe him anything anymore. If something happens with Mark this weekend, then I'm not going to fight it. I'm in love with him and I'm pretty certain that he's in love with me too. I'm going to be staying in the house where it all began, socialising with his friends like we did when we were together, and I made sure to pack my best lingerie. In fact, I know that something will happen with Mark this weekend, and I'm nervous... and very excited.

I decide I can't leave it much longer, so I disturb Jacob and knock on Carolyn's door. I hear Cooper barking, and when she opens the door, he jumps at me and tries to lick me all over. I push him down as I'm not sure how he'll be with Jacob, but it's good to know he's missed me too. Carolyn embraces me and then gushes over Jacob, who would normally be a bit overwhelmed, having just been woken, but it seems he's as taken with Cooper as I am.

We spend the afternoon catching up. I brought her a lemon drizzle cake that I made earlier in the week, and after eating a bit too much we decide to take Cooper out for an early walk. Jacob is in the pushchair and Carolyn and I link arms as we walk. It's nice to be walking around my home town again, and I almost get lost in the familiarity of everything, when she suddenly sighs and says, "My sister is getting worse."

"Oh, Carolyn, I'm so sorry to hear that," I tell her, giving her arm a squeeze.

"I've decided that I need to move in with her. I'm going to sell up, or rent the place out — I've not decided yet, but it's got to be done," she tells me, then she pauses for a moment to collect herself. "I can't take Cooper with me," she says, close to tears.

"Oh no!" I reply and I feel my own tears forming. I know how much she loves that dog and the thought of him being given away is just heart breaking.

"Ava, will you take him?" she asks.

"Me?" I ask in surprise. I love Cooper and have looked after him a lot in the past, but I've never really thought about having a dog of my own.

"Yes. You told me yourself that you predominantly work from home with the writing, and if you're baking in the tea rooms... Well, it's not like you're there all day every day, and you always go out for walks with this little chap. I think you have the perfect set up for a dog, actually," she says. "Cooper already knows and loves you. You love him too, don't you?" she asks hopefully.

"Yes, of course, I do."

"So, what's stopping you?" she asks eagerly.

"Well... I guess I'd better check with my landlord, I didn't really look at the part about pets in the contract. Here..." I move for her to take the pushchair. "I'll text him now."

By the time we get back to Carolyn's it's dinner time and I have a reply from my landlord, Curtis, telling me that he's absolutely fine with pets. He's also confirmed that the locks have been changed and the new keys are with my parents — which is a massive relief. I tell Carolyn what Curtis has said and she immediately bursts into tears.

"So, you'll do it then? You'll take him back with you on Sunday?" she asks, and I agree. I guess I'm now the proud owner of a dog.

We eat and then bath Jacob together, and after not really napping all day, he pretty much crashes as soon as I sit down with him. When I join Carolyn downstairs, I find a nice glass of wine waiting for me. I welcome it and soon realise why it's there — she wants to get me to open up about Mark.

"So, you're going to be staying at his, tomorrow?" she asks, smirking.

"Yes..." I reply, giving her a pointed look. "You know, we have spent the majority of weekends together for the last month?" I tell her.

"Yes, but he wasn't sleeping in your house and you still had a boyfriend," she says, still smirking.

"And your point is?" I ask, already knowing exactly what her point is.

"It's his point I'm thinking about, actually. His point in you, to be specific."

"Carolyn!" I squeal, practically spraying wine everywhere.

"What?" she replies laughing and giving me an innocent look. "You're in love with him. It sounds like he's in love with you. You're adults, you're going to be alone — save for Jacob..." she leans into me and asks, "Are you actually going to try and make me believe that you've not thought about it?"

"Carolyn... it's pretty much all I've thought about since I saw him again," I tell her, but then I hesitate, and she notices.

"So, what's the problem?" she asks.

"Honestly, I'm scared," I reply, sipping my wine.

"That's natural, there's been a lot of hurt—"

"That's not why I'm scared. Honestly, you should see him, he's all sculpted and muscular and looking better than he already did! And me... I've had a baby."

"Ava, come on. You look fantastic," she admonishes me.

"Well, thanks... but—"

"But what?" she asks eagerly.

"What if I'm different... you know... down there?" I point down to my crotch to emphasise what I'm talking about and she bursts out laughing.

I let her laugh it out for a moment, even though I'm being completely serious. There were no real complications with Jacob's birth, it was vaginal, and there was no intervention. I never had any complaints from Lucas, but he'd not slept with me pre-childbirth. It seems like a legitimate thing to be concerned about to me, but she's still laughing at me.

"Carolyn, come on, I'm being serious," I implore her, whilst trying not to laugh along with her infectious giggle.

"Oh, sweetheart. It's been a while for me, but I do remember having children. It's a muscle, it firms back up and you're young," she tells me. "To be quite honest, I think that he is going to be so eager to get back in there, that even if you have changed, he'll be too preoccupied to notice," she says bluntly and then she laughs some more.

"Well, thank you, but on that note, I think this conversation is over," I tell her, and we both laugh again.

We talk some more about what I've been up to in Clovelly. Like everyone else she tells me that I'm strong, that I've done well, but I've honestly never felt that way. I just did what I had to; I couldn't fall apart. Well, I did for a while, but it's a luxury that you can't afford when you have a baby. Besides, my love for Jacob made me strong and it gave me a sense of purpose like nothing ever has before.

Carolyn tells me more about her sister and she's right, she can't take Cooper with her. She really is going to have her hands full with her care, and as her children are off on their own adventures, they're not going to be able to take him on. I just hope this City dog can learn to love life by the sea.

We head to bed around ten and I sleep well for the first time all week. I'm not sure if it's being back at my true home, or being far away from where Lucas is. I just feel at peace here, and I wake in the morning feeling refreshed — even though Jacob woke up twice in the night. I receive a message from Mark at around eight O'clock telling me to come over whenever I'm ready, and my body becomes a nervous and excited mess again. I've made sure to put on my most 'unmumsy' underwear this morning, just in case.

I'm a bundle of nerves as I park up in Mark's street. It's been a long time since I was last here but the memory of what was said is still with me. Luckily, I manage to park fairly close to his house as my car is full. I carry Jacob to his door, my stomach churning with nerves, and as I reach for the doorbell the door opens — he'd been watching for us.

"Hello, you two," he says, reaching out to hug us both. As we hug, I kiss him on the cheek without thinking and then I realise what I've done and step back, embarrassed, but Mark only smiles at me.

"Do you want to take him while I fetch the things from the car?" I ask him.

"No, you two come in and get warm, I'll go," he says.

I walk into his house, it's just like I remember. I look at the sofa where it all began so passionately, and then into the kitchen where my heart broke into a million pieces. I take a deep breath and push away the sad memories, trying instead to focus on the happier ones. Mark comes back in with our bag over one shoulder, Jacob's travel cot over the over, a high chair tucked under an arm, and a big smile on his face.

"Ava... do I want to know why there is a big cage in the boot of your car?" he asks, laughing.

"Ah, yes," I laugh in response. We put Cooper's cage in the boot ready for tomorrow to make sure it fits. "It seems that I now have a dog."

"You do? Since when?" he asks, still amused.

"Since yesterday. Or tomorrow, technically. Carolyn can't keep Cooper anymore and she's asked me to take him back to Clovelly."

"That's lovely," he says looking genuinely happy for me.

He shows us up to a spare room and I get Jacob's travel cot set up while he plays with him downstairs. The door to Mark's room is open and I peek in as I pass, and I can't help but smile thinking about the things that we got up to in there. I head downstairs and we spend the morning playing with Jacob, who is loving getting stuck into Mark's nonchild-proof house. I'm just thankful he doesn't have as many ornaments as Carolyn does, because I was on edge the entire time, worrying about him breaking something.

After lunch we decide to head out for a walk so that Jacob can have a nap. I really have missed the bustle of London, and I've definitely missed the boutiques and cafés that Crouch End has to offer. We stop at a little independent coffee shop and grab a drink to go, and I bring the cup to my nose to inhale the aroma — it smells heavenly.

"Don't ever tell my mum I said this, but I have missed good coffee," I smile while taking a sip. "Mum's coffee is probably the best in Clovelly, but it's not quite like this."

Mark smiles and takes a quick look at Jacob. "He's asleep," he tells me. "Do you want to sit?"

I nod and we head over to a bench by a little green. I position Jacob's chair in front of me so that I can keep an eye on him, because I've still not quite shaken off all of the 'what ifs' after last Saturday night. Mark sits close to me, we're touching, and my body instantly warms.

"So, I know what made you break up with Lucas when you did," he says, "but you mentioned that you were going to do it anyway... why was that?" he asks innocently, taking a sip of his drink.

I give a little laugh because Mark knows exactly why I was planning to break up with Lucas. There is no denying the tension that has been surrounding us this last month, you can practically touch it when we say our goodbyes each Sunday. I wonder for a moment whether to toy with him and keep him guessing, but then it occurs to me that we've already wasted enough time being apart.

So, I take a deep breath and say, "I tried to make it right, but I realised that I wasn't in love with him." I look right at Mark and tell him, "I'm in love with you."

In a split second his lips are on mine. His kiss is urgent and I welcome it with the same need. He puts his hands in my hair and holds me in place as he pulls back to rest his forehead against mine.

He looks me right in the eyes and says, "I have never stopped being in love with you. Not for a single moment."

I feel the tears start to fill my eyes and we continue to kiss, until a group of teenagers walk past and shout, "Get a room!"

We pull apart, giggling and he stands up and reaches for my hand, "Let's head back," he says.

We walk back hand in hand, and at a much quicker pace than we left, and I'm very thankful that it's not a long walk. I put Jacob in the kitchen, leaving him sleeping in the pushchair and take off my coat and boots, and when I turn around Mark is looking at me with such intensity that I'm instantly aroused.

"How long will he sleep for?" he asks me.

"Hopefully long enough," I say, smiling in reply.

We walk towards each other and start kissing passionately, there's no gentle exploratory kisses this time — not like the last first time. We already know each other's bodies and we know exactly what we want. He picks me up and carries me to the sofa and we instantly start to pull at each other's clothes. I finally get my hands on his body and it feels as good as it looks.

"I like this," I tell him leaning down to kiss his chest.

He pulls my top off and buries his head in my chest. "I've missed this." He cups my breasts and I giggle and squirm away.

Mark pulls back looking concerned. "What's wrong?" he asks.

I wrap my arms around my chest and tell him, "I can't

quite get my head around these being sexual while Jacob's feeding, so—"

"Say no more," he says smiling. "I know other ways to torture you."

He starts kissing lower down, making his way down to my stomach. He pulls at my trousers and continues to kiss lower and lower, and my desperate body practically starts grinding against him. He pulls my underwear aside and smiles at me as he feels how wet I am for him.

"I don't want to ruin the moment, but do I need to get—"

"I have the implant now," I say, pre-empting what he was going to ask.

"Good," he says, "I want to feel every part of you."

He unbuttons his trousers and pulls them down, taking his boxers with them. He is as ready as I am, and I quickly pull him down and wrap my legs around him because I can't wait any longer. It occurs to me for a moment, that even though Lucas is younger and bigger, my body never responded to him like this. I never wanted him as much as I want Mark. Then all thoughts of Lucas disappear as Mark pushes inside me.

It feels amazing and I squeeze myself around him so that I can feel him even more. We fit together perfectly and we both groan at the sensation of finally being back where we belong. We kiss hard and deep, our tongues entwining as he continues to thrust inside me. I thrust back against him hard, letting him know that I need him deeper and faster, and he instantly responds.

Neither of us can hold out for long and after a few minutes we cry out our release together. Then we lay there kissing and panting for a few minutes, completely unable to stop smiling at each other. He looks at me seriously and says, "Ava Swan, you are still completely perfect."

Any fears I had vanish and I kiss him deeply, but after a while I pull back and let out a sigh.

"What are you thinking?" he asks, as he runs a finger gently along my cheek.

"I used to tell myself that we worked so well together... that it was this good between us because we were in our own bubble," I tell him. "That it wasn't real life because we were a secret and didn't really have to deal with other people," I pause to kiss him. "I think that's why I kept trying to make things feel right with Lucas. I had Jacob, and he's always been my priority. So, you know... it was bound to be different," I say shrugging. "I just thought it was normal, but the moment I saw you in the kitchen that day, I felt things that I hadn't felt for a long time — since I was last with you," I admit, and he kisses me. "Leaving you hurt so much," I tell him, pushing the pain that memory brings away. "So, I think I just eventually made myself believe it, because it was easier to accept than the truth."

"What was the truth?" Mark asks, running a finger along the side of my body and making me shiver.

"The truth was that I was never going to love anyone as much as I love you," I confess and then we kiss some more until Mark eventually pauses.

"Ava... I never told you this, but you were my world. When you walked away, I fell apart," he says sadly. "I should have let you know that I had done something to stop them — I planned to, but you were right that day — I was pathetic. When you said that to me it changed things and I acted," he admits. "I thought I'd get myself sorted before reaching out to you. Then I found out that you'd left. I tried to contact you, but your number was dead and you'd disappeared from social media. I wanted to go to Clovelly, but Darren convinced me that I needed to respect your choice to go... so I did. I never stopped loving you though. I never stopped missing you," he tells me sincerely.

"We made a real mess of things didn't we... living in our bubble?" I say closing my eyes, and as I do, he strokes my cheek, and I open them again to look into those blue eyes.

"Then I guess it's a good job that I happen to think that we work pretty well in the real world," he says. "The three of us together... it feels right. It feels complete."

"I feel that too, but we're still keeping secret."

"We can change that whenever you're ready," he says. "It won't be the same as last time, I promise you that."

"No, it won't," I say firmly. "I'm sorry to say this because they're still your children, but I no longer care what they think."

"I don't blame you for that, what they did was unforgivable," he says honestly. "You left to save my relationship with them, but what they did to you broke it anyway. I love them, obviously, but it's never been the same."

"I'm sorry," I tell him, and I kiss his forehead.

"Don't be. It was their doing, not yours," he tells me. "And I mean it, if they do just one thing to upset you, or make you worry about Jacob and I will cut them off."

"Oh, you don't need to do that," I tell him, smiling. "I'm not the same girl they knew then. There's not much more they can do to me, and if I thought for a second that they'd do anything to Jacob... I mean, I know they wouldn't harm him," I admit. "But if they do anything to try to sabotage his life in any way, I will go full Tiger Mum and kill them."

We both laugh at that, although I am a little serious. I will not sit back and just take their crap this time.

"Does that mean you want to tell them?" he asks.

"Soon, I guess, but not quite yet," I say, stroking his chest. "You know, I really do like this new you. I liked the old you too, mind you," I tell him lovingly. I look up at him and I can see from his eyes that we both want the same thing. He lowers himself onto me and starts kissing me again, but then I hear noises from the kitchen signalling that Jacob is now waking up. I groan a little and say, "Speaking of being a mum."

I kiss him again, shuffle out from under him, put on my clothes and go to greet our son.

30

We spend the rest of the afternoon playing with Jacob and being as close to each other as possible, touching as much as possible, and kissing as much as possible — when Jacob isn't getting into trouble, that is. It's lovely and it feels natural. In truth, I'm not in a rush to let his family know, but that's because I'm not especially keen on having them in my life again, but I know it has to happen eventually. They are part of Mark's life — Jacob's too — and being with Mark, really being with him, means being in the open. I may not be relishing the idea, but I don't fear it. Not this time.

"I've been meaning to ask you..." Mark says, snapping me out of my thoughts. "It was through Carolyn that I found out that you'd left London, and she made it clear that she knew about us," he grimaces. "I always wondered what made you tell her and nobody else."

I burst out laughing and hide my face with my hands. "Oh my God! I'd forgotten about that," I tell him laughing.

"What?" Mark asks, laughing with me.

"Well... I didn't actually tell her," I say as I cringe at the memory. "She knew because it would seem that Vi — who lives in the house behind her — has an excellent view into her kitchen." I raise my eyebrows at him and watch in amusement as the penny drops.

"No!" he says, giving a full belly laugh. "She saw us?"

"Oh, yes."

"What did Carolyn say?" he asks, aghast.

"Let's just say she approved and leave it at that," I tell him, still laughing.

We carry on playing with Jacob who continues to ignore all of the toys that I brought for him in favour of Mark's stereo. Then I notice the time — it's quarter past three — Darren and Lilly are due to arrive at four.

"You seem nervous," Mark says.

"I am..." I pull my hair behind my ears and ask, "Does Darren hate me?"

He smiles at me and asks, "Why would you think that?"

"You mean other than the fact that I hid your baby from you for a year?" I look at him seriously, and continue, "You two are like brothers. You forgave me because you love me, but Darren's loyalty is to you."

"Darren had... let's say, strong feelings when Lilly told us — I won't lie, but Lilly defended you, and you know how much her opinion matters to him," he says genuinely.

"That doesn't sound reassuring," I say, hugging my knees into my chest a little.

"Darren knows that I was at my happiest with you and my lowest without you," he tells me. "Honestly, he just wants us to be happy. I assure you he bears you no ill will. He wants you to be happy and safe, just like I do."

"Safe?" I ask, confused. "Why would you say that?" I think I see Mark stutter a little, but he regains himself so quickly that I wonder if I imagined it.

"I just mean that he wants things to work out for us. You know, drama free," he says.

"Drama free? Hmmm... I don't think that's something we'll achieve," I reply, giving a shaky laugh.

"Perhaps not, but I know one thing for certain, I won't let you leave me this time," he tells me firmly, kissing me quickly before we have to intervene in Jacob's attempts to dismantle his stereo.

I'm still feeling nervous when Lilly and Darren ring the doorbell. I pick Jacob up and go to greet them with Mark. I don't really need to take him — he's happy playing, but it gives me something to hide behind. Lilly comes straight in for a hug, telling me how good it is to see me, but it's Darren's reaction that I'm watching for. I see him hug Mark, and some words pass between them that I don't catch. Mark gives him a big smile, which Darren responds to with what appears to be a knowing grin and slight head shake. I may not have any siblings of my own, but I've spent enough of my life around Ted and Will to gather that during their almost wordless interaction, Darren has figured out that we've had sex this afternoon.

Darren is still smiling when he turns his attention to me and I'm expecting to see it fade, but it doesn't.

"Ava," he says, reaching out to squeeze my shoulder, "I can't tell you how good it is to have you back."

I'm a little taken aback, to say the least, but I manage to smile and say, "It's good to see you again, Darren."

He nods and looks at Jacob. "My God, he really does look like you, Mark — poor sod," he exclaims, and we all laugh. "And not just the eyes like the others."

"He has Ava's smile," Mark adds affectionately.

"You think so?" I ask. I've never really thought about it. To me Jacob's smile is just his.

"He has something going for him, after all," Lilly adds innocently, and I give her a grateful smile.

It seems like old times — well, not quite old times — since we are sat on the floor engrossed with Jacob, as opposed to drinking copious amounts of alcohol. They came around early so that they could spend time with him before bedtime, and we are going to get a takeaway once he's asleep. I'm sure the wine will flow then, but right now, it's the conversation that is flowing. I feel a bit awkward when they ask me questions about Jacob's past, knowing that some of the information is new to Mark too — but I only ever sense genuine interest from them.

"So, how was the birth?" Lilly asks.

"You know, I never asked about that," Mark adds.

"Oh, well…" I feel guilty again now because Mark should've had the chance to be there. "I guess it was quite straightforward as far as unplanned home births go. I was thirty-eight weeks and two days pregnant and feeling really ready for him to just come out," I tell them. "I was living with my parents and I woke up that morning with a few pains, but nothing that made me think that the whole process had started. I decided to bake a cake because I was basically doing that every day at that point, and I was mixing some chocolate frosting when my waters broke." I laugh a little, at the memory. It really was such a shock. At first, I thought I'd wet myself, but I'm not going to tell them that.

"I called my mum as she was at the tea rooms," I continue, "and my friend Julia — who was also my doctor at the time. Everyone was telling me to relax because it was my first and it would take ages, but Julia said she'd come over to see how dilated I was before deciding if we should go to the hospital or not."

"You two are very close friends then?" Darren adds laughing.

"Ah, yes, she knows me very well." I smile, then continue, "Mum was with me while we were waiting for Julia, and I was starting to feel like things were happening, and naturally, Mum told me that I was overreacting." I roll my eyes at the memory. "When Julia arrived and examined me, she told me she could feel his head. So, we called for an ambulance and got prepared for him to come and he did — pretty quickly and before the ambulance arrived," I tell them, laughing a little. "We went to hospital, but everything was fine, and we were sent home a few hours later."

"Was it just your mum and Julia that were with you?" Mark asks, and I can see what he is thinking.

"Yes, it was... Lucas did come around," I say honestly. "We weren't together then and I'm still not sure how he knew that something was going on, actually..." I shake my head still puzzled by the memory. I never did remember to ask him about that. I'm sure I see Mark and Darren share a look, but I carry on thinking nothing of it. "I told him to go away," I continue, "and Julia swore at him a lot. Or maybe that was me... but either way he left. It was just Mum and Julia as Dad was out, but he joined us at the hospital and brought us home."

We continue to talk and play with Jacob some more, but after a while Darren and Mark disappear to the kitchen. Lilly seems completely taken with Jacob as we sit and play, and it occurs to me that I've never asked why she and Darren never had any children — but then I guess that's not my business. Jacob is clearly loving the extra attention and is very much enjoying passing the ball with Lilly on repeat. Lilly seems quite content too, but then she turns her attention to me.

"Mark mentioned a bit about the break-up with Lucas," she tells me. "He's a pretty imposing person, it must've been scary standing up to him like that?"

"Honestly, Lilly, I was so angry I didn't even think about it," I reply, just thinking about it has my heart racing again. "I actually think he was still too drunk to realise what was going on. I physically shoved him out and he didn't even react," I tell her. "My neighbour stayed with me until my parents came over — you know I really must go and see him; he was petrified..." I suddenly remember, and I laugh a little at that. Then I continue, "I didn't realise at the time that Lucas had just stayed there staring blankly at the door. The first I knew of it was when my dad arrived and told him that he had thirty-seconds to leave before he called the police. He left then."

"Have you seen him since?" she asks.

"No, I asked the landlord to change the locks. An emergency locksmith would've cost a fortune, so we waited for an appointment and I've stayed with my parents all week," I tell her. "He has a key... so I didn't want to risk him coming in."

"That's understandable," Lilly says, "he certainly scared me."

"I've been keeping a low profile to be honest, because after my shouting and Jeff coming to help, everyone knows about it," I say, with a wry smile. "I really am so sorry about that day."

"Don't be," she scolds me. "It wasn't your fault."

We sit together for a while longer — just the three of us as Mark and Darren are still in the kitchen. Lilly tells me a bit about what she's been up to while I've been away. Which includes more Golf sessions with Darren, which she's clearly not impressed about? She tells me that the only time she's enjoyed it is when I was there. We laugh a lot at the memory of that day, but then I realise what the time is.

"Well, this guy is going to be ready for his dinner soon," I say, rubbing Jacob's hair — it's getting long and he has his dad's curls. "I brought something with me, so I'll just go and reheat it," I tell her, and I get up and head to the kitchen.

As I walk in, I see Mark and Darren standing close and talking quietly. Whatever they're saying I cannot hear but it seems pretty intense, so I clear my throat to alert them to my presence.

"Sorry, I was just coming to warm up Jacob's dinner," I tell them apologetically.

They separate, but I see Darren giving Mark one final look of concern and the panic sets in — perhaps he isn't as happy about me being here as Mark let me believe. Then he looks at me and smiles before going to join Lilly and Jacob in the snug. Mark turns to me with his arms open and I walk towards him. He wraps them around me tightly and it starts to feel like it did when I left him — when he held me tight to try to stop me from going. I try to push those thoughts away. I don't want to think about that day.

"Is everything OK?" I ask. "I thought Darren was OK with me?" I add more quietly.

"He is," Mark tells me, pulling back so that he can kiss me. "That was just about a bit of joint business. Darren was just reminding me of some risks, that's all."

"But everything is OK?" I ask apprehensively.

"It will be," he says looking at me with such love and passion that I feel my knees go weak. "Trust me," he tells me.

"I do," I say and it's true, I really do. I trust him with my life.

We start kissing and it is so hard to pull myself out of his arms, but Jacob needs his dinner, so I pull away from his body but keep hold of his hand as I walk to the fridge.

"What will I be wearing tonight?" Mark laughs, as I take the container out.

Bedtime is a bit of a challenge tonight. It's another new setting for Jacob and another day of excitement and new faces. Eventually, he gives up and falls asleep in my arms and I ever so gently and slowly lower him into his travel cot, silently praying to the Gods of Sleep that he doesn't wake up. I've done it. He stays asleep so I quietly change out of my food-covered clothes and go downstairs to join the others.

Now it's starting to feel like old times. We eat, drink, and I sit on the sofa in Mark's arms. We never had to hide our relationship from these two, which is good because we can't stop looking at each other. I may be sitting against him but it's not enough, we touch and stroke each other constantly and when he whispers in my ear that he loves me, it sends tingles through my entire body.

By eleven, Lilly is a little worse for wear. I'm more or less sober having made my two glasses last, and Mark has been taking it steady too — for reasons I hope to find out soon. Darren decides that it's best to call it a night and calls a taxi, and I sit with Lilly while we wait — she's a truly lovely drunk and I can't help but laugh at her affectionately.

"You two are made for each other," she tells me, trying to look as serious as she can.

"I think so too," I say, and she leans in for a big hug. While her head is on my shoulder, she adjusts it a little so that she's against my ear and she whispers something that sends chills down my spine. I want to question her but it's too late, their taxi is here, and she's whisked away by Darren. We all say goodbye and when Mark closes the door, he looks at me with concern.

"What's wrong?" he asks.

"Lilly just said something that spooked me a bit," I say, wrapping my arms against myself for protection from the chill that I can't seem to shake. "I guess it was nothing really... she just told me to 'be safe' — that's all. I guess it was the way she said it and maybe because of everything that's happened."

"Yes, perhaps... she's also very drunk and cares about you a lot," he replies, making light of it and pulling me in close. "Shall we head upstairs?" he asks, looking at me darkly.

I smile cheekily, and say, "That sounds like a good idea, I'm really tired." I give a mock yawn and stretch out my arms for added emphasis.

He picks me up and puts me over his shoulder and I can't help but giggle like a schoolgirl. "Sleep can wait. I have other plans for you."

He picks up Jacob's monitor on the way and I feel the familiar glow that I have when I see him with Jacob. Even now, he's being a dad.

He takes me to his room and lowers me onto his bed, he holds himself above me and starts to undress me slowly. First, he rids me of my top and bra and then my trousers and underwear. He says nothing and barely touches me, except for his lips that are now on my neck. He traces kisses down my entire body, he kisses me between my breasts, without actually touching them and moves lower and lower at an agonisingly slow pace.

Then he's at my centre, but he pauses to look at me — to see the utter need in my face, before he starts — slowly at first, licking, kissing, nibbling, and holding me in place to stop me from moving away. He slips his fingers inside me, knowing exactly where to go. He pushes them in and out, firmly rubbing exactly the right spot as he picks up the pace with his tongue. I let out a loud moan and grab at his hair with one hand, and with the other I grasp onto his shoulder for support, as I feel my body losing control. Moments later it happens again — just like the first night. My release is hard, long and very wet, but this time I feel no embarrassment.

He moves up and kisses me, then smiles as he tells me, "I'm not going to be done with you until these sheets are soaked through."

I smile at his words that are all too familiar to me — just like he is, just like this is. Then, just like the first time we were in his bed I flip him over and sit on top of him.

He smiles, thinking that he knows what's going to happen, but I don't plan on taking him in my mouth right now. Instead I lower myself onto him, taking him into me deeply. I squeeze him tight and he groans. I lower my shoulders and lean forward so that we're face to face and tell him, "I'm never going to be done with you. Not ever," and then I start riding him, fast and hard.

As he gets close, he pulls me into him, grasping me firmly so that our entire bodies are rubbing together. My own climax starts building again with the change of position, so he holds back until I'm finished, and then cries out as he reaches his limit too.

I collapse on him and we stay like that for a few minutes, breathing heavily. I reluctantly slide off him, go to the ensuite, and then quickly climb back into his arms. Then, true to form, I hear Jacob on the monitor, so I get up and slip my knickers back on. I know Jacob will need a quick feed before he nods back off, so I grab Mark's shirt as it'll give me easy access.

I sit on the bed in the dark with Jacob against me and

Mark quietly comes through the door. He sits behind me and rubs my back and I gently shuffle backwards so that I'm leaning against him. Lucas saw me feeding Jacob all the time, but he was never really a part of it. Right now, Mark is right here with both of us, looking down over my shoulder at his content little boy.

"How do you do it?" he whispers.

"Do what?" I ask.

"Go from Sex Goddess to Earth Mother in a matter of seconds?" he asks in admiration.

I turn to face him and see that he is looking at me with complete adoration, but I don't know how to respond, so I just kiss him and then turn my attention back to our son.

We stay like that until he's settled again and then sneak back to Mark's room. At first, we just hold each other, but then our bodies yearn for each other once more and we gently make love. I fall asleep in his arms and that's where I wake up when I hear Jacob chatting to himself at seven O'clock the next morning. Mark gets up first and greets him, picking him up from his cot then sitting with him on the bed. I follow him in and put on some pyjamas before joining my family for an early morning snuggle, feeling more content and at peace than I ever have before.

31

I barely eat any breakfast because I'm already missing Mark and I haven't even left yet. As if sensing what I'm thinking, he asks me, "What are your plans for tomorrow?"

"I don't have to do much, actually," I reply. "I did a lot of baking at my parent's last week and I was having trouble sleeping, so I made a good start on a magazine project that's due on Friday. So other than getting Cooper settled, it will be a lazy Monday for me."

"Have I told you how proud I am of you?" he gushes. "The way you put your life back together... after my daughter tore it apart," he adds more remorsefully.

"Well, I had to, I don't just live for me," I reply seriously, looking at Jacob. "Besides, Hattie didn't get to any of my freelance contacts so there was no damage done there," I add more lightly.

"Hmmm... still—"

"What were you going to say about Monday? Are you busy?" I ask, interrupting him. I know he wanted to say more but I hate the fact that we're going into dark territory when I'm already feeling sad about leaving him.

"I am actually, I'm at a client's all week," he replies.

"You're working a lot more at the moment," I tell him. "Did you get bored of semi-retirement?" I tease.

"I did after you left," he says, giving me a sad smile. "Anyway, it makes sense right now — I have another one to look after," he says ruffling Jacob's hair. "I'm asking because I was going to suggest that you stay tonight and you can just head off tomorrow morning when you're ready... if you'd like to?" he asks, smiling hopefully.

"Another night with you?" I ask, smiling seductively. "I think I could be persuaded."

"Well, given that we have this one to look after," he says, nodding to Jacob, "I think you have to agree now without persuasion... and then I get to show you why you made the right choice later," he smiles just as seductively.

"Hmmm... there is just one thing."

"And that is?" he asks, still smiling.

"How do you feel about having a big Labrador bouncing around your house?" I ask him with a grin. "I need to pick Cooper up from Carolyn today. She'll have been psyching herself up for it so I can't really postpone her."

"As long as I don't have to face Carolyn again that's absolutely fine," he says, laughing nervously.

"Oh, and speaking of looking after Jacob..." he heads to a drawer and pulls out an envelope. "I opened up a savings account for him. It can be accessed instantly in case of emergency — only by me at the moment. I'll need to get you to a bank to set you up as a signatory, but I've put all of the online login details in here so you can still get into it if you need to," he says, handing it over to me.

"Oh, well, on behalf of Jacob, thank you." I tell him

gratefully. "I shall have to lock these details away then, won't I."

We spend another lovely morning all together and after lunch I take Jacob with me to see Carolyn. She opens the door and I can see that she has been crying.

"Oh, Carolyn..." I hug her with one arm as I'm holding Jacob. "Are you sure you want to do this?" I ask her.

"Yes. It's the right thing," she says, trying to gather herself back together. "Even without the move, I can't really give him what he needs. He'll be happier with you. Wherever you end up living," she adds more casually as she steps aside to let me in.

"Where I end up living?" I ask.

"Yes. I can see by the glow surrounding you that you had a fun night," she says smirking at me. It's impossible not to smile back at her, which only confirms her suspicions. "So, I guess you're not going to have a long-distance relationship forever?"

"Honestly, Carolyn, you always manage to get me thinking about the things that hadn't even crossed my mind yet." I give her a fake scowl, it's not possible to ever be angry with her. "I'm just living in the moment for now, we can tackle the future another day. My brain can only cope with so much." My brain, and my heart too.

We have tea together and some more of my cake, and I think Cooper can sense her sadness because he doesn't leave her side. I know this is breaking her heart and it breaks mine just thinking about what this is doing to her.

"Carolyn, you can come and visit him whenever you want to, I hope you know that?" I tell her. "And now I've done this trip once, it's not so bad... I can bring him to you for visits too."

"I'd like that, thank you," she smiles at me. "It's strange how things work out isn't it?" she says.

"How so?" I ask.

"You went away from this place broken and I thought you'd go off and find some happiness — but that didn't happen, did it?" she asks me.

"I've not exactly spent the last year in a state of depression," I reply laughing.

"No, I'm not saying that. You built yourself up again. You became a mother, and I can see that it suits you completely, by the way," she says, smilingly adoringly. Then she continues, "You were content, maybe you even thought that you truly were happy, but it's clear that your happiness was always waiting for you here, wasn't it? You never took your heart with you. You never took it back from Mark."

A tear falls silently down my face and I sigh, and say, "You are a very wise woman Carolyn, and I miss you very much." I lean in to kiss her and we both have a little cry.

When it's time to go she holds onto Cooper while I put Jacob into his seat and then he jumps happily into the cage in the boot.

"This isn't goodbye... you're not rid of me yet young man," she says to him as she fastens the cage door. "Now, you be a good boy for your new mummy."

With that said she closes the boot, and I'm standing here in tears just watching how brave she is. Cooper became her companion when she lost her husband and now, she's letting him go. I know it's right, it is for the best, but I'm utterly humbled by her bravery. We hug one last time and then she goes into her house, unable to watch us leave.

I get back to Mark's with Jacob and Cooper in tow and as soon as he opens the door, I burst into tears again. I'm crying because of Carolyn, I'm crying because of Cooper,

I'm crying because of the time that I lost with Mark, and his time with Jacob — time that I took from him. I'm crying because of all the pain, loss and love that I've felt over the last two years, and I'm crying because now I can. It's safe to let it all out now. It's safe to acknowledge all of it. Because Carolyn is right, my happiness is wherever Mark is, and I never took my heart back from him. Now I know all of this, now that I know that there is no other love for me. I'm crying because I'm scared to death of losing him again. Because if he goes, my heart will go with him.

After a little while I get myself back together and I try to explain to Mark as best as I can where my emotional outburst has come from. Like always, he understands. He lost me too and his pain was as real as mine.

We take the rest of the afternoon easy; Jacob is yet to nap so we go for a walk, bringing Cooper along too. I can't help but think about what Carolyn said about living arrangements, but it feels a bit too soon to actually have that conversation with Mark. We may have picked up where we left off, but we have some hurdles to overcome too — the same hurdles as last time.

Thankfully, Jacob goes to bed a little easier than last night, and it's a nice, mild evening, so I sit on the patio sipping some wine while Cooper runs around the garden. Mark is cooking tonight, and it smells delicious. I could definitely get used to this. Tomorrow's drive home was always going to be long. Jacob needs breaks so I can't do the whole journey in one go anyway, but they'll be needed even more now that Cooper is with us too. Now, it's also the fact that I'm reluctant to leave that is making me dread the journey all the more. I knew that I was in love with Mark before I came here this weekend, but now I've allowed myself to acknowledge the true depth of my feelings, I just don't want to be away from him. I can't help but give a little laugh at the fact that I was so reluctant to come here, and now I don't want to leave.

We eat together, we sit together, and when we decide it's time to go upstairs, we make sure Cooper is settled, and, more importantly for Mark, that he cannot destroy anything. Then, as promised Mark is quick to show me why staying an extra night was definitely the right choice. Not that I ever had any doubt.

Mark's alarm wakes us at six and I turn to look at Jacob on the monitor, through my tired, bleary eyes. He woke a few times in the night but he is currently sleeping soundly. Mark rolls over and nuzzles into my neck.

"Shower with me?" he asks, sleepily.

Jacob is pretty consistent at waking at seven these days, but we bring his monitor into the bathroom — just in case. At first, we just stand holding each other, feeling the warm water rushing over us. We kiss, and then we proceed to have the best shower ever. An element of washing does actually take place, and afterwards Mark quickly dresses and takes Jacob's monitor downstairs, leaving me to dry my hair in peace. Once I'm done, I go to the spare room to dress and I see that Jacob is gone. This is something that would normally make me panic for a moment, but not here, not with Mark, and it's not long before I hear them both in the kitchen. Once I'm dressed, I walk down the stairs as quietly as possible, because I can hear them chatting away — Mark chatting, Jacob babbling — and I don't want to interrupt them. I peek around the corner and see Mark holding Jacob in his arms.

"I'm going to miss you and your mummy very much," he tells him. "I'll be seeing you very soon, and I love you both so much." He kisses him and Jacob giggles in return.

My heart completely melts watching them together, but then the guilt comes back. Mark doesn't ever mention what I did, but I honestly don't think I'm going to ever stop feeling guilty about keeping them apart for so long. My only relief is that at least Jacob won't remember it.

"Sorry to interrupt," I say, finally letting them know that I'm here.

Mark turns and smiles at me — I am going to miss him so much. "As much as it pains me, I have to go," he says, putting Jacob into his high chair. "What are your plans?"

"Eat, take Cooper for a walk and then head home," I tell him, but the word 'home' no longer seems to sit right. Home is with Mark.

"Make sure you let me know when you get back," he tells me.

"I will, but don't hold your breath. I've no idea how many times I'll need to stop," I say.

"My bed will feel very lonely tonight," he says sadly, kissing me.

I let out a deep breath. "Saying goodbye here. It's starting to feel too much like the last time," I tell him, shakily.

"It's nothing like last time," he says firmly. "I will be coming to you on Friday. You're not getting rid of me that easily."

"The last time wasn't exactly easy."

"No, it definitely wasn't," he agrees and kisses me deeply. I hold him tight, not wanting to let him go, but he starts to pull away saying, "I really have to go, we have a meeting first thing."

I know I have to let him leave, so I reluctantly release him. We both walk over to Jacob and without thinking I ask,

"Do you have a 'bye, bye' for Daddy, Jakie?" Jacob squeals in return and bangs his hands on his high chair.

"Daddy?" Mark asks, elated. "I thought you wanted to wait?"

"I... I honestly didn't think. It just felt right," I tell him sincerely.

"Thank you," he says, and he kisses me.

"There's no need to thank me, it's who you are," I tell him.

"God, I have to go," he groans.

"I know. Go. We'll talk later and I'll see you in four days... four long days," I say, pulling a sad face.

"I love you," he says, and he kisses me deeply. He then kisses Jacob and leaves for work.

We eat quickly, I tidy up, and then get all of our belongings together, remembering to put the information about Jacob's savings account into my suitcase. I put Jacob into his sling, and we head out for a walk with Cooper. While I'm out, I try to figure out how I'm going to get everything into the car. I decide the best approach is to put Cooper back in the garden, keep Jacob in the sling while I pack the car up, put Cooper in his cage, and then put Jacob in his car seat. That works. I can figure this dog and child thing out.

It is a long journey home, with three stops. Jacob sleeps a lot but also squeals at Cooper a lot, who is in return barking a lot. I just want to get home and get settled again, but I have no keys, so I need to go to my parents first to get the new ones. As I pull into their drive late in the afternoon, I message Mark to let him know that I'm back. I miss him so much already but I'm absolutely exhausted. It was a long drive, and I did not have much sleep this weekend. I smile at that though, it was a completely amazing weekend and I have four nights of relatively undisturbed sleep to recover, before seeing him again.

Mum is at the door before I get out and she gives me a hug before going to get Jacob out of his seat. Dad comes out a few minutes later and comes to meet Cooper, who is ridiculously excited to meet another new person.

"All right, sweetheart?" Dad asks, giving me a kiss. "You look tired."

"I am. It was a long drive and I'm definitely ready for a coffee."

"Come in then, love. We thought we'd cook dinner for you tonight," he tells me innocently.

"Oh," I say, and the memory of the last time they cooked for me comes flooding back. They haven't cooked for me since then. I look at my dad to try to see if I can figure out what he's thinking, but I can't, and that's not because it was an innocent offer and I'm over thinking it. I can't read him because he's wearing his mask, and a feeling of dread takes over me again.

32

Mum is fussing over Jacob and Dad is playing with Cooper, and once again we look like a picture-perfect, happy family. However, as amazing and helpful as my parents are, they don't tend to cook for me, not unless they have something to say.

"Do you want to ask me about Mark?" I ask, and I don't miss the quick look that they share.

"Do you want to talk about it, darling?" Mum asks looking up at me.

"That's not what I mean... dinner. You're cooking me dinner? I've been here a week and I've either cooked for you or we've had takeaway," I say. "No offence, but you don't tend to just cook for me unless there's a reason."

They say nothing but they glance at each other again.

"Oh, come on, just come out with it, please," I practically beg.

"OK," Mum says. "I'll take these two out, it's best you're not distracted."

"Well, that doesn't fill me with dread at all, Mum," I say slumping down on the sofa.

"I'll be back in a bit," she says, and she heads out with Jacob and Cooper.

It's just me and my dad now, so I look right at him and ask, "Do you not approve of me being with Mark? Because you're the one that was suggesting that I go to London in the first place."

"It's not about Mark," he says calmly, sitting down next to me and putting a grey file on the coffee table in front of us. "And as it happens, I do approve of him."

"Oh..." I wasn't expecting that. "So, what's going on?" I ask him apprehensively.

"Last week I visited Tony, as you know," he starts. "Only, when I got there, he wasn't alone. Mark was with him, as was his friend Darren and a colleague of his — of Darren's — that is."

I'm completely confused. "Why would Mark and Darren be at Uncle Tony's?" I ask him. As far as I'm aware Mark doesn't know my Godfather. "And more importantly, why would neither of you tell me about this?"

"This file here," Dad says pointing to the file on the coffee table, it looked inconspicuous before but now I'm not so sure. "It was given to me by Darren's colleague. He's a private investigator. A private investigator that Mark asked to look into Lucas."

"What?" I say utterly shocked. "Why?"

"Because of Lilly's gut feeling about him, and because of how Mark saw him treat you. He was worried," Dad says, with his own worry clearly visible too.

"Right, and it's been a week, and nobody has told me this, because?" I ask, feeling irritated.

"Because I asked him not to. Because I thought you had enough on your plate, and I just wanted you to have a nice weekend without worrying," he tells me sincerely.

I reach for the file, but he stops me. "Not yet, Ava," he says gently.

"I am not a child!" I protest.

"I know, but that doesn't stop the people that love you from wanting to protect you," he says more firmly.

"From what?" I ask, worried now. "Let me have that file, Dad."

"Not yet. Please let me explain and then we can sit and go through it together. It was hard enough for me to get my head around... please, darling," he practically begs. "I've done nothing but think about the right way to do this all week."

The love and concern are clear in his eyes, so I relent a little. "Fine," I say.

"I'm going to just tell you like it is, in plain English. Then we can go through it, OK?"

"OK," I reluctantly agree.

"You see, Lucas has been lying to everyone. He's not who he claims to be," he says. I instantly feel the bile rising, so I breathe deeply to try to push it down. "He has an identical twin — well, he had one. It was the two of them — Lucas and Jamie O'Connor," he tells me, and then pauses to make sure I'm following. "Lucas was the Lucas we know — the one the whole town loves. Happy, charming, funny... only, Lucas died when he was seventeen," he pauses to look at me again. I'm still following, I feel like I'm in an alternate reality, but I'm still following. He continues, "Jamie wasn't... Jamie isn't like Lucas. He's more volatile and he got into a lot of trouble and fled Ireland to England about eight years ago. When he got here, he became Lucas, in name and character... do you understand what I'm saying Ava?" he asks me.

I feel like I might actually be sick, and I put my hand over my mouth in preparation, but nothing happens.

"Ava, do you understand what I'm saying?" he asks again.

I take a deep breath and nod at him and the tears fall down my face. "Yes," I tell him. "Yes... you're telling me that the man that I let into my life, into my bed. The man that I left alone with my son..." I say, and I let out a sob at that. "Is Jamie O'Connor, not Lucas O'Connor. It's all been a lie!" I shout, feeling panicked. "All of it, from day one and I'm the mug who fell for it."

I put my head in my hands as the realisation hits me full force. I let this man; this imposter be alone with my child so many times. I trusted him, and he was lying to me the entire time.

"No. You must not think like that," Dad says firmly. "He fooled everyone. Everyone here and everyone in the other places he's been before here. I suspect he's even fooling himself. He probably even believes that he is his brother."

"I let him into my bed, Dad. I let him be a father to my son. I'm supposed to protect Jacob, I'm supposed to know better," I shout through my tears.

"You did know better. The investigator suggested that the behaviour we started to see was the real him — was Jamie — and you didn't stand for it. You sent him packing. You did protect your son," he implores.

"I just can't believe this. It's mad. It's just mad!" I get up and pace around the room, but it doesn't help so I sit back down. "So, what the hell is in that file that's worse than what you've already told me?" I ask him, now terrified of what he's going to say.

The rest of the conversation is a bit of a blur, because I'm sitting here feeling like I can't trust my own senses. I don't know if I can tell what's real anymore. Everything Lucas has ever said to me plays over in my mind. I'm looking for clues, looking for anything that I missed. I barely asked him anything about his past. I know he has sisters, but I never pushed him for information. After all, I had my secrets. If I wasn't sharing, then how could I expect him to?

I'm vaguely listening to my dad because my internal dialogue is my main focus, he's just in the background, but certain words or sentences stick out occasionally, pulling my attention to him — "following you" is one of them and I regain my focus to look at the photos he has placed in front of me. They are photos of me and Jacob doing completely insignificant things. Then I see him, in all of them, lurking in the background, just watching. How did I not see him? How have I been so stupid?

I feel violated, I feel like the biggest idiot on the planet. Oh my God, the clues were there that very first day when I met him, and it occurred to me, just for a moment, that he might be mad. It was there, but I shrugged it off, totally taken in by his looks, charm — even his accent. "Dangerous" I hear my dad say, and he gets my full attention again.

"He's dangerous?" I ask him. "Dangerous to whom? Would he hurt Jacob?" I ask, and my tears fall and my voice cracks when I say my child's name.

"The investigator doesn't want to rule anything out—"

"He might hurt Jacob?" I jump up ready to run out and find my son, but my dad grabs me and pulls me back down.

"No, Ava. No. Listen to me. There's nothing in his past to suggest that he'd do anything to hurt a child, or you even — but he's also doing things here he's not done anywhere else," he says.

"What do you mean?" I ask him. Dad sighs.

"He's stayed longer. He's got into a relationship... these are all things that it looks like he's avoided in the past," he tells me. "His track record is to do cash in hand work for a year or so, be friendly, charming, and get people to like him. Then he always moves on before questions are asked."

"So, what's different about Clovelly?" I ask him.

"You, sweetheart. He loves you," my dad says, reaching for my hand.

I sit for a moment and take it all in. Or at least I try to. I've never doubted Lucas' love for me, he made it clear from the start. I almost feel sorry for him. He lost his twin. I may not have any siblings of my own, but losing a twin? I can understand how that might push you over the edge. Then I came along and he fell in love with me. I gave him a child — a ready-made family. Then I took it away. This is all my fault I start to think, then I suddenly remember what my dad had been talking about.

"You said he was dangerous?" Dad nods. "If not to me or Jacob, then who is he a danger to?"

He rubs his face. "At this point the investigator — Mike his name was — he doesn't want to rule out the possibility that he might hurt you. Just so that we're being cautious," he adds, trying and failing to reassure me. "Chances are he's more of a danger to himself, and to..." he pauses.

"Just say it, please, Dad."

He swallows hard then says, "There's a chance he could target Mark."

This time when the bile starts to rise, I know it won't be contained and I run to the bathroom and throw up in the toilet. Dad follows me and grabs my hair, and I hear him run the sink and wet a flannel for me. When I know that nothing more is going to come out, I reach for the handle, flush the toilet and then I lean back against the bath. Dad lowers himself next to me and passes me the wet flannel. I put it over my face letting it shield me for a moment before wiping myself clean.

“Does Mark know this?” I ask him.

“Yes, Mark knows everything,” he replies calmly.

“I can't believe he's just let things escalate between us — he should be running a mile,” I sob.

“Mark's not going anywhere. He loves you.”

“And that might get him, what? Beaten? Killed?” I ask hysterically.

“We don't know anything for certain—”

“Where is he?” I ask, and then I jump up. “Where is Lucas, or Jamie — whoever he is? I need to find him. I need to straighten things out.”

“You're not going anywhere near him,” he says firmly, standing to block my path. “Besides, I've been keeping an eye out all week, nobody has seen him.”

“What?” I ask.

“Travis came around. He's not been on the boats, he's not been seen in his workshop, the pub, anywhere,” he tells me.

“He's probably passed out with a bottle of whiskey in his flat,” I say bitterly.

“I don't know. I went there—”

“You went there? You know he's dangerous and you went there?” I shout at him.

“I can take care of myself, you know that,” he counters.

“Well, did you see him?”

“No. I couldn't see signs of much, but then there's only so much you can see through his letter box.”

"So, he's just gone?" I ask, hardly knowing what to think.

“Maybe... it is what he does,” he says, clearly hoping this is the case.

An idea suddenly comes to me. “I need my phone,” I say, and I brush past my dad and head back to the living room. I grab my phone from my bag and call Lucas. "It's ringing," I tell him eagerly.

"I know, love. I've left a message asking him to call me," he says calmly.

I hear Lucas' voice and panic sets in, but it's just his voicemail, so I hang up. I don't know what the hell to say to him right now anyway. So, I just sit down on the sofa and rest my head in my hands.

"So, what do we do?" I ask him, he always knows what to do. "Do we tell the police about him? Show them that he's been following me?"

Dad reaches for my hand. "I've thought about this and I've asked around. He hasn't done anything to you so they're not likely to be much help with regard to keeping him away," he says. "Using a false identity and not paying taxes is another matter — if Clovelly's local bobbies will take that on... I don't know."

"So, what then? We just assume he's gone and move on as if nothing has happened?" I ask, feeling scared again. "How can I bring Mark back here knowing he has a target on his back?"

"No, I'm not saying we do nothing. I may not be holding out much hope of them doing anything, but we need to tell the police what's going on here."

"Just in case," I say, guessing what he's thinking.

"Yes. We do need to try and move on, but we're not burying our heads in the sand. We'll do it by the book and be cautious," he assures me.

He sees that his words have done nothing to calm me and continues, "This may be hanging over our heads for a bit but I'm certain we'll be able to put it to bed soon. In the meantime, your locks have been changed and you've got a big bloody dog now," he laughs a little at that.

I laugh at that too. Cooper is more likely to lick a person to death than actually be of much use as extra security.

I sit back and close my eyes; exhaustion has just completely taken over me. "When did I make such a mess of everything?" I ask him.

"Look at me," he gently commands, and I look him right in the eye. "You've not made a mess of anything, love. This isn't your doing," he says sincerely, then he pulls me in for a hug.

I stay in his arms for a while and then we hear Mum come through the door. She looks in cautiously, but Cooper bounds over to me and starts licking me. I give him a big fuss and look over at my mum and Jacob, who is looking a bit grumbly in his pushchair.

"Are you all right, darling?" she asks with concern.

"I have no idea how to begin to answer that, Mum," I say, and I manage a half smile. I look at the clock, it's five. When did that happen? "I should go home and get Jacob some dinner," I say rising.

"No, sweetheart, stay. I know you think we only cook dinner when we want to ambush you, but let us take care of you right now, OK?" she says kindly.

"You've been taking care of me all week."

"Well, as a mother yourself, you know that's my job. No matter how old you are, you're my little girl," she says, and I feel new tears starting to fill my eyes.

"Thank you," I eventually manage to say.

I let Mum take over dinner time with Jacob and I sit outside with Cooper for a bit. I've pretty much done all the thinking I can do. My body and brain are exhausted, so I just sit clutching my tea, staring blankly ahead of me. I can smell the food and my stomach rumbles loudly, reminding me that after my vomiting session earlier, I'm completely empty. I'm about to head inside when my phone rings, it's Mark. Up until now I've been sitting here feeling numb, but seeing his name flash up on my screen sends a rush of warmth to my heart.

"Hello," I say.

"Hello to you, too," he says. "You sound exhausted."

"I am."

"Are you at home?"

"No, I'm still at my parent's house. They're cooking dinner for me... it's been quite an afternoon," I tell him.

There's a slight pause, then he asks, "You know?" a little apprehensively.

"If you're talking about my ex-boyfriend impersonating his dead twin brother and stalking me, then yes," I tell him calmly — I literally don't have the energy to get worked up.

"Oh, Ava. I hated keeping this from you," he says, sounding concerned. "Your dad asked me to let him handle it. Are you mad with me?"

"No," I say quietly but honestly.

"Are you sure? Because you sound distant."

"I think I've just used up every emotion that I'm capable of feeling this week. I'm out of tears," I tell him, attempting to laugh a little. "And I'm really not angry with you. I'm glad I didn't know until today. I wouldn't have changed this weekend for the world."

He sighs in relief. "I love you so much," he tells me.

"I love you too. We're going to go to the police tomorrow — they need to know the truth about him. Dad doesn't think they'll really do much, mind you," I say.

"Perhaps not, but it's the right call. Ava, really you sound strange, how are you really with all of this?" he asks, the concern clear in his voice.

"Honestly? I feel like an idiot. I feel like I've let Jacob

down. I feel violated. I feel like he's watching me right now," I tell him, and I wrap my arms around myself a little. "I'm angry at him, and I'm sad for him."

"Why are you sad?" Mark asks.

I let out a breath. "How much pain must a person be in to impersonate their dead brother?" I ask, but Mark says nothing. "You think I'm stupid for thinking that don't you?"

"Not at all," he replies quickly. "It's just what makes you, you. It's what makes you good."

"I'm also scared, Mark," I tell him, unable to hide the fear in my voice.

"There is no way that any of us will let him touch you, Ava," he says firmly.

"I'm not scared for me, I'm scared for you," I tell him. "You can't come here. Not until we know where he is. Not until we know it's safe," I tell him, and the emotions that I thought had been completely drained kick back in again. I am truly terrified for him.

"Nothing and no-one will stop me from being with you. I am coming to you on Friday," he tells me firmly.

"You can't," I tell him more urgently. "I don't want you hurt." Just thinking about it has the tears forming again and I try to swallow down more sobs. "We'll come to you again," I tell him.

"You're welcome here whenever you want, but I don't want you to have to do that drive with Jacob all the time. Also, I can't guarantee you won't see them," he says, and he doesn't need to elaborate, I know who the "them" is that he is referring to. "Are you ready for that?" he asks.

I let out another breath. "If you'd asked me that this morning I would have said 'bring it on', but I'm not so sure now. I just feel like I'm questioning myself and I can't be weak around them," I admit.

"Then I'm coming to you."

"No! No. I couldn't... I can't risk anything happening to you," I say, and this time a sob escapes.

"Ava, I need to see you. Both of you."

"I know. I do too," I tell him, and then an idea comes to me. "What about the Cotswolds? Would Darren and Lilly let us use their place for a few weekends? It's more or less in the middle, anyway," I ask.

"That's actually a brilliant idea, I'll talk to him later," he says, sounding happier.

"This is what you and Darren were talking about in the kitchen, wasn't it?" I ask him.

"Yes," he admits.

"He thinks it's too risky being with me—"

"No. He thinks being together is the best thing for both of us," he replies firmly. "Although, he does have concerns about my safety there."

We're silent for a few moments then for some reason I feel compelled to say, "I did love him, you know? It was never the same as how I love you, but I did feel something," I admit. "He was what I needed, when I needed it. He was always there for me. He made me feel like I had someone on my team at a time when everyone had turned on me... and I loved him for it. Sorry."

"You don't need to apologise, it's completely understandable," Mark replies.

"When I saw you in the kitchen that day, I realised where my heart really lies — whether I admitted it to myself or not. Does that make me a user?" I ask, genuinely wanting to know.

"No, Ava. I'd say it just makes you human," he says kindly.

We sit quietly again and then I ask, "Did you see any other women after me?"

"Do you really want to talk about this now?" he asks, giving a slight, bewildered laugh.

"Why not? It seems like a good time for putting everything on the table," I reply.

"OK..." he says, but he sounds uncomfortable and I brace myself for what's to come. "About six months after you left, Darren told me that I wasn't allowed to mope around anymore, and he set me up with a woman from the gym."

I have no right to, but I instantly feel jealous, "What was she like?" I ask.

"Well, she had light brown hair, in her early thirties... attractive. Her name was Jenny and she was a graphic designer," he pauses to clear his throat and then continues, "We went for a drink. She seemed very eager and I just sat there comparing her to you... let's just say she didn't match up," he says. "But..."

"But?" I ask and that one simple word has my stomach churning.

"But..." he repeats, "a couple of weeks after your father came to see me, I bumped into Helen. She suggested we go for a drink, and I accepted. I just started to think that we seemed so good on paper, that perhaps I should give it another go. I knew you had a boyfriend then... so, I tried to move on," he tells me cautiously.

My jealousy hits a new level, but I try to contain it and ask as casually as I can, "How did it go?"

"I tried to make it work for a few months. She was pleasant company, after all, but it never felt like it felt with you. Like it feels with you," he tells me gently.

"Why did it end?" I ask.

"Because I never stopped loving you, Ava," he replies,

and I sigh, relieved to hear those words coming from him. "Also, because I told her about us," he adds.

"You did? Why?" I ask.

"Hattie and the others were round for Sunday lunch. They were actually nice company," he says, laughing a little. "Everyone was drinking, and out of the blue a slightly drunk Will, asked if anyone ever wondered what you were doing."

"He did? How did that go down?" I ask dryly.

"Well, Helen asked who you were, and Hattie replied saying that you were 'nobody,'" he says, sounding disgusted. "I just looked at her. I just stared at her blankly for a few minutes, just trying to figure her out."

"Good luck with that," I scoff.

"I just hated the idea of another person thinking badly of you. So, after Hattie and the boys left, I told Helen what had happened between us," he says.

"How did she take it?" I ask.

"She just looked at me and said, 'you're not over her, are you?' I told her that I wasn't sure that I ever would be, and that was that," he says calmly.

"Dinner is ready, sweetheart," Mum suddenly calls from the back door.

"Thanks, Mum," I call back.

"I'll let you go," he says, "I'll talk to Darren and call you later. I love you."

"I love you too," I tell him, and I go inside.

33

In the end I practically inhaled my dinner. My parents wanted me to stay but I just wanted to be in my own home, so they insisted on staying with me instead. I put them in my room, and I had the futon in Jacob's. My tiny two bed thankfully has spacious rooms. Mark called at around eight O'clock to tell me that we could go to the Cotswolds for the next few weekends, and the knot in my stomach finally loosened a little. We could be together safely. I went to bed not knowing if my mind would actually switch off, but exhaustion won, and I fell asleep almost instantly.

I wake up at seven O'clock to Jacob's singing and the realisation that we've both slept through. This does not happen often, so I say a silent thank you to the Gods of Sleep for showing me mercy, and for a moment that's all I think about — but then it all hits me. Lucas isn't Lucas. He's a liar, probably sick in the head and he could hurt Mark, and the knot in my stomach tightens once more. I know it's true — all of it. I've seen the photos, driving licenses, even the death certificate, but it's still hard to believe this is actually happening — but it is.

Dad and I are going to have breakfast and then go to the police station. They may not do anything, but it feels like the first step towards trying to get this all sorted — or at least going some way towards taking control.

I don't really know what to expect as we arrive at the station, especially as Lucas is drinking buddies with many of the officers. Dad has the file, and as he's the one that spoke to the investigator first-hand, he's the one who is going to do the talking. After a little wait we eventually get into a room with PC Harris, otherwise known as Joe. Joe's a similar age to me, a bit of a lightweight, loves my French Fancies, and pretty much hero worships Lucas. I can't help but feel a little bad that we're about to crush his world.

He's a bit standoffish with me to begin with, naturally, the whole of Clovelly is talking about how I've broken Lucas' heart and run off with my ex, after everything he did for me. Dad talks, Joe listens, then he listens again, and again, making Dad repeat himself about three times, because he can't get his head around it either. Dad shows him the file and he just goes over each piece of paper again and again. He looks at me and I just shrug at him. What more can I add?

"I need to go and speak to the sergeant," Joe eventually says, and he leaves the room.

We sit alone for about twenty minutes, someone comes in and brings us a coffee, but it's disgusting so neither of us can actually drink it. Eventually, Sergeant Moore comes through the door. He's another familiar face and he looks upset, shocked and upset, which isn't surprising considering that Lucas built his new fence four months ago. Joe has obviously filled him in on what we discussed, but we go over it all again. He sends Joe off to verify the documents that we've brought. He asks me to think of anything — everything — no matter how insignificant it might seem. Anything that could shed some light. I've got nothing, but I promise to keep trying.

After a while, Joe pops his head through the door and Sergeant Moore leaves the room. He's only gone a few minutes, then he comes back and tells us, "These all check out."

Dad and I didn't need to hear that, we never doubted it, but he clearly needed conformation. Then we go through the motions. He confirms what we thought, that they can't do much about him following me, but he advises me to take precautions and to get an attack alarm — Dad's already ordered one.

As we leave, Sergeant Moore lets out a deep sigh and I turn to look at him. "My wife made him a plum crumble," he tells me, shaking his head. "From our garden, they were."

"I remember," I tell him, smiling. "It was delicious."

He looks as messed up by this as I am. He thought he knew him, just like I did, just like everyone else did. However, I know he definitely thinks that he should've known better, above all else. I have no doubt he'll be beating himself up for some time over this, perhaps even more so than me.

It's lunch time when we finally leave the station and we're starving. I call my mum to check that she's still OK with Jacob, and then we go and get fish and chips. We sit on a bench looking out at the sea, and just eat and take it all in.

"I'll miss you," Dad says to me, and I look at him, puzzled. "When you go back to London. It's been so lovely having you both here."

"What are you talking about? Are you sick of all my drama and banishing me?"

"Never," he says smiling. "You keep things lively, that's for sure, sweetheart." Despite myself I laugh at him. "I just mean you and Mark."

"Now you sound like Carolyn," I tell him, rolling my eyes.

"Good," he says, smiling triumphantly. "She's a very smart woman."

"That she is," I agree.

"You and Mark though, you're the real deal," he continues. "Have you talked about living together?"

"Dad... We've literally just got back together after over a year of being apart, his children ruining my life, and me keeping a baby hidden from him," I say, shaking my head at him. "Funnily enough we've not talked about living together yet."

"Yes, but it's going to happen isn't it?" he asks seriously.

"I think for now it's best that we just take life one drama at a time, don't you?" I look at him, raising my eyebrows. "Let's face the potentially psychotic ex-boyfriend situation, then his definitely psychotic-daughter situation, and then we'll talk about living arrangements, OK?" I say it realising that I sound strangely calm about the whole thing.

"You seem to be handling this well," he tells me.

"Do I?" I ask, laughing. "Honestly, I think I'm just compartmentalising it all. It's a bit much really, and I definitely do not get enough sleep to be able to deal with all of this," I say, and he laughs with me too.

"Can I ask you about Hattie?" he asks cautiously.

"I guess that depends on what you want to know?" I reply, eyeing him questioningly.

"How will you deal with her?" he asks, seriously.

"I think I'm just going to have to go full Nanny Mae and take that bitch down."

I say it seriously, but then I look at him and smile. Then we laugh and chat for a bit longer, then decide that we've eaten enough and walk home to Mum and Jacob, with our leftovers.

The rest of the week goes by in a bit of a blur. I have a project to finish and baking to do and now that I have Cooper I'm out walking lots too. Sergeant Moore checks in with not much to tell me. I talk and text with Mark all the time, but I miss him. I'm rarely alone but when I am, especially if I'm out, I'm always watching. I find myself looking into parked vans as I pass them to make sure nobody is hiding, and I'm constantly checking behind me as I walk down the street. I feel safe in my home as Lucas no longer has a key, and although Cooper may be more of a lover than a fighter, he'll certainly let me know if someone comes in. The paranoia is exhausting, and I'm relieved when I make it to Friday afternoon, and I pack up the car to drive to meet Mark.

The drive to the Cotswolds takes about half the time of the drive to London and I make it without stopping, thanks to some serious napping on Jacob's part. Cooper is staying with my parents, so he didn't distract him this time. As I pull up to the cottage, I see Mark's car and I instantly feel the nervousness that has been my constant companion this week, becoming replaced with excitement. Then he comes out to meet us with that smile of his on his face, and I'm completely flooded by love.

We spend the next three weekends at the cottage, and I love every moment of it. There we're free to be just us, to be open without fearing who we may be about to bump into, or who might be watching. Yet, as amazing as the seclusion together has been in order to give us the time to heal, and to learn how to be a family. We both started to feel like we've been hiding away, like before — and that's something we don't plan to do this time.

It was during our second weekend at the cottage that we started to talk about what the next step would be for us, and we agreed that it would be to stop hiding. We were lying in bed after both just having had a pretty intense orgasm, and he said to me out of the blue, "I choose you, Ava. I choose you and Jacob."

"What do you mean?" I had asked.

He looked me right in the eyes and said, "When we tell them, no matter what the repercussions are — I will choose you," he said passionately. "I love my children, I do, but I've experienced life without you already and I won't do that again. So, promise me — no running and no self-sacrifice, because I choose you."

I kissed him deeply and told him, "I couldn't leave you again, even if I tried."

Then we kissed until we needed more, and I felt the completeness I feel when he's inside me, once again. I would never be able to leave Mark again, I knew that, but I was still scared that he might be taken from me.

It's been almost four weeks and there's been no sign of Lucas this entire time. I haven't checked to see if his phone still works since that first day, as Sergeant Moore advised me not to, and they have no leads as to where he might be. Mark has been suggesting that it's time he came back to Clovelly and I've actually agreed. I'm still scared, but I've agreed. So, he's coming here tomorrow, and next week... Well, next week I am taking Jacob to London. Mark is going to invite Hattie, Ted and Will over and we're going to tell them everything. No more secrets, no more hiding, and this time I won't be the one leaving.

It's Thursday afternoon, and Mark's not working tomorrow so he'll be travelling down in the morning and I really need to do a food shop. Dad has Jacob, he's not a bad shopping companion but it's definitely quicker to do it solo, and I also need to have a clean-up at home. I hadn't really thought about the extra cleaning needed when I took Cooper on. I grab everything that I need quite quickly and load everything into the boot, then I return the trolley and get into my car.

I throw my bag into the passenger foot-well and put my seatbelt on, then my passenger door opens startling me, and I turn to see Lucas get in and close the door, and I'm instantly so scared that I can barely breathe. I think about my attack alarm but it's in my bag and that's now been pushed further out of reach by his feet. I just stare at him. He looks clean, like he's taking care of himself, not dishevelled like I've been imagining. He smiles at me, the same smile I've seen so many times, but now it looks so out of place on his face.

"Hello, Ava darlin'," he says calmly.

I am frozen to the spot but inside everything is in panic mode. What should I do?

"Did you want to speak to me?" he asks. I manage to let out a sound, but no words form, and he smiles again. "You called me the other week? Sorry it's taken me a while to get back to you, but I've been busy," he says calmly, still so calm. "What was it that you wanted? Are you bored of the old man already?" he asks me, and then his smile turns into a smirk, and I'm taken back to how he acted when Mark first arrived.

"I... I don't want you here," I manage to say. "Please go or I'll call the police."

"And tell them what? Your ex-boyfriend came to see why you've been calling him?" he asks as he sneers at me.

"I only called you once, and it was because I think you need help."

He laughs maniacally and leans in closer to me, my back is already pressed against my door and my seatbelt is still fastened and I have nowhere to go.

"Why, Ava? Because you broke my heart?" he asks bitterly. "Don't worry. In my opinion women are only good for two things — cooking and fucking," he tells me, and he smiles again. "Now, don't get me wrong, you're pretty exceptional at both, darlin', but I'll get over it."

He leans back again, and I summon the courage to challenge him. "That's not why I think you need help... Jamie."

His head snaps to me and he looks angry. "What did you just call me?" he asks harshly.

"Jamie... because that's your name. Your real name," I say, shaking a little.

"Well, well, well... not just a pretty face after all," he says as he looks me up and down. The sneer is back as he asks, "Did you get that information from the old man?"

"It doesn't matter how I know — but I know. You're Jamie O'Connor. Lucas was your twin brother and he's dead," I tell him, and as he shuffles uncomfortably, I start to think that I have a way to reason with him. "I'm really sorry for your loss—"

"I don't need your pity or your help!" he spits at me, and then he leans closer again. "You know, it was always amusing to watch how Lucas could work people. So, when I came to England, I decided to give it a try, and I liked it. People are pathetic," he says, smiling unnervingly. "A good-looking face, a smile, a bit of charm and they're putty in your hands. Do you want to know what I was thinking the first time I saw you standing there, just looking at the sea?" he asks. He pauses for me to respond but I say nothing, so he just smiles again and continues, "Here's another mug. Another mug who I wanted to fuck, yes — but still just another mug. Then... I saw you smile... and I felt something," he says and for a moment I think I see sadness there.

"I'm sorry..." I start to say, but he isn't listening to me.

"You made me feel something, Ava — I can admit that. Only you weren't just another mug, were you? I had to admit defeat that day and that's something I don't do lightly," he says, shaking his head as he laughs a little. "I knew you'd be back at some point though, what with your parents living here. Then you actually moved here. Only, you were heartbroken and pregnant," he says, laughing a little more cruelly this time. "Got to tell you, I thought you'd be an easy target. A bit desperate perhaps, and I'd never had sex with someone that's pregnant. Still haven't, have I?" he says, and he nudges me a little as if we're sharing a joke.

"So, it was all just a lie then? All just some game?" I ask him coldly. "You may not think you're sick Jamie, but you certainly make me sick," I tell him angrily.

"Oh, don't be like that, Ava. I love you," he says with sincerity, and I can't help feeling a little guilty about causing him more pain. "You did that to me. Made me feel — made me weak. You loved me too, I know that," he tells me. He had been struggling to maintain eye contact, but he looks at me now as he says bitterly, "Then he came back."

"It wasn't Mark's fault — it was yours," I tell him, firmly. "I loved who I thought you were and when you could no longer pretend, I no longer liked what I saw."

"You see, I think part of the problem is that a girl like you might actually prefer the real me — the real Jamie," he says, smiling again.

"I doubt that very much—"

His hand is around my neck in a split second and I can no longer speak.

"I bet Jamie could make you happier than that old man does," he says, his face so close to mine that I can feel his breath on my cheek. "Perhaps you and Jamie should get better acquainted?" he asks quietly and coldly.

He's squeezing my neck with one hand and rubbing firmly against my groin with the other. I can't push him away because he's too heavy and I'm struggling to breathe, let alone scream. Fear floods through me as his hand starts to creep over the top of my jeans and I do the only thing that I can think of. I let go of the hand that I've been failing to prise from my neck and hit my car horn. It lets out a long, loud blast taking Jamie by surprise.

He moves back a little, but he still has his hand around my neck, so I continue to push at my horn. He lets go, and I gasp for air and turn to see that I've now got people's attention, they're turning to look; trying to work out what's happening. So, I continue to push the horn as Jamie jumps out of the car and runs off. I don't know what to do so I keep pressing the horn and then I jump out of my skin as a woman and her husband knock at my window. My relief spills out of me in tears and she opens the door and unhooks my seatbelt so that she can assess me. A crowd starts to form, a security guard pushes to the front, and they take me inside to an office and call the police.

When PC Joe Harris walks into the office with his colleague and sees me in floods of tears, he knows exactly what's happened. He comes over and moves my hair out of the way so that he can look at my neck. I haven't looked yet, but when they made the call, I heard them saying that there are red marks in the shape of fingers there.

"Was it him?" he asks me urgently, and I nod my reply, since I'm still unable to find my voice. "I think we need to get you to hospital to make sure everything is OK. We'll take your statement there," he tells me, and he looks at me with such concern that I know whatever ill feelings he may have harboured are completely gone.

The doctors check me over immediately and Joe stays with me the entire time. They're satisfied that it's just superficial bruising and that there's no damage to the vocal cords — but it will hurt for a while. As the doctor leaves I hear my dad's voice outside the room.

"Where is she?" Dad shouts — he sounds so scared.

Joe goes to meet him and seconds later my dad bounds over to me, fear and concern etched onto his face. He looks at my face first, then he focuses on my neck and I see him boil over.

He turns to Joe. "Is this enough for you to do something?" he shouts. "Is this enough for you to consider him a threat?"

Joe assures him that they are looking for Jamie, but Dad can't hear it, he just wants Joe gone, but they're yet to take my statement, so he stays. His colleague returns and I do my best to tell them everything through the pain in my throat. I tell them everything he said, every look he gave me and every way that he touched me, and my skin is crawling just thinking about his hands on me. I keep thinking about how he looked at me, his laugh, his smile and I can't tell if he's mad, or just cruel... and I honestly don't know which is worse.

Dad drives me home and tells me that Sergeant Moore had an officer bring my car home when they went to pick up the CCTV footage from the supermarket. The angle of the camera didn't show what happened inside the car — that will end up being my word against his — but it showed Jamie getting in and then it showed him running away. Jacob is with Mum at my house, Dad had to call her to come and take care of him when Sergeant Moore came knocking at the front door.

I hear them both crying as we walk in, and when she sees me, she breaks down even more and rushes over to me. I manage to tell her that I'm OK and I take Jacob from her. Dad engulfs her in a hug while I take Jacob to the living room, and as we sit together, he feeds and is instantly calm again. I smile at him, in spite of the pain that I'm in and how I'm feeling inside, I smile — but I can't help but wonder whether he's truly as oblivious as I like to think he is.

I don't text Mark, this needs to be either done on the phone or in person, though I know he'd want to know right away. Mum takes over the cooking and sends me upstairs to rest, and I just lay in bed going over and over what happened. I close my eyes, but I can still see his face, I can feel his breath on my cheek, and I can smell him. Then I realise that part isn't just a memory — I can actually smell him because his aftershave rubbed onto my clothes. I quickly head to the bathroom, strip them off, get into the shower and let the hot water wash him away.

Jonathan

Jonathan helped his wife in the kitchen, all the time watching her, the woman he adored trying to hold it together so that she could paint on a brave face, a happy face, for Jacob, but she was breaking over this and he knew it. They knew the threat, but it seemed so unlikely that

Jamie would target Ava, that they had dismissed it. They'd let their guard down and their little girl had been hurt. She'd been violated, and by the sounds of it, things could have been much worse had she not reacted the way she did. He walked up behind El as she stirred the soup and put his arms around her. He didn't say anything, he just knew that she needed some comfort right now.

He heard Ava's footsteps heading towards the bathroom and the boiler kicked in as she turned the shower on. Without really thinking about it, he went to her bag and picked up her phone. It's password protected but he knew it — "in case of emergencies" she'd said when she'd told him the code.

"What are you doing?" Eleanor asked him.

"He needs to know," Jonathan replied, and she gave him a slight nod. He scrolled down the contact list, pressed the call button, and after a few rings it was answered.

"Hello," Mark said warmly, "I was just thinking about you."

"It's me – Jonathan, so don't start whispering your sweet nothings," he said, attempting to put some humour in his voice.

"What's going on? Where's Ava?" Mark asked, concerned.

"She's in the shower. She doesn't know I'm calling you right now."

"What has happened, Jonathan?" Mark asked with more urgency.

Jonathan cleared his throat and tried to keep himself calm and collected as he told him, "He showed up today... and he hurt her."

Mark said nothing as Jonathan explained what had happened, but he could hear him breathing hard. After

Jonathan had finished, Mark remained silent for a few more moments, then he said, "I'm on my way," and hung up.

After about half an hour Ava came downstairs in comfy trousers and a jumper which was covering her neck. She went straight over to Jacob and gave him a big kiss. Jonathan loved watching the two of them together. When Ava's world crumbled, becoming a mother was the making of her. While Ava had thought that she'd let them down when she came to Clovelly, watching her with Jacob had never made her parents prouder. He looked at her closely. Even though she'd been through hell that day and wasn't wearing makeup, he was in awe at what a beautiful girl — or woman — she was. He knew he wasn't just biased, she had the looks, but there was just something else about her too.

He remembered his dad telling him one day when Ava was about ten, "She's going to be a looker, she is. Got that smile that your mum has too — you'll have nothing but trouble with this one." Jonathan could see what he meant but it never really amounted to much, she never was any trouble, not really. She had boyfriends growing up, but she also had a good head on her shoulders, so there was never really any drama.

Well, that had all changed now. The situation with Mark may have been unusual and brought her pain, but Jonathan could see that their love was real, and he knew it would last. They would have problems to face, what with Mark's family, but Jonathan had been confident for a few weeks now that they'd get through it.

Now Lucas, well, Jamie — that was another matter. Her looks and character had drawn in a right wrong 'un there, that's for sure... and he had hurt her. Jonathan's blood started to boil again but then Ava looked at him and gave him a gentle smile, forcing him to smile back at her.

"I made you some soup," El said, passing Ava the bowl.

"Thank you, Mum," she replied croakily. She started to stir it but then put her spoon down and said, "I should probably call Mark, but I don't want to freak him out..."

Eleanor looked at Jonathan, but Ava was watching her soup, so she missed their silent communication.

Jonathan sighed and said, "There's no need to, love." Ava looked up at him with a questioning look in her eyes, and Jonathan continued, "He's on his way."

34

I hear Mark arrive at around nine O'clock. I've been in bed for about an hour and I'm exhausted, but I haven't slept. I've just been lying in the dark with my eyes open, because every time I close them, I see Jamie's face leaning into mine. I still can't believe this happened. I had allowed myself to believe that he had just gone. That's what he did. Why would I be so important? He said he loved me but what happened today didn't feel like love. I don't know what it was, but it is clear to me that he blames Mark, and now I've seen what he's capable of that scares me more than ever before.

My parents wanted to stay until Mark arrived and I can hear them talking now — not the words — just the voices. I wanted to stay up to meet him, but I was just so tired, and I needed a break from their looks of concern. My neck is hurting, and my throat is sore, but the doctors said this was to be expected. I want to see Mark, and I want some more pain relief, so I drag myself out of bed and go downstairs.

Like always, the stairs creak with every step that I take, but right now I like the fact that my house is noisy — it means that there are no surprises. Unfortunately, it also means that they hear me coming and they've stopped talking about whatever it is that they were talking about in anticipation of my arrival. I step into the kitchen and I see them standing around the table — my parents still look so worried. I can't quite tell how Mark looks; there's fear, anger, pain, but also love — always love. He comes straight over and wraps his arms around me. I put my arms around him too and hold him tight, and then I feel safe for the first time all day.

"We thought you were asleep," Mum says.

"Can't sleep," I manage to croak out. "Need some more Ibuprofen."

She goes to the cupboard for the pills and gets me some water. Mark hasn't said anything yet, he's still just holding me, and Cooper has also got up and settled himself at my feet. Poor chap, he thought he was coming for a quiet life by the sea. Mum hands me the water and tablets and Mark and I let go of each other so that I can take them.

After making sure that I'm OK my parents say their goodbyes, and Mark follows them to the door to ensure that it's locked behind them. He then goes around the house making sure all of the doors and windows are properly locked. He gives Cooper a quick fuss and sends him to bed, then he picks me up and carries me back upstairs and into bed. He takes off his clothes and even in my sorry state the view makes my body flutter, but that's definitely not on the agenda for tonight. He gets into bed with me, still not having said a word, and when he pulls me close, I can feel his heart pounding.

"Are you OK?" I ask him.

"You're asking me if I'm OK?" he replies, astonished. "Ava… are you OK?"

"I'm better now you're here," I tell him honestly. "Thanks for coming."

"Are you kidding? It is my job to make sure you're safe," he says incredulously. "I just... I'm just so sorry about what you went through today. It makes me feel sick," he says, his emotions spilling over.

"I'm OK. It could've been worse... people have been through worse," I tell him.

"It doesn't make what happened to you any less significant," he says seriously. "Honestly, I'm not letting you out of my sight again. I want to kill him. I actually want to kill him."

"Can you just hold me?" I ask him. "I know this is hard for you too, but I don't want to think about him."

He holds me close, but his racing heart tells me that he's in no way calm.

"I'm scared," I say, quietly.

"We're not leaving you alone for the time being," he tells me firmly. "I'm sorry, I know you don't want to feel like you're being treated like a child, but we're not and that's just how it is," he says, and his tone makes it clear that there's no point in arguing.

"I'm scared for you. He blames you and I don't know what he's capable of," I tell him as my tears spill over.

"Nobody is going to take me from you, Ava. Nobody," he tells me firmly. Then he gently kisses me on my forehead, my cheeks and my lips, and then he holds me in his arms, and after a while, I finally fall asleep.

When I wake up in the morning, I'm in exactly the same position — in Mark's arms. I wish I could say that I stayed there all night, but Jacob woke up twice. The first time Mark had told me to stay where I was and he managed to rock him back to sleep, but only mummy would do the second time. Thankfully he's still asleep, because I don't want to move right now. Here feels safe, not just for me but for Mark too. I can feel his slow breathing and steady heartbeat. He's warm. He's safe. Oh God, I can't lose him.

I lie awake in his arms thinking about the events of yesterday. It would almost feel like a dream were it not for the pain. I need more pills. I gently move away so that I don't disturb him and go down to the kitchen. Cooper greets me affectionately and I let him out the back door. Normally, I'd leave it open for him, but today I lock it straight away. I walk around checking everywhere is still locked, and it is — everything is as we left it.

I take some pills and go back upstairs, but I don't make it to my bed as I hear that Jacob is now awake, so I take him back downstairs instead. Cooper gets my attention from the living room window letting me know that he's ready to come back in and have some breakfast. I let him back in and feed him. I boil the kettle and get a pot of coffee ready, and I start making Jacob his breakfast. I'm doing all of the things that I'd usually do, only today it's all being done with a cloud of fear looming over me.

Sergeant Moore comes around later in the morning, they're looking for Lucas — no Jamie, because he's no longer Lucas — but they have no leads yet. Of course, they don't — he knows how to disappear. My parents come over and everyone fusses over me. Everyone's worried about me, but I'm just worried about Mark. The police speak to him too. They want to make sure that after what happened, and what was said, that he's cautious. Half of me wants him as far away from here as possible, but the other half doesn't want to let him out of my sight.

At some point during the morning Mum goes to the tea rooms, but the gossip mill is working overtime and she couldn't cope with all of the looks and questions. The truth about Jamie is out, as is what he did to me. So, she called Linda to take over and has been keeping a low profile since — just like me. Dad has been taking Cooper out for walks. He's not concerned about crossing paths with Jamie — I actually think he wants to. In general, we're all trying to keep things as calm and entertaining as possible for Jacob, whilst not leaving the house.

Mark is on his phone a lot, and most of the calls he takes out in the garden. He tells me he's talking to Darren, but also to Hattie and the boys. All this time he's been visiting me, he's been telling them that he's been entertaining clients, or going away with Lilly and Darren, but it isn't cutting it anymore, and they're suspicious. At one point, when we're sitting on the sofa together, I see Mary's name flash up on his phone. He just tuts and sends her to voice-mail, it's a small thing, but it makes me smile and he sees it.

"The kids aren't hearing what they want to so they're sending in their chief interrogator," he says. "My life is absolutely none of her business." He kisses me, letting me know where his allegiance lies.

Mark told me that things went from being amicable to outright frosty with his ex-wife after we broke up. He hated the way she talked about me and half thought that she was encouraging Hattie in her mission to wreak havoc on my life. If she wasn't actively encouraging it, she certainly wasn't doing anything to discourage it. Unfortunately, it doesn't seem to stop her from sending the occasional drunken message asking if he wants "no strings" sex with her. They always go unanswered, and yet she persists. Poor Tom, he really is too nice for her.

The entire day is spent in hibernation, as I have no desire to face the world outside these walls just yet. Julia comes over late in the afternoon to check my neck — it's now looking more purple than red but it's apparently nothing to be worried about. Mum and Dad join us for a takeaway in the evening, and for the first time since yesterday things don't feel forced. It feels like they're all actually enjoying being here, rather than being here to keep an eye on me. The conversation between Mark and my parents seems natural, and I don't sense any hint of them being in the slightest bit unhappy about our relationship.

Saturday is much the same, we stay in, we play with Jacob, we play with Cooper, and Mark spends more time in my garden on his phone. He looks preoccupied but he doesn't say why, but if he's speaking to Darren then I know that he's going to be trying to use his contacts — just like before. He'll be trying to find a way to fix this, and a way to find Jamie. He wants to make me safe, but all I care about is him being safe.

On Sunday, Mark declares that I need to get out. I need to face the world at some point, and he would rather I do it with him here to support me. He has to go back to London later to sort some things out, but he plans to travel back on Tuesday and work from here for the rest of the week. I'm both saddened and relieved that he's leaving. I don't want him gone but I also don't want him here. Here he can be found. Here he can be hurt.

We head out after lunch with Jacob in the pushchair, and we end up sitting on a bench by the beach. Clovelly really is such a lovely place, and what's going on right now doesn't seem to fit with the beauty of it. The few people we've seen have stared, given me a sympathetic smile, and then started whispering when they think they're too far away for us to hear. I can't find it in me to care that they now see me as the victim instead of the villain.

We sit for a while, and then Mark lifts me onto his knee and kisses my ear and the sensation sends tingles down my spine. All we've done this weekend is kiss and hug. We've never spent this much time together without having sex before, and now the soreness in my throat is subsiding a little, the rest of my body is letting me know what it's been missing. I kiss him on the lips, and I can feel that he's missing my touch too.

"Have I told you yet today how much I love you?" I ask him.

"You know, I don't think you have," he says seriously, but then smiles. "How much do you love me, exactly?"

"An excruciatingly painful amount," I tell him, kissing him deeply. I feel his body react and then Jacob squeals as he drops his toy, bringing us back to the world — to our world. As I bend down to pick it up, I see a large set of man's legs walking towards us and I instantly jump in panic, Mark's hands tighten around me, and we look up and see that it's just my dad and we instantly relax.

"Don't sneak up on me like that, Dad!" I admonish him.

"Sorry, love... sorry, I didn't think," he says putting his hands up as a show of peace. "It's just me. No need to be alarmed," he tells me as he bends down towards Jacob. "Hello, little man," he says to him, then he looks at me again. "Your mum and I thought we'd take him back to ours for a bit — give you two... you know," he clears his throat, and looks very uncomfortable, before continuing, "you know, a bit of space before Mark heads back."

I can't help but laugh at his embarrassment. Mark is also smiling at him, but then he looks at me and his eyes turn lustful and I know that we want the same thing.

"Thanks, that would be nice," I tell him, trying not to

show the excitement building in me. "He could do with a sleep, but a bit of a walk ought to send him off."

"No problem," he says, taking the handle of the pushchair. "What time are you leaving?" he asks Mark.

"Around five," he replies.

"I'll bring him back for four then," Dad confirms, and then he leaves looking just as uncomfortable as when he arrived.

It's half past twelve — that's three and a half hours of alone time with Mark. I'm still sitting on his knee and I look at him and see the same excitement in his eyes that I know is reflected in mine. I stand up, take his hand and we walk quickly back to mine. When we open the door Cooper barks, and it's a sound that I'm very thankful for right now — if someone comes in — he barks. I lock the door behind us and then Mark picks me up and I wrap my legs around him.

"What are you thinking? Every room in the house?" I ask, and I raise my eyebrows, challenging him to accept.

He kisses me and as his tongue reaches mine, I can't help but let out a slight moan. My body is aching for him, but he breaks away and says, "Not today..." he pauses to kiss me again. "I'm taking you upstairs..." More kisses. "I need you to be comfortable."

As we move from the utility to the kitchen, Cooper jumps up at us, excited by our return. "Bed, Cooper," we both say in unison, and then we make our way upstairs. He's still carrying me and when he lays me down on the bed, he asks, "Are you sure you're OK for this?"

"I am more than OK," I tell him honestly. "I need this. I need you."

He lowers himself onto me and we kiss passionately. He then pulls away to gently undress me, and once I'm naked he undresses himself at a quicker pace, but he never takes his eyes off me. Feeling self-conscious, I move my hair across my neck to try to hide the worst of the bruising.

He leans over me and moves my hair away again saying, "You never need to hide anything from me." He strokes my face and kisses me gently. "I will never stop wanting you, and I will never stop loving you."

I pull him onto me so that I can feel him, I need his touch, his warmth, and I need to feel his heartbeat. I love this man with all of my being. "I don't ever want to be without you," I tell him. "I love you so much."

We make love for the next couple of hours, taking breaks in-between climaxes to kiss, and rest, and just feel. He's gentle with me, he explores my entire body, kissing and stroking as if I'm something to be worshipped. To him, it would seem that I am. Just like he is to me.

By three O'clock we're both feeling hungry and we go downstairs. Mark checks his phone and sees that he's got four missed calls from Hattie and a text message asking him to call her.

"I should call her back... just in case," he says.

I nod in agreement and he goes into the living room. I hear him ask if everything's OK — which it is. There's no drama and no need for panic, so he walks back into the kitchen.

"Then why all the calls?" he asks her, and I hear her shout in response from where I'm standing.

"Because nobody knows where you are, or what you're doing all the time," she yells at him.

He looks at me, he's clearly irritated by her. "Am I not allowed a private life, Hattie?" he asks her.

I don't hear her response, so she's stopped shouting at him, at least. I hate that he's being put under this pressure and having to lie at a time when we are technically ready to tell the truth. I notice the notepad and pen on the side. I pick it up, and after a moment I show him what I've written — **Shall we just tell her about us now?**

"Hattie, just give me a moment," he says, as he puts her on hold. "Are you sure?" he asks me, looking right into my eyes to make sure he can see the truth.

"It's not the way we planned to do it, but they're not going to leave you alone," I tell him honestly, shrugging a little.

"I'm ready if you are," he says, and he kisses me as we sit down at the table together. He goes to take her off hold but pauses. "I'll put her on speaker phone, but do me a favour and let me do the talking to begin with?" he asks with a little smile.

"If that's what you want," I say, secretly pleased by his request.

He takes her off hold and puts her on speaker phone. "Hattie," he says.

"Dad!" she snaps, and I flinch at the sound of her voice. "Did you just put me on hold?"

I've not heard her voice in almost two years, and it sounds alien to me now. After all the time we spent together as best friends I had half expected to feel something for her, but I don't — nothing positive anyway. She doesn't sound like the Hattie that I once knew and loved. If anything, she sounds like her mum.

"Yes, I did," Mark replies calmly, "but you want to know where I've been going and I'm about to tell you."

"Oh... good," she replies calmer now. "That's good."

"Helen and I..." I shoot him a questioning look, but he just smiles at me and puts his finger to his mouth. The glint in his eyes is telling me that he is up to something, so I say nothing and let him continue.

"Helen and I have recently got back together, and we've been seeing each other outside of London so that we could keep it private for a while," he tells her. He's still smiling at me, but I still have no clue where he's going with this.

"Oh... well... that's really great to hear," Hattie says, sounding thrilled. "I'm not sure why you'd not tell us, but I'm really happy for you."

"You are?" he asks.

"Of course," Hattie replies genuinely. "All I want is for you to be happy."

"That's good to hear, darling," he says fondly. "Because I am happy. I'm the happiest I've ever been and I'm very, very much in love," he says looking at me adoringly. He takes my hand in his and kisses it. Hattie is saying something but I'm too focused on Mark to take it in.

"Now Hattie," he says, his tone a little firmer, "I want you to do something for me."

"OK...?" she asks, sounding a little confused.

"I want you to remember what you just said about wanting me to be happy, and what I just told you about being happy — about being in love," he tells her. "Then I need you to think about what I just told you about being in a relationship, and then I need you to replace the name, Helen..." I start to smile as the penny drops, "with the name, Ava."

Hattie gives a confused laugh. "What are you talking about?" she asks. "Ava? I don't get it, Dad."

Mark speaks more firmly this time. "Take the information that I gave you about being in a relationship with Helen, but replace Helen, with Ava," he tells her again.

Silence. Hattie is silent — for a moment at least, but then she laughs in disbelief.

"Are you actually trying to tell me that you're back with Ava? Ava Swan, that is?" she asks, unable to hide her anger.

"I'm not trying to tell you, Hattie, I am telling you," he says calmly. "We were planning on doing this face to face, but you've all been pretty persistent this weekend, so here we are."

It takes a few seconds for her to speak but when she does the venom in her voice practically seeps through the phone.

"You got back together with Ava?" she asks, incredulously.

"Yes, I did," Mark replies, and it thrills me that there is no hint of an apology in his voice.

"You've been going off to see her?" she asks bitterly.

"True again, Hattie," he replies. "That's OK, isn't it? Because you just want me to be happy... that's what you said, isn't it?"

Mark looks at me and I can't help but give a silent laugh. Hattie is furious and the fact that I don't care is quite liberating. Plus, I have to admit that I'm absolutely loving the way he has just played her.

"Is she there now?" she manages to get out through gritted teeth.

"She is," Mark says warmly. He looks at me and nods towards the phone, letting me know that he's done what he wanted to do, and it's my turn to speak if I want to. I do.

"Hattie," I say calmly, but without the slightest hint of warmth. "I'd say it's nice to speak to you again, but that would make me a liar, like you."

I can hear her breathing hard, she's trying to speak but she seems unable to form any coherent words, so I speak again instead. “Yes, well, it's been... interesting,” I tell her, “but you're actually interrupting so we're going to go now,” I hit the end call button without saying goodbye.

Mark looks at me and says, “I think that went rather well, don't you?”

We both laugh and he leans in for a kiss, then we look at each other with the look we share so often, and all thoughts of food are forgotten, as once again we're only hungry for each other

35

Mark left at half past five yesterday evening and said that he was likely to make a stop or two, and therefore wouldn't be home until close to midnight. So, he suggested that I should go to sleep without waiting to hear from him. I tried to stay up, but I was physically and mentally exhausted, and I fell asleep on the futon at around ten O'clock. True to their word, my parents are not leaving me alone, so they took my room again and I made sure to flip the mattress when I put on fresh bedding for them.

When I wake up in the morning I'm surprised to see that there's no message from Mark letting me know that he got back, but I assume he was so exhausted that he must have just crashed — I know this is all taking a toll on him too. I decide to send him a text instead of calling, because he's likely to be rushing about to get out early for work, and an hour later, I brush off his lack of reply as being down to early morning meetings.

Dad tells me that I need to continue to try to get out of the house. So, after we've washed and eaten, we take Cooper out, leaving Jacob with Mum. It's after nine, and because most people work outside of Clovelly, my street is pretty free from parked cars during the day. That's why I spot it so easily. I freeze to the spot for a moment and then rush over in panic, looking into the windows.

"What's the matter?" Dad asks, running after me.

"This..." I struggle to speak in my panic. "This is Mark's car!" I manage to squeak out.

"What? Are you sure, Ava?" he asks me, clearly concerned too.

"Yes!" I shout. "This is Mark's car. Why is it here? He went home... he's in London. He went home." I grab my phone and call him, and it immediately goes to voicemail. "Mark! Are you OK?" I ask, sounding frantic. "Your car is here. Where are you? Please, please call me. Please be OK. I love you... I love you," I hang up the phone and burst into tears.

My dad pins me by the shoulders and looks at me hard. "Ava. Are you absolutely, one hundred percent certain that this is Mark's car?" he asks.

"Yes," I sob out. There is no doubt.

He turns us around and walks us back to my house, taking out his own phone to call the police.

Sergeant Moore sits at my kitchen table across from me. They've run the plates, it's been confirmed as Mark's car, and given what's already happened they are taking this seriously. They're requesting access to CCTV and they're sending out the Coast Guard. I just sit here. I hear them speak and I sense their urgency, but all I can focus on is my own fears. It hurts to breathe. My heart is beating too hard and I can barely catch my breath.

It's his car. He didn't get into his car. I know there's only one thing that would have stopped him, and we're near the sea and they're sending out the Coast Guard. They already think the worst. I want to cry again but I'm scared to, because if I start to cry now, I don't know if I'll be able to stop.

Somebody is saying my name, I can't tell who, but they keep saying it. My dad touches my shoulder and I turn to look at him. It isn't him speaking though, it's Sergeant Moore, so I turn to look at him.

"Ava, according to the DVLA records, a Darren Barton is listed as his next of kin?" he's telling me, but he's asking too. I nod and force the words out.

"Darren is his best friend... they're like brothers."

"We are going to make contact with him," he assures me. "Do you know how to get in touch with any other family members?" he asks, and I shake my head in response. "Anyone at all?" he asks me.

My dad steps in for me. "There's history there... they're not on speaking terms," he tells him.

"I remember where his ex-wife lives," I say vacantly. I give him the details, and he asks me more questions.

"What was Mark's frame of mind when I last saw him? Was anything said to give any indication that he may be going somewhere else?" I focus on his words, and I answer as best as I can, but the whole time I'm telling myself, "Don't cry, don't cry, don't cry." If I let the pain in it will overwhelm me, and then I'll have to admit what everyone else in the room is already thinking.

Somebody comes in, there's a police mechanic here and they're going to open up Mark's car. Sergeant Moore goes out. I stay exactly where I am at the kitchen table. I'm just focusing on breathing. Breathing, and not thinking. I pick up my phone and I call him again.

Voicemail.

I listen to his voice, but I don't leave a message this time. The tears are already forming, and I know if I speak, they'll spill over.

Sergeant Moore comes back in and shows me a bag — Mark's bag — I confirm that for them. We now know that he got to his car and put his bag in it, but something stopped him from getting in and driving away.

Somebody else comes into the kitchen. They can't get hold of Darren and by the sounds of the dial tone he's abroad. More questions follow. "Do I know where he is? Is there anyone else they can call?" Then I remember Lilly.

I pick up my phone and call her and she answers after a few rings, sounding happy to hear from me.

"Ava," she says enthusiastically. "How are you?"

"Lilly..." is all I manage to say before I break down in tears.

I can't stop them now and I can't speak so Dad takes my phone from me and walks into the living room, where Mum has been hiding Jacob away.

I sit at the table with my head in my hands, crying like I cried in my flat the day I lost him. I can't stop, I want to, but I can't. I'm aware of arms around me, holding me tight. It's my mum. She holds me close and says nothing, but I can feel that she's crying too. I hear Dad's voice again. He's told Lilly what's going on and she'll keep trying to get hold of Darren, but will contact Mary herself if she can't track him down.

Sergeant Moore goes back to the station to review some information, but he leaves an officer with us. I have no idea how much time has passed, but Lilly calls back and Dad takes the call for me. They speak for a few moments but then he puts his hand over the mouthpiece and looks at me.

"She wants to speak to you," he tells me, and I take a deep breath and take the phone from him.

"Lilly..." I try to say, but it comes out as a whisper, so I clear my throat and try again, but it doesn't come out any better.

"Oh my God, Ava..." she sounds broken too. "I don't know what to say. I finally got in touch with Darren and he's on his way to Clovelly... he wants to be involved with the investigation. He should be there first thing tomorrow," she tells me, then she hesitates. "I'm going to see Mary now and I'll travel tomorrow as well. I... I imagine they will too, but I'll let you know."

I still haven't spoken. The tears are waiting to fall, and my throat is tightening, but I eventually find my voice. "They've sent the boats out, Lilly," I tell her. "They think he's in the water..." I say, and a sob escapes me.

"Ava, you listen to me," she says firmly. "Mark is a strong swimmer. Really strong. If... if he went into the water then there is a good chance he got to safety," she tells me. "There's a good chance he's waiting to be found."

I let out a deep breath. "I want to believe that — I do, but... I've lost him, haven't I?" I ask, and I let the tears fall freely. "We wasted so much time," I say through my cries. "And I've lost him."

"Ava, please, please try to be positive," she says, crying now too. "He loves you so much. He would not leave you without a fight."

I breakdown at her words, because a fight is exactly what I fear has happened.

"Ava... I'm sorry but I need to go to Mary's now," she says reluctantly. "I'll call to check in later, but please have someone call me if there's anything new."

I'm crying too hard to speak now so I hand the phone back to my dad and he says our goodbyes.

I fell asleep on the sofa. I don't know how. I just lay there because my head was hurting, and I couldn't sit at the table anymore. Usually, when you wake up you get a short, sweet moment where you forget what is going on — but that didn't happen. The reality of what is happening hit me straight away, because it never left.

I can smell cooking and the clock tells me it's almost five — Jacob needs dinner. I've not been much of a mum today. I've cuddled him when he's wanted me and I've fed him when he's wanted it, but there was no engagement with him — I just stared at the wall. Mum has been with him keeping him happy, but at this moment I feel awful for not being there for him. I walk into the kitchen, he's in his high chair but his dinner isn't ready yet, so when he gives me an excited giggle, I put a smile on my face and take him out. I don't say anything to anyone, I just take him to the living room and hug him.

"I love you, Jakie Baby. I love you so much. I'm here for you. I'm here..." I say, whilst kissing him — but he wants to be put down, so I let him go and he goes over to his toys, and I sit on the floor and play with him as best I can. Then Dad comes in with a cup of tea for me.

"Has there been any news?" I ask him.

"Not much," he says swallowing hard. "They've gathered the available CCTV footage and are working through it."

I take a deep breath and ask, "And the boats?"

He shakes his head. "Nothing, sweetheart. They'll... they'll have to stop for the day soon... no light," he tells me.

I look at him in a panic. "They won't look through the night?" I ask him, horrified.

"They can't... they don't—"

"What if he's hurt? If he's resting on some rock or in some, I don't know, some cove then he'll have to face another night," I cry out and the tears fall again.

Mum walks in and picks up Jacob. "Dinner is ready, little man," she says to him brightly. She quickly takes him back to the kitchen, but I see from his face that my outburst has startled him, and I instantly feel like I'm failing him again.

Dad moves to my side and tells me, "They are doing everything that they can."

"What about me?" I argue back. "I'm just sitting here waiting and being an utterly shit mum," I say, waving my hand towards the kitchen.

"Hey... listen to me," he gently commands, and he holds onto my face so that I have no choice but to look at him. "There's nothing you can do right now," he tells me. "We have to let them do their job, and that boy... your son adores you. You can do no wrong in his eyes, and you can't put pressure on yourself like that, sweetheart." He pauses for a moment before continuing, "This is... what you're going through right now is most people's worst nightmare... and you're living it. Your mum and I are here for both of you. Jacob is being looked after," he reassures me. "You need to focus on you so that you can be strong for him, but right now, it's OK not to be." My tears fall even faster and he wraps his arms around me. "It's OK not to be," he tells me again.

He holds me as I cry in his arms, but after a few minutes my mum comes in. "I've made soup," she tells me. "I know you probably don't feel like it, but you need to eat, you're feeding Jacob, so come and eat something... please."

I don't say anything, but I don't resist as my dad leads me to the kitchen. I start to eat the soup because they want me to, but as soon as it hits my stomach my body lets me know that I need it, so I finish my bowl and then my mum refills it. I eat that too and my body feels a little better, but my soul feels more destroyed than before. Because with each mouthful that I took I thought about Mark. I thought about the fact that he wasn't eating. That he was cold. Hurt. Scared. Alone. Yet, as much as those thoughts crushed me, I hung onto them... I'm hanging onto them, because as terrible as they are, they are better than the alternative.

After dinner, I decide to have a bath with Jacob, because I want to show him that I'm still here for him. We splash and play, and I smile when he giggles, but I ask Mum to dress him for bed because the bath was too cool for me, and I need to lose myself in the warmth of the shower. Once I've got him to sleep, I go downstairs to see if there's any more news. Dad tells me that there's nothing from the police, but Lilly called to say that she will be arriving tomorrow, as will Mary, Tom, Hattie, Ted and Will. They're all coming... of course they are, but Lilly has promised that I won't have to face them alone, and my parents make the same promise to me also.

I feel helpless and exhausted. My world is falling apart and there's nothing I can do, so I go to bed. I take my phone and I call him for the twentieth time. Each time I've allowed myself to hope that this will be the time he'll answer, but the voice I hear — his voice — is always a pre-recorded one.

Always his voicemail.

I dial a few more times so that I can hear him, then I open my messages so that I can read his words, but it's not enough. It suddenly occurs to me that although I stripped my bed after he stayed, I didn't get around to washing it. I go to the laundry basket hoping that my mum hasn't decided to be helpful and put a wash on today. She hasn't. I find what I'm looking for and take it back to Jacob's room. I put my pillow inside the pillowcase and lay there taking in his smell. Silent tears fall, I wrap my arms around myself and eventually, I fall asleep; breathing him in.

36

Jacob wakes me at seven O'clock and I bring him into bed for a morning feed. I don't want to get up yet. I don't want to think about what else might have happened while I've been safe in my bed. I can hear my parents downstairs though, and after Jacob has finished, I force myself to face the world. It's early so there's no update, we only know that the boats went back out at first light. I force food into myself again, then I wash and dress so that I'm ready to face whatever is coming next.

We get a call from PC Harris at half past eight telling us that they've reviewed the CCTV footage and they need us to come in and "confirm the identity of the person in the images." Those are the words he uses. This means they've seen him on camera, and this means that they know something, only, they're not telling us because they need to tick all their boxes first.

Dad and I get there for nine, leaving Jacob and Mum once again. We're shown into a basic interview room which contains a table with four chairs, a camera on the ceiling in the corner and there's a recording device on the table. PC

Harris walks in with a file — I was expecting to see the actual footage, but it would seem they're only bringing photos. My heart sinks. I wanted to see him moving. I wanted to see him living.

Joe greets us, and then gestures for us to sit down as he sits across from us and turns on the tape recorder.

"Ava, this is just a formality," he tells me. "We believe we know the identity of the person in the images I'm about to show you, but for the avoidance of doubt we need you to confirm it. Is that OK?" he asks.

"Yes..." I force out, my heart pounding again.

He opens the file and places four different images of the same man in front of me. The same man, but in different locations around Clovelly. I stare at them and then look back at Joe.

"I don't understand... this isn't Mark."

"We know," he replies, "but we need you to tell us if you recognise the man in these images."

"You know who it is," I say, voice raised. Why has he brought me these photos? I was expecting to see Mark.

"Ava, please... I know this is so hard, but can you please tell us who is in these images?" he asks again more gently.

"It's Lucas..." I pause to correct myself. "It's Jamie O'Connor," I confirm for him.

"Thank you, Ava," he says, turning off the tape recorder and standing to leave.

"What? That's it?" I ask, astonished. "Is that all we're here for?"

"We just—"

"No, Joe! You need to tell me what this means," I shout at him. "Are these photos from Sunday night? Was he here then? Where is Mark? Where are the images of Mark?" I burst into tears and my dad puts his arm around me.

"Come on, Joe," Dad implores. "You can't leave her hanging like this, it's cruel."

"We have found images of Mr Davidson on CCTV," he tells us, looking up at the camera — he's clearly not supposed to tell us more, "and Mr Barton has identified him from them."

"Darren is here?" I ask urgently. "Can I see him?"

"Mr Barton is currently helping Sergeant Moore with our enquiries—"

"Joe!" I shout through my tears. "You know something. Please, please, tell me," I plead.

A knock at the door startles us all and in walks Sergeant Moore, with Darren right behind him. More tears flow at the sight of him. I'm scared but I also feel a little relieved, because Darren gets things sorted. Darren will always protect Mark. Darren can find him. He walks over to me and pulls me in for a hug. We've never hugged before and it should feel strange, but right now he's the only thing giving me hope and I don't want to let him go.

"Are you OK?" he asks me.

"No," I say through my sobs. "He won't tell me what's going on."

Darren pulls away from me and moves me towards a seat, then he gently pushes me down so that I'm sitting. He pulls a chair out and sits right in front of me and takes my hands in his. He is holding them tightly and a feeling of dread overwhelms me. My heart feels like it might actually burst out of my chest, and the rush of blood to my ears is making me feel dizzy.

"Ava... please just listen for a minute," he tells me, and I can see his concern for me is genuine. "The CCTV footage gathered shows that after Mark left your house and put his bag in his car, he walked to the beach and stood by the railings," I start to open my mouth to ask a question, but his eyes are asking me to just listen, so I do.

"He stood there for about an hour. He walked around a bit, checked his phone, but he stayed in the same area. We think he was trying to lure him out. To lure Jamie out." I let out a sob, because I know it worked — I saw those railings in one of the images Joe showed me. Please, no.

"It worked," Darren says, confirming my fears, and I pull my hands away so that I can cry into them. "Please try to hear me, Ava, please..." he pleads again, and I find the strength to look at him, but I can't stop crying. "Jamie surprised him from behind. Mark went over the railings and into the water, but he took Jamie with him..."

"Dad!" I cry out, and he's there in a second wrapping his arms around me as I completely break down. I fall off the chair onto my knees and he sits on the floor with me as my heart shatters and my world completely falls apart. I have never felt pain like this before. It's hard to cry because it's hard to breathe, but somehow the sobs escape me, and the tears won't stop. It's over. He's gone. He had my heart completely, and now he's gone.

Darren is still speaking. He's telling me what a strong swimmer Mark is. How there were boats out there that night. He could have swum to one. They could have taken him somewhere. They're going to check the hospitals now — but I know the boats are still out. The boats are out because he went into the water. That's all I can think of "he went into the water," and I squeeze my eyes tightly shut to try to rid myself of the image of his lifeless body floating in the dark.

After a while, I stop crying enough to be able to support my own body, and Dad takes me to the car and drives us home. I don't know how long we were on that floor for, but my knees hurt, and my legs are stiff. I sit with Jacob in the living room as Dad speaks with Mum in the kitchen. Darren is here too; I hear him on the phone to Lilly — she'll be here in half an hour, but I just sit watching Jacob. I know I'm in the room, but it doesn't feel like it. I feel numb now. I don't know which emotion I should be feeling more, pain, loss, or fear, so I push them all away and try to lose myself in nothingness. I have no idea what to do next. I focus on Jacob because he needs me to, and because he's the one thing that I have left to live for. Nothing else feels worth it anymore. Mark's gone and my heart is gone with him.

Lilly is next to me now; I didn't even hear her come in. I look at her vacantly and she holds me, she kisses my cheek and whispers in my ear, "Have faith, Ava... don't give up on him."

My tears roll silently down my cheeks and I watch as one lands on the floor. It just sits there for a second before sinking into the fibres of the carpet, and once again I have to shake off the image of Mark sinking deeper and deeper into the cold, dark water.

My dad's voice brings me back to attention, he sounds urgent and annoyed. I look at him, trying to see what he wants to say. Has he just received news? I didn't even hear the phone.

"Ava..." he says, clearly unnerved and I feel my heart ready to rise to my throat again. "They're here. In the tea rooms — all of them." His eyes narrow and I realise who he means. "They're refusing to leave until they see you."

So, they're here — I knew it was coming. They're here and they're making their demands, yet again, and they're making a scene in my mum's tea rooms of all places. I feel my body coming back to life. I'm no longer numb. I'm absolutely furious

I splash some water on my face, but it does nothing because there's been too many tears. My eyes are red and swollen and nothing is going to change that. I look at myself and realise once again that anger feels good. Anger is so much easier to bear than pain. Mum reluctantly agrees to stay with Jacob, and Darren drives the rest of us to the tea rooms. As promised, Lilly is with me. We're in the back of the car and she's holding my hand, letting me know that I have their support. I'm anxious, but not because I'm scared of them. This is going to be the showdown that was always going to happen, and that would've happened sooner if I'd just stood up to Hattie in London. Mark should be with me — we were going to face them together. Once again, I'm facing them when my heart is breaking. Only, this time I won't be weak. He wouldn't want me to be weak.

Once out of the car, I take the lead, feeling compelled to get there as soon as possible. The others rush to catch up with me and it's Dad's hand that gets to the door handle before mine. We pause and he gives me a nod, he's telling me that I can do this. I look back at Lilly and Darren and their faces and smiles remind me that they have my back too. Mark isn't here, but I'm not in this alone.

They all watch as we walk in, and I move further into the seating area so that I'm ahead of them and they're closest to the door. I look at all their faces and I can see their pain and fear, and I'm reminded that this is going to be killing them too. Then I see the disdain, it's in all of them and then I stand face to face with her. With the woman that destroyed my life — with Hattie. I see her anger and I remember my own, and I make sure that she can see it in me too.

"I'm here," I tell her. Only her.

It was always going to come down to me and her eventually.

“Is that all you have to say?” she asks furiously.

“What would you like me to say, Hattie?” I ask her, managing to keep my voice calm even though my heart is pounding, and the rage is making my skin feel like it's burning.

“I want to know where my dad is!” she shouts back. “I want to know why he was here.”

“I wish I knew,” I reply honestly. “I wish he was here with me, safe — and you know why he was here because we told you, and I know Lilly's filled you in on the rest.”

“If by ‘the rest,’” Mary barks out, “you mean that you had his baby and kept it a secret for over a year, then yes. We know.”

I don't even acknowledge her, and I don't take my eyes off Hattie.

“How could you do that?” Hattie asks bitterly. “And more importantly, how could he forgive you?” She's getting louder but somehow, I'm keeping my calm.

“He forgave me because he loves me,” I tell her, “and because he understood why I would want to keep my child...” I move closer so that I can get right in her face, “far away from a poisonous bitch like you!”

She looks startled and my dad puts his hands on my shoulders to move me back again.

“How dare you!” Ted shouts. “Do you know what we're going through?”

“I do actually, Ted,” I turn to face him full on, “because I'm going through it too. Besides, I thought you were all on board with kicking people when they're down?” I look at them all and then focus back on Hattie and say, “When they're hurting more than they've ever hurt before.”

“It doesn't matter what you say, this is your fault.”

I was expecting that, it's what I've been telling myself, but it still feels like a slap in the face coming from her.

"He was here because of you!" she shouts, pointing a finger at me. "That man went after him because of you!"

She bursts into tears but then she quickly pushes them away to allow the anger to come back. Hattie finds anger easier, just like me.

My own tears fall now too. "You're absolutely right, Hattie," I say, and that shocks her. "He was here because of me and Jamie went after him because of me..."

"Ava..." Lilly protests, but I look at her and put my hand up to reassure her that I need to say this.

I look Hattie in the eye again and tell her, "I will take whatever blame and guilt is coming my way and I'll bear it as best as I can."

Even in this situation I can see that she feels triumphant, like she's got the upper hand. Can't she see that there are no winners here?

"But, Hattie," I say more firmly, "you seem to be forgetting one crucial thing."

"And what's that?" she snarls.

"Why am I here?" I ask, and her face pales. "Why did he need to track me down here? Why am I not in my flat, that I loved, in Muswell Hill, instead of here?"

She says nothing, but Mary does. "I don't think we need to go into that here, do you?"

I look at her and then glance around the rest of the tea rooms to see who else is here — I didn't even look when we arrived. My eyes settle on Jessica Miller and I let out a bitter laugh.

"Actually, Mary, I think now is the perfect time," I tell her. "You see, there were many, many rumours circulated about me when I arrived here, but none of them really touched on the truth — but you see we have Jessica Miller here..." I turn and point at her and she shuffles uncomfortably in her seat, "so we can guarantee that anything said here will be around the village in five minutes flat. So, let's put them all out of their misery and tell them the truth," I say, and I glare at her so hard that even she backs down.

I look at Hattie again and see that she's uncomfortable too. She's never met this version of me before, which is funny considering she created it. "I asked you a question, Hattie. Why am I here?" I ask again. She swallows hard but says nothing.

I guess this is all on me then. "I'm here, Hattie, because I fell in love with your dad. We didn't want to hurt anyone, it just happened, and we couldn't stop it — but we did hurt people in the process. We hurt you... all of you," I add, looking at Ted and Will. "And when you found out, you did exactly what I knew you'd do. You asked him to choose — his children or me. Only, I didn't let him choose, did I?"

She's struggling to maintain eye contact and I push on. "I chose," I remind her. "I chose you. I chose to not hurt you anymore. I chose to not destroy his relationship with you. I. WALKED. AWAY!" I shout at her. Then I take a moment to regain my calm, once again. "You saw me that night," I say. "You saw how much it hurt me. You saw that my heart was breaking."

Her tears start to fall now but they no longer affect me, so I carry on. "You asked me not to contact our mutual friends for a week. You said you needed them, and I agreed. You asked me to promise not to tell anyone about Mark, and I agreed — like you knew I would. Good old Ava... always doing what Hattie asks," I say sourly.

"So, there I was, feeling the most pain I'd ever felt... until now," I clarify, and my voice cracks, so I take a deep breath and force myself to continue. "I'd lost the man that I was in love with, and I'd lost the person that could've helped me through it. My best friend... you. And at the end of that week — that most horrendous week... Miri and Tasha came to see me, and they told me what you had said." I swallow hard at the memory of that day. "That we'd fallen out because I was sleeping with both of your brothers."

I look at Ted and Will now. "And you both backed it up, making it all the more believable," I scoff at them. "What was it? Wishful thinking? Or were you just pissed off because your dad managed to do in one day, what you'd both been failing to do for years?"

Ted opens his mouth to speak but then I see him look at my dad. I don't turn to see for myself, but I imagine he gave him a silent warning, and Ted listened.

"I thought of you two like you were my own brothers," I tell them, and they look down, clearly feeling the shame that they ought to.

I turn back to Hattie. "It was perfect Hattie, well done." I give her a little clap. "Miri had been in love with Ted for years and Tasha follows where she goes — but just to make sure that she did, you said that I'd kissed her ex — yet another lie."

She swallows hard and I continue, "And the whole time I couldn't really defend myself because I kept my promise, just like you knew I would. So that was Tasha and Miri gone — friends I'd had my whole life," I say shrugging my shoulders at her. "So, that left me with my closest friend at work — Amanda, and you know, she actually helped. She almost got me to the point where I thought that I might actually be able to get through it. You couldn't have that, though could you?" I pause for a moment and then say, "Feel free to chip in at any time,

Hattie. Do correct me if I say something wrong," I scathe at her.

Hattie looks around the room and I imagine she's not seeing many friendly faces, then she just shakes her head at me.

"You had your new boyfriend — our manager — mine and Amanda's that is," I clarify, "tell her that we'd fallen out because I'd had an affair with a married man. And you knew what that would do, because you knew how her marriage ended, because I'm the one that told you," I remind her. "And stupid, loyal, me, still didn't tell her the truth." I raise my hands in exasperation at the memory of my own foolishness.

"I didn't give up, because we worked together so she couldn't avoid me. I thought I'd get the chance to win her over," I tell her. "So, you had your boyfriend try to manage me out of my job with more lies. And I know they were lies," I point at her, "because Amanda told me so — and she'd have gladly told me if I'd messed up at work at that point."

Hattie takes a deep breath and tears stream down her face. Her defiance is gone but she still says nothing.

"So, I did the only thing I could think of," I tell her. "I went to Mark and I asked for his help. For him to get you to stop — only, because he was hurting as much as I was, and because you made him think he'd lose you too — he told me he couldn't. Obviously, I know now that he did," I say, shaking my head at her, "but I didn't know then, so I got angry and I decided that I wasn't going to let you take anything else. I cut my losses. As I'm sure you know, I quit my job that night. The next day I saw the estate agents about renting out my flat, and two weeks later I came here."

I pause to catch my breath before continuing, "I didn't plan to stay here," I tell her. "I thought I'd travel. I don't know, heal, and then figure life out. Only, during those two weeks, when I felt strong for the first time since that night, and only because I pushed the pain away and replaced it with anger." Anger I made sure she could see was still present. "During those two weeks I started paying attention to my body, and I bought a pregnancy test because I'd missed three periods."

I pause and turn to Jessica, who is unashamedly enthralled and tell her, "You should know, Jessica — for when you tell this story — that it's perfectly normal for me to not have a period for a few months when I'm under a lot of stress."

She gives a slightly embarrassed smile and looks away.

I turn back to Hattie. "I avoided taking the test until the morning I was leaving, because deep down I knew it wouldn't be like all those other times. You remember?" I ask. "When you would sit on the bathroom floor while I peed on a stick, and then three minutes later we'd open a bottle of wine when it was negative." A tear escapes her again. "This time it was positive. So, when I came here, I didn't leave after a few weeks like I planned. I stayed. I stayed because I needed the two people that have never let me down more than I ever have before."

I take two steps closer to her, but this time she doesn't flinch. "So, Hattie, the answer to my question — is you. Your dad was here because of me, because of our son — but I'm only here in the first place because of what you did to me. I'm here because of you, Hattie."

She looks away from me now, and I lean in and say more quietly, "I will take the guilt that is coming my way, Hattie, but I will not now or ever relieve you of yours. And if I've lost him again... if he's not coming back to me this time..." I pause as my tears fall and I put my hand on my stomach as my pain starts to overwhelm me again. Then I find the strength to say, "I will never forgive you."

I turn to my dad and let it all out. Anger, pain, fear, guilt — it all floods out as I cry uncontrollably in his arms. I'm falling apart but he holds me tight and I let my heart break in front of everyone. I think my dad is going to say something, but he just holds me, and it's Darren that eventually speaks.

"I think you should all leave," he tells them, and moments later the bell above the front door jingles, letting me know that they have.

37

The rest of yesterday afternoon and evening is a bit of a blur. I was completely physically and mentally exhausted after the confrontation in the tea rooms. I know I cried a lot. I know Dad asked everyone to leave and Linda brought me an overly sweet cup of tea. I think I remember Jessica actually looking sad for me as she left, but I could have been imagining it — I had some very strange dreams last night, after all.

I know Darren and Lilly came here, and Julia stopped by too. Cooper slept on my bed all night — I'm not sure if I invited him or if he sensed my sadness and took it upon himself to look after me. I'm now staring at my coffee and there's been no more news. People are trying to tell me that's a good thing, but I'm not sure how. To me it just means he's lost. The sea just swallowed him up and now it won't give him back. I need him back. I need him back alive, but if that can't happen then I need him back so that I can kiss him goodbye one final time.

Dad thinks I need to walk, to get some fresh air, so I reluctantly agree to take Cooper out with him this morning.

I put Jacob in his baby carrier; I know he'll want to get out and explore once we get to the beach, but it'll be easier than taking the pushchair there. Besides, I want to keep him close. I don't really want to go to the beach, that's where he went in, that's where they both went in, but Dad tells me that watching Cooper chase the waves is hilarious. He thinks, or at least hopes, that it will make me smile a little bit.

As expected, as soon as we get to the beach Jacob wiggles around — he wants out. He tries to help my dad throw the ball for Cooper and I watch them playing for a bit. Jacob is squealing with joy and that at least, makes a small smile form. Then I turn to look at the sea; it looks calm, but I know the currents that flow unseen are strong and have a will of their own. It looks cold and it looks dark, just like I've been picturing. A tear rolls down my cheek and I send out a silent plea. I'm not overly religious, so I guess I'm talking to the sea itself. I ask it to bring him back — to please bring him back to me.

"Ava?" I suddenly hear, and I turn around in surprise. It's an Irish voice and that scares me for a moment, but it's not Jamie, it's a woman. She's older than me, tall, and has dark hair and green eyes, just like her brother, and I instantly realise that standing before me is one of Jamie's sisters.

"You are Ava Swan, aren't you?" she asks.

"Yes," I answer her quietly, unsure how she is going to react to me.

"I thought so," she says, smiling a little. "You're just like Jamie described. I'm Fiona by the way... Fi — Jamie's sister."

I have no idea what to say to her, so I go with the obvious. "It's nice to meet you... I'm so sorry for all of this."

She takes a step forward and I instinctively step back, she notices and pauses, putting her hands up and smiling to show me that she means no harm. "You don't need to be. I don't blame you, Ava," she says sincerely.

"How can you not?" I ask her in disbelief.

"Can I ask you something?" she says, and I nod in reply. "Have you ever heard of me?"

"No," I reply honestly. "Lu... Jamie mentioned that he had three sisters, but he never said much more. And in truth... I never asked," I tell her.

"He has one sister," she replies solemnly. "Just me. And I used to have twin, baby brothers... but we lost Lucas — I think you know about that now?" she asks, and I nod at her again.

"I really don't blame you for this Ava," she says again. "Jamie was a tortured soul — even before we lost our brother. I've not seen him since he left Ireland, but we always talked." Another thing I didn't know. "I know that you brought him happiness... and love."

"Not enough though," I reply solemnly.

"I knew it would never last," she says. "I knew it the day he told me that you'd finally got together. He told me what you said to him. Do you remember what you said, Ava?" she asks.

I think for a moment, it feels so long ago. "I said, 'Lucas O'Connor, I think I'm in love with you,'" I tell her.

She smiles and nods at me. "Exactly. He said that to me word for word, not even realising that he'd said Lucas instead of Jamie." She wipes a fallen tear away and continues, "You see, I thought the change that I sensed in him was brought about by you. By being in love. But I realised then that my brother was living a lie. He was lying to you by pretending to be Lucas, and he was lying to himself if he thought that it could last. Truly being Lucas..." She shakes her head. "That's something Jamie could never keep up for too long."

She takes another deep breath. "I love Jamie, but he was never like Lucas, not deep down. He was putting on an act, and it was only ever going to be a matter of time before Jamie came out," she says, shrugging. "Perhaps I should've pulled him up on it then?" she asks.

"No, this isn't on you," I tell her, "and for what it's worth I did love him. I loved who he pretended to be, at least." I take a deep breath of my own. "Then Mark came back, and I'd never fallen out of love with him, you see. And Jamie — well the cracks started to show," I tell her, and she nods in understanding.

"I'm sorry about what's been done here," she tells me. "I'm sorry about your man, and what he did to you." She points to my neck; some bruising is on show.

I try to tell her thank you, but my tears fall, and I feel the pain rising again and I cannot form the words. She steps closer and this time I don't move, then she reaches out her hand and I take it.

She smiles kindly and says, "I truly hope he's out there somewhere, waiting. I hope you get your happily ever after, Ava."

"I hope..." I start to say, but she shakes her head at me.

"No, Ava," she interrupts, "I know my brother is gone... I can feel it." She puts her hand on her heart then continues, "My only hope for him is that he's at peace."

We both cry, and then she gently squeezes my hand before releasing it and walking away.

Later in the afternoon Dad receives a call from Sergeant Moore. He takes it in the kitchen, and I can't hear what they're saying, but when he walks back into the living room he is as white as a ghost. I just look at him and slowly shake my head. I don't want to hear it. I don't want to know, but he tells me anyway, with tears in his eyes and his hands shaking. A body has been found on the beach in Morwenstow — it's a male with dark hair.

We drive there in silence but it's loud in my head. I just keep saying on repeat, "Please don't be Mark, please don't be Mark, please don't be Mark..." It's still not very warm outside but I keep the window open because I need the air blasting into my face to stop me from being sick. My heart is pounding, and I have to keep letting out a sigh because it hurts to breathe. When we arrive at the beach there is a crowd and a police cordon, but Joe is waiting for us. He takes us through, and people all stare at us whispering... wondering. I see Darren with Mark's family and he waves us over. Mary says something to him, it looks like she's objecting but he clearly silences her.

My legs are like lead, making it hard to walk and I'm gripping my dad's arm so hard that I'm probably hurting him — but he says nothing. I don't look at the others as I pass them, and I stand on the other side of Darren, next to Lilly — they both act as a buffer between me and them. I look around and I see Fiona. She's alone and she looks scared, just like we are. We can't see the body from here as there are screens up, but I see Sergeant Moore step away from it and call Joe over to him, and then Joe walks over and goes behind the screen too. Nobody is saying anything, and I don't look at any of them, I just stare at the screen and try to focus on breathing. In and out. In and out. Keep breathing.

Joe and Sergeant Moore both step out and they start scanning the crowd. Their eyes stop on me for a moment and my heart stops beating. They linger for what feels like minutes but are only seconds in reality, but then they carry on looking before stopping again, this time for longer. I follow their gaze and it leads to Fiona, and then they start to walk over to her, and I see her raise her hand to her mouth. She looks around, and as our eyes meet, I see the pain and realisation in hers. I open my mouth to try to speak but only manage to let out the breath that I've been holding.

They get to her, say a few words, then start to walk her over to the screens... to the body. I let go of my dad's hand and step forward without thinking, but he reaches for me and stops me.

"No Ava," he says. "Don't do this to yourself!"

"She's his sister," Darren adds, "she's the only one that's needed for formal identification."

I just look at them both and tell them, "She's on her own," and continue walking. She's moving slowly so I catch up to her easily and I reach for her hand.

She turns with a start, but then gives me a grateful smile, and I put my other hand on her shoulder as they pull back the screen and we step behind it.

Darren

Darren watched as Ava went over to the woman being led to the body. He knew who she was, Mike had put her photo and details in his file. Fiona Munroe — formally O'Connor — Jamie O'Connor's older sister.

"I didn't think Ava knew his sister," he said to Jonathan, who was watching his daughter with concern.

"She doesn't," he replied. "Fiona approached her on the beach this morning. They talked for a bit, that's all."

Darren understood what his best friend saw in Ava

Swan. Yes, she was very beautiful, and he teased Mark about her age when he had first told him about their relationship. Yet, he knew there was much more to her than that. He knew it the first time they met. She just had a way about her, and it was plain to see that she was as in love with Mark as he was with her. Lilly said she was a "good soul" within about the first twenty minutes of meeting her, and that was all the endorsement he ever needed.

She'd done more and more since then to reinforce his admiration of her. He wished she'd not walked away from Mark when they were first together. He knew Mark would've fought for the relationship regardless of the price, but she had ultimately sacrificed herself. Mark was devastated and he wished he could take that away, but he'd always admired her bravery that day. Ava had thought that it was the right thing to do and so she did it, in spite of the cost to herself. Now, she was dealing with her own pain again, and yet, she had just walked off to help someone she'd only just met through theirs. This was the woman his best friend loved, and he completely understood why Mark had gone to the lengths that he had to be with her, and to make her safe again.

He looked at the people on his right — Mark's family — his family too, really. They had started to relax a little in the knowledge that the police obviously didn't believe that the body on the beach was their father. The boys looked relieved and had started a conversation with each other, but Hattie was focused on the two women that were walking away hand in hand. He'd heard Hattie breathe a sigh of relief when the police walked over to Fiona. He knew she loved her father, and he knew this was hard for her too, but that wasn't what was concerning her right now.

Darren had never really discussed with Mark his

thoughts on why Hattie did what she did to Ava. Mark had put it down to Hattie's pain and anger at what she perceived to be a massive betrayal on Ava's part, but Darren believed there was more to it than that.

Mark went to Japan with his family's blessing and he made a big effort to make sure that he was still involved in their lives. They talked all the time, and he travelled back to the UK more than most would — but he didn't get to see the day to day like Darren and Lilly did. They made a point of being involved in their God-children's lives, and they'd even seen Ava before at family gatherings. Although Mary would often give her jobs and Hattie would dominate the rest of her time. He had never properly met her before that weekend in the Cotswolds, but he watched, and he listened. Hattie would talk about Ava a lot — the boys too — but Hattie in particular, and she'd let a few things slip that she perhaps wouldn't have — if Darren was not as good as he was at getting people to open up.

Hattie clearly adored Ava, and it was mutual — they'd been thick as thieves since they were five. There were similarities between them, but also some fundamental differences. Hattie wanted people to adore her and generally they did, however, she had to work for it. Ava, on the other hand didn't seek it out, but people were naturally drawn to her, and from what he saw he didn't think she even realised it. Hattie did realise it though, and she used Ava's ignorance to her own advantage. As popular as Ava was, there was only ever really Hattie, Tasha and Miranda that she truly called her friends, and that's because they were 'Hattie approved' — as Darren thought of it.

Darren was quite certain that Ava didn't realise that Hattie had either directly, or indirectly interfered in new friendships that Ava had started to form in the past. She had said herself when they were in the Cotswolds that she "didn't make friends easily." She had no idea that a big part of her life had been controlled by the person she considered to be her best friend.

That's why Hattie did what she did. She had felt betrayed by Ava, but it came down to something more basic than that. She didn't want to share her, and she didn't like losing control. She lost Ava that day, and if she couldn't have her in her life, then she decided that Ava couldn't have anything at all in hers. So, she took, and she took, and in the process of doing so she started to feel like she'd clawed back the control that she had lost. Until Mark finally hit his children where he knew it would hurt — when he threatened to take their inheritance away. Still, the damage was done — she'd wrecked Ava's life, but then Ava claimed that control back when she moved to Clovelly and rebuilt it.

Now, Hattie was remembering that she had lost a loyal and caring friend. A good soul that puts other people before herself. Hattie had thought she'd won and for a while she had. Now she could see that she hadn't destroyed Ava, after all. That was proven at the tea rooms when she had given them both barrels. Hattie hadn't expected that. Ava showed them exactly how angry they'd made her, and Hattie probably walked away thinking that her once, loving friend was now bitter, but now Hattie was seeing that Ava was still full of love, it's just that she no longer had any for her.

~

Ava

They pull open the zip on the body bag to reveal his face and Fiona instantly doubles over as the pain of seeing her brother hits her full force. I keep my hands on her back, letting her know that she's not alone, but I can't take my eyes off his face. It's Jamie, I can see his green eyes — they're open — but the water has done damage and he doesn't quite look the same. I'm looking at him but I'm thinking about Mark. Is this what it will be like when the sea eventually spits him back out?

I stay next to Fiona until her crying lessens and it becomes clear that she wants some time alone with her brother. So, I walk away towards the sea and sit on the sand, wrapping my arms around my knees which I've pulled close to my chest. I'm not sure how long I've been sitting here for, but eventually Fiona joins me. She's quiet now, she's all cried out. I can relate to the feeling, only, it never lasts long — the tears always return.

"They're together again now. Lucas will take care of him... the water... it took them both," she says, and as she breathes deeply a single tear falls.

"I am truly sorry for your loss, Fiona," I tell her.

"Thank you," she replies.

We sit in silence for a little longer, then she speaks again. "They hope to do the post-mortem in the next day or so," she tells me. "Then I ought to be able to take him back home."

"What are you going to do?" I ask her.

"I can't wait here," she says shakily. "I need my husband and my babies to hold right now. I'll go home tomorrow and return when he's ready."

"That's probably for the best," I agree.

"I don't want to remember him like that," she chokes out.

"Did you drive here?" I ask her.

"Emm... no, Sergeant Moore brought me," she replies.

"I hope we don't have to stay here too much longer," she adds with a shudder.

"If you'd like you can come back with us?" I ask her. "You shouldn't be alone and, well, I threw away the hard copies of the photos I had of Jamie after..." I look at her and see that she understands, I don't need to repeat what he did to me, right now. "But everything is backed up digitally. So, if you wanted to see some photographs of him when he was happy?"

"I'd really like that," she says quickly, reaching out to me. "Thank you, Ava. Thank you."

We help each other up, and I wait as she tells Sergeant Moore what our plans are and then we walk over to my dad. He's standing next to Lilly in the same spot that I left him, he smiles warmly at us and reaches out to pull me in for a hug.

"Dad, this is Fiona," I tell him, and he smiles and extends his hand to her. "I said we'd take her back to Clovelly. She's going to come to mine for a bit," I tell him.

I can see that he understands, and he puts out his arm for her to lean on. I let them walk ahead a little and then turn to Lilly, and she immediately puts her arms around me

"That was really kind, Ava," she tells me. "That must've been so hard."

"I don't want to see him like that." I tell her, as the tears fall down my face. "I don't want to think of him like that."

I cry in her arms and she holds me tight, and then I feel another hand on my back — it belongs to Darren. He leans in a little and looks at me with sincerity as he says, "You won't, Ava. I promise you — you won't."

38

Fiona stayed for a few hours and we sat and went through photographs from my time with Jamie. Although when I looked at the photos it was hard not to think of him as Lucas. That's the person he was then, whether it was real or not, it felt like it at the time. I explained where photos were taken and what we'd been doing, and we both smiled, laughed and cried. I created an album for her, and she told me that she would keep me updated on all the reports, and eventually, his funeral arrangements. She asked me if I would go and I told her I'd think about it, but I knew that I wouldn't. I'd already done my grieving for Lucas — for the man that I thought Jamie was. I said my goodbyes when we were going through the photos, and I didn't feel the need to see him put into the ground. I told her that it would depend on how things were, and she understood. She had her closure, but I was still waiting for mine.

That was two days ago. Two days have passed since Jamie's body washed ashore and there is still no sign of Mark. Darren and Lilly are still in Clovelly and they come around every day. I know Hattie and the others are here too, but our paths haven't crossed again. Darren is getting a lot of information that people in our situation would usually have to wait for. He has friends in the force in London and they've made sure that Clovelly's police are going above and beyond for him. This morning they are due to inform Fiona of the results of the post-mortem, and Darren is at the station now being briefed. I don't even know why it's important. Jamie drowned. He's dead. What else matters? Yet, for some reason it seems very important to Darren.

I've spent these last two days going through the motions. Sometimes I get lost in the tears, other times I sit here feeling completely numb. I play with Jacob, I fuss over Cooper, and all the time I'm trying to stop myself from admitting the inevitable. Deep down I know that at some point soon I'll need to accept that he's gone and is never coming back — but accepting it means dealing with the grief that will follow, and I'm so scared of doing that. I'm scared to believe that he's gone. That I'll never see his smile, stroke his hair, kiss him, smell him, hear his voice — all of it. He was it for me.

I tried to move on with my life after we broke-up, but it didn't work. It was always him. It will always be him, and it's not just my loss that I'm afraid to grieve for — it's Jacob's too. He will never remember his dad. He'll never remember feeling the love he had for him. He'll grow up without the man that ought to guide him, and he'll look in the mirror and see Mark's face in his own, but he won't remember the original.

It's eleven O'clock when Darren unexpectedly knocks at the door, and when I let him in, I'm surprised to see that he looks happy. For a moment, I want to ask him if Mark's been found somewhere safe and alive, but the pain in my gut reminds me not to. It reminds me that there's no chance of that happening now — it's been too long. So, I invite him in and show him to the living room where my parents are playing with Jacob.

"I've just been with Sergeant Moore," he tells us. "The post-mortem confirms drowning as the cause of Jamie's death. There were no significant defensive or inflicted injuries found, so there will be no suggestion of foul play," he says smiling. "Given that they have the CCTV footage of him falling into the water when he pushed Mark..." he says it so casually, how can he say this so casually? "The coroner will determine it was an accident of his own causing. There will be no blame on Mark," he finishes, looking pleased.

He looks at us all and my parents nod at him, but I can see that they're confused by this too. Darren's smile fades a little as if he was expecting us to share his enthusiasm, and he looks at me expectantly.

"Did you hear that, Ava?" he asks. I was watching Jacob, but I look at him now.

"Yes, Darren, we can all rest easy knowing that Mark died an innocent man." I walk out the door leaving them all behind.

I walk to the beach — I've no idea why I always come back to this spot. This should be the place I want to avoid, but it was the last place he was seen, and something keeps pulling me back here. I look out at the sea once more, but I don't talk to it — I don't see the point. It isn't listening to my pleas, and it isn't going to grant me my wish. I hear crunching in the sand behind me and I turn, expecting to see Darren or one of my parents, so I'm a little taken aback when I see Mary walking towards me. I let out a huff and wipe the tears that had been falling away — she is the last person I want to see.

"What do you want, Mary?" I ask her, keeping my back to her and letting her know exactly how much her presence irritates me.

I spent so long having to hide how vile I think this woman is because she and Hattie are so close. Not now though. I look at her briefly and I can see that she wishes that she was dealing with the old Ava. The Ava that used to take everything she threw at her and wore her best smile in the process, but that Ava no longer exists. However, Mary is still Mary and she's not one to back down.

"Are you sure your son isn't imaginary, Ava?" she asks, snarling. "Only, I've never seen you with him."

"If I was out with him and saw any of you coming, I would run in the opposite direction," I tell her, sighing a little. Then I look right at her and say, "I don't want him to start believing in monsters at such a young age." She laughs a little, but I can see she's annoyed. "What exactly do you want, Mary?" I ask more bluntly.

"Well..." she starts, a little nervously, "I think it's clear that we're at the point where we need to start accepting things, and I have my children to think about."

"You mean that you want to help them deal with the loss of their dad?" I say to her bitterly, knowing full well that isn't the direction that she wants to take this conversation in.

She stutters a little but brushes it away to carry on. "Of course, I will do that!" she snaps. "But I have to be practical too. Your boy... naturally, he has a claim, but I'm hoping to appeal to you to do the right thing."

"I beg your pardon?" I practically spit at her. "We don't even know for certain that he's gone, and you're already concerned about the fact that his money might be split four ways instead of three?" I cannot believe this woman. "Oh, Mary, my mum had you pegged from day one." She frowns, sensing what's coming. "You really are a piece of work, aren't you?"

"I'm just suggesting—"

"Go away, Mary," I tell her calmly, trying my best not to let her see how angry she is making me.

"So, you want his money then, do you?" she snarls at me.

"No, Mary!" I shout at her now. "I want him. I want Mark. I want him back. Nothing else matters."

"So, I'm supposed to believe that your love for him was always pure, am I?" she asks bitterly.

"Why? Wasn't yours?" I snap back.

"Yes! But I'm not twenty years younger than him." She clearly thinks that she is getting one over on me, but she doesn't know that I know what I know.

"Is that so hard to believe?" I ask calmly now, knowing that I have the information to put her back in her place. "He's a gorgeous man. A kind man, a funny man... you think it too," I tell her. "In fact, I think you quite recently told him that he was a 'damn sexy man' in one of your drunken texts that you so often send asking him for sex." I smile at her and she shuffles on the spot clearly unnerved. "What? Did you think he wouldn't have told me?" I ask, laughing at her.

She starts to clear her throat, but I can see that she has no idea what to say, so I carry on. "I think my favourite one was when you told him that... and I believe I am quoting the text correctly — 'A man like you needs a woman, not a girl.'" I laugh at her. "We laughed a lot about that one. Especially considering just how hard I had made him cum only half an hour before."

She looks embarrassed, and I'm about to say more but then I glance a little further behind her, and see Tom. I didn't know he was there but by the look on his face he just heard everything that I said. Mary sees my shocked expression and turns to follow my gaze towards her husband, and she gasps.

He looks between us, and I say guiltily, "I'm sorry Tom, I didn't see you."

Tom is a nice man, and he's only ever shown me kindness. I have no problem ripping Mary apart as she's only ever shown me contempt. I wanted her to know that I knew so that she would back off and leave me alone. I hadn't intended to cause any damage to her marriage.

He looks at me sadly but still manages to give me a small smile. "It's OK, Ava. You're not the one in the wrong here," he says, and then he walks away.

Mary looks at me and I just shake my head — she looks scared, not angry, neither of us knew he was here. She goes after him and I put my head in my hands and let out a loud groan. There is enough pain here. I didn't intend to add to it.

I walk home and sit at the kitchen table with my head in my hands. I never thought I'd feel guilty about Mary. Though in truth, it's Tom I'm upset about hurting. I suddenly realise how quiet it is in my house and I'm about to get up to see where everyone is, but then Darren walks in from the living room and startles me. He sees my questioning expression and tells me that my parents have taken Jacob for lunch at the tea rooms.

"I'm sorry about before," he says. "I realise that may have been confusing." I just nod at him — I'm still processing what happened on the beach.

"Are you OK?" he asks.

"Um... no..." I say, honestly. "I think I just destroyed Tom and Mary's marriage."

"OK... how?" he asks, looking confused and a little amused.

"She confronted me on the beach because she wanted to

talk to me about money," I say, and I start to feel the anger rise again. "She tried to insinuate that was all I ever wanted from Mark. I didn't really let her say what she was going to say, but it was along the lines of telling me that I shouldn't try and get anything for Jacob."

It was Darren's turn to look annoyed now. "That woman... seriously!" he says with his fists on the table. "So, where does Tom come into this?"

"Well, I challenged her, telling her that if she was still attracted to him then why shouldn't I be? I take it you know about her texts?" I ask, and he rolls his eyes and nods his head. "I pulled her up on them and told her about one in particular, only..." I pause as the guilt kicks in again. "I didn't see Tom. Neither of us knew he was there, but he heard everything."

Darren walks around the table to me and puts a hand on my shoulder. "That's on her, not you," he says firmly. Then he looks at me seriously. "I know Mark set up a savings account for Jacob. Have you even looked at it?" he asks me.

"No," I say honestly, "it's for Jacob. He gave me some paperwork and I've got it filed in the office," I tell him. Then I add shakily, "Darren, I don't want to go down this path. I know at some point that we'll have to go through the formalities, but not yet. Please, not yet..." I beg him. "That means admitting..." I can't finish the sentence as the sobs are choking me and the tears are falling again.

"Ava..." Darren says calmly, "my wife is right. You are a good soul," he says, and I feel the weight of his sincerity. "I know your love for Mark is real, just like his is for you."

I swallow hard as the tears spill out with more force. "I've told you from the start to have faith, Ava," he tells me, looking at me intently. "I told you he's a strong swimmer. I told you there were boats, and I promised you that you'd never see him lying on the beach like Jamie." I'm confused by his words and he sees it. "Look at Jacob's savings account," he tells me. "You have the access details in the envelope. Take a look."

I'm still baffled by what he has just said to me, but I nod at him in agreement.

"I have to go back to London now, there are some things that I need to sort out," he tells me. Then he pulls me in for a hug, and when he lets me go, he says, "Make sure you go online and look at that account."

"I will," I tell him, more to appease him than anything, he is so determined about it, but I still don't understand why.

He asks me to put his number in my phone and says his goodbyes, letting me know that I can call him whenever I need to. After he's gone, I call my mum to ask them what they're doing. They're still having lunch and suggest that they'll take Jacob for a walk afterwards — if I'm OK alone that is. I reassure them that I am and after I say goodbye, I go to the office and unlock the file that I put the envelope in.

I open it and look at the starting balance — it's £200,000! I was expecting more like £2000 at the most. I know Mark has money, but I've never known exactly how much. Is this what Darren wanted me to know? That Jacob would be taken care of no matter what Mary did, because this money is in an account specifically for him? Still, he told me to log on, specifically to go online, so I pull the account and login details out of the envelope. They're handwritten and I run my fingers over the words that he wrote before opening up my laptop. I look at the screen and the first thing I see is the balance, it's £156,250 — not £200,000. Mark told me that only he and I have access to it, and he wouldn't have dipped into this account. I open the transaction history and see that all the transactions have taken place in France. The first is a £35,000 cash withdrawal that appears to have been authorised by a bank in Bordeaux. Then the rest are just smaller amounts, but all in the same area — a place called Saint-Guilhem-le-Désert — which I have never heard of.

I search online and find a truly gorgeous little town near Montpellier, and I instantly think that there's fraudulent activity going on. I'm furious! Somebody, somehow, is taking money from Mark when he's missing. How? I look again and I see the dates, all of the transactions have taken place after Mark disappeared, the large amount in Bordeaux was two days after he went missing.

I just don't get this. I'm about to call Darren to tell him, but then something draws me to the account settings. I click on them and pull up the address, expecting to see Mark's address in Crouch End, but it isn't, it's an address in Saint-Guilhem-le-Désert. I put it into the search engine and a beautiful woodland cottage appears on my screen. What the hell is going on? Think, Ava... think. Darren told me to look at this for a reason. He wanted me to see this. He also promised me that Mark is not dead. He didn't say that exactly, but he's alluded to it — more than once. I wouldn't see him on the beach like Jamie, he said. He said it twice.

I go back over conversations Mark and I had in the past — has he ever mentioned France? I can't think, this is too much. I'm clutching at straws, wanting to believe that he's there. Then there's Darren... Darren has never once looked upset. Mark is his best friend, he's like a brother to him and he's not once looked upset. I didn't notice before because I've been too focused on my own pain.

I sit trying to recall anything ever being said about France. It's possible Mark talked about buying in France when we were first together, but I could be imagining it — or wanting to believe it. I can't tell what's real and what's wishful thinking right now. I've no idea how long I sit like this for, but I hear my parents come back in and realise it's three O'clock already... time keeps disappearing on me.

I shout for them to come into the front room and they can see that I'm freaked out, so their first thought is that there's been news on Mark. I tell them that there isn't, but maybe there is. I'm confusing them, so I tell them everything that Darren said to me, everything he's insinuated from the beginning and what I've just found online.

"Have you seen him look upset?" I ask them. "Even once?"

They look at each other and shrug but they're clearly more worried about me than Darren. They think that I'm jumping to conclusions. That I'm fighting the truth with some fantasy that will soon be crushed. Maybe I am.

I show them the bank account and just like I first did, they assume that it's fraudulent and suggest we call the police.

"No," I tell them. "I know this sounds mad, but Darren was so insistent that I look at this."

"Ava..." Mum starts to say, but she stops and sighs and moves towards me.

"No, Mum, don't!" I shout, and she pauses and looks at me with even more concern. "Darren knew that this is what I would find when I looked. He knew. He knew, and he wanted me to know, don't you see that?" I plead.

"I think we need to take a breath here," Dad says calmly. "This has been a truly hard time for you darling... for everyone," he adds looking at my mum. "I'd love to believe that Mark is alive — that all this is pointing to that, but let's just take some time to think things through... you know, clear our heads a little before getting excited."

"But, Dad..." I try to protest.

"Ava, you know we only want the best for you. Go with your mum, get dinner ready, do something, anything to try to distract yourself from this," he tells me. "I'll go through this, OK. I'll see if there's anything more that I can figure out," he says gesturing towards my laptop.

We have a silent stand-off in the room, until I eventually, and reluctantly agree to let him look into it, and I head to the kitchen with my mum.

Dad stays in the office for an hour, I don't know exactly what he's looking for, more clues? I don't know, but Mum and I more or less stay in silence in the kitchen. I know we're going over everything in our heads though. I look at her every now and then and I see a little frown. Or, she'll pause and just look out of the window, lost in thought. We're cooking shepherd's pie together and it occurs to me that we haven't cooked together like this since I was little. We've cooked in each other's presence often, but not like this. It's nice, but it's definitely not distracting enough.

"Do you mind if I take Jacob and Cooper out for a bit, instead?" I ask her.

"Not at all," she replies. "I've got this under control."

She's talking about the cooking, but it suddenly occurs to me just how much she has had things under control. The amount of times I've walked off, or gone to the police station, or had a show down in her tea rooms, and she's just stepped in and taken care of Jacob for me — taken care of me. Have I even thanked her? I decide to do it now and I wrap my arms around her and squeeze her tight and she reciprocates, squeezing me just as hard. I always hug my dad, I guess he's always been my hero. He steps in and he makes his voice heard, but I realise now that my mum is my hero too — she's just a bit quieter and less imposing in the process.

"I love you, Mum," I tell her. "Thank you for everything you do for us."

"I love you too, darling," she replies, and her voice starts to crack. We are all just a mess of emotions right now.

I take Cooper and Jacob out to the park instead of our usual trip to the beach. I can't face the water today and I don't want to bump into anyone. It's a good choice if my aim is to kill time because Jacob loves the swings and could stay on them for hours. Unfortunately, when Cooper is around, you get about fifteen minutes maximum before he gets restless and wants to get on the move again. It's slow going today because Jacob wants to hold Cooper, and although he's as good as gold for him, it isn't exactly the pace he needs. Thankfully, we have a large dog-friendly area that he can blast around for a bit.

We get home around five O'clock and when I open the back door, I can smell that dinner is ready. I've tried my best not to think about Mark and France, and the possibility, but the question has always been at the back of my mind — could this be real?

Dad's now at the kitchen table and I can tell he is weary, he's clearly been busy trying to work things out for the last two hours, but I can't let him rest. I trust him and I need to know what he thinks about all of this.

"Well?" I ask him. "Have you found anything else?" I start to put Jacob in his high chair, but I watch my dad's face the entire time. I can't read him though because he's wearing his mask — like he always does in these situations.

"I honestly don't know what to think," he tells me, shrugging his shoulders. "In truth, I don't know what I've been hoping to find," he admits. "I know this is a lot to ask but can we just eat dinner, get Jake in bed and then sit down and talk this through, together?" he asks.

I put my head in my hands and let out a loud groan in frustration. He's asking me to wait. Just a few hours — but to wait. All I've done is wait. I've waited for news, waited for a body, waited to start grieving, and now I'm waiting to allow myself to hope.

"Fine," I say reluctantly, "we'll wait." What else can I do right now?

Time moves even slower than usual. I just keep watching the clock slowly tick by as I wait for it to be time to take Jacob for a bath. I eventually get him to sleep and make it downstairs at around eight O'clock. I find my parents sitting silently in the living room, and I waste no more time getting straight to it.

"Right," I say as soon as I enter the room, "what are you thinking?"

He sighs for a moment then starts to speak, only to pause again. He's trying to get the words right; I can see that.

"OK..." he eventually says, "this is what we know." Finally. My dad has done what he does and has come up with an answer. I try my best not to get my hopes up as he continues, "Mark and Jamie went into the water at the same time, in the same place." He pauses and I nod. "And yet, Jamie is the only one to have come ashore. All the hospitals within a one-hundred-mile radius have been checked. All of the islands and coves have been searched, but there's no Mark." I nod again, encouraging him to continue, and he does.

"Then we have Darren..." he says thoughtfully. "We know he was out of the country when Mark first disappeared, and he's never said where he was."

"God, I'd forgotten about that," I say honestly. "Although, we never thought to ask," I add.

"No," Dad replies, "but still, it's a piece of the puzzle — and you're right — those two are like brothers and he's not once looked upset. He's only ever said to have hope. And what he came to tell us earlier... well, I thought it was a bit odd at the time, but now it seems to fit," he says cautiously.

"So, what are you saying?" I ask eagerly. "Do you think it really could be him?" I ask, almost daring myself to truly believe it.

"Ava..." he says, looking at me with concern. "I am petrified... truly, truly petrified of being the reason that you may believe this... just in case it's not true," he tells me. He starts to choke up as he continues, "I'd hate to see you crushed like that." He looks right at me with those eyes that let me know how much he loves me. "But... but, it is starting to look that way," he tells me. He says it cautiously, but he still says it. "And what it comes down to is this... that man loves you. There's nothing he wouldn't do to make you safe," he tells me, sincerely. "And I doubt there's much Darren wouldn't do to make him safe."

My heart is beating like crazy. I want to hope but I'm scared to hope. I want to believe it, but I'm scared to. Yet at the same time I know that I have to follow this path. I have to know once and for all where it leads.

"I know what we need to do," I tell them, and I pick up my phone and find Darren's name. I put it on speaker phone as I call him, and we hear three rings before he picks up.

"Ava... hi," he says as he answers. "Is everything OK?"

"I'm not sure," I answer honestly. "My parents think I need a change of scene for a while. They think we should go away for a bit," I tell him.

"OK, where are you thinking of going?" he asks.

"We're undecided," I reply, "somewhere quiet..." Then I take a deep breath before saying, "We've heard that there are some beautiful areas in the Montpellier region." I swear that I hear him sigh in relief.

"There are," he confirms calmly.

"Could you recommend anywhere in particular?" I ask him with my voice shaking.

"Yes, Ava, I'd be happy to," he tells us. "Saint-Guilhem-le-Désert is particularly beautiful this time of year." My heart stops beating. "I think you'd like it there. I think you'd be very happy there."

I try to speak but nothing comes out and I look at my parents, who have heard it all and they both have their mouths hanging open. My mum lets out a breath and clasps her hands over her mouth in utter shock. It's true. It's really true. How did this happen? How is he in France? Why hasn't he contacted me? I don't know how long we're silent for, but Darren's voice comes over the phone again, asking if I'm still there.

"I am..." I reply, sounding as utterly shocked as I am. "Thank you, Darren," I say, and I end the call.

We go straight to my laptop and I open up the search bar to look for flights, but I'm shaking too much to type so my dad takes over. The air of sadness that has filled my house since Monday morning has been replaced with a nervous excitement. I'd been preparing myself to admit that he's gone, and now it seems that all signs are pointing to him being alive. It's too much, and I start to feel like my heart will actually explode. It's beating so hard and so fast and I can't catch my breath. I start to panic, and my mum sees, and she quickly forces me to a chair. She sits in front of me and holds my face in her hands forcing me to look at her.

"Breathe, Ava," she tells me, calmly but firmly. "Breathe,"

she says again. "Let the air in. Let it fill your lungs... I'm going to count to six and then you can breathe out again... OK?"

I nod at her, but I'm still freaking out. She repeats it again and again, whilst reassuring me that I'm safe, and I slowly start to catch my breath again. We continue until I've slowed my heart rate too, and then I fall into her and she holds me. I've never had a panic attack before, but my mum has seen them many times, because she got her own mum through them too.

While my mum was helping me, my dad was on the laptop and the flights were booked and we fly to Montpellier in two days.

I go to bed feeling hopeful, but when I wake up in the morning, I feel the doubt creep back in and I start to question it all again.

Why am I doing this to myself? Why am I prolonging the inevitable? Surely, he's not really alive? Surely it was all just a dream? It wasn't though, it was real. I look up the address again, just like I did last night. Until about six months ago the house had been on the market. I could see Mark liking this property and I could see him buying it, it's beautiful. If I let myself, I can even picture him there, but I'm still terrified to truly believe that I'm going to see him there. That I'm going to see him tomorrow.

When Dad booked the flights, he allowed for us to be away for two nights. He told us afterwards that he decided on two because one night might not be enough after we've got there and got organised — but then if Mark isn't there, would we really want to stay longer than two? We couldn't really discuss it at the time, what with me being unable to breathe, but I guess it makes sense. He's also booked a bed and breakfast in the town itself, about thirty-five minutes away from where we believe, where we really want to believe Mark is staying.

Today is about getting things organised. We all need to pack, and I need to get Jacob sorted too and I'm utterly relieved that I decided to get him a passport a few months ago. I go to see Julia to ask if she can look after Cooper for a couple of days and my gut churns when I lie to her. I have to lie to her. I hate lying to her, but I can't tell her the truth, because I don't know if the truth is really the truth. Also, because if it is — then I don't know what the repercussions will be. So, I tell her that we are going to Ireland for Jamie's funeral. Thankfully, the timing is right, but I have already told Fiona that I won't be going.

39

We fly out early the next morning, and when we arrive at Montpellier airport it's busy and I can't help getting annoyed at all the people that are in my way. The woman at the car hire company is lovely and she's just doing her job, but she's asking us if we want things we do not want. She's trying to up-sell when we just want to get out. Mum can see and sense the tension coursing through me, and she gives me a reassuring squeeze, and I do my best to smile at the woman when she finally hands the key over to my dad.

By the time we get to Saint-Guilhem-le-Désert it's nearly lunchtime, but I've been pumping Jacob full of snacks all the way here, so I'm hoping that we can get to what I hope is Mark's house, where I hope Mark is waiting, alive and well, without stopping. My stomach is churning and I've no idea what I'm actually going to do or say when I see him. If I see him, I still can't allow myself to fully believe that this is definitely happening.

I'm desperate to see him. I want him to be safe, and in

my arms, again. I want to smell him and kiss him, and to see him looking well in order to destroy the image of him looking like Jamie. The image that has been haunting me. Then, I realise as we drive that I'm also angry. If he is there — if he's been there all this time — all this time that I've been worried that he's dead. Then he is going to have some explaining to do.

We pull up a little way from the house so that we're close enough to see, but not be seen. It looks just like the pictures I found from the listing, but it's been improved. Somebody has been working on it. We have a quick look around from within the car — there are no neighbours in the immediate proximity and there's no car in the driveway. It looks quiet and it looks safe, but Dad is still apprehensive about me going there alone, but I insist that I have to — this has to be just me. He parks up and as I get out, he puts my attack alarm in my hand and steps out of the car with me. He's going to wait there to make sure that he'll hear me if I need help. It takes a minute for me to get my legs to work but eventually, they do, and I walk up the driveway towards the front door.

My stomach is in knots and I still have no idea as to what I'll say if it's Mark that answers the door. If it's not him I'll pull the release on the alarm, and we'll call the police on the person that's been stealing his money, but if it's him, if it's Mark, then I have no clue. I get to the front door. It's solid Oak and it's old. The whole place is old and is clearly undergoing a renovation — could this really be his place?

I don't see a doorbell but there's an old knocker. I slowly put my hand on it and then, taking a deep breath, bang it three times. Then I wait.

Nothing.

I wait for another minute and then I try again, banging with more force this time. Still nothing. I've come all this way, and nobody is here. I can't leave it like this, so I give the handle a try and to my surprise the door is unlocked. I let it open and slowly take a step in.

"Hello?" I call out, shaking. "Hello... Mark?" I try to call a little louder, but I choke up when I say his name.

What was I thinking? He's not here. It's not going to be him, but regardless I am not leaving until I find out who is here. I can smell coffee, so I follow the aroma towards an old, country-style kitchen. I see a half empty cafetière on a worktop and go over to touch it. It's cold. That's good. Hopefully that means that whoever made it is out, as opposed to hiding, and that gives me a little more comfort.

There's an open laptop on the table and I go over to it and touch the mouse pad, and when I do, I see myself. Me, Jacob and Mark to be precise. It's a screensaver — a photograph of the three of us that Lilly took when we were in London. I'm about to let the hope I've been keeping at bay find its way back in, but fear quickly takes over as I hear the large Oak door creak open, and then close loudly seconds later. There's only one door into the kitchen and the footsteps are getting louder — they're coming this way. There's nowhere to go so I back away to the far wall and I make sure that I have my finger positioned ready to set off the alarm. Then I stand there, trying to breathe while I wait to meet whomever is about to walk into the room.

He walks in. He's carrying something, a letter perhaps, so he's not looking up as he stands in the doorway for a moment — but I see him. His hair is looking a little unruly and I can see enough of his face to see a bruise under his left eye. Then he looks up. He looks right at me and I look right into his blue eyes. Mark jumps at the sight of me at first, and he drops the bags he's holding on the floor. Then his tears fall, and when he says my name and smiles at me, I can see the relief flooding out of him.

I stand watching him, no longer breathing. I take him in, completely unaware of the tears that are streaming down my face. I feel my heart pounding, and I hear when he says, "You're here! Thank God, you're here!" but I can't make it feel real.

He is alive. I haven't lost him. I let those words sink into my consciousness and then I finally take in a large breath and double over as a loud, animalistic cry escapes me. I cry and I cry and then his hands are on me, holding me, and then he falls to the ground with me as my legs buckle underneath me.

"Ava..." he says, trying to soothe me. "Ava, I am so sorry about all of this. About what you've been through." I'm still crying with my hands over my face, and he's trying to pull them away so that he can see me, but I can't move them. "It wasn't supposed to happen like this, it wasn't," he tells me. "I wasn't supposed to leave you. You weren't supposed to think..."

He can't say the words, but I can — I have to. I move my hands away, wiping my tears with them and I fight the sobs back enough to be able to say, "I thought you were dead. I thought I'd lost you."

I break down again, but he takes hold of my hands so that I can't hide, and he pulls me into him so that he can hold me properly. Despite everything I'm feeling — my internal fight between fear, anger and relief — I hold him back. I hold him tight, because I don't ever want to let him go again. We hold each other like that for a while, both of us crying. Then I manage to find the strength to speak again.

"What happened?" I ask him through my tears.

"Ava... I'm so sorry, I can explain everything."

"Then explain!" Dad demands harshly, and we both turn to see him standing in the doorway. He looks like he might kill Mark himself. "And make it good," he adds. "Because the pain she has been in... it had better be good."

"Just give us a minute," Mark says to him.

"Mark—"

"A minute, Jonathan!" Mark snaps back, and I'm shocked for a moment because I've never heard anyone stand up to my dad before. "Please, Jonathan," he adds more calmly, "just give us a minute."

"Fine," Dad replies, clearly disgruntled. "I'll go and get El and Jacob and then you talk."

Mark pulls away and puts his hands on my face, and he looks right at me as he says, "I love you so much, Ava." A tear falls down my cheek again. "This wasn't supposed to happen. I never meant to leave you and I never meant to put you through more pain," he tells me sincerely, and then he slowly leans in and gently kisses me.

I respond by wrapping my arms around his shoulders and I pull him in closer so that I can kiss him fully. My body comes alive for the first time in a week because this isn't a kiss goodbye, this isn't the last kiss — the only kiss that I thought I'd ever be able to give him again.

When my parents come back in, Mark and I finally get up from the kitchen floor. Jacob is so excited to see him that he lets out a little squeal, and as Mark takes him from my mum, I let out another sob and everyone turns to look at me. I wave them off and wipe my tears away letting them know it's OK — I'm just relieved because Jacob hasn't lost his daddy, after all. When we go into the living room, I'm surprised to see that it has big, floor to ceiling windows looking out onto the back garden. It's so light. I wasn't expecting this. From the front, with its small windows I was expecting it to be darker. Then I've been imagining Mark shrouded in darkness for days.

Mark sits down, Jacob wriggles off him so that he can go and explore, my mum and dad sit on the sofa opposite Mark, and I stay standing for a moment. I don't feel like my heart and brain have caught up with each other yet. Should I be annoyed and sit across from him with my parents while he explains? While he tells me why he's let me think he was dead? Or should I give him the benefit of the doubt? Should I show him the same forgiveness that he showed me when he found out about Jacob? All of these questions are going around my head as Mark looks at me. Then he puts out his hand in a gesture for me to come to him and take it, and my feet decide for me. I go over to him and sit, taking the offered hand and holding it tightly in my own.

"What the hell happened?" Dad asks firmly.

Mark sighs, then says, "Things went wrong."

"What things?" Dad asks.

Mark squeezes my hand and looks at me. "We had a plan to draw Jamie out. We just wanted to find him so that we could get him arrested," he tells me. "

"Who's the 'we?'" I ask him.

Mark sighs again and tells me, "You're not going to like some of this."

I laugh a little in response, because I think it's safe to say that I'm not going to like any of it.

Mark

Mark hung up the phone to Jonathan, and was shaking with anger. He hurt her. He had his hands on her throat... he tried to... Mark couldn't even begin to think about what almost happened. He just needed to get to her as quickly as possible, but there were things to do first, so he called Darren and he answered almost instantly.

"Mark. I've been in meetings, but I've just heard—"

"What happened?" he shouted at his friend. "They were supposed to be watching."

Neither Ava nor her family knew that Mike and his team were still working for Mark. They didn't believe that Jamie would just walk away after Ava broke up with him, but they couldn't find him. They went over all of the ground that he used to cover, even previous residences — but there was nothing. So, they took the decision to watch Ava. Not to spy or to take photos, but to see if Jamie was still watching her. To see if he'd try to reach out to her. They needed to locate him so that they could alert the authorities of his whereabouts. They'd pick him up for tax avoidance, if nothing else and then he knew he'd be gone. Jamie had been good at hiding in plain sight, and they suspected that he was still lurking somewhere, but it had been weeks and there had been nothing.

Darren sighed. "I know, OK. I know," he replied. "It seems that they made the decision to just watch because at first he was just talking."

"And when he put his hand around her throat?" Mark asked angrily. "They decided to just watch then too?"

"They were going to intervene," Darren assured him. "But when Ava started beeping the horn, she got people's attention. People were going over to the car and he backed off," he told him. "So, they followed him instead."

"So, they've found him?" Mark asked anxiously.

"No..." Darren replied, sighing again. "They lost him."

Mark couldn't believe what he was hearing. He was paying these men to keep her safe and they'd taken the decision to just watch as she was being hurt, and for what? They'd lost him.

"These guys are supposed to be the best, Darren," Mark said seriously.

"They are," Darren replied firmly. "But this guy is a snake. He's been on the run for eight years and he knows what he's doing." He sighed again and asked, "How is she?"

"I've only spoken to Jonathan, but I'm going there now. She's shaken, bruised, and sore but there's no serious damage," he told him. "I suppose from where they were sitting, they didn't see what he was doing with his other hand?"

"Fuuuuck...." Darren groaned out, understanding immediately.

"It didn't go far because she acted... it could've been worse, but I swear... if I get my hands on him!" Mark said, full of rage.

"No, Mark. You need to keep your head and we need to be smart."

"He blames me. He'll come for me," Mark told him.

"I know, and I know you have to go there," Darren replied, "but you need to do as I say."

"Darren—"

"No," Darren said in a way that allowed for no objection. This was the Darren that criminals turned to in order to stay out of jail. "You do exactly what I say, when I say it," he told him. "You lay low until I say, and before you go, I need you to get some things organised for me to collect."

Mark didn't ask Darren for an explanation when he'd given him a list of instructions. It was for a backup plan that he didn't think would be necessary, and he didn't really want to know the details of. He just wanted to get to Ava. He wanted to hold her and make her feel safe again, and the only way he was going to feel calm ever again was to feel her heartbeat and to have her close. In his arms she'd be safe. He wouldn't ever let anyone hurt her again.

When Mark arrived in Clovelly, Ava was in bed, but her parents were waiting for him. They talked a bit about how she'd been but then they heard her coming down the stairs. She walked in wearing pyjamas with her neck on show and Mark lost the ability to speak. The love of his life stood before him with a red hand mark around her throat. She walked up to him and wrapped her arms around him and he held her tight, and he waited for the calm that he thought would come from being near her to settle him, but it didn't. Seeing her injuries and seeing her look so vulnerable had only made him angrier. He loved this woman so much. She was brave and strong as always, but she was so much smaller than both he and Jamie. Her quick thinking had stopped anything more from happening in that car and he was so grateful for that, because she would never have been able to fight him off physically.

He took her to bed and held her close all night. He'd tried to help with Jacob when he woke so that she could rest, but he wasn't going to accept anything other than his mummy when he woke for the second time, and Ava had come in to take over. He'd stayed in the room with her, watching her in awe, as he always did when she was with Jacob. She was just being a mother, doing what mothers all over the world do. Yet, he'd seen Mary with three of his children, and it had never stirred those feelings in him.

On Friday they stayed in all day — Ava was clearly still in pain, even though she was trying to put on a brave face for everyone. Darren was on the phone often giving instructions, as he still didn't want Mark leaving the house. Saturday was much the same, but it wasn't an issue as Ava seemed in no rush to go out either. Jonathan went out often with either Cooper or Jacob, and Mark knew that he wanted to get his hands on Jamie just as much as Mark did. Part of him hoped that he would. Jonathan was formidable to say the least, and after what was done to his daughter, Jamie wouldn't stand a chance. Though, at the same time, he knew he needed to take Darren's advice. They needed to do this right, and they needed to be smart.

He was on the phone to Darren a lot on Saturday as plans were progressing, and Mark always took the calls in private. Darren was relatively light on the details, only telling Mark what he really needed to know, and although Mark was nervous, he trusted Darren. If he was going to offer himself up as bait, there was no way that his best friend was going to let him do it without an element of protection. "Precautions" Darren had called them. Just precautions. Mark was impatient though. He wanted to find Jamie, and part of him wanted the confrontation, but Darren was insistent — he wasn't to step out of that house until everything was in place.

That wasn't the only reason his phone was ringing all weekend though — his children were calling him too. He'd been away practically every weekend for almost two months without much of an explanation and they now wanted to know why. Hattie, in particular, was calling and texting constantly. He took the occasional call but kept it brief but all that did was make them worse. They even had Mary call him. He knew that was why she was calling. They didn't talk often and if she did get in touch out of the blue it was usually when she'd been drinking, and at night.

On Sunday morning, Darren called and told him that things were in place. "Do I want to know?" Mark had asked him. "Best not" had been Darren's reply, but he did tell him that they'd spotted Jamie around Clovelly, and that it would be good for Mark to be seen out with Ava. If they were to draw him out, then they needed to get his attention.

So, Mark had suggested that Ava get out of the house. He hadn't liked deceiving her, but it was mainly true. He had wanted to be the one to be with her when she eventually faced the world again — and it wasn't just about drawing Jamie out. When she kissed him and had given him the look that she gets when she wants him, a look he cannot get enough of, just like he cannot get enough of her — the feelings that came over him were completely genuine. Then when they went back to hers, completely alone, all thoughts of Jamie had disappeared, and it was all about Ava. All about the love, pleasure and completeness he felt when they both surrendered themselves to the other entirely.

Hattie's call had been amusing, he knew he shouldn't take pleasure in annoying his own daughter, but he'd never truly forgiven her for what she had done to Ava, and there was no way he was going to let her, or anyone else, stand in their way this time.

Not long after he and Ava had gone back to bed, Darren had sent him a message.

He saw you both & he was angry. Very angry! Everything is in place. After you leave Ava's tonight go to the railings and wait. He'll come to you, I'm sure. There will

be people waiting to intervene, but watch your back. Be safe. D.

Saying goodbye to Ava had been harder than ever, but he was also eager to leave. He wanted to play his part in making her safe again. He wanted to draw Jamie out. He would come for Mark and when he did, he'd be ready. Jamie was a talker. He'd talk before he acted, and when he did there'd be people there to help take him down and hold him down while they waited for the police. That was the plan. Lure him out. Take him down. Call the police.

Only, it didn't go to plan. Jamie didn't talk and he didn't make his presence known. One-minute Mark was alone, the next he was being knocked over the railings. He only had a second to think and in that second, he reached back, grabbed hold of Jamie's arm and pulled him into the sea with him.

After that it was a bit of a blur. Mark's ribs hurt and a fist landed on his face knocking him under. He remembered the sea being calm, he was grateful for that, but it had been cold, very cold. He'd kicked out and felt his foot connect and then he'd resurfaced. It was so dark, and he couldn't see where Jamie was, but he heard the engine start and he saw the light, and so he swam towards the boat.

He didn't know until he was pulled aboard that the men on it were Mike's men — most of them anyway. He hadn't known that they had been waiting there for him, just in case. They had looked in the water, all of them. They shone the lights and called his name but there was no sign of Jamie.

Mark was ready to go back to shore, to call the police and get a search party out for him, but the boat was going further out to sea. He'd argued with them, but they'd simply told him that they had instructions to follow. He'd tried to grab one of them, to make them see sense, to make them get help, but had been hit by a wave of pain from his ribs. They handed him some tablets and water, for the pain they told him, but within five minutes of taking them Mark was out cold.

The sleeping pills he'd been given were strong and when Mark finally woke up, he was in Bordeaux, anchored slightly away from the shore, and Darren was there, shaking him. He was so confused and so thirsty, and Darren had given him time to clear his head, before explaining everything. This was the backup of the backup plan — Plan C. The plan Darren hoped wouldn't be needed, but he'd prepared for all the same.

Mark was furious and had asked to be taken back immediately, but Darren had told him that it was too late. As far as they could tell, Jamie hadn't come out of the water, and Ava had already alerted the police after finding Mark's car, and they'd already tried getting in touch with Darren. Things were now in motion and Mark had no choice but to ride it out.

Mark struggled to get his head around it all, as Darren explained what would happen next, and handed him a case that contained everything that he needed to enter France — everything that Mark had been instructed to leave for Darren before he went to Clovelly last Thursday. They would travel to Mark's secret hideaway in Saint-Guilhem-le-Désert and he would wait it out. If Jamie was dead then he would be found soon, and a post-mortem would need to be done to clear Mark of any wrongdoing. Only then would Darren entertain bringing him back.

Even in his battered and exhausted state, Mark had tried to argue. He needed to speak to Ava, he needed to let her know that he was OK — but Darren had refused. The police had already seen her in a state of panic, so if she were to all of a sudden appear calm then it would raise suspicions — it could get her in trouble and would ruin the plan. Darren was adamant that she couldn't know the truth, not yet, but he would go to Clovelly as soon as possible and help her as best he could, and when the time was right, he would point her in the right direction. He would help her to find her way to Mark.

40

We all sit in silence, apart from Jacob who is completely happy exploring his new surroundings. I heard everything Mark told us, but it was like hearing someone read out extracts from a story. It was like a movie. Who makes things like this happen in real life? Darren Barton does. Darren and the people he knows — the people that want to keep him on side.

I asked Mark about Darren's job when we were first together. I had a vision of criminal lawyers as being dirty, sweaty, seedy types that would do anything for money. Men without conscience keeping criminals on the streets because they could pay, but as far as I could see Darren never fit that mould. That's not the sort of man that Mark would call his best friend, and definitely not the sort of man that someone like Lilly would love.

Mark had told me that Darren was very particular about the sorts of cases that he took on. If you were a violent thug or a rapist, then he wouldn't touch you. It was the more complex cases that he'd take on, and yes, sometimes he knew that the person was guilty, but it all stemmed back to his father.

Darren's father had been involved with a few criminal elements and he wasn't squeaky clean, but he got sent down for five years for something that he didn't do, and all because his representation wasn't good enough to pull apart the holes in the police's case. It had taken four years to finally clear him, but it had damaged him, and he wasn't the same man afterwards.

Darren was driven to study law to help men like his father — the wrongly accused. Although it was true to say that his motivation had changed a little along the way, Darren ultimately saw his role as keeping the police honest. He knew there were good ones out there and he even called some his friends. If they'd done a good enough job and Darren couldn't see a way of fighting the charges, then he would advise his client to plead guilty, and he'd do his best for them. However, if there were errors. If the police had been lazy, or worse, if someone on the case was known to him for being corrupt. Then he'd fight it, and he'd usually win.

That's why people did favours for Darren. That's how he got a crew for a boat that would take a man they didn't know to France under the radar. That's how he was going to get Mark's details onto the database of a hospital in Bordeaux — because that's where the fishermen that had pulled him out of the water when he was far out at sea had taken him. That's what the records will show anyway, along with the fact that Mark had been in and out of consciousness for a few days — or however long it takes for Darren to believe he can be brought back to the UK safely.

"So, what... you just go back to England and all is forgotten?" Dad asks him

"Not necessarily," Mark replies, "it's possible that the police might want to make some charges against me," he tells him, and I feel a new wave of dread wash over me. "But, the official coroner's report will clear me of any wrongdoing. The hospital records will give me an alibi, and then there's the matter of the embarrassment the force will face over Jamie."

"What do you mean?" Dad asks. I'm glad he knows what questions to ask right now because I certainly don't.

"Jamie deceived them all. Sergeant Moore even employed him — paid him," Mark says. "If it looks like they want to dig into this then they will find that their colleagues in London will advise them better of it."

"So, you've got it all sorted, then?" Dad asks, he's still annoyed but I can see he's a little impressed too.

"Not me, no," Mark replies more solemnly. "This is all Darren. I'm following his orders, but I do owe him my life. It could've gone very differently."

"You really could have died..." I say sadly and he turns to me, taking my face in his hands.

"But I didn't," he tells me firmly. "He didn't take me away from you, Ava. Nobody ever will," he assures me, and then he kisses me, and we stay like that until my parents remind us that they're still in the room.

I sit in the garden watching Jacob play, Mark is in the house with my parents — they're preparing lunch and seeing what can be salvaged from the bags that Mark dropped on the floor earlier. I asked them for some space because it would seem that I've developed my dad's need for thinking time recently. Not that my brain really has the capacity to think right now. So instead, I'm just watching Jacob play and finding some peace in his innocence and happiness.

I recognise Mark's walk as he approaches and when he reaches me, he sits facing me, and takes my hand in his. His touch is warm.

"I understand if you're angry with me," he tells me, apologetically. "I know you've been through hell. I promise you that not a day has gone by where I haven't wanted to reach out to you, but I had to put my trust in Darren."

"I'm not mad at you," I tell him honestly, still watching Jacob. "Anger is one of the emotions that I've felt during all of this, but that's before you explained." Then I turn to him and look him in the eyes, and say with sincerity, "I'm not mad now."

"I can't read you right now, please don't hide away from me," he pleads. "Tell me what's going on in that beautiful head of yours."

I let out a little laugh at that. "Honestly, Mark, my head is screwed up. This whole thing is a total mind fuck!"

"I know. Believe me, I can relate," he replies sadly.

"For days I've lived in pain and fear," I tell him. "On the one hand I've not allowed myself to think that you were gone, but it's been there in the back of my mind, occasionally creeping in... I saw Jamie dead." He winces at that. "And from that moment on I've expected to see you that way too," I say, and then the tears fall, and I can't help the sobs that escape me. "I've been picturing you, pale and lifeless in the cold, dark water, even though I've tried to fight it," I admit. "And then when Darren told me to look at Jacob's account, and when I told him we were thinking of coming here, and he encouraged it... it gave me hope." I pause to swallow back the cries that want to escape again, and continue, "But I've been scared to let that hope completely in. Scared to really believe I'd find you here, just in case it all got shattered again."

I take a breath and look around to make sure Jacob is still safe. He is, he's happy. Still happy. Then I turn back to Mark.

"It's mad. Because even though I can see you and touch you and kiss you, I'm petrified of being happy." I tell him honestly. "I'm scared of losing you all over again. I'm even starting to think I've gone completely insane and this is all a dream." I manage to laugh through my tears.

Mark isn't laughing though; he's looking at me with concern and love. "If it were the other way around, I would be feeling exactly the same," he reassures me. Then he picks up my hand and puts it against his heart. "Do you feel my heart beating?" he asks, and I nod my reply.

He moves my hand to his cheek and asks, "Do you feel my warmth?" I nod again and another tear falls. Then he puts my hand on his mouth and takes a few breaths. "Do you feel my breath?" he asks, and once again all I can do is nod at him.

Then he leans closer and says, "Ava... I need you to kiss me."

My body moves in response without any thought, and his lips are on mine once again, breathing life into my soul and healing my heart. When we eventually pull away from each other I finally smile at him. I finally succumb to my happiness, to my complete and utter relief. He is alive, and I can finally let myself believe it.

We all eat lunch together, and my change in mood has impacted my parents and they are starting to relent a little. I know they're finding this whole situation as difficult as me, as Mark is too, but seeing me finally happy again — that's all any parent wants. Ultimately, they understand what Mark did. He tried to rid me of Jamie. He tried to do it the right way, and never intended for it to happen like this — for

Jamie to die, but they tried to predict how an unpredictable man would act and it backfired.

Perhaps it didn't have to happen this way — if Jamie had gone under Mark could've possibly made it back to safety by himself. Then again, perhaps he wouldn't have — he was injured after all. Yet, even though it has caused so much fear and pain, I am glad that Darren did this. He took action to make sure Mark was safe, and now he's doing what needs to be done to make sure that he can live his life. He's gone above and beyond, and then some. We all have to trust him now.

As Mark and my parents clear up after lunch, I take Jacob away to try to get him to sleep, and once we're alone I take my phone out and write a message.

I'm not sure that these words could ever be enough, but thank you, Darren. Thank you so much.xx

As evening approaches my mum suggests that she and Dad should have Jacob overnight at the bed and breakfast, and that I stay with Mark at his cottage alone. My initial reaction is to feel a bit freaked out because I've never had a night away from him. Dad then joins in telling me that we need space, even if it's only for one night — Mark and I need to be alone — just the two of us with no distractions. I can tell Mark is quietly encouraging it too, and so eventually, I agree. It's so hard to say goodbye, and although I know I'll be worrying about him, he has an amazing relationship with my parents. I know that if he wakes, they ought to be able to settle him and they've promised to call if they really can't.

Mark says his goodbyes too, and when he closes the door I lean against the wall, completely exhausted.

"What would you like to do?" he asks, smiling at me expectantly.

"I want to do what every mum wants to do when they get a night off," I reply. "I want a nice, long soak in a hot bath."

Mark laughs a little, but his rueful smile tells me that he was hoping that I'd say something else, but he nods and says, "I'll go run you a bath."

"No," I tell him. "You can run us a bath."

"That sounds even better," he tells me, then he kisses me gently and leads me upstairs.

I'm very glad to discover that he has a giant bathtub. I'd want him in with me regardless, but it's good to know we'll be comfortable instead of trying to find somewhere to fit our legs. We lay there together for a long time, me with my back against his chest. It's warm and I can feel his heart beating and I don't want to move away from him.

"I was thinking the other day, when you're sixty, I'll be eighty," he tells me.

I can't help but laugh a little, because my thoughts have been much gloomier than that these past few days. I didn't think he'd see his next Birthday.

"What do you think about that?" he asks me.

I give his thigh a little squeeze and tell him, "That's why Viagra was invented." We both laugh and he flicks water at me. I tilt my head back letting him see my smile and we kiss.

"No, but really, what do you think about that?" he asks again more seriously.

"Are you asking me if I see us growing old together?" I ask him.

"Yes," he replies, sounding cautious.

I turn around so that I'm now facing him, and I rest my head on his chest.

"If we look at things objectively, then the reality is that since we first started our relationship, we've been separated for longer than we've been together," I tell him, and I feel his heartbeat change as he starts to fear what I'm going to say. "We were apart for over a year after only being together for six months. During that year I tried to move on. I really tried, and then you came back into my life and I knew that I still loved you," I say honestly. "After all that time apart. After everything that happened. I still loved you." I breathe a kiss into his warm, wet chest.

"You've talked about you and Helen being good on paper, and I guess that if you apply that to us, then we probably don't look like we would work," I continue. "But we do. There are people that will want to get in our way, but I know they can't anymore. I lost you once, but I got you back. And then I thought I'd lost you again, forever... and I've never known pain like it."

"I'm sorry..." Mark starts to say but I shush him and lean up to gently kiss his lips.

Then I look him in the eyes and tell him, "That's how I know — how I can be sure that you're it for me." I kiss him again then smile as I say, "So I guess I'm stuck with you... saggy balls and all."

I burst out laughing and he laughs along with me, but I know he's not going to let me get away with that one. I try to escape him, but he holds onto me. He's laughing, but the dark look is back in his eyes and I'm instantly aroused. He stands up and gets out of the bath, bringing me with him, and carries me to his bed and lays me down. I'm soaking wet in more ways than one, and as he rests himself above me, he tells me, "Well, I definitely don't need Viagra yet."

I feel the truth in his words pressing against me as he lowers himself onto me. He starts kissing me and I welcome his touch greedily. We make love throughout the night, both of us seemingly unable to get enough of the other. When I finally drift off in his arms, feeling his heartbeat, I know there will be no bad dreams tonight. No pale face and dark water to haunt me. Just peace, rest, and love.

41

My parents are due to come over at nine O'clock and I'm desperate to see my boy. We needed last night. After everything that's happened, we needed the time alone, but having Jacob back with us makes everything complete — it's the three of us.

"Why haven't you told anyone about this house?" I ask Mark, while he's getting breakfast ready.

"I planned to bring you here as a surprise at some point," he tells me, "but it still needs work."

"It's lovely." I tell him genuinely.

"Yes, but it's not quite finished yet."

"Why not tell your children?" I ask.

"You may have noticed that I don't confide in them that much these days," he replies, moving over to me. "I bought it with the intention of it being my place to escape to when I needed to get away," he says. "Then I got you back and I wanted to make it a special place for us," he tells me, and he kisses me gently.

I start to feel the familiar tingling in my core, and I glance at the clock to see if there is time. He sees what I'm thinking, and he lifts me onto the table. He slowly starts to lower me down, and then three loud bangs at the Oak door put a very abrupt stop to things. I groan in frustration but then I jump up to go and get our son.

Jacob seems perfectly happy, but he has a big feed to make up for what he missed out on last night. My parents look tired, but they insist that he only woke once and then my mum got in bed with him. Though I guess that it's hardly surprising that they look tired. Everything I've been through since Mark disappeared; they've been right by my side through it all.

During breakfast, Mark suggests that we go into the town to have a look around. He tells us how beautiful and unspoiled it is, and as soon as we arrive, I see that he's right. I've never been anywhere like it, and it's breathtaking. I didn't know places like this still existed. Mark takes charge of Jacob's pushchair so that I can take it all in, and all of a sudden, I'm being dragged over to an antique jewellery store by my mum.

Mum has always brought me into these sorts of shops. I used to hate it when I was younger, but then one day a shop owner told us the stories behind the jewellery; the love, loss, happiness and pain, and I was completely taken in. We both only really know a basic amount of French. Enough to be polite and order drinks, so that's not going to happen today, but still, we take it all in, feeling the energy of it all, instead.

I move over to the counter where there is a selection of rings on display. There is one that I'm completely drawn to, it has an almost woven effect to it with tiny diamonds inset along each weave, and then in the middle a blue stone — which I assume must be a sapphire. It's absolutely beautiful but I suspect it's the blue that has pulled me in. It's the same blue as Mark's eyes — Jacob's too.

The owner walks over to me smiling and he opens up the cabinet and hands the ring to me so that I can see it properly. I was expecting it to feel heavy but it's light. He gestures for me to try it on and at first, I decline, because it looks far too expensive, but then Mum encourages me to do it too. It looks like the right size for my ring finger and I start to slip it onto my right hand, but he stops me and gestures towards my left hand, and he says something that I don't understand whilst pointing to my ring finger.

"He's telling you that this was an engagement ring and he wants you to try it on properly," Mark says, as he walks up behind me.

I look back at him and then to the shop owner before me, he's still smiling at me encouragingly, so I do as he wishes. It fits perfectly and it truly is the most beautiful and unique ring that I've ever seen. He then goes back to the cabinet and shows me another more simple, woven band and again Mark translates for us.

"That's the wedding band that goes with it," he tells me, but the man doesn't hand that one to me.

I hold out my hand to examine the ring on my finger more closely. "It's the most beautiful thing I've ever seen. Don't you think?" I ask, looking at Mark.

"Almost," he replies, and he leans in to kiss me.

It's silly, but I feel sad as I hand the ring back and I listen intently as the owner — Gérald, tells us all about it via Mark. It's a love story, but not like any I've heard before. There is only love. No loss and no pain. The woman that was given this ring had a blessed life and the ring stayed in her family for many years, but it was never again given to another as a promise of forever, and eventually, when it needed to be done — it was sold.

I can't help but think about who she was, what she

looked like and who she loved as we walk to a café for lunch. I'm still in a bit of a dream world as we sit, but then before we even have a chance to look at the menu Mark receives a call from Darren, and I come crashing back into my reality. He goes off to speak with him and we order some drinks and snacks while we wait. He's gone for quite a while and I start to feel apprehensive again. I had let hope in, I trust Darren completely, or at least I want to, but the longer Mark is away the more concerned I get. He's given me the impression that it will be straightforward, and straightforward doesn't require long and secretive phone calls. However, when he finally comes back, he's smiling, and I push the fear and doubt away again.

"Darren says just three more days and I can go back," he tells us eagerly. "He's going to travel to Bordeaux, and I need to meet him there. Everything that needs to be in place is set," he says, but then he looks more solemn as he tells me, "Sadly, that does mean that you need to leave."

The pain returns and I have to fight back the tears as I ask, "When?"

"Tomorrow, as you originally planned..." he replies, and his eyes are filling up now too. "I wish you could stay longer, I really do."

I know it's good news. Darren is positive that Mark will not be charged. Yes, the police will want to speak to him, but it should just be a case of clarifying what happened so that they can close the case nice and neatly. Still, the thought of leaving Mark again has me feeling completely vulnerable and I'm so scared that something will go wrong. I just got him back and now I'm supposed to say goodbye, again? I try my best to contain my concerns as we eat our lunch — it's delicious but I struggle to find enjoyment in it. Given the news my parents suggest that they should go sightseeing for the rest of the day, leaving the three of us alone, and that perhaps they should have Jacob overnight again.

This time it's Mark that objects. "That's very kind," he tells them, "but I'd like to keep both of them with me tonight."

He looks at me and I nod and smile in agreement. As much as I enjoyed my time alone with Mark, Jacob is part of our team. We're a family.

"I think you two should still spend the afternoon here without us," I tell them. "You deserve some time alone too, but we should all have dinner together later?" I suggest.

It's agreed. We go back to Mark's leaving them to it and we spend the afternoon just the three of us. It feels like my first trip back to London again. We'd just got back together then, and I've just found him again now, but just like it has been throughout our entire relationship — there's a time limit. We have to say goodbye again tomorrow morning and I'm so tired of saying goodbye to him — especially as it doesn't have to be that way. Not anymore.

"How would you feel about me moving back to London?" I ask him. "I've literally just thought of this by the way," I quickly add, "so I've no idea where I'd live, but..."

"You'll live with me," he tells me, smiling. "I would absolutely love you to move back to London. If it's what you want? If you're ready?"

"I'm ready," I tell him honestly, "and I'm so sick of saying goodbye to you."

"You're not worried about Hattie and the boys?" he asks.

"Not anymore. Did you not hear about our eventful confrontation?" I ask him in surprise, then I add, "It was quite the talk of the village," with more amusement.

He smiles at me. "I heard. Darren described it as you

giving them both barrels and then dropping a grenade on them for good measure," he says laughing.

"I think there's a chance that I went a bit too far. They're hurting too," I tell him, honestly.

"I know, and I feel awful about that too, but you had every right to say what you did," he says genuinely. "I'm just sorry that you had to do it alone."

"I wasn't alone," I reassure him. "My dad was there, and Darren and Lilly were great too," I tell him and then I pause for a moment before asking, "Will you tell them the truth about all of this?"

"No. The less people that know the better," he replies seriously. "It gets messy otherwise and it's not just me that would be implicated."

We put the gloom of that conversation, and of the pain that we know Mark's family is feeling to the back of our minds and have a lovely afternoon — just the three of us. Eventually, I leave the two of them alone to play while I prepare dinner. As I do, I let everything sink in, and not just what has happened, but what's going to happen too. I'm moving back to London and moving in with Mark. I don't feel scared, because home is wherever he is — the location doesn't matter.

When my parents arrive for dinner, I'm pleased to see that they look more refreshed than when I left them, but I feel a pang of guilt about the fact that I'm going to be moving back to London and taking their grandson with me. Then I recall the conversation that I had with my dad by the beach and I realise that they're already expecting it.

We enjoy dinner together with a considerable amount of wine and lots of chat, and for a short time it seems like we've all forgotten what has brought us to this place, and what awaits us when we return home. However, it all comes crashing back when we say goodbye to my parents and discuss our plans to leave the next day. It's a morning flight which means I'll need to leave early. I'll be saying goodbye to him again in a matter of hours and then I'll have to wait. Wait for him to be brought back, wait for the police to make their decisions and wait to start our new life together. At least there is light in that thought — we will have a life together. I would wait for him even if he was sent to prison — I have no doubts about that.

We put Jacob to bed and just lay on the sofa holding each other. There's no denying the sexual attraction between us and that may be how we started, but that has never been all that there is to us. I feel like my soul is entwined with his, and I never feel as safe, or as comforted as I do when I'm in his arms. I'm still exhausted in both mind and body and for a moment I feel like I might actually drift off, but then he sits up.

"I have something that I want to give you," he tells me, and I smirk at him in response. "Not that, you horny little minx," he smiles at me. "And although I'd like you to have it now you are going to have to keep it a secret for a while... if you want it, that is?"

"I'm intrigued."

"Well, you aren't getting it for free," he tells me, and I smirk at him again. "Will you stop looking at me like that?" he chastises me, laughing. "I can't concentrate when you look at me like that."

"Sorry," I say, trying to swallow down another smirk.

"It comes with a question."

"OK, then ask away," I reply to him, completely clueless as to where this is going.

"Well, you see... the thing is, it's taken me so long to find you, but you're it for me too," he tells me lovingly. "Nobody has ever made me feel the way that you do, and I'm well aware that we still have challenges to face... but I think that I could do anything with you by my side."

He looks nervous and my heart starts to flutter, as he continues, "So, my question is this... will you make me the happiest man that has ever existed and agree to be with me forever — Viagra, saggy balls and all?" We both laugh and he moves from the sofa and goes down to the floor on one knee, as he pulls a box from his pocket. "Ava Swan, you are my world. Will you marry me?" he finally asks.

"Yes!" I squeal jumping onto him and sending him flying backwards. He's lying on his back and I lay on top of him, smothering him with kisses. "Yes, yes, and yes again!" I tell him excitedly. "Just in case you missed it."

He pushes up from the floor, smiling the biggest smile I've ever seen. "I'm supposed to give you a ring now," he says, laughing at me.

"I don't need a ring," I tell him, kissing him again. "I just need you."

He pushes my hair behind my ears and kisses me gently on the lips. "Perhaps you'd like to see it before you decide that?" he asks, smiling at me. "Close your eyes," he gently commands.

I do as he asks and close my eyes. I keep them closed as he takes my left hand and I feel the ring being gently pushed onto my finger. It fits perfectly and it feels familiar.

"Open them," he tells me, with a smile clear in his voice.

I open my eyes and I immediately understand why the ring feels familiar; it's because I'd been wearing it earlier in the day. It's the ring that brings happiness. At least it did to the woman who first accepted it as a symbol of love so many, many years ago. I take in the diamond encrusted weaves and the beautiful blue gem that reminds me of the eyes that mean so much to me, and a tear rolls down my cheek.

"Now it really is the most beautiful thing I've ever seen. It's a shame that you don't want it," he says, feigning seriousness as he starts to take it off my finger.

"Don't you dare!" I squeal as I bat his hand away. "Thank you, this is so perfect. I love it. I love you."

We kiss gently, sealing the promise that we just made to each other, but as he starts to deepen the kiss, I push him back and say, "I have a question of my own... two, in fact."

He raises his eyebrows at me but he's smiling as he says, "Go on."

"Did you use money intended for our son to buy me this?" I ask him.

He looks at me seriously. "It's the only account I've been able to access under the radar, but I am going to put it all back as soon as I'm home," he tells me with sincerity.

"You do realise that I may be tempted to see how much you spent on this?" I ask him, smiling. "Given that I have access."

"Ah... I hadn't actually thought about that," he laughs a little. "Well, I would've paid double," he tells me smiling, then asks, "What's your second question?"

"Oh, well, that's a little more troubling," I say seriously. "My dad's quite traditional in these matters—"

"I know he is," Mark jumps in. "Which is why I asked his permission before he left," he says, smiling at me.

"You did?"

"Of course. I recently had a brush with death. I wasn't going to risk my life again when I have you to grow old with," he tells me. Then he kisses me and asks, "Can I ask you another question?"

"Yes..." I reply.

"Can I take you to bed now?" he asks, kissing my neck.

"Yes, Mr Davidson," I reply smiling, "you can."

He looks at me darkly and smiles as he says, "You're going to regret that."

"I don't think I am," I tell him and I kiss him deeply as he carries me up the stairs.

42

Tomorrow.

Mark is coming back tomorrow. I've no idea what that actually entails but Darren is in Bordeaux, Mark is too, and at some point today, Darren is going to call Sergeant Moore from the hospital to tell him that he found Mark. That Mark finally regained consciousness, remembered Darren's number and called him, to be precise. There's even going to be a nurse there that will confirm Mark's been there this whole time. That £35k has been well spent, that's for sure. I am so nervous. We've all been hiding out as much as possible since we got back from France — or Ireland as people here believe.

The last time people saw us we were all scared, hurt and exhausted, and it's so hard to fake that now we know the truth. It's perhaps a little easier for me than it is for my parents, because I am scared about what's coming next. I'm scared it won't be as easy as Darren wants us to believe it will be. I also still have my red eyes thanks to the tears that I shed when I said goodbye to Mark, and the tears that I cry into the pillow that still smells like him at night. I miss him so much already and I can't even pick up the phone to speak with him. No contact Darren has said — just in case.

So, when I'm out and about with Cooper, like I am now, people still see pain. Although in truth, nobody is really looking at me anymore. They lower their head when they walk past me and they avoid making eye contact. As far as they're concerned, I'm the girl whose ex-boyfriend murdered her lover and died in the process. I'm the girl waiting to start grieving. I'm the girl with a world of pain yet to come. So, they don't look. Perhaps they're worried that tragedy is contagious.

"Is that Cooper?" a voice behind me asks, and I turn with a start, and see Will walking towards me.

Cooper runs back with the ball he just caught, and I throw it again. It lands in the sand near the shoreline, and he splashes through the water in a rush to get it.

"Yes," I reply as he becomes level with me.

"Are you looking after him for a bit?" he asks awkwardly.

For a moment, I want to be rude to him. I'm still angry with him and I'm not sure that I want him near me, but then I remember that he's in pain. He probably thinks his dad is gone, because unlike me, he doesn't know the truth. I also remember that I'm about to become his step mum. He's going to be in my life whether I like it or not, and it will be easier for everyone if we can be amicable. So, I swallow down my gut reaction and try my best to be polite.

"No, he's mine now," I tell him, still watching Cooper, then I look at him without scowling, take a deep breath, and just talk. "Carolyn doesn't feel that she can give him what he needs, so she asked me to have him," I tell him calmly.

He doesn't say anything, but when Cooper comes back and drops the ball at his feet, he picks it up and throws it for him.

"Did you come to London to get him?" he eventually asks.

"Yes, you were all on holiday at the time," I tell him.

"Right," he says quietly. "So, I guess you stayed with my dad?" he asks.

"I stayed with Carolyn," I reply, "and your dad. That was when we got back together."

"Oh, I thought it had been longer than that," he says. "He's been disappearing for some time."

"He's been coming here to see Jacob," I tell him, "but we didn't get back together straight away. I was still with Jamie — well, he was Lucas, then."

"But you knew you were still in love with him, didn't you?" he asks me in a way that I can't make out.

In fact, I'm not really sure where this conversation is going at all, so, I ask him, "What do you want, Will?" in a far gentler way than I asked Mary.

He looks awkward and starts to jiggle on the spot a little. Cooper brings the ball back and he throws it for him again, and then he turns to me and says, "I want to apologise to you. I have for a long time, actually."

He sees the look of surprise on my face and smiles a little. "I can understand that you'd feel that way. You probably think we're all evil?" he asks.

I let out a deep sigh and reply, "Not all of you."

He smiles a little at that. "I didn't know that Hattie was going to take things so far," he tells me with remorse. "I was only involved with the lie about me and Ted."

"That did enough damage—"

"I know!" he almost shouts, not letting me finish. Then he regains himself and continues, "Believe me, I know."

He pauses again and I can see that he's struggling with

what he wants to say, so I say nothing. I just wait. I'm so good at waiting these days.

"You see, you just thought I had a crush on you," he says, not really looking at me. "But it was always more than that. I thought that if I just kept at it then one day, you'd see me, and not as a brother-figure." He's looking at me now and I can see the pain that I saw that day. Not just the pain he's feeling about Mark, but the pain that I caused him too.

He takes a deep breath. "Then you fell in love with my dad," he says, laughing sadly. "I was hurt but I was also humiliated, and I wanted to punish you, but you didn't deserve that, and I'm sorry." He turns away again, but I see him wipe a fallen tear from his cheek.

"Thank you," I tell him gratefully. I could add that I'm sorry for hurting him, but I said that a long time ago and I don't feel like I need to say it again now.

He throws the ball for Cooper again then asks, "I may be a glutton for punishment, but can I ask what it was about him?"

I want to correct him and tell him that it's what it 'is' about him, not what it 'was' — because he's still here. I can't do that, so instead, I smile at him a little as I say, "Will... sometimes you can't specify exactly what it is that makes you attracted to someone. There's no one thing, it's just a combination of everything. Sometimes your heart just lands where it falls." I shrug a little and he smiles at me, and in that moment, I realise that I've missed Will's smile. So, I bite the bullet and add, "Besides, the sex... just amazing!"

He practically chokes on the spot and I laugh at him. "Sorry, I couldn't resist," I say, still laughing.

"Bitch!" he replies, but he's laughing now as well.

We stand quietly for another minute or so. Cooper seems to be alternating who he's giving the ball to, so we take it in turns to throw it for him. Having us both in the palm of his hand — he's completely in his element.

"What was it like?" Will suddenly asks, and I look at him quizzically. "Being pregnant? Going through all that alone?"

"I was living with my parents, so I wasn't really alone. I had a lot of help," I tell him honestly.

"Yes, but..." he pauses again, then blurts out, "I'm going to be a dad."

This time it's my turn to choke on the spot, but he looks terrified, so I quickly regain myself.

"Oh... congratulations?" I ask, rather than say. "Is this a good thing?" I add cautiously.

He looks right at me and says, "I'm in my third year at university and I've only been with her three months. Do you think it's a good thing?"

"It's not really my place to say. What do the others think?" I ask him.

"Nobody else knows," he tells me. "I only found out just over a week ago and it's not really been the time to talk about it, has it?"

"But you're telling me?" I ask him, shaking my head a little in disbelief.

"Ava... you are the closest person to my dad..." he says, and I can see that he means it. "What would he say to me?"

"Oh..." I say, unsure how to answer, then add quickly, "Well, for starters he'd probably tell you not to propose." I laugh, and he laughs too.

"Do you love her?" I ask him seriously.

"I'm not sure," he replies.

"Have you talked about it properly with her?"

"Not really," he admits, raking his fingers through his hair, just like Mark does when he's anxious. "She told me she's keeping it, but she knows what's going on here, so she's not tried to talk about it again."

I feel sorry for him because if he's turning to me above anyone else in his life, then he must be really going through it. So, I decide to do my best for him, and for Mark too.

"Look, Will, you need to treat the relationship and the pregnancy as two different things," I tell him.

"Well, that sounds simple," he replies sarcastically. "And how do I do that?"

"I'm not sure exactly," I reply honestly. "I just mean that you need to see if the relationship — just the two of you — is actually something that you want. If you and she actually want each other, as opposed to sticking it out because there's a baby," I say. "At the same time, you need to absolutely let her know that you're there for her," I tell him firmly. "That no matter what your relationship status ends up being, that you are going to be a father."

He nods at that.

"Can I give you some insight?" I ask him, and he smiles and nods at me. "She's going to be scared," I tell him. "Scared and angry. She's going to be feeling like the future that she had mapped out is gone, and that everything that she's been working for is now out of reach."

He nods again, understanding.

"So, when you speak to her, you need to let her know that it isn't," I say kindly. "It's just going to take a bit more time for her to get there, but it will be worth it in the end."

He smiles back and looks like he's about to say more but my phone rings, stopping him. It's my mum letting me know that Jacob is awake and in need of me. I call Cooper and get him on the lead and start to say my goodbyes to Will, but then he stops me.

"Can I come with you? Can I meet my baby brother?" he asks hopefully.

Despite all we've just shared my guard immediately goes back up. "Why? So, you can get a sample for a DNA test?" I ask him defensively.

He laughs nervously and replies, "As much as my mum would love that, no. Anyway, Darren and Lilly say he's a carbon copy of him... of my dad..." he says sadly. "I'd just like to meet him, that's all."

I wrestle with myself for a minute, but eventually I come to a decision. "OK, but I should warn you that my dad is there," I tell him, giving him a smirk.

"Shit!" he says laughing nervously.

"It's OK. After I shouted at you all like I did, I don't think he feels the need to do so anymore," I say, smiling at him reassuringly.

We start to walk back, but before we're off the beach I turn to him and say, "Will, don't give up on him."

He puts his head down and gently shakes it. "Ava..." he starts to say, but I stop him.

"No, Will. Don't give up on him."

He clenches his jaw and nods at me, but I see a fresh wave of pain wash over him and I wish I could take it away. Soon he'll see. Soon he'll be happy.

On the way home I text my dad to let him know that Will's going to be arriving with me, partly because I do want to make sure he's on his best behaviour, but also so that they know that they need to be on their guard again. They need to pretend that we don't know what we know.

As we're walking Will laughs a little and says, "You know, you're not my mum's favourite person at the moment."

"Will, I've never been your mum's favourite person," I reply seriously, although still laughing.

"Well... you've always been one of mine," he says, giving me a kind smile.

I smile back as I give him a little nudge and it starts to feel like one day, I may actually get my baby brother back.

When we get in, I find Dad alone in the kitchen, Mum is upstairs changing Jacob, and I can hear him fussing. I look at my dad and give him a silent plea to be nice, and thankfully, he obliges and offers Will a drink as I go upstairs. I stay there for a while to feed Jacob, and when I go back downstairs, they're all in the kitchen, and Will is crying as he looks down at the picture in his hands. It's the same one that was on Mark's laptop in France of the three of us together, looking completely happy. I leave Jacob in the living room with his toys and go over to Will.

"Do you want to talk about it?" I ask him.

"No..." he replies, but then quickly adds, "he just looks so happy. I took that away from him once. I hope I get the chance to apologise one day."

He wipes more tears away and tries to get himself together. It's so hard seeing him hurting, especially when he doesn't need to. I look at my parents and they see what I'm thinking and they both give a slight shake of their heads. They're right, I can't tell him. So, I take the photo from him, put it back on the dresser, and then I take him to meet his brother.

Will spends the next few hours playing with Jacob happily, but then he gets a call from Mary and he's summoned back. He thanks me as he leaves, telling me that he needed this. He needed to try to build bridges with me, and to meet Jacob. He was completely in awe of just how much he looks like his dad and it brought him some comfort. Surprisingly, I actually enjoyed his company.

Despite his past agenda we always got on. I genuinely

adored him from the moment he was born, but only ever platonically. Although as nice as it was, I'm relieved when he's gone. We don't need to pretend when it's just us and we all give a collective sigh of relief as I close the door. Now I can focus on what's bothering me — when is Darren going to call?

I get my answer at four O'clock when I see his name on my screen. "Darren!" I practically shout down the receiver. "What's going on?"

"It's me," Mark says warmly, and on hearing his voice I slump into a chair and let the tears fall.

"Mark," I breathe out. "I've been so worried. What's happening?"

"Everything is going as planned, so far," he says reassuringly. "As far as the police are concerned, I've just been released from the hospital in Bordeaux and Darren and I are currently travelling to Calais — which we are. We'll be getting the Eurostar to London first thing and then we'll travel to Clovelly."

"And then what?" I ask him, nervously.

"We need to go straight to the police station to give a statement," he says.

"Then we wait and see."

"Whether they arrest you or not?" I say for him.

"It won't come to that," he replies confidently.

I let out a deep breath and for a moment I can't speak because my emotions are still all over the place. I'm not going to feel completely happy until this is all over. Until he's in my arms again and I can be sure that nobody is going to take him away.

"What should I do now?" I ask him. "Do I act surprised when the police get in touch?"

"No, it's OK. They know I'll be contacting you," he tells me.

"Have you spoken to the others yet?" I ask.

"No, I called you first," he answers lovingly.

"You should call them now," I tell him. "I spoke to Will today and he's in bits."

"You spoke to Will?" he asks with surprise.

"Yes, he apologised for what happened. Then he asked to meet Jacob," I say apprehensively.

"Did you lynch him on the spot?" he asks, laughing a little.

"No..." I say laughing with him. "I let him, actually. They played together for a few hours. It was nice... he needed it, I think."

"Thank you for that, Ava," he says adoringly.

"As much as I don't want to let you go, you should really call them. When can we speak again?" I ask him eagerly.

"I'll call when we arrive at the hotel. Give Jacob a kiss from me. I love you."

I put my phone down and put my head on the table. I feel so out of control of everything. Yet again, all I can do is wait. So, while I wait, I boil the kettle, I go upstairs and open the drawer next to my bed, I open the small blue box and I put my ring back on my finger where it belongs. I go back to the kitchen and make a cup of tea for myself and my parents. I play with Jacob. I give him his dinner. I bath him, and I feed him to sleep — then eventually, my phone rings and my heart comes back to life again.

43

Mark called when he got to his hotel yesterday evening, he'd been on the phone with his children for a long time and he sounded completely drained. I don't know if he ever really let himself think about what this was doing to them, and for some reason he was surprised by the depth of their love for him. It seems that because of the divorce, because he went away for so long, and then because of everything that happened with me — it seems like he felt that he wasn't that significant to them. I wish he'd opened up to me about this sooner because I know exactly how much they love him.

Selfishly, this made me worry, because he'd told me that he'd choose me. That if it came down to that again, then he'd choose me and Jacob over the rest of his family. He'd obviously sensed what I was feeling when we were speaking last night, and he told me point blank that it changes nothing.

He used the time he had with them to tell them in no uncertain terms that I am going to be in his life. He'd been on speaker phone with them all at the time and it was of course, Will that had told him that he was absolutely fine with it. Hattie and Ted said nothing, but I guess I should forgive them for not having a clue what to say, having just found out that the father that they feared dead was alive, and on his way home.

There was one request made of me, and that was that I stay away from the police station while he's there and give his children that first meeting alone. I couldn't exactly argue given that I'd already had time with him in France, but it was going to be hard. He promised that he or Darren would keep me up to date on what was happening as much as possible, but ultimately, yet again, I was going to have to wait. However, he promised me that he'd be coming back to me, and that when he did it would be the start of our new life together. So, I allowed myself to hope again.

Not long after speaking with him there was a knock at my door. Dad opened it and was startled to see Sergeant Moore on my doorstep. Mum and I were in the living room drinking wine and she gestured towards my ring, and I had to quickly put it in my pocket before he walked in. It was a truly horrendous twenty minutes. The man was shocked, he was happy, but he was shocked — it wasn't the outcome that he'd been expecting. I kept feeling like he was trying to gauge my reactions, but Dad just kept reminding him how shocked we all were.

I tried to talk at one point but burst out crying instead, and that seemed to help the situation. If I'd been acting then I ought to be in line for an Oscar, but I wasn't, I've been on an emotional roller coaster for the past two weeks and the tears are never far away. So, glass of wine in hand, my emotions just spilled out of me, and then they carried on for a little longer.

He wouldn't tell us anything about what was going to

happen next, only that they would be taking a statement and going from there. My tears may have been real, but I did have to lie to him, and it pained me to do so. As he was leaving, he asked about Jamie's funeral and I told him what I told Julia — that when it came to it, we didn't feel like we could face it — it didn't feel appropriate. He understood and he left without asking me anything more.

I barely slept last night, the anticipation of everything is even worse now that he's so close to coming home. In fact, he is home, well, he's on UK soil anyway. He's sent me a message to let me know that he's arrived in London and now they have the long drive to Clovelly. I have no idea what to do with myself so I'm hiding away in the kitchen at the tea rooms for a bit. I've been neglecting my baking duties recently and there is a lot to do — which thankfully, means a lot to keep me occupied.

Mum and Dad are going to have a fun day with Jacob — it was their suggestion. I think they're preparing themselves for what's coming next too — for when they will no longer see their grandson every day. So, I plan to stay here most of the day.

Somehow, people seem to have heard the news. I don't know how, but then the Clovelly gossip circle is a mystery to me, anyway. Luckily, there were no customers here when I arrived, but I received a massive hug from Linda and the girls when I walked in, and had to quickly escape before I became a blubbering mess again.

So, my agenda for today is to bake scones, bake sponges, make fruit tarts, tidy up, and then tidy up again — whilst constantly checking my phone for news.

Time tends to fly when you lose yourself in baking and before I know it, Linda walks in with some sandwiches letting me know that it's lunch time. The look on her face alerts me to the fact that I've already caused carnage in the kitchen. So, after I've eaten, I dutifully tidy up before getting started with making more mess. Linda wanted to talk to me, I could tell, but the minute I saw the look on her face she saw the tears forming in my eyes, so instead, she smiled kindly and left.

I've been in this kitchen for a good three hours and I'm in need of a change of scene, so I'm heading home to take Cooper out for a bit. He's got so used to us all being around the house, so I think that being alone will be a bit of a shock to the system. He's also got quite used to sleeping with me, as I have with him. He's been my little guardian angel watching over me at night, saying nothing — since he can't — but giving me a slight nudge whenever the tears have started to flow. I hope he doesn't feel too pushed out when Mark comes back and reclaims his place in my bed, because there will definitely be no room for him then. As soon as I put the key into my back door my phone rings. It's Darren's name that flashes up, but I know whose voice I'll hear when I answer.

"Hello," I say warmly.

"Hello, you," he replies in the same tone.

"Where are you?" I ask.

"We're just about to pull up to the police station," he says calmly. "It feels so weird being so close to you but not knowing when I'm going to see you again."

"Soon," I say, sighing. "Really, really soon. That's what I keep telling myself, anyway," I laugh a little.

"We're here... Jesus, they're all waiting," he tells me, and I know he's talking about Hattie and the others. "I have to go. Darren will keep you updated, and I will see you soon," he tells me firmly. "So, no worrying, OK?"

"I'll try. I love you."

"I love you too," he replies and then I hear the elated welcome he is receiving from his family before he hangs up the call.

No worrying. How can I not worry? He's about to talk to the police. He and Darren are about to try and sell them the story — the lie. Mark didn't kill Jamie. The only time he even touched him was in self-defence and the coroner has confirmed that. Mark didn't ask to be dragged away to France, he wanted to go back, he wanted to be taken ashore — but his best friend had wanted to protect him from Jamie, and from any police investigation that might follow — so, he squirrelled him away.

That is the only thing they can possibly pull him up on — that he left the scene and their time was wasted searching for him. I hope that Darren has everything as tightly wrapped up as he thinks he does, but at least he won't be leaving Mark's side. He's not just there with him as his friend, he'll be acting as his legal representative too — should it be needed. At the end of the day, Darren is the best. So, I try to push the worry away and I grab Cooper's lead from the utility and open the kitchen door. He practically knocks me over in his excitement as I open the door, and he's even more uncontrollable when he sees that I'm holding his lead.

"Come on, you nutter," I tell him affectionately, as we head out of the door.

After I walk Cooper, I go back to the tea rooms to do some more baking. It's the afternoon and it's busier than when I left, and everyone stops what they're doing to look at me when I walk in. Great. Now I'm not so tragic, everyone wants to stare at me again. They've obviously heard on the grapevine that Mark is here. I guess the welcome that his family gave him was never going to go unnoticed — not here anyway. I start walking to the kitchen and give those that are still looking at me a polite smile — they are customers, after all — but I'm relieved to be tucked away in the kitchen again. I've barely taken my coat off when Linda comes in.

"Why are you here?" she asks in surprise.

"I'm baking..." I reply, a little puzzled.

"Yes... but why aren't you at the police station waiting for him?" she asks, shaking her head. "Surely that's where you'd rather be?"

"Actually, no." I tell her, and she looks, shocked. "Here I have something to distract me. There I would just have a bunch of people that don't want me around. And I'm not just making assumptions — it was an actual request," I tell her as I give a slight shrug.

"You have the right—"

"Linda, he's here. He's back," I tell her, smiling. "After all this time. After everything that we thought — I'm going to see him. I'm going to be with him, and they won't get in the way of that," I tell her resolutely. "I'm just respecting their needs right now."

She seems to relax then and she walks over and embraces me in a big hug, and as she does the tears start to fall. I really hope there will come a time when they aren't always in the background.

"Is this really happening?" I ask her. "Life feels like a dream right now." I'm not lying to her, I'm not playing my role. Part of me is still wondering if I may have gone a bit mad.

"Ava, Ava, Ava..." she sighs. "It's happening. I don't know how, but it is." She holds me tighter for a moment, then adds, "Be happy, sweet girl. You deserve to be happy."

She holds me for a little longer before going back to the

customers and I try to get myself together. I try to get myself together and focus on tarts — apricot tarts to be precise. That ought to keep me occupied for the next few hours at least — and it does. I check my phone constantly; I have even sent Darren a message. After two hours I couldn't take the silence, so I asked for an update and it took thirty agonising minutes for him to reply, and all he said was —

Going through the motions... hang tight. D

So, I'm waiting. Baking and waiting, but not for much longer. The tarts are done, and I've cleaned the kitchen — scrubbed it to within an inch of its life, in fact. You'd never even know that I've been in here all day. Mum would be proud. Unfortunately, I'm running out of ways to distract myself, so it's amazingly perfect timing that Mum has just sent me a message telling me that they're back from their trip, and I don't hesitate to grab my coat and go straight home. I barely look at anyone as I leave, but Linda catches my eye and we share a smile.

I practically run home and when I get in, I immediately reach for Jacob. He loves spending time with my parents, but thankfully, he is always pleased to see me, and after a day away from me he's always eager to reconnect — always eager for a feed. Today, I feel like I'm getting as much comfort from him as he is from me.

Baking was a distraction, but this is real. Jacob is real. He is me and he is Mark, and when he came into my life, he gave me back the sense of purpose that I lost when my life fell apart. Nothing feels more important than knowing that I'm giving him what he needs. It's the one thing that still makes me feel empowered when I feel utterly powerless about everything else — like I do now. My parents come into the room and they can tell without asking that there's been no update. So, they tell me about their day, about what they all got up to, and it's clear that they loved spending the time with Jacob — and probably getting out of Clovelly too. The eyes are on them as much as they are on me and I often forget that I'm not the only one going through this. I may be an adult, but I'll always be their child and they feel my pain as if it's their own. I know that now, because I know that love too.

When they're finished, they sit down, looking shattered and I tell them that they should sleep at their own home tonight, in their own bed. It's not that I want the night alone with Mark — I have no idea if he'll even get out tonight. It's just that all this time they've been staying with me because we didn't know where he was. Then we thought he was gone, and then we knew the truth, but still needed to keep up appearances. I may still be scared, and I may still be a bit all over the place emotionally, but I'm no longer hurting.

My heart started to heal in France, in a warm bath, in his bed, when he asked me to grow old with him, and when he asked me to marry him. I can be alone now because I know I'm not alone — and they need their rest. They need to reclaim their space and their life. They're apprehensive, but I think secretly they appreciate me releasing them, but they insist on staying for fish and chips, and they'll say their goodbyes after I've put Jacob to bed.

I don't want to be an annoyance, but I send Darren another message before I start Jacob's bath. It's been hours. Hours since I heard from Darren and even more since Mark arrived at the police station. There must be some news? They must know something, but I hear nothing from Darren this time and the worry starts to creep in again. He'd reply if he could. If he knew what to say to me. If he wasn't too busy to. I want to call but I know I can't. If they're in the interview room he won't answer and if

Mark's out, if he's with his family — then I promised to stay away.

I feel so insecure about the fact that he'll be seeing them first. I know he loves me, but this has all been so crazy. He's going to see just how much they've missed him and how much they love him, and no doubt they'll be pushing the blame for all of this on me. How can I really expect him to choose me over them? I didn't expect him to all that time ago, so why did I allow myself to believe he would now. I fetch my engagement ring from my box and put it back on my finger. I've been afraid to wear it at home since Sergeant Moore surprised us last night, but now I need to feel it. I need to remember what Mark said to me when he gave it to me and how it feels to wear it. I need to hold onto the fact that this ring brings only happiness, and that I will get my happy ending too.

I try to push these thoughts aside as I bath Jacob, because I'm driving myself insane. I don't even recognise the insecure way that I'm behaving, but the pain that I felt when I thought I'd lost him is still lingering and it's making me doubt everything. I thought I had become more practised at waiting than this.

I leave my phone with my parents in the living room because I cannot bear to keep looking at it, and I try to get my head in gear and be present for Jacob. Once again, I splash, smile and laugh with him — but my mind is elsewhere. It's in the police station with Mark, it's in France, it's in Mary's dining room and it's on the beach looking at Jamie's dead body. I close my eyes tight to push that last thought away, because I don't need to fear that now.

Jacob falls asleep easily after a busy day with my parents, but I sit in his room for a bit longer. If I go downstairs and find that there's no news, I might just scream. I can't hide away forever though, and there might be some news, so I leave my boy sleeping soundly and go downstairs. Whatever small hope I allowed to build up is instantly crushed when I walk into the living room and see my parents' faces.

"Nothing?" I ask them in frustration, checking my phone for confirmation. There's nothing. No text and no missed call.

"I'm sure Darren would have got in touch if there were any issues," Dad says, trying to reassure me. "I bet they've just got tied up with his family."

"Then surely, they'd call to let me know that, instead of leaving me to pull my hair out?" I ask in annoyance.

Dad just shrugs at me; this isn't his fault and I'm not really mad with him. I let out a growl and almost do pull my hair out. "Should I call, or go there?" I ask them.

"Just sit tight," my dad says, and I glare at him in response. "I know. Easier said than done, but what can you do? March over to the police station when we don't know what's going on and have them ask you questions too?"

With that I glare at him some more. I need solutions not more questions. No. I need Mark. I'm about to tell them to leave because I'm not good company right now, but a knock at the front door stops me in my tracks. My parents jump up from the sofa and for a moment we all just stand there looking at each other. Then I rush to the door with my heart ready to jump out of my chest and a smile waiting to take over my face — but that soon subsides when I open the door and see only Darren standing in front of me, looking serious.

"Darren," I say, unable to hide my disappointment. "What...? Where...?"

I can't even bring myself to ask the questions because

I'm not sure that I want to hear the answers. So, I just look at him as the tears start to fill my eyes again — then suddenly he smiles.

"Don't look so disappointed Ava, I'm almost offended," he says with humour.

I try to speak again without really knowing what to say, but he gets there before me.

"Do you think I'd come here empty handed?" he asks, breaking into a full-blown smile.

He looks to his left and steps aside and Mark appears before me, smiling in a similar manner to Darren. The tears fall now, and I let out a sob as I grab him by his coat and pull him into the house. He wraps his arms around me, and I squeeze him hard. I'm never going to let him go again. Then just like that, just like always, all the fear, all the worry and the uncertainty, disappear as soon as I'm in his arms.

Darren follows him in and shuts the door and I hear my dad asking him questions. He's asking the questions that I should be asking but I'm not, because I'm scared that speaking will break the spell. So, I just hold him, and I cry with relief. Darren's words are coming through though — "It's over", he's telling them. They believed the story, or so they say, and even if they didn't, they aren't taking things any further. Mark's free. Mark's back, and I let out a sigh of relief as I pull away a little and look up at him, and see that he's still smiling at me.

"I've been going crazy," I tell him honestly, with my vulnerability clear for all to see.

"I'm sorry. My family grabbed me as soon as we got out of the door, and in truth I wanted to surprise you," he says, then realising from the look on my face that it may not have been the best decision, he adds, "Sorry, baby," and he leans in to kiss me.

It's a gentle kiss because my parents are in the room, but I don't care about that right now. He starts to pull back, but I put my hand around his neck, and I pull him down to me and then I kiss him more forcefully. It's a kiss that tells him how scared I've been, a kiss that tells him how much I love him, and as we both open our mouths to deepen the kiss further, it becomes a kiss that lets him know just how much I want him. He reciprocates and he wraps one arm around my waist pulling me in as close as he can, holding me firmly against him, and with the other he's holding my head in place so that I can't escape him either.

I'm vaguely aware of a few throats being cleared, footsteps leaving the room, and then the door closing — but neither of us pull away. We continue to kiss passionately and then my hands go to his coat and I unzip it and pull it off him. He pushes me against the desk, and I can feel that he's hard, and it's in that moment that a cupboard door in the kitchen is slammed, and my mum calls out to ask who needs a drink — reminding us that we're not actually alone.

We pull away and laugh at ourselves, but the dark look is in his eyes and I can't help but look down at his crotch where his erection is visibly on show.

He looks down too and gives me a rueful smile and then whispers in my ear, "That is completely for you and it always will be, but it will have to wait until later."

I smile and shudder as his words excite me and his breath tickles me.

"But right now I need you to move away from me so that I can get myself into a fit state to be able to face your parents," he says, and I kiss him gently and unashamedly take in his erection once more, then walk away still smiling at the promise he just made.

He shakes his head and mouths "Minx" at me as I leave the room.

When I get into the kitchen Mum is still busying herself with the glasses and I give her an apologetic smile. I hadn't realised that they'd bought Champagne while they were out today, but it's definitely a welcome sight. I take some glasses through to the living room where Darren is sitting with my dad and he gives me a cheeky smile. I put the glasses down and reach for him and he stands up, knowing what I want, and I hug him tight. That's what Darren and I do now — we hug.

"Is everything really going to be all right now?" I ask him.

"Yes, Ava," he tells me confidently, "he's a free man." Then he steps back and smiles at me. "Well, actually, not for long, I hear," he says as he takes my left hand to appraise my ring. "That is very nice. So, when is the big day?" he asks.

"As soon as possible," Mark says, standing in the doorway holding one of the bottles of champagne. "Before she comes to her senses and changes her mind," he adds, popping the cork.

"I think she's a lost cause," Darren says, looking at me affectionately. "Well, I guess I've got one hell of a best man speech to write," he adds, laughing.

I laugh at that too. "Hmmm... I think it might need to be heavily censored this time," I tell him as Mark walks over and fills my glass, along with everyone else's.

"I had to censor the first one," he says laughing, and then he leans into me conspiratorially and says, "I didn't much like the bride," and we all laugh with him.

"What are we drinking to?" Mum asks.

"Where do we start?" Dad asks, laughing. "I'm not sure I bought enough champagne to cover all the bases."

I clear my throat and look at Darren and say, "I suggest that we start with great friends," and I tip my glass towards him. "Family... the best family," I say, looking at both my parents. "And epic love," I add, looking at Mark.

He smiles at me and reaches for my hand and he pulls me into him, so that we're standing together as we all take a drink.

"To getting it right the second time around," Darren says looking at me and Mark.

"To new beginnings," Mum adds smiling.

"And to a lot less bloody drama," Dad quickly adds, laughing.

"I'll definitely drink to that," I say, taking a big gulp.

Mark tops up our glasses again then looks at me and says, "To finally being happy... forever."

We all take another sip from our glasses, but Mark and I seal that one with a kiss too.

We carry on drinking until the second bottle is gone — well, in truth it's mainly my parents and Darren that are drinking it. Mark is laughing along with everyone, but I can see that he's exhausted. Eventually, my parents announce that they're leaving and having offered Darren a bed for the night, he leaves with them. Mark and I see them out and then we walk back to the sofa and just crash on it together, holding each other close.

"You look exhausted," I tell him. "What was it like?"

"I could tell that Darren didn't want to alarm me, but it was clear that they were a little suspicious — at first anyway," he says. "They checked everything, and they were thorough — but thankfully, so was Darren... it ends here," he says, letting out a deep breath. Then he adds, "I'm sorry I left you hanging — that was misjudged." Then he brings the hand that he's holding up to his lips and kisses it.

"I started to think that you'd chosen them over me," I tell him honestly. "That you'd realised how important they are."

"Ava, they are important. But so are you and Jacob," he says passionately. "It was intense, and I did lose sight of how much pain this was likely to cause them — but then I didn't plan it..." he adds, sighing. "We're all going to meet up back in London as a family and as far as I'm concerned, that includes you."

"Not as far as they're concerned," I reply.

"Honestly, they didn't really mention our relationship, or even Jacob. I think they were just relieved and in shock. They're heading back to London in the morning, but they know that I need to stay and sort a few things out — my car needs collecting from a police impound, for one," he says, rolling his eyes. "They know I'll be with you, but then I need to go back, and I want you both to come with me. When we meet as a family, it will be as the family that we're going to become," he says, and he kisses my hand again. "They can meet their brother and they can meet my future wife — my entire future. My entire world," he says smiling at me lovingly.

Then he looks serious, as he says, "And anyone that has a problem with that can walk out the door — anyone."

I bury my head in his chest as a few tears escape and fall down my cheeks. "Are you sure about this? About me?" I ask, and he pushes my head away from his chest so that I can see from his face just how absurd he thinks my question is. "I've brought you nothing but trouble," I tell him.

"No, Ava," he says, shaking his head at me. Then he kisses my forehead, my cheeks and then my lips. "You brought me back to life. Yes, there's been pain — for both of us — but there's no reason for there to be pain now. Nobody has ever made me happier than you do," he says with complete sincerity. "Nobody can separate us this time."

He pulls out my left hand and rubs his finger over my ring. "When I gave you this it was with complete clarity. I'm not bewitched by some beautiful young woman and I'm not having a midlife crisis. It just took me forty-four years to find my soul mate, because whomever has control over this universe thought it would be funny to make her twenty years after me."

"I love you so much," I tell him, reaching up to kiss him. "Yes, I'll come to London with you." I hesitate for a moment then add, "I'm not sure I can ever forgive her..." he nods understanding who I mean. "I won't go out of my way to be difficult, but I don't think we are likely to ever be on good terms — even if she wanted to be — which I doubt."

He kisses me again. "I don't expect you to," he says genuinely. "The only thing I expect you to do is stay by my side and allow me to make you the happiest woman on the planet," he says, smiling.

I laugh at him and ask, "Do you think you're up to the challenge?"

"Well, I know I'll spend every day of the rest of my life trying," he replies, kissing me again.

"Well..." I say, looking at him seductively. "Unless you're too exhausted, I believe that you may have promised me a certain something earlier on? That's definitely something that makes me happy," I say, unable to stop the smile spreading across my face.

He looks back at me with lust in his eyes and says, "I haven't forgotten."

He leans down and we start kissing, continuing with the same level of passion as when we abruptly stopped when he first arrived. He pulls my top off and kisses my chest and I start to unbutton his shirt, I'm just about to pull it off when we hear Jacob over the monitor.

"Jacob...." I groan. "Really? Now?" I practically hit the sofa in frustration, but then we both laugh. This is our life, after all, it's not just the two of us that make up our family, it's Jacob too, and everything that involves.

"Shall I go?" Mark asks, lifting himself off me.

"It'll probably be quicker if I go," I tell him, knowing that a quick feed ought to settle him.

"Can I come with you?" he asks, and then I take his hand as we go upstairs to see our son.

I was right — a quick feed settled him even though he was delighted to see his daddy. Mark sat behind me as I fed him, keeping us both close. Then I slowly put Jacob back into his cot, we tiptoed out of his room, carefully closed the door, and then we ran to my bedroom like naughty teenagers, rapidly stripped off our clothes, and made love passionately — until we were disturbed again.

44

I wake up the best way possible — in Mark's arms, and I peek at the clock and see that it's half past six. We're both completely naked after making up for lost time during the night, and as I nuzzle into him, running my fingers through the dark hair on his chest, the rest of my body starts to wake up too.

Part of me knows that I should let him rest, but I also know that he's not likely to complain about being woken up for sex. So, I lift myself up and slowly start to kiss his neck and nibble at his ears, and the position of my leg alerts me to the fact that I'm managing to wake him up, in more ways than one. His arm starts to move, and he pulls me closer and gives me a sleepy smile.

"I was having a lovely dream,'" he says, opening his eyes to look at me. "My beautiful wife-to-be was in my arms kissing me," he says, laughing a little.

I smile up at him. "Well, I'm sorry to have woken you," I say, and then I go back to kissing his neck.

"I could happily get used to being woken up like this," he tells me as he rolls me over so that he's now on top of me.

He starts kissing me now, my cheek, neck and my ears, and I start tingling all over. He pushes into me gently, slowly, kissing me constantly, making me feel completely cherished.

"If there is ever a day when your body isn't ready for me, it will be a sad day indeed," he says, as we continue to move together.

"I've never wanted anyone like I want you," I tell him honestly. "Nobody has ever had this effect on me... just you," I gasp as he picks up the pace and I feel the warmth rising up my body, promising the orgasm that will follow, and like always — it does.

We lay in bed for a while holding each other close, it's still early but there will be a lot to do today. Darren will pick Mark up early and take him to collect his car, and then Darren will go back to London. I need to pack, but only for a few days, because we need to sort a few things out before I move there properly, and I can't leave my mum completely in the lurch. My tenancy will end in a few months, so I need to speak to Curtis and give him notice too.

Jacob may be little, but he doesn't travel light, and I have accumulated a lot of stuff. Packing up my life last time was hard work, but this time it will be even harder, because in truth, I'm also a little sad. I want to be with Mark, and I realised when I stayed with him that I missed London. Yet, unlike my last move, I don't feel the need to escape Clovelly.

This place grew on me and considering some of the things that have happened here, I probably ought to want to leave. There are good memories here too and there are more people here to miss, than there were when I left London. I was only going to miss Carolyn and Cooper then — but here, there's my parents, there's the life I created for myself and my son, and there's Julia. Julia may have only been in my life for a short time, but her friendship has felt more real and more genuine than Hattie's ever did.

Mark speaks, snapping me out of my thoughts. "Have you thought much about what sort of wedding you'd like?" he asks me. "I've done this before, so I'm happy to do whatever you want to do."

"I want a really big, expensive wedding," I tell him seriously. "Haven't you heard that I'm only with you for your money?" I look at him and we both laugh.

"Honestly, I've not given the details much thought," I tell him. "But I think a small wedding in a beautiful French town — there's a really nice one near Montpellier, did you know?" I ask him teasingly. "Followed by a party with lots of food and wine, at a beautiful woodland cottage... that would be lovely," I tell him with sincerity. "Just family and real friends, and as I don't have many of those it ought to be pretty cheap," I tell him, laughing a little.

"That sounds perfect," he replies genuinely as he leans in to kiss me. "There's another thing I wanted to talk about," he says. "I've been a 'Mr and Mrs Davidson' before and it wasn't the best experience. I was wondering how you'd feel about being a Davidson-Swan?"

"You want to take my name too?" I ask him a little surprised — though I don't know why.

"Yes," he replies. "Jacob has always been a Swan and your parents are such an important part of his life... I guess I don't want to take that away from him, or them."

I push off him a little so that I can look at him right in the eyes, and he can see how truly touched I am by his gesture. "Ava Davidson-Swan," I say smiling. "I like it." I lean in to kiss him again but then hear Jacob over the monitor signalling that our time in seclusion has ended, and our day has well and truly begun.

Mark takes Jacob down for breakfast while I shower and then we switch places when I'm finished. I'm struggling to know where to start today. I'm eager to start my new life with Mark, but it's a case of which job to do first. I guess I can keep it simple to begin with — we're just going away for a few days to meet with his family and to get the ball rolling, but I feel that I at least ought to give Curtis as much notice as I can, considering he's been such a great landlord.

I go into the office to get the rental contract out so that I can double check all the details before I make the call, and as I'm going through the files, I spot the envelope that holds Jacob's birth certificate. I pick it up and take it to the living room and I hand it to Mark.

"I wanted to put your name on it, but I couldn't without telling you," I say, and I feel the guilt that I think I'll always feel, creeping back in. "I'd like to rectify that as soon as possible."

"Don't worry about it," he tells me, stroking my face. "It's a piece of paper that can be easily changed. I'm here now, we're a family and that's all that matters."

Moments later Darren arrives to take Mark to get his car. We have no idea how long that task will take, but I'm going to use the time to pack up what we'll need for the next few days. My parents will be coming over too so they can help entertain Jacob, and that will definitely make my job easier.

I make the call to Curtis and though he said he'll be sad to see me go, he had expected it to happen. I can't help but feel sad after I speak with him — this really is going to be the end of an era. It's the start of something that I know will be even better, and I'll finally be getting the life with the man that I love, but still... Jacob was born ten minutes away. I fell in love again here — not the same as with Mark but it felt real enough at the time. Then there's my parents... not seeing them practically every day is going to take some getting used to again. Still, there is darkness here too and this house was once full of lies.

My parents take Jacob and Cooper out for a walk while I get all of our things together. Cooper is going to be staying with my parents this time, but he will be coming back to London with me. Jacob loves him as much as I do, and I don't want to be without him. I wish I could take Julia with me too, but I know that's not an option. She tried London once and it wasn't for her, and even though her bad memory still lives here, she loves this place. It's always been home to her.

As I think of her, I decide to pick up the phone and give her a call. Like the rest of the village she knows that Mark came back and was at the police station yesterday. She called me a few times, but I couldn't face lying to her, and had instead just sent her a message letting her know that I was fine — but I need to see her now. I need to let her know what's happening and to share my news. It will be nice to be able tell her something happy for once. She comes over twenty minutes later with a bottle of Prosecco in hand and I can't help but laugh at her.

"Well, it is a time to celebrate, isn't it?" she asks, smiling at me innocently.

"In more ways than one," I beam back, holding out my left hand for her.

"Jesus! You guys didn't waste any time, did you?" she says, examining the ring closely.

"Actually, we wasted a lot of time..." I tell her more sombrely. "I'm moving back to London."

She sighs at that and looks at me sadly. "I guessed as much... I'm going to miss you," she tells me, pulling me in for a hug.

"I'm going to miss you too," I tell her, and a tear escapes me.

Then Julia gets to business. She asks where Jacob is and if I need to drive anywhere today, and once she's satisfied with my answers, she gets some glasses out and pops the cork. As I've finished packing everything that's needed and I'm just waiting for Mark, I decide that it's OK to enjoy the moment guilt-free. We talk about wedding plans and I ask her to be my maid of honour — to which she wholeheartedly agrees.

We talk about how, and where we can meet up in order to avoid constantly making a five-hour journey whenever we want to see each other — and I thank her. I thank her for taking care of both me and the baby growing inside me. I thank her for bringing him into the world safely, and I thank her for showing me what real friendship looks like.

"I was just doing my job," she smiles at me modestly.

"Oh, Julia, you were always doing much more than just your job," I tell her and we both lean in for another hug.

Mark clears his throat in the doorway, and we break away. For a moment, I forget that they've never met because I've talked about each one to the other so much. So, I finally introduce them to each other now.

"So, you're the one who's been causing all the trouble?" Julia asks him seriously, but then she smiles as she shakes his hand. "I'm glad to see that you're alive and well, Mark. Someone up there must be looking out for you," she adds, laughing a little.

Mark and I quickly share a look and I know we're both thinking the same thing — that it was someone very much of this realm that was looking out for him.

"It's lovely to meet you," Mark says smiling at her

warmly. "Ava has told me how much you've done for her and what a great friend you've been."

"Well, she makes it easy," Julia says fondly, and they both turn to me and smile.

Just then my parents walk in the door with Jacob, it's almost lunch so we decide to eat now and then leave shortly after, so that Jacob can nap along the way. Mark tells me that he's spoken to Mary — tomorrow is Monday but nobody will be going to work, so we'll be having our meeting then. It's going to be all of us in the house together, including Tom, who has apparently forgiven Mary. Darren and Lilly will join us too, and, if needed, will act as mediators — but are really there so that we don't feel outnumbered. That's what Lilly said in her message to me anyway. Then there will be Jacob.

The thing that I've wanted to avoid his entire life will be happening — he'll be in a room with all of the people that I've always wanted to keep him away from. I know that I can trust Will to be good with him, Tom too, but if the others even look at him the wrong way, I think I'll lose it. Mark knows my concerns because they're his too.

He hasn't told them that Jacob and I will be there. On the one hand, we assume that they'll be expecting it, but we don't want to say it outright, because we don't want to give them an excuse not to come. If they think it's just Mark, they'll definitely show up, and we need them to show up. We need this face to face if we're going to start our new life together. Our new life out in the open, as husband and wife. I don't see us putting the past to bed in this one meeting, but they need to know what the future holds — and most importantly, that there's nothing that they can do to stop it.

45

It was always going to be a long drive home, especially as I couldn't help but cry as I said goodbye to Julia and my parents. It isn't 'goodbye' yet though, I'll be back soon. In fact, it will never be goodbye as they'll always be in my life, but it is the start of something new and the end of life as I know it. Life has been intense these last few months. Intense highs and intense lows and I realised as I hugged my parents that it has taken its toll, although, the Prosecco probably didn't help. I hope, really hope, that once we get past this next obstacle, that I am saying goodbye to all of that uncertainty for good.

Jacob had a long nap, but we ended up stopping twice, so it was after his usual dinner time when we got home. Thankfully, Lilly had let us know that she'd been in and stocked up the kitchen, so we rustled up something very simple for him before bathing and putting him to bed. Mark and I just crashed on the sofa in the snug after dinner. There was some comedy on that neither of us were really watching, but we just felt like we needed some background noise.

This whole situation has had an impact on him too and we both just wanted to welcome something simple — mundane even. Although it wasn't long before tiredness overcame us, and we decided to have an early night.

It's almost eleven O'clock now and Darren and Lilly will be over soon. The plan is for us to have lunch with Jacob and then get him to sleep before the others arrive at one O'clock, and I really hope he cooperates with the plan. We think that any shouting or general nastiness is more likely to happen when they first arrive, and we're hoping that by the time he wakes up we'll be at a calmer level. Then again, you know what they say about the best laid plans. Knowing our luck, they'll scream blue murder and wake him up and I'll have to try to calm a tired and grumpy toddler amidst the chaos.

For now, at least, things are going to plan. We had lunch with Darren and Lilly, Jacob fell asleep twenty minutes ago and any minute now the doorbell will ring, and it will all begin.

My stomach is in knots. I'm not afraid of these people, I just don't know how this will go — well, there are a few certainties. Darren and Lilly will have our back, and Mark and I will still be together by the end of it — that I do know. It's just the insults and squabbling in between that I'm dreading.

Thankfully, there's no time to dwell on it too much now, because they're at the door. I sit at the large dining table with Lilly and Darren, and for a moment I can't help but wonder why showdowns always happen in the kitchen, when there are so many dangerous objects to hand? Luckily, there will also be a very large table between us all, and at the end of the day, this feels like a formality. They've not come over for a cup of tea and a cosy chat, so sitting around a big table is appropriate, really.

Mark leads them all into the kitchen and when they walk in, he and Hattie have an arm around each other, but as soon as she sees me, she breaks away from him.

"I thought this was a family meeting?" she asks him.

"It is," he tells her calmly. "Ava and Jacob are my family too."

They all stand back for a moment, but then Will says, "This is so stupid," and walks over and gives me a big hug, surprising me as much as everyone else in the room.

He then places himself on 'our side' of the table, leaving the chair next to me free for Mark. Mark beams at him and we all look expectantly at the others. After a few minutes Tom walks over to the table and sits down in the seat opposite me, which is something I will be eternally grateful for. Eventually, the others follow suit, sitting on either side of him, and then Mark comes and sits next to me.

"Where's the imaginary baby?" Mary asks, smirking, and then Mark, Darren, Lilly and me all instantly turn to her and give her a look that lets her know exactly what we all think of her.

"Jacob is sleeping," Mark tells her bluntly, "and if you are going to insist on taking that attitude with my child then I suggest you leave now."

Mary shrugs her shoulders and looks at me, but then quickly looks away again, because if looks could kill she knows full well that she'd be six feet under right now.

Mark clears his throat. "I wanted you all to come here today because we have been through so much. All of us," he says looking at them all. "There has been more pain in the past two years than anyone ought to have to deal with in their lifetime," he tells them sadly. "I don't want to discuss that today, there's no point. It's done and it can't be changed. It's the past," he adds, and I can see that nobody has missed the meaning behind his words. "Regardless of the individual feelings of the people around this table," he continues, "this is what our family will look like moving forward — Jacob included, naturally," he adds, looking at Mary.

He takes hold of my left hand which had been resting on my lap out of sight and brings it onto the table, and holding it in his, he makes sure that my ring is on show. "This woman here is the love of my life and we are going to be married," he says lovingly. He looks at me and we smile at each other, and then all hell breaks loose.

Hattie jumps up, pushing her chair backwards, sending it scraping across the floor and shouts, "How can you do this to me, Dad?"

"This isn't about you, Hattie," he tells her calmly.

"How am I supposed to come and see you if she is here?" she says pointing at me.

"Then we can meet up at yours, can't we?" he replies just as calmly as before.

"How can you choose her over me?" she asks him as her tears fall. "I'm your daughter!"

Mark lets out a sigh and says, "Hattie, I'm not choosing Ava over you, because I'm not drawing those lines. I love you both. You are my daughter and Ava is my happiness. She is my future." He squeezes my hand before continuing. "I am choosing what my future will be," he tells her more firmly. "If you say that you can't be a part of it, then that is a choice that you are making — not me."

"So much has happened, Dad," Ted says, always backing up his big sister. "There's been so much hurt..."

"Yes, Ted, there has," I interrupt. "You all caused me a lot of pain and only one of you has had the decency to apologise."

Both Hattie and Ted look at Will questioningly — they clearly weren't aware of that. "In an ideal world I would never have to see your faces again," I tell them honestly. "However, that's not the world we live in. You are important to the man that I love, to the man I want to spend the rest of my life with," I add looking at Mark again. "So, I suggest that at best, we find a way to make our peace with the past, and at worst, we just learn to tolerate each other. The choice is yours," I tell them shrugging. "Because I'm not going anywhere, and to be quite honest, your decision will have zero impact on my happiness."

Mary scoffs, "So you expect everyone to just pretend to like you?"

"I managed it with you for the best part of twenty years, Mary," I reply in a similar tone. I see Darren moving in the corner of my eye and I turn just in time to catch him smiling. I'll always have an ally in him when it comes to Mary.

Everyone is silent for a moment and then Tom speaks, "I may only be part of this family through marriage to Mary, but I think of each of you as my own children too," he says, looking at Hattie, Ted and Will. "I didn't say anything at the time, but it was a terrible thing that was done to Ava. To Mark too," he says looking at Mark. "You were a different man when you were with her, and I see that you're a better man now because of her," he nods at him. "I personally wish you both happiness and I truly hope that the right thing is done, here today," he says, looking at the others again, then he turns to me and we share a smile.

"Me too," Will adds. "I have apologised to Ava and I've

spent time with my baby brother too," he says, looking at his older siblings defiantly. "Dad..." he adds more shakily, turning to Mark. "I owe you an apology too — we all do," he says, looking at his brother and sister again. "We had no right to interfere in your life... Ava knows why... we talked... I don't want to go over that now..." he says looking down a little. "Dad, I am sorry. We should have never split you two up. We shouldn't have tried to destroy what you had, and I'm glad that in the end, we didn't."

Will looks down but Mark reaches for him and pulls him into a hug. They stay like that for a few minutes and I feel the tears start to form as I watch them. When they eventually release each other, I see Will wiping away a few fallen tears, and then he looks at me.

"So, Ava... if you can tolerate seeing my face," he says, giving a little smile. "I really want to be part of your lives."

I smile back at him and try to hold back the tears as I tell him, "Your face is tolerable, Will."

He laughs a little and I turn to Mark and say, "I guess that's one more to add to the wedding list." He gives a little laugh and takes my hand once more.

"Don't expect me to be there," Hattie blurts out, and the mood is once again brought down.

I let out a deep sigh and look right at her. "Hattie, just stop," I tell her, shaking my head. "Let it go, you must be exhausting yourself. Don't you see?" I ask her, but she doesn't respond. "You can't hurt me anymore."

She looks away but remains standing and everyone is silent for a few minutes. Then we hear Jacob over the monitor and my heart jumps into my throat. I look at Mark and he immediately sees the dread on my face. The people in this room are the reason I hid Jacob from him. He squeezes my hand and gives me a reassuring smile and I slowly leave my chair and go to him.

As I walk up the stairs, I hear Mark saying, "I strongly recommend that you do nothing to make her feel like she needs to defend him." I'm not sure who he's speaking to, whether it's an individual or to all of them, but then he adds, "Because if you do, I won't be the one holding her back."

I smile a little at that. I truly hope it doesn't come to that but at least I have a great lawyer on standby if it does.

Once in his room, I lift Jacob out of the travel cot and I'm relieved when he immediately asks for a feed because this will give me a little more time to prepare myself. After ten minutes, I walk down the stairs and turn into the kitchen, Mark stands up as soon as he sees us and walks over to give us both a kiss. Jacob buries his head into my neck, and I hold him tightly as I sit back down in-between Mark and Lilly.

"What have I missed?" I ask apprehensively.

Mark sighs, "Not a lot, unfortunately. I guess we're at a stalemate," he replies.

I roll my eyes and look at Hattie and Ted disapprovingly. They're both staring at Jacob and I study them for a moment, trying to figure out how they're going to react to him. They don't look threatening, if anything they look intrigued.

"I guess it was a bit much to expect that we could sort this in one afternoon," I say, to nobody in particular. "Though as far as Mark and I are concerned that wasn't really what today was going to be about," I add.

"So, enlighten us," Mary adds snidely. "What is the point of this?"

"The point, Mary," Mark says bluntly. "Is to make it

clear to you all how we feel about each other, and to make it very clear, once and for all, that Ava and I will be together, regardless of how any of you feel about it," he takes a deep breath to calm himself again. "I also want to tell my children that I love them. I love them very much and I want them in my life too," he says, and tears start to form in his eyes, "but I will not be held to ransom, by anybody."

At that moment Jacob perks up and leans over to Mark, who then takes him and holds him close. Will gives him a tickle and he giggles, and then Hattie's chair scrapes across the floor once more as she pushes away from the table and walks out. Mary quickly follows, Ted appears to think for a moment, but then leaves too without another word. Tom lets out a deep sigh, shakes his head and gives us an apologetic smile, before saying his goodbyes and going after them.

The rest of us sit for a moment and then Darren says, "Well, that was disappointing. I didn't need to referee at all," he laughs a little, then he walks over to Will and embraces him, telling him "Good lad," before releasing him.

Lilly takes Jacob and Mark and I instinctively reach for each other, and I look him in the eyes as I tell him, "I know that was a big thing for you and I'm proud of you."

"I love you," he replies and then leans in to kiss me.

We continue to kiss until Will clears his throat and Darren laughs, telling him, "Don't worry, you get used to it."

Mark and I both laugh, but then I catch the look on Will's face. He's nervous and uneasy and I realise that he's plucking up the courage to speak to Mark about the baby. I give him a reassuring smile and then turn to Darren and Lilly and ask them to join me and Jacob on a trip to the park. At first, they don't look keen, but I try my best to signal with my eyes that we need to leave them to it, and eventually they understand, and we head out.

I sit on the bench with Lilly watching Darren push Jacob on the swing, when she suddenly says, "You've never asked about me and Darren not having any children." She looks at me and smiles. "It's one of those questions usually asked to women my age, but you never have."

"Honestly, Lilly, when I've seen you with Jacob the question has crossed my mind," I tell her. "However, I know from my mum's experience that as common a question as it is, it's not always an easy one to answer." She smiles again, but this time I see sadness. "You just never know what a person has gone through. Or, if it's purely a choice, then nobody has the right to question it either."

She breathes out a little then says, "We did try for a while but there were complications and, well... that put an end to it." I give her hand a squeeze. "We thought we were settled on it but recently we've been thinking about it again and we're actually looking into adoption," she says brightly. "Our age may make it a bit of an issue... but if we can't do it here then there are children all over the world in need of a family."

"Any child that gets you as their mummy will be the luckiest child in the world."

She smiles, but a tear escapes too and so she walks over to Darren and takes over pushing Jacob on the swing, and Darren comes over to sit with me.

"I guess she's told you our plans?" he asks.

"Yes, I'm really happy for you, you'll be great parents," I tell him.

"Thank you," he says, sincerely. "Speaking of parenting, what's going on back there that we needed to be away for?" he asks, clearly intrigued.

"Ha! Well... I guess you'll find out soon anyway," I laugh. "Will's girlfriend is pregnant," I say, grimacing a little.

"Bloody hell!" he says, somewhat annoyed, but then adds more jokingly, "I swear these Davidson men ought to be selling their sperm. That or they just need to have a bit more care about where they put their d—"

"Hey!" I say, stopping him from finishing what he was going to say. I give him a slight shove on the arm to let him know that I'm mortally offended, and he laughs again.

"Don't worry, Ava, you are the exception," he says smiling at me.

"I should think so," I reply, pretending to still be annoyed.

We continue to watch Lilly and Jacob for a while longer and then Mark comes up from behind us and sits on the bench next to me, letting out a deep breath as he does.

"All right, Grandad?" Darren asks, and we all burst out laughing.

After a few moments we regain our composure and Darren asks, "What did you tell him?"

"Not to propose," Mark replies laughing. Then he looks at me adoringly and says, "But apparently, he's already been given that instruction, along with a few other pearls of wisdom." Then he takes my hand and kisses it, looking me in the eyes the entire time.

"Well, I guess always hanging around with old people has made me wise," I say. Then I quickly try to run off to Lilly, only to be grabbed by Mark and pulled into him.

He's laughing as he leans into my ear and says, "You do realise that you're going to be a grandma, don't you?"

Darren bursts out laughing again, and then Mark pulls me onto his lap and turns me so that I'm leaning into him, and asks, "Have I told you yet today how much I love you?"

"I don't think you have. How much do you love me?" I reply. "An excruciatingly painful amount... but you're worth it," he tells me.

We both move in closer and begin kissing. Darren says something I don't really hear and goes off to Lilly, and we stay as we are until both Darren and Lilly bring Jacob back and instruct us that we're all heading to the pub.

46

It took six weeks to completely move out of Clovelly, and it was so hard saying goodbye to my parents. It's not like I've always had them physically close to me. I went to university and they moved to Clovelly not long after I graduated, so it's not new to me. Still, they rescued me and became such a big part of my world with Jacob, so not having them just up the road is going to be a bit of a shock to the system. They were in tears too but for Dad it was bittersweet, because now he'll have an excuse to visit London more often.

Mark has seen Hattie and Ted but always at Hattie's or out for dinner, because they still refuse to come here when he suggests it. He knows I don't care about seeing them, and I think he likes keeping them away from me so that he can shield me from their wrath, but he is starting to feel irritated about their refusal to meet Jacob. He may only be their half-brother, but he's as much Mark's as they are and their negativity towards him is starting to become an issue.

Thankfully, Will is totally on-board with everything. He comes over for dinner some evenings and even comes over to see Jacob and me when he doesn't have lectures. I actually enjoy spending time with him again now. We were always friends, but the fact that he had feelings for me was always lingering beneath the surface. Thankfully, that's no longer an issue, as he is now very much in love with Bex — his pregnant girlfriend.

Bex has been over a few times on her own too and we're actually pretty good friends. I could see that she was terrified the first time he brought her over, but then that could've been due to the fact that she had already met Mary. Mary, who has made sure that everyone is aware of how unhappy she is about the pregnancy — the hypocrisy of which hasn't been lost on anyone.

I can relate to a lot of what Bex is going through, and as her own parents are also a little displeased, she often confides in me. I never tell her that I think that what she's going through is actually scarier than what I did, but I think they can do it. It will be hard, but Mark and I have promised to help as much as we can, and as the plan is for me to continue doing freelance work, I'll be around to help with childcare when she starts studying again too.

Mark's house or, "our house" is in a state of chaos. Unpacking hasn't really proven to be that easy because Jacob sees every box as a new adventure and sabotages my attempts to be productive. Plus, it's not just a case of finding a place for items to be stored, because Mark already has everything we need here. So, unless something is of sentimental value there's no point in keeping it. Really, the job involves opening a box and then putting the items into other boxes depending on whether I can sell or donate them — and I've not even started on the things still in storage yet.

Currently, Mark is at work, Jacob is having his afternoon

nap, I've banished Cooper to the garden because he's more of a saboteur than Jacob, and I'm actually feeling like I'm getting things done. So naturally, the doorbell rings and interrupts my flow.

When I open the door, I know who they are immediately. I've never even seen a photograph of them, but I can see Mark in their features — if not their demeanour. Apparently, he has his mum's eyes — I had always assumed that they would be from his dad.

"Mr and Mrs Davidson," I say politely, stepping aside to let them in. "Mark didn't say that you'd be visiting — he's actually at work..."

"We didn't tell him we would be visiting," his dad replies, interrupting me, and as they step inside the temperature in the house instantly drops a degree or two.

This is the worst possible day for a surprise visit from Mark's parents. He's in project meetings all day and has warned me that I might have difficulty getting hold of him. I take a deep breath and invite them into the kitchen, apologising for the state of the house — and of me, for that matter.

I know that they know about me. Mark spoke to them when we came back to London and told them everything, and to be honest, I had expected them to come sooner. They knew that he was missing because Mary was keeping them informed. Their only child could've died, and it's taken them six weeks to come and see him. I can't help but feel annoyed at them on his behalf, but at the same time, I can see why he's been in no rush to see them — they really are cold. His grandma must have been very special indeed.

They sit at the table and I offer them tea — thankfully, my time spent in the tea rooms means that I know how to brew a good pot, and how to set things out. I even have some lemon drizzle cake on hand that I made for Carolyn when she visits tomorrow. It seems a shame to waste it on them, but they definitely need sweetening up a bit. I slice it up and lay it on the table then step out of the kitchen, letting them know that I'll call Mark. As expected, it goes through to voicemail, so, I decide to send him a text instead of leaving a message as he's likely to pick it up sooner.

I don't want to alarm you, but your parents just arrived! Don't worry. I'll be fine. I can handle it, but call me when you can. Love you.xx

I walk back into the kitchen and see that having heard the doorbell, and now, seeing two strangers in the kitchen — Cooper is going crazy at the patio door. Mark's dad doesn't hide his disapproving look and I say nothing as I go over and let him in. Cooper is actually a very obedient dog, but he's excitable, inquisitive, and loves people, so I keep hold of him by his collar to stop him from running over to them. Then I get down to his level, give him a fuss and calmly ask him to sit — and he does. I went to the puppy training sessions with Carolyn, so I know how to handle him, and as soon as I feel that he's calmed down enough, I release him and ask him to go to his bed.

Thankfully, he doesn't show me up and does as he's told. He goes off to chew his favourite and most disgusting teddy, and when I turn back, I almost think I see a look of approval from his dad.

I explain to them that I've contacted Mark, but that he's not likely to pick up my message straight away, and then I bring the teapot over to the table — noticing that the cake is still sitting there untouched.

"Did you drive down?' I ask them.

"Yes," his dad replies politely, but definitely not warmly

I'm starting to feel like I'm going to need an extra jumper.

"Where are you staying?" I ask.

"We're in a hotel," he replies in a similar manner.

"I understand that you write?" his mum asks.

"Yes, I do," I reply, smiling, "freelance for a few publications."

"Are you working now?" his dad asks.

"I am, but with the move I've not been able to take on too many projects recently," I reply.

"You can survive on that financially, can you?" his dad asks, and I instantly understand where this line of conversation is going.

I channel the polite smile my mum made me practice for difficult customers, and reply, "Well no, that alone doesn't pay the bills." He sneers a little, and then I add, "Thankfully, I receive a regular income from the flat that I own and rent out in Muswell Hill."

He forces a smile and takes a sip of his tea and I look down at my own cup, desperately wanting to add, "So put that in your pipe and smoke it," but manage to resist the urge.

"And the child—"

"Jacob," I say, looking at him firmly. "Your grandson's name is Jacob."

Then right on cue I hear him murmuring over the monitor. It's two O'clock, so yes, it's time for him to wake up. If only he knew that he'd be better off staying asleep right now. I stand to make a move to go and get him, but then stop and turn to them.

"Jacob will probably want a feed, so I'll be up there for about ten minutes," I tell them. "So perhaps you could use this time to think, or to rethink why you've come here today."

They sit more upright, making it clear that they're not used to being spoken to like this, but I'm not finished.

"If you're here to show me your disapproval of me, then you've succeeded," I tell them. "But... if you're here to attempt to break us up then you need to be aware that we have been through and survived much worse than you."

They look at each other and the shock is clear on their faces.

"So, if that is the case, then please feel free to use this time to quietly leave without a scene or embarrassment," I add, smiling politely. "But," I continue, "if you're here to reconnect with your only child. A child that you very nearly lost mere weeks ago, then stay. Drink your tea, eat your cake, make yourselves comfortable," I tell them. Then I shrug my shoulders and smile as I say, "You may even get a cuddle from your new grandchild."

With that said, I practically run upstairs to Jacob and to warm up a little. Ten minutes later Jacob is ready to face the world and I can see that Mark hasn't yet picked up my message. I didn't hear the door while I was up here, but that doesn't mean that they haven't gone, but when I come downstairs and turn into the kitchen, I see them still at the table. His mum is drinking tea and eating cake, and his dad is sat stroking Cooper — who has left the safety of his bed and ventured over to the table. They meet my gaze and I smile at them and I get a small smile, and slight nod in return. It's an improvement — I'll take it.

"This cake is delicious, Ava. Where did you buy it from?" his mum asks politely.

"Actually, I made it. So, thank you," I add.

"Oh," she says, unable to hide her surprise.

"Is he bothering you, Mr Davidson?" I ask, gesturing to Cooper.

"Not at all, he's a lovely dog," he replies genuinely. Then he adds, "We have two Red Setters at home."

Well, they like my dog and my cake so this could be going worse. I notice Mrs Davidson looking at Jacob, who like always is cuddled up to me, so I suggest that we move into the living room. It'll be more comfortable and there will be toys for Jacob to play with, and they'll be able to interact with him, if they want to. I invite Cooper along too as he now has a role in this whole thing as a buffer.

We sit quietly for a while but as Jacob moves away from me to go to his toys, Mark's mum lets out a little gasp. I look over to her and she's just staring at him.

"He's the spitting image of him, isn't he?" I say, smiling at her. She smiles back at me.

"It could almost be him, couldn't it, George?" she says lovingly, and I realise that there is a heart in there after all.

She then goes over and plays with him, while Mark's dad and I continue to sit in silence, but after a while I can't take it anymore, so I take a deep breath and say, "Can we just address the elephant in the room?"

They both turn to look at me. "Yes, I am twenty years younger than Mark. Yes, he first met me when I was five... but as you know, we hadn't seen each other for ten years when we met again," I quickly add. "Yes, I was formerly Hattie's best friend, and yes, the journey we've been on to get to where we are today has been messy and complicated... to say the least."

I take a breath and they look at each other, clearly wondering how I can possibly think that what I'm saying can be interpreted as positive.

"When it comes down to it," I continue, "when you

break it all down. What Mark and I have is the most uncomplicated thing out there. We love each other," I smile at them and shrug. "There is no hidden agenda, we just love each other. We complete each other and we each make the other stronger. We're happy. That's it," I tell them with sincerity.

They look like they want to say something but my phone rings, stopping them. It's Mark, and I go into the kitchen, leaving them to distract themselves with Jacob and Cooper once more.

"Please tell me that message was a joke?" Mark says as soon as I answer.

"Nope. Sorry. Absolutely not a joke," I reply, apologetically.

He lets out a groan, then asks firmly, "Have they been rude to you?"

"No," I reply honestly. "I've had to adjust the thermostat, but no," I reply, laughing a little.

"Well, if there's anyone that can thaw them, it's you," he says affectionately.

"Defrosting a little perhaps," I reply, "I wouldn't go as far as thawed."

"I'll be home in an hour," he says, and I can hear the smile in his voice. "Will you be all right?"

"Yes, don't worry."

"I love you," he tells me.

"I love you too."

I go back into the living room and they're both now playing on the floor with Jacob, so I just sit and watch them, and other than making more tea for them, they don't interact with me much more. I don't mind though, because they appear to be at ease with Jacob, and I feel like they may actually have taken what I said on board.

When Mark eventually walks in, I go to greet him and as he holds me, he checks again that I'm OK. There isn't really time to fill him in on what's been said because his mum comes straight over. So instead, I offer to take Cooper and Jacob out and give them some time alone — a gesture that doesn't appear to go unnoticed by his parents.

I get back at half past five — I couldn't really leave it much longer as Jacob needs his dinner and I was already stretching it out. When I get in, Mark comes to meet me, and as he's already got something ready for Jacob, I'm invited to sit at the table with his parents and have some of the wine that they've been drinking. They seem happy, but I can see that there's been tears. They stay a little longer but leave before bath time, and as we close the front door Mark pulls me in close and kisses me deeply.

"I didn't think I'd be saying this to you," he tells me with a baffled expression, "but that's two more to add to the wedding list."

47

It's May now, Mark and I have been married for almost a year. So much has happened and for once I can say that most of it was good. We married in June last year and Mark's parents did accept our invitation, and they even looked like they were having a good time. They're clearly not good at expressing their emotions, but I've at least discovered that they do have them. They clearly love Mark, and all their grandchildren too. Will and Bex both came along and I felt like Will took one for the team, as he spent most of his time with his grandparents. Hattie and Ted didn't come, but they were never actually invited — we only ever wanted people there that were happy for us.

The wedding was exactly as we talked about that morning in Clovelly. A small ceremony in a beautiful space at an old restaurant in Saint-Guilhem-le-Désert. Which was then followed by a party at Mark's cottage. We hired a marquee and had a dance floor, but we kept it simple. The closest friends, the closest family, lots of food and alcohol, and dancing — lots of dancing. Dancing like I've not danced in a long, long time, with the best friends a girl could ask for in Julia and Lilly.

It was a very emotional day and neither of us could hold back our tears as we said our vows to each other, and Dad's speech completely broke me. I was an emotional wreck by the time Darren stood up with several pieces of paper in hand. I knew he'd not talk about the secret that we all shared, but he still had enough on us to cause embarrassment. Thankfully, most of the banter was aimed at Mark, and I was mostly spared — mostly.

It was the happiest of days, followed by an extremely memorable night. My parents had Jacob for that one night, but we didn't have a honeymoon in the traditional sense. We just stayed on as a family for a few more weeks, enjoying our time together before we went back to life in London.

We christened Jacob. It wasn't really that important to me, but as all of his other children have Godparents, Mark wanted to carry on the tradition. It did have some significance for me though, as a way of celebrating Jacob becoming a Davidson-Swan — just like us. Keeping with tradition Darren and Lilly are Godparents, as are Julia and my own Godfather, Tony. In return, Mark and I are Godparents to Hugo — the baby boy that Darren and Lilly adopted in December. He's completely gorgeous and they seem to have taken to parenting like ducks to water. Although, we do have to laugh when we get together and they nod off at nine O'clock. Long gone are the days of Lilly battling to stay up drinking until the bitter end.

Bex and Will had been staying at Mary and Tom's, but it was becoming a serious source of stress for them. Luckily, about a month before she was due, my tenant's in Muswell Hill moved out. So, after speaking with Mark I offered them the flat for a few years rent free — just until they're earning and on their feet. I didn't do it to score points, but I know Bex will be eternally grateful to have been able to escape Mary and her judgmental gaze.

At the time, Will had taken me aside and asked me if I was sure that I wanted to do that for them. So, I'd reminded him that my parents had given me that flat to help me when I was getting started in life, and as his step mum, I started to say, but he'd stopped me there. Will is finally on board with thinking of me as a sister, but step mum he's finding a bit weird. I tried to tell him that thinking of me as a sister was even weirder given that I'm married to his dad, but he left the room with his hands over his ears, so we never really finished that conversation. I'm yet to tell him that there's not a room, and barely a surface in that flat that Mark and I didn't have sex in or on — especially as my furniture came out of storage for them. I'll just have to save that information for the next time he's a bit of an arse.

Although I was completely happy to help them, I did feel awkward about the fact that it meant that I wouldn't be able to contribute financially. Mark still gets frustrated with me on this subject, and not long after we were married, he showed me exactly what the state of *our* finances are. I finally understand why he tells me that I don't need to worry, and why Mary was so concerned.

Still, I've always paid my way in life and being told that I no longer need to takes some getting used to. I'm still writing though, and Mark's still working, though he's gone back to only working on projects or with clients that he finds interesting. Happily, that means that we get to spend lots of time together as a family, so as far as married life goes, I really can't complain.

I'm now twenty-seven and a grandma, which is a constant source of amusement for Darren. Bex gave birth to a healthy and beautiful baby girl in November, and they called her Anna Mae Davidson. Anna after Mark's grandmother and Mae after mine. They said that they wanted her to be named after strong and loving women who fought for what they believed in. Mark and I both practically cried when they told us, but I know that Mary, on the other hand, doesn't share the sentiment.

Hattie and Ted have started to give way a little — with Jacob at least. They eventually agreed to come to our house and spend time with him, and now it's a relatively regular occurrence. I either go out for a bit, or I hide in the kitchen either cooking or writing with my headphones on. I don't mind them being here, and I do actually think it's important for Jacob to have a relationship with them. I even go as far as to be nice to them around him so that he doesn't pick up on any tension. However, they've still not apologised to me, and although I'll never do anything to make it awkward for Mark or Jacob — I'm definitely happy to keep my distance.

It's also been a very educational and informative year. After I'd sorted out all of my belongings and I finally felt settled, I started to take Jacob to some local toddler groups so that I could try and make some 'mummy friends.' It was a really big step for me, as in the past I've struggled with new friendships, but I was told that there was a lovely group at a local church in Crouch End, so I forced myself to go along one morning. When I walked in my name was shouted and I was instantly greeted by a familiar face.

Lucy Warren had been on my course at university and we hit it off in the early days, but then she seemed to pull away and I never knew why. Yet, the day I walked into the church she was all smiles and took me under her wing, introducing me to the other mums there. It took me a couple of weeks to pluck up the courage, but as we were tidying up the toys I asked if she wanted to come to lunch. She agreed and after I'd plied her with cake, I eventually asked her why we stopped being friends. She looked at me apprehensively, but then gave me a one-word answer, “Hattie.”

My jaw dropped to the floor as she told me that Hattie had lied to her about me — all sorts of random, crazy stuff. Lucy said she hadn't really believed it, but thought it was best to not get involved with someone like Hattie, and so she turned away from me. I couldn't believe what I was hearing. Yet, as Lucy talked things started to click into place, and I started to think of the other people that I thought I was connecting with, but who had just disappeared. It was all Hattie. Being possessive all this time, just like Carolyn had said.

Hattie and I were supposed to go to different universities. She had suggested going to the same one, but I'd had my heart set on Bristol and the course that I took there. Hattie was supposed to go to Bath, but in the end, she came to Bristol through Clearing. I was so nervous about going at the time that I was actually relieved that I'd have my best friend with me, but it was always the two of us. We didn't share a house with anyone else because she “felt uncomfortable” with it, and I never questioned it. I never questioned it because we always had a good time. We always had people around us when we were out — but then it stopped there. Everything makes sense now. Although, at the same time it doesn't, because I still don't understand why.

My education in all things Hattie didn't stop with Lucy. I bumped into Miri at the supermarket one day — I was with Jacob and she knew straight away that he was Mark's. I filled her in on the rest, well... I glossed over the details on that first meeting and went straight to the fact that we were married. She asked me to meet her and Tasha for a drink, and at first, I wasn't sure that I wanted to. They dropped me, just like that. I know I didn't help the situation, but I had believed that they thought more of me than that. In the end though, I decided to meet them, I wanted to know why, and I wanted to talk to them about what I'd learned about Hattie.

It seems that they were as taken in by Hattie as I was. Looking back now they could see and question certain things, but at the time they'd completely gone unnoticed, just like they had with me. When I asked them why they didn't stick by me, they admitted that Hattie's lies about her brothers and Paul had been a big part of it — she had targeted their vulnerabilities, but there was more to it than that. Apparently, they had always felt like I was indifferent to them. I think that they could see from the look of shock on my face that it clearly wasn't the case. I adored those girls and the memory of watching them walk out my door still haunts me.

When I asked them why they felt that way, and they really thought about it — it all seemed to go back to the same thing — Hattie. Amongst other things, it seems that Hattie met them without me on a number of occasions, telling them that I didn't want to join them, but these were occasions that I knew nothing about.

Sitting with them that evening, listening to the things that they told me, the things that had been going on for years. I just couldn't believe it. No wonder I'd been taken in by Jamie so easily, Hattie had been doing a number on me for years and I had no clue whatsoever. I trusted her completely and I loved her. I gave Mark up the first time for her, and why? All I ever was to her was a puppet. A shiny toy that she didn't want to share. I thought she was the best friend a girl could ask for, but she was never a friend, I see that now.

I have no idea what to do. I know I have the right to ask her and I've spent time torturing myself, trying to work out why, and what her motives could have possibly been? Yet, at the same time, what difference would it make? I already know her true colours. I already know that she destroyed my life and I've said my piece to her. The only thing now is that I know even more. I know what and I know how long for — I just don't know why.

I talked to Mark about it, and he has said it's up to me whether I confront her or not, but if I do, then he'll support me all the way. He didn't see this behaviour himself. He didn't live with her during the teenage years, and it wouldn't have crossed his mind to think she would do that when she was younger, and yet he believes it, and he's not surprised, because Mary is the same. Mary manipulates.

Mark has told me that he's always wondered if Mary getting pregnant at university had truly been an accident. It's always been there, lingering in the back of his mind, but he's never asked because he can't regret it. He could never regret his children, so there's no point in dredging up the past.

Thankfully, we don't have to see too much of Mary. There are many family gatherings, most I manage to stay clear of, but today is Will's birthday and they're throwing him a garden party again, and he's specifically asked me to come. So here we are, about to knock at the door of the house where my world once started to crumble, and just like last time I'm arriving with Mark, and I've even baked. Though, unlike last time, we're arriving hand in hand, with our new, shared name, with our wedding rings proudly on show, and with Jacob — the child that I was unknowingly pregnant with the last time I was here.

We're not entirely free of secrets though, because just like the last time I was here, I'm pregnant. I'm eight weeks pregnant, but we're keeping it quiet until we have the twelve-week scan. This time it was no accident. I'd been thinking about it for a while, but I wasn't sure how Mark would feel about having a fifth child, but when I asked him, he couldn't have been more thrilled by the idea.

So, I had the implant removed and we got busy in the bedroom. He was there when I took the test and we sat nervously together as we waited for the result. This time he'll be right by my side through everything, like he should've been the first time.

It's Tom who comes to the door, so we're greeted with a friendly face. I take the cake through to the kitchen and then we all head out to the garden. Darren and Lilly are here with Hugo, and like always, we go over to them. Bex is with Mary, looking uncomfortable as Mary proudly shows off Anna to her friends. Our eyes meet and I give her a supportive smile and she starts to relax a little.

I've promised myself that I'll never make life awkward for Mark with his children — so I would never do anything to cause a scene. Thankfully, I don't think I'll ever need to, because Mary is now wary of me, even here, in her home. She knows that I have fight, and she knows that what Mark and I have is stronger than anything she ever had with him. More importantly, she knows she's lost whatever game she was playing.

Bex is like the old me. The me that never did anything to rock the boat — the me that let Mary push her around. She told me that I've inspired her to believe that one day she'll too be able to put Mary in her place. I'm sure that she will, I just hope she doesn't need to go through what I did to get there. Actually, there's no need to worry about that, because I'd never let that happen.

The party is nice, but that's mainly because we're sticking to the people we like. Will is tipsy as he always is on these occasions. Ian Simmons keeps topping up his drink, and occasionally I see him giving Mark a nervous look. Ted's here too and he's got a girlfriend now called Natalie. I've not met her properly because Ted and I don't really mingle. Mark says that she seems nice enough, but Lilly's not keen, so naturally I'm trusting her judgement more. Hattie is here with Miles, and I'm not surprised they're still together; they're very well suited. I always said that Nate was good for Hattie, but now I realise that he was too good for her.

The downside to being pregnant and at this party is that I can't drink because I'm doing it by the book this time, and I keep needing the loo. I don't think anyone has really noticed my multiple trips, but as I step out of the door after the third, I'm stopped in my tracks. Because there, leaning against the wall waiting for me, is Hattie. She gives me an uncertain smile and I return it with a polite one and start to walk away.

"Can I talk to you?" she asks hesitantly.

"What about?" I reply, turning to face her. She looks nervous, she's twiddling with her hands and is hardly able to make eye contact.

"Do you think you could ever forgive me? Do you think we could ever go back to being friends?" she asks, hopefully.

I let out a little laugh and look at her in disbelief, as I say, "Hattie... I don't even know where to begin with that." I walk a little closer to her. "People that ask for forgiveness, usually show remorse first. They usually apologise before they ask to be forgiven."

"I'm sorry," she says, and it actually looks like she means it. "I really am sorry."

"For what?" I ask her bluntly.

"What do you mean?" she asks, confused.

"I mean, what exactly are you apologising for?" I ask. "For what I did..." she says shakily, "for the lies and for making you leave."

I stay silent for a moment and she looks uncomfortable. "And what about the rest, Hattie?" I eventually ask her. She looks at me questioningly, and I continue, "What about Tasha, Miri, Lucy Warren, and all the other Lucy Warrens out there? What about all the people you stopped me getting close to? What about the twenty years of lies and manipulation?"

She turns pale, I see the tears form, I see the guilt, and I see the acknowledgement that what I've just said is true, before she looks away.

"Yes, I've known about it for a while now and I've thought about it a lot. Mainly about one thing... why?" I tell her. "But, I've also come to realise that it doesn't matter."

She looks up at me again now, but she still says nothing.

"I don't need you to tell me why, Hattie, so let me instead, answer your questions," I say. "Firstly, the one about being friends again? The answer to that is no, Hattie," I tell her seriously, as I look her right in the eyes. "We could never be friends again, because I'm not the same person that I once was, and neither are you. Actually..." I pause a little, "it's probably more accurate to say that you are the same person — it's just that I now know who that person really is." She looks down again and I say more gently, "But thanks to a strange twist of fate, I'm now your step mum." I laugh a little at that. "We're family now, Hattie. So, whether I like it or not, you're in my life... and that's probably going to be the best that I can offer for quite some time."

"As for forgiveness," I say, shrugging a little, "I honestly don't know if I can ever truly forgive you for all of this... I really don't, but I have made peace with it," I say, smiling a little, and she meets my eyes again. "I've made peace with it, because I actually need to thank you."

She lets out a shocked laugh and she looks like she's about to speak, but I push on. "I need to thank you, because the moment that you decided to cut me out — the moment that you decided to destroy my life. Well, what you actually did in that moment was set me free. It was a truly horrendous and incredibly painful time in my life," I tell her, and I see the guilt again. "But I'm finally where I'm supposed to be because of it. Or in spite of it... depending on your perspective," I clarify, then continue, "I'm with the man that I'm supposed to be with. I know what true friendship looks and feels like." She looks away again. "I know more love now than I ever thought possible, and I am so very, very happy."

I pause and smile at her again. "I finally know who I am, and most importantly, I finally know my own worth, and in some completely messed up way, that's actually because of you, Hattie."

I smile at her again and turn to walk back to my husband and son, and as I do, I breathe a sigh of relief — because I've done it. I've finally put Hattie and everything that happened exactly where it all belongs... behind me.

A NOTE FROM THE AUTHOR

Did you like my story? If so, **please leave a review** —especially if it's going to be a nice one. Reviews mean everything to an indie author, like me and help us to be noticed.

Firstly, I'd like to say a massive thank you to Alison Ward for using up her free time to help me with the initial proofread of my manuscript, and for pulling me up on all my grammatical errors. I was always better at English Lit than grammar at school and for only asking for chocolate in payment. Also, to Jessica Runyard for taking on the task officially. Thanks also has to go to Leah Wright and Jessica Galvin for reading the story in the early days and giving me their honest feedback.

Sometimes things work in your head but they don't always come through on paper, and when you know the characters inside out, and you can feel the depths of their emotions, you need that outside perspective to make sure that you've managed to communicate them properly. Feedback in this area led to an almost complete chapter re-write to show that there was more to Ava and Mark than just a lot of sex, because at first it was only me that knew that they were completely in love and not just in lust.

Well, if you've made it this far then thank you to you too. Thanks, so much for reading my first ever attempt at writing a novel. I hope you enjoyed immersing yourself into the world of Ava and Mark as much as I enjoyed writing it. In fact, I really, really hope you enjoyed it because I plan to try my hand at this writing lark again.

Do you ever have a dream that sticks with you and then when you go to bed the next night you try to clear your head of all the reality of the day, and try to go back to and build on the dream you'd had the night before? Well, I do. I do it often and it is how the story of Ava and Mark came about — a kinky dream about a girl getting it on with her best friend's dad. I've always enjoyed writing and I genuinely believe that I'm better in text form than real life. Writing a funny text is much easier than telling a joke in person, unless I have a drink in hand. Clearly, I like to hide away a bit as I'm also writing under a nom de plume. I've wondered for a few years now if I've actually got the ability to write a novel. Whether I could take an idea, or a dream and build on it and make it into something interesting, and not just in my head. To also write it down and tell it in a way that other people would find interesting too. I've got to admit that I've had a few false starts over the years.

There's been a couple of attempts to put pen to paper and to create something in the past, but they all led to nothing. However, this idea stuck with me, and so I just told myself to do it. I'm thirty-seven years old, I have two children and a million excuses for not doing it, so I forced myself to commit, and I did... in secret. That's right, I didn't even tell my husband. He's very practical and I didn't want to risk it being seen as a waste of time because I know it would have put me off. The dream was to write it, self-publish it, sell a few copies and then turn around and say, "Hey! Look what I've done." If you're reading this then I sold at least one, right?

So, how do you secretly write a book? Well, I would sit in the car whilst my youngest child had a nap and just tap away on my phone. I'd burn the midnight oil whilst writing in the dark in my children's bedroom — because I always end up sleeping with them. I'd even tap away on the sofa in front of the TV when my husband was present, but because we both tend to "zone out" a bit and play on our phones in the evening instead of chatting. We should perhaps work on that. There were only a few occasions when I had to tell a little lie when he asked me what I was doing. So, I didn't tell anyone. Not until I got some friends on board to read a book that, "A friend" was writing so that I could get some outside perspective. It was only after they'd read the story and had given me their honest feedback that I told them that it was actually my work. Although, as one of those selected was my sister and another an old friend, they did ask me if I was the author, because for those that know me there were a few tell-tale signs that it was my voice, but I just denied it.

I never wrote a formal plan for the structure of this book and didn't have a plan as to what would happen and when. The story just evolved as ideas, conversations, characters and new ways to add depth came to me. The plot just seemed to evolve naturally, and I found that I'd set characters up from the beginning to take on roles in the future that I hadn't really planned for. Darren Barton is an example of this, as I'd written him in as a criminal lawyer long before I thought about Mark being hidden in France and everything that Darren did to help him. So as cheesy as it might sound, it really felt like things were just clicking into place, and this really led to my enjoyment in writing the story and spurred me on to see it through.

However, the story did take on some quite big changes from the original concept. In fact, when the idea first came to me, I had thought that Ava would run off somewhere with Lucas, having found some elaborate way to disappear, whilst making sure that the truth about what Hattie had done would come out, and she'd be punished. I was even thinking along the lines of faking deaths. Then, as I started to write Lucas, I realised that I was writing about a man that was too good to be true and the cynic in me couldn't allow that.

I picture Mark as a younger Rufus Sewell, who I've fancied long since before Victoria and The Man in the High Castle. As I started to write Mark's character — that first encounter with Ava in particular, I really felt their connection. I felt the anticipation about where their journey would go from that very first meeting and I never felt that when I was writing about Lucas. I was getting horny from my own writing. It was then that I decided that I wanted Ava and Mark to end up together.

That meant some serious thought needed to be put into Lucas, because he was such a good man — how would it be believable for Ava to choose Mark over him? So, I basically assassinated his character. He couldn't just be broken and vulnerable because that would invoke sympathy, he needed to be an all-out baddie and he needed to do the unforgivable.

I brought in his sister, Fiona, in the hope that if she could understand it all, and not hold Ava accountable, then you wouldn't either — just in case there were people out there that thought that Ava had done Lucas wrong somehow.

Although this is Ava's story and it is told predominantly in her voice and from her perspective, I thought that it was important to give other characters centre stage at times too — especially Mark. He was absent from Ava's life for a long time and had his own story to tell, and I felt like he needed to have that time dedicated to him. I also felt like this would give him the opportunity to explain himself for why he let Ava down so badly, and to also have the chance to win you over, and I hope he did.

That's also why I gave some time to Lilly too. She may only really be a supportive character, but she is someone that goes through Mark's journey with him, and is someone that loves him. As someone that was a genuine friend to Ava and knew the truth about her past, I thought Lilly was the perfect go-between.

Jonathan Swan is a guilty pleasure of mine. I'm a lover of Guy Ritchie films and also having read a few Martina Cole books I couldn't help but bring a bit of "gangster" to the book — even though he is far from that. I think he's every girl's dream dad. Loving, fun and supportive, but hard as nails and will always have your back — or is that just me? He too needed some time dedicated to his story because he's such a strong person, and such a strong presence in Ava's life. I guess I should confess that it was also the only way I could drop the 'C-bomb'! Sorry... again.

He took on the role of protector and the visit with Mark had to be told from his perspective so that I could do his character justice. I also felt that it was important to hear directly from him what he thought of his daughter being with a much older man — a man that in reality had known his daughter since she was five — which might be weird to some. I hoped that the story of his own parents meeting would add insight into why Ava and Mark were also destined, and why he would understand and approve that love sometimes comes at you from where it is least expected.

Darren had a little bit of time given to him too at a very pivotal moment. As a smart and very practical man, I thought it would be good to share his view of Ava, but to also get some perspective into Hattie — especially as we don't ever unearth exactly why Hattie behaved the way that she did. Well, except the fact that she inherited her mum's skills in manipulating people. I also wanted you to hear from him what Ava wasn't hearing. He was trying to subtly tell her that Mark wasn't dead, but Ava never took it on board because she was too scared and in so much pain. However, he was giving her clues, or at least trying to, and I wanted to give you one too, and so that had to come directly from him.

As a mum that doesn't really have the brain capacity for anything too 'high-brow' or challenging, I have to admit that I've read quite a few "soft porn" books — as my husband calls them. Lots of bad boy biker stories and that sort of thing, and I guess they fuelled my desire to add an element of kink to this story — but then that is also how my brain works.

I really wanted to make it real too. Ava is gorgeous but she's also a mother and anyone that's had children knows that a sex life post-children is never the same as it was before. Not in the early days anyway. I really felt like there needed to be an element of reality to it, so I added the no-nipple touching issue, and of course the fact that sex can be painful after having a baby for a few months. This is the reality that many mums face when they try to get their sex life back on track. I mean, I didn't want to totally kill the mood, but if other mums like me, were going to be into this book, then I wanted it to strike a chord and be something that they could relate to, as well as fantasise to.

That's why there's talk of breastfeeding too, because it really can dominate your life, especially in those first few months, and I wanted to reflect that. It's also been, and still is to this day a big part of my life, and normalising breastfeeding is important to me and I wanted to reflect that in this book. It's not a "breast is best" book by any means, but it's what I know and was fundamental to parts of the story.

For example, I'm sure that I'm not the only one out there that has had to quickly switch from being in bed having some "adult time," to having to throw on some clothes and head to a room to soothe a crying baby. I remember when my husband and I were trying for our second baby and it was a night when we were "supposed" to have sex, and my non-sleeping first born interrupted us three times. To clarify, that wasn't three separate sessions in one night. I know, that was some serious dedication to the cause and she's worth it, although she doesn't really sleep either.

Finally, the story needed to have a happy ending. We needed clarity and closure on a few things, and Ava deserved to be happy. She went on a journey, a journey that could have broken her, but instead it made her stronger. There was part of me that felt like I could have spent more time on Hattie and exploring what her motives were, but part of Ava's journey and growth as a person, was that she escaped Hattie. Ava could've easily spent her whole life under Hattie's thumb, but she met Mark and she followed her heart.

Some might argue that she did do the dirty on Hattie and that it was wrong. Still, it set her on her path to freedom and as hard as that path was at times, she ended up where she was supposed to be. So, in the end it didn't seem right to dedicate too much time to Hattie, because it would contradict the fact that Ava no longer cared for her and could no longer be hurt by her. Hattie no longer had control and will most likely spend the rest of her life on the outside looking in. She'll be watching Ava be happy but will have little involvement in it herself, and I felt like that was a fitting punishment and a fitting ending.

If you like what you've read, then don't forget to leave a review for this first-time, wannabe author.

ROXANNA C REVELL
THE BENEATH
BEHIND THE WALL BOOK ONE